The Last Independent

Vince L. Marcanti

To Carol - a great Friend

Vince L. Marcanti

Enjoy

Avid Readers Publishing Group
Lakewood, California

This is a work of fiction. The opinions expressed in this manuscript are those of the author and do not represent the thoughts or opinions of the publisher. The author warrants and represents that he has the legal right to publish or owns all material in this book. If you find a discrepancy, contact the publisher at www.avidreaderspg.com.

The Last Independent

All Rights Reserved

Copyright © 2010 Vince L. Marcanti

This book may not be transmitted, reproduced, or stored in part or in whole by any means without the express written consent of the publisher except for brief quotations in articles and reviews.

Avid Readers Publishing Group

http://www.avidreaderspg.com

ISBN-13: 978-1-935105-85-5

Printed in the United States

Author's note

I wish to express my gratitude to you for having enough interest to open my book. The sole purpose of this story is to amuse you and perhaps consider the possible consequences of our current, unlimited growth, economic ideology. As author I would like to challenge you with one request: read no further unless you are devoted to reading the entire story with an open mind, no matter how outraged you may become over a character's beliefs or actions or political predictions, (may I remind you that the truth is much stranger and more malevolent than any fiction writer could create).

If you read all 129,955 words, you may understand that this story is not about class warfare or the unequivocal political divide that exists in our culture. It is about the biggest obstacle to peace and equality: human nature.

This book is dedicated to the people who fought and still fight to change our corrupted two-party system; the independent and third party candidates that speak the truth about the dismal state of our government and try to enlighten us to the obvious solutions, **like no more private campaign donations.** They are inevitably ignored, but still fight to be heard. Don't quit!

Thank you, Burney Sanders and Ralph Nader. But most of all to you, for reading my story from start to finish. I would be overjoyed if it gave you amusement and was worthy of your precious time.

Thank you!

Contact me at Vinnywaters@aol.com

PROLOGUE

In the foreseeable future-

The United States of America still claimed to be a democracy, but after decades of donations from the wealthy minority, used to persuade political policy, the U.S was more aptly described as a veiled plutocracy.

For too long the working class struggled to keep up with the cost of minimum credit payments, while corporate profits were maximized by exploiting low wage foreign laborers with no rights and importing finished goods with minuscule tariffs. Wealth was redistributed upward and hoarded by the plutocrats. The leisure class became obscenely rich and under taxed, while common Americans became unemployed and destitute.

The government did very little to advance alternative energy technology to curb the addiction to dwindling, finite oil or invest in sustainable infrastructure. Credit lines from the banking monopoly were used by average citizens just to survive, setting the stage for another credit default meltdown. Despite high unemployment, politicians and the media being subservient to multinational corporations, deceitful waste in tax dollar appropriation, loss of economic protection to the masses and increasing public outrage over government debt, **a revolution never arose...**

Within the enduring effort to subdue public uprising, the wealthy plutocrats that bought all three branches of government with unrestricted donations to members of congress, supreme court justices, and of course, the president, also finance the murder of free media. After a series of perplexing terrorist bombings of public libraries, the corporate media ignored the lack of investigations and pushed pro-war propaganda. After forty years of polarizing distractive and trivial mainstream news, things got worse when all media outlets became united in pushing the governments' maniacal foreign and domestic agenda. Most common citizens are isolated from truth while their world view is continually manufactured.

The fatal downfall began in September when America suffered another economic collapse. This one struck so deeply that virtually all commerce froze. The short term financial growth that preceded the collapse inevitably occurred in the absence of uncorrupted legal, regulatory, and supervisory frameworks. The voracious executives and title holders in the banking and insurance sectors amassed insurmountable liabilities because working class citizens began defaulting on mortgage and credit card payments.

Foreign credit dried up due to loss of confidence in the dollar and the astronomical debt the government had run up.

The banker's cabal, who ran the Federal Reserve, had the power to create money for too long, and again they conjured more to bail out selected cronies in both sectors and bought all their toxic assets once again. The Federal Reserve kept the numbers a secret, but it was clearly trillions they were chasing down the drain.

The plutocrats were counting on a new world arrangement set up by the central bankers and other billionaires in this transnational group. They would issue a single world currency, set interest rates and control the entire monetary economic system, beginning in North and South America and all countries in the European Union. The stage was set for the greedy minority to take over the world's monetary system, once the current fiat currency died an awful death.

The American people would easily go along, believing it would save them from depression. Greedy acts perpetrated on the American people by the influential rich since the Federal Reserve act in 1913 had culminated to this.

But the people of Great Britain united against the central banker's plan. Through protests and civil disobedience, they eventually ejected all the sell outs in their fallen government. This left America stuck with its debased dollar and rising oil prices, hence, the next collapse.

China and other U.S creditors demanded reimbursement in the form of food and services instead of dollars. It was then that the U.S Government publicly declared total isolation from the world! They ceased all exports, and all military members were brought home, abandoning three wars. For the first time in well over a hundred years, no American troops occupied foreign soil.

All imports ceased. More jobs evaporated, and all non-affluent people were devastated. With the absences of foreign oil, the government rationed it. As a result, fuel prices became unaffordable to the masses. Nearly all commerce ceased, and when food was not delivered to grocery stores, it was only a matter of weeks before the social order broke down. The rules of society changed from respect thy neighbor, to survival of the fittest.

The Government quickly focused on protecting factory farms and the affluent communities.

The only federally funded project was quickly put in to law. Its plan was to build tall, electrical, security gates around the richest towns where the leisure class lived or quickly migrated to.

Those who were rich enough to own property in the gated communities made up about twelve percent of the population.

These chosen cities are protected by police and military members.

Conversely, in lower and middle class towns across the country, people looted and rioted over remaining food on store shelves.

In a desperate urge to stock up, some people became murderous fiends during the anarchy. People who owned guns recklessly used them as their means of survival. Before order was restored, millions of innocent, maltreated Americans lost their lives.

Eventually the government, safe inside the guarded capital, approved funding for a radical new plan. Under martial law, they created and put in effect the Government Action Plan. It ordered every citizen who went broke to join the plan.

All privately owned firearms were banned. Each citizen

was registered and crudely analyzed for job placement.

The plan attempted to give every penniless American a job and a residence by herding them together into the major Service Cities. There they would work in factories or other facilities. After decades of outsourcing for cheap labor in undeveloped countries, manufacturing jobs were being done in America once again and for low wages. The millions of citizens that were arrested under martial law or already in prison worked twelve hours a day. They were under the supervision of low wage armed guards in penitentiaries that were converted into manufacturing plants. The Penitentiary Plants were highly successful in manufacturing clothes, shoes, and other things that had been imported from other countries for decades.

Newly enrolled citizens were assigned one-room units in newly built government housing buildings or old buildings converted into mass housing projects. They were placed within walking distance or a short bus ride to their jobs, thus solving all transportation problems. America would have to quickly become self-sufficient to survive in the world.

Most people joined the plan and praised America's first successful third party, the Compatriots, for their bold action. But there were those who refused to enroll in the G.A. plan and remained in the wild with no electric, no filtered, running water, and no prepared food. They were deemed fanatical criminals by the servant media and became know as The Scavies; a purposely demeaning word derived from scavenger.

The British are coming

Brigadier Roger Gilmore thought about his mission while he tried to fall asleep in his slightly damp sleeping bag, which lay on the hard wooden floor of an old, abandoned American house. He was honored to be chosen for this imperative mission. A high probability of death never discouraged him for a moment. The Prime Minister and all the young members of the newly transformed parliament expressed faith in him. Allowing him to choose five men to comprise his team, he picked five officers in the British army that he personally knew would be honored to join his mission.

The World United Nations going to war with America seemed unavoidable, and therefore a nuclear holocaust was inevitable. Only one solitary effort to disrupt the maniacal American government would be risked, and it fell onto him. The six brave British men were flown to Ontario, Canada where their Canadian allies helped them launch a top secret underwater vessel into Lake Superior. They crossed into America undetected, landing in Wisconsin at the Ottawa National Forest. Then they carefully traveled south through the whole state and into Illinois Their destination was the town of Rosemont, just outside of Chicago. Australian intelligence swore that a trusted American spy informed them that Rosemont was where the Government secretly moved for defensive reasons.

The Brigadier carried the new state-of-the-art rocket launcher himself, and each of the sergeants carried a rocket. The five rockets were highly advanced technological wonders conceived by a transnational team of biological scientists and military weapons experts. They were constructed to penetrate walls of virtually any material before exploding into the interior of the target. The explosion would spread toxic gas that instantly attacks the lungs of anyone one who inhales even a single breath.

So much work and money went into devising these rockets, Gilmore often thought, *and it's me they trust to deliver them.*

He and his men would probably be caught and killed after they fired the missiles, but recently optimism for survival arose.

As they came closer to their destination, they caught sight of a group of grubby people living in the wild. They carefully observed their behavior for half a day before the brigadier decided to make contact with them. As usual, he was right; meeting the scavies was indeed the right decision. These grubby renegades called themselves The Emancipators. They had an impressive system of survival in the illegal wild where they could be killed on sight if discovered by military or law enforcement search teams.

Surprisingly to the British, there were many of these Americans opposing the government living in the abandoned wild, and they were well organized too. They kept well spread out and had a network of communication they employed by using eight stolen and unregistered keyphones, using runners to deliver messages to local groups. The scavies, as the rest of the country called them, set up an outpost in a town called Crystal Lake. The brigadier met with the leaders there.

He truly respected how these Americans had a magnificent sense of pride for their country and patriotic duty. Their leaders saw the arrival of the British as a signal to act and wanted to help them on their mission.

They would travel on different paths and meet in the forest preserve near the Rosemont Convention Center. The Emancipators must witness the rocketed attack and attempt to overthrow and take over the government in the aftermath. The brigadier admired the scruffy bold men, but he kept in mind they would only serve as perfect cover for him and his men to flee back to Wisconsin to try and make it out of this God forsaken country alive. Sleep would come a little easier for the brigadier tonight because he could finally envision his future. The plan was set. Tomorrow he would do his risky duty and send a coded satellite transmission to inform his anxious superiors of the updated plan.

Chapter 1

Today, Wednesday, the ninth of September, was his enrollment date and thus the beginning of his campaign to overthrow the most powerful entity in the world. Former Senator Louis Rizzo sat near the back of a G.A. bus as it drove eastward toward Service City, Chicago. He sat motionless while the peril of war loomed in the very ether surrounding the planet. Its presence was thick and muggy in America but still unidentifiable to the common citizen.

Lou knew the plutocrats planned for this two-class society in America. They had to know the economic policies they bought from the government and their monopolistic control would eventually bankrupt the nation. But the ultimate, transnational plan of getting the countries to agree to a new world economy had failed. What was the plan now? What role will the power brokers choose for America to play? Lou suspected the worst.

It was a typical, hot, humid, late summer day in north east Illinois. With a gaze, he squinted out the window, audaciously looking directly into the blazing sun and enduring the burning in his moist brown eyes. The side of his forehead was resting upon the glass, knocking it lightly each time they hit a bump in the road, and he welcomed the mild pain with every collision.

Lou boarded the bus at the government command building in the small rural town of Byron, Illinois. Unlike the big cities that turned to chaos after the economic collapse, some small towns like Byron remained relatively peaceful. It was a factory farming town with a minute population, protected by the military, as was every factory farm around the country.

This morning the tall trees and slowly flowing Rock River looked particularly serene. Lou forced himself to have a final peaceful moment before leaving to catch his bus. His home was being seized by the state for delinquent property tax payments, and he was scheduled to join the G.A. plan today. He relaxed on his back porch swing, gazing at the river and trees and blanking his mind from the trouble to come. He became mindful in that moment and meditated awhile. Six years ago he wisely fled the big city area, anticipating an economic collapse, to live quietly until his money ran out.

He wasn't a frugal man; he enjoyed giving more than saving . . . like employing Lena, his attractive, 26-year-old, beautiful, Latina maid (who did more for him than just cleaning) for two hundred and fifty dollars a week, right up until two weeks ago when he had one last party with Lena's family and friends, who were still employed at the town's factory farm.

It was at this party that he learned the government moved from Washington D.C. to the Chicago area. Ronnie was in charge of dispatch at the factory farm and a friend of Lou's who attended the party. He told Lou he was in charge of getting the best food to Rosemont because the government now resides there. Ronnie was told to tell no one, but he had to tell Lou because, good old Louie knew more about politics than anyone. It made sense to Lou immediately; *they don't want the rest of the world to know where they are.*

There were a few years of recession after he, Independent Senator Louis Rizzo, was removed from office in a special recall election during his fifth year of serving Illinois. The market was on shaky ground, and unemployment was being reported at twelve percent, though in reality, it was closer to thirty-five percent. Unpredictably, five years ago in September the American government announced to its people that it would no longer trade with any country and would immediately begin manufacturing all its goods at home.

However, Lou was one of the few citizens, not on the government payroll, who knew that was just an excuse. It was a brilliant subterfuge used to cover up the truth. In reality, the rest of the world's major powers had enough of America bringing down world markets with their unregulated financial sector and borrowing trillions to fund pre-emptive wars to secure dwindling foreign oil interests, while always claiming it was to fight terrorism.

In response, a new organization was born; the W.U.N. (World United Nations). It included every civilized country in the world save America. They quickly passed a treaty, ordering America to abide by new world trade regulations, and they must pay restitution for the tragic death toll and refugee situations caused in each of their pre-emptive wars. They were not ordered to pay with the debased dollar, but in goods. The treaty was a bold act to make demands on the most militarized country in the world, but it was essentially fair.

It asked for things the U.S. was in abundance of, like whole grain and fresh water, both of which could save millions of lives if distributed properly.

The U.S refused this treaty, shocking the W.U.N. The following year the W.U.N drew up another treaty the U.S refused to sign. The nuclear weapons ban treaty. Every other country agreed to it and singled out the U.S. as the most likely to start a nuclear holocaust. As a result the rest of the world agreed to cut off all commerce with the United States until they signed the treaty; however the U.S. government reported it quite differently to its people, saying that "by choice we are taking an isolationist foreign policy to stabilize the economy."

When foreign trade was blocked, gas prices skyrocketed affecting everything. It wasn't long before most people had no disposable income to stimulate the economy.

Rich executives bought up thousands of tickets to sporting events and awarded them to lucky, struggling, lower class workers, in an effort to keep professional sports alive.

Sports were still a popular distraction from their bleak futures, filling up plenty of corporate controlled network news time, but nothing could stop the approaching storm September would bring.

During Lou's six years in Byron, he spent time breaking national laws by observing world affairs. He accomplished this by means of his laptop computer and an illegal disk which could gain prohibited access to the world internet without being traced. He observed real foreign news and had contact with a foreign diplomat who informed him that war was inevitable if the U.S. didn't change its foreign policy.

The illegal disk was painstakingly arranged for him to obtain and also a risky endeavor because America had a homeland security budget that was immense, all geared toward one thing: keeping all foreign contact and factual information away from the populace. Having all the specialists in communications on the homeland security payroll made it unproblematic.

The people's tax dollars paid for a quarter million re-educated employees to maintain information flow. The main objective of the wealthy leaders was to suppress unfiltered information from common citizens and feed them only pro Compatriot party, fabricated and filtered news. Yet through unwavering dedication, Lou received this disk that contained satellite access codes without it being detected by homeland security. It was made possible by the only sympathetic man still in the Senate and his only rich friend, Senator Ralph Durbin.

Senator Durbin was a good man inside, but on the outside he remained callously conservative in Washington, where he enjoyed a cozy lifestyle, protected from the working class by towering security gates and armed guards. Daring to help Lou was his only way of feeling some sort of self-worth.

Bribes were paid, and a man died in the aftermath because he had a big mouth, but the transaction was completed, seemingly still in secret.

Tony Swan, the Deputy Prime Minister of Australia, was his foreign contact. He was a man whom Lou had met on ten occasions, all of them very constructive interactions between two enlightened minds.

They first met as diplomats to their respected countries. Lou was first sent there eleven years ago as Illinois' newest senator, who was seated on the foreign relations committee in his first year. It was intentionally given to him to distract him from his home agenda of demonstrating how the country was in for disaster if his protectionist bill was not passed.

That first trip to Australia was the first time Lou ever left the country. Currently, it is impossible to leave or enter the country. President Bud Burns approved the emergency homeland lock down act once the W.U.N. approved a global trade blockade on the U.S.

Foreign communication of any sort was cut off and banned overnight. The government succeeded in totally isolating its people.

Only domestic news was available from the internet network, F.F.A. (Freedom Forever Network) and the television and radio network, American Airways.

The government and the bankers took ownership of nearly eighty percent of all publicly owned middle and lower class properties in the country, leaving the homes vacant and transplanting the people into one-room government housing.

Lou had known this day was inevitable. Now that it had arrived, he still felt unprepared to endure what was to come. The government eviction team came yesterday and dropped a storage pod off their truck onto his front lawn. New evictees were allowed to bring only what they could fit into the moving pod. Lou had a hard time squeezing his things in. He took his precious laptop, his twin size mattress, a dresser, clothes, and hundreds of books and d.v.d documentaries. They were undamaged items found in the rubble after the library in his home town of Des Plaines was bombed by terrorists. It was publicly linked to Muslims, but Lou suspected domestic terrorists did the bidding of those who wished to end the privilege of public libraries that Ben Franklin conceived so long ago. He was not sure if they would allow him to keep the stuff, but he had to try to preserve them.

Presently the bus continued making more stops in small towns along the way. It began to fill up with more disheartened people.

Lou continued to gaze into the sun, fighting to keep his eyes open long enough to be blinded and oblivious to every occurrence in the bus.

As they added miles, he began to daydream. His mind was replaying how he answered his son, Mario's, tearful question at the airport six years ago.

"Why won't you come with us to Australia, dad?"

He wanted to go and question himself everyday why he didn't.

"I can't leave my country, Mario; look around most people are dummies because they've been listening to lies for so long, but I know the truth, and it's my duty as an informed citizen to try to tell people the truth.

If the people are united they can change the government. You understand, right?"

The boy wrinkled his face and sobbed in short breaths. "Then why can't I stay with you, dad," he suddenly cried out and threw his arms around his father . . . not so much a hug as it was a desperate grab to stop his father before he walked away, possibly forever.

Lou pried the boy's arms off of him, still holding his wrists; he squatted so he would be eye-to-eye with him. "Because your job is to get educated, and you can't get that here. You're gonna be an intelligent kid, Mario." He rubbed his hair and smiled down at his son. "Don't be sad. I want you to have fun, play golf, and study hard in school; and don't forget to learn more about American history, okay buddy. You'll form your own opinions. Then, when it's safe, you can come back here and help us rebuild America." Tears blurred his vision and he wiped his eyes. "We're gonna need smart people like you. Then we'll be together again, but you have to be strong." He glanced up to his ex-wife who wasn't sporting her usual frown. She smiled sympathetically.

That was the saddest moment in his life, and his mind conjured up the same feelings now. His face wrinkled up, his stomach went queasy. His unwavering spirit that drove him through all adversities felt like it was dying. He wished he had left this Godforsaken land and was on a beautiful Australian golf course with his son. Finally, he closed his eyes and took in a deep breath. Reality washed over him, and he sought a reason to live. *I have to go on and try to create a movement,* was his prevailing thought. Then his sad, despairing counter thought answered, *The only movement I can create anymore is a bowel movement.*

The bus was more than halfway to Service City, Chicago when it stopped at the government command building in Elgin. A large group of people got on, filling the bus almost to full occupancy. Now a mix of Americans shared the G.A. bus. There were white people from small farming towns like Byron, some Hispanics, and now black people from this larger suburb.

The bus was presently full of voices chattering. Some of the black men were shouting. All of them seemed to be talking at once.

Lou never moved his head as if he was in a daze. Voices were just background babble until one was speaking directed at him.

"Man! What's this boot doing sitting in my window seat," a large, burly black man said. Lou heard this but never moved an inch. He had no remaining spirit to even react. He heard blacks had started calling whites boots because they put on their marching boots and voted the Compatriot party into power, the year of the great party switch six years ago.

His voice grew in aggression, "What's with you, boot? You deaf or just stupid?"

Lou felt a minor impulse to move but ignored it. Feeling so distraught, he didn't care what happened to himself, slightly suicidal perhaps.

Suddenly a powerful left hand struck against his chest, forcing air out of his lungs! This abrupt awakening made Lou's heart jolt while he let out a high pitched shriek. Then his lean body was violently pulled up out of his seat.

The moment was surreal to him.

The powerful black man pulled him into the isle and pitched him to the ground like a slender sack of potatoes. Banging his hip on a metal seat bar on the way down, pain and anger flooded over him at once. Lou rolled to his back, rubbing his hip.

The bus driver glanced in the mirror to see if there was a fight. Seeing one body in the isle didn't warrant a response. He drove on.

Long suppressed dread washed over Lou. He began to weep uncontrollably. "Goddamn it! How did it come to this!" he cried out.

The question was rhetorical; he knew quite well how it came to this.

Before his downfall, he was well respected by the people. When he was a senator, he inspired the apathetic and challenged the establishment itself, but even a well liked man could have his career destroyed if the ones who control the media are persistent enough. The attacks came at him even from the start of his campaign because of his open discourse on the looming economic crisis. His candor and relentless effort got him the votes he needed, and he won the senate seat twelve years ago despite massive corporate voter fraud. His votes were from the majority of people who usually didn't even bother to vote and voter turn out broke state records that year. He was a man of the people, and the only non-millionaire in politics. He was the last Independent ever to serve in congress.

He led a one man charge to clean up government by writing a bill to stop private campaign donations. He fought for retired people in his state, those losing their houses for not being able to pay their property taxes. He also began to work on a public school solution that made sense and exposed the fraud.

He was a hero to the people, but when he decided to address the wasteful state budget, that sealed his fate.

The crooked diversion of funds was shocking to him. Lou ignored bribes and death threats and still probed deeply. He made public speeches promising to expose the corruption in the state senate. He also vowed to expose the federal budget that would appall the public if they knew the wasted funds.

People were listening to him; they were talking about having an honest man in the senate, and they wanted to become involved in their government once again. The American people were in the early stages of creating a movement to take back their government, and Lou was their leader.

Most congressmen would hold their seats until they were ready to retire or died, while the majority party would switch by a slim margin every cycle. Lou made people aware that both parties were bought by the same lobbyists and common people must run for office and replace them. This made Corporate America very concerned about the next election, and a new party was invented. They pretended to be the third party answer to democrats and republicans, one that was truly for the working class.

They were called the Compatriot party. With their promise of change and the hatred the people had for the government, they gained on incumbents in every election they ran in. Amazingly, they won a majority of seats in the house and senate in the next election.

In reality, they were just rich, corporate, conservatives, vetted and chosen by the financial royalists themselves. But their newly contrived rhetoric made them sound like working class and somewhat honest.

The compatriots first and main agenda was to demonize Lou. They claimed that Senator Louis Canti was the biggest threat to government unity; he was destroying the senate and the country by making outrageous claims that could lead to terrorism. The media ran with it for weeks.

He was finally invited to appear live on the FOX news network.

"So Senator Rizzo, is it true that you're an atheist?" was the first question the beautiful blond news lady asked.

Without even acknowledging her, he looked right into the camera and pleaded with the country. "The Compatriot party is no different from the republicans!" he shouted. "They won't even look at my protectionist bill, which we need to pass immediately to avoid a depression. People, we need to take back our government this year. Go to my website and learn the facts."

The interview was cut off there. Lou was never allowed to appear in the privately owned media again. His website got shut down days later.

The ruling elite worked through the media and congress to destroy Lou. They successfully demonized him, calling him the biggest fool ever to serve for wanting to cut some of the military budget. They affirmed cutting the military budget even by one percent would endanger our country in this time of increasing danger. Because of sporadic acts of terrorism, Muslims living in caves on the other side of the world were made out to be a continuing threat that warranted an enormous military budget. They actually planned on increasing military spending. Defense contractors were demanding bigger contracts from their congressional servants. All was going as planned for the ruling elite. Despite the national smear campaign against Lou, they still couldn't convince people in Illinois, who knew him best, that he was a fool. They would continue to support him, and his re-election was inevitable.

That's when it got really dirty in Chicago! A story broke that Lou had an extramarital affair with a young, beautiful woman that worked as a health insurance lobbyist. The woman shamefully acknowledged it was true on FOX news. Lou's constituents found it hard to believe, not about the affair, but that Lou would have anything to do with a health insurance lobbyist.

He always claimed health insurance corporations were barbaric in their profit driven motives. The story was profoundly untrue. Lou never met the woman they claimed he had the affair with. However, it was a problem for him because it was known in certain circles that he did have affairs from time to time. He and his wife weren't a happy couple, almost to the point that Lou loathed her. She never supported him in his endeavors to be in politics, and she didn't understand much of anything he discussed. They were both undereducated victims of the neglected public school system, which was where they met. But Lou self-educated himself with the aid of the city library, his computer, and a hunger for knowledge while sustaining himself by working as a house painter. He and his wife lost any connection intellectually. She preferred to live in ignorant bliss and let her health decline by overeating processed food. Their love for their son kept the marriage going, despite the differences. Lou compromised by having affairs. This made it more difficult to defend himself against the allegation, and more attacks kept coming. They said he was a chronic marijuana addict because he was caught on a street light police camera smoking pot in his car, and the grainy pictures were made public.

After the anti terrorist act (the super patriot act) was again revised, the government could look into anyone's phone and internet records at will if they were suspected to be in contact with terrorists.

They traced everything Lou did on the internet.

Then the major news networks broke the story that consumed all media for weeks: Senator Louis Rizzo has been viewing pornographic websites, and he had installed a concealed camera in his maid's bedroom to view her undress while at his office computer. The pretty Latina maid, who worked for Lou's wife, quit her job and became a media darling. Over and over the country viewed her explaining how violated she felt after undressing every night and not knowing she was being watched by a perverted, sex-crazed man.

The word, pervert, stuck to him after it was repeated for weeks. The nick name Peek-a-boo Lou was given to him, and he became a national joke.

All the while the economy drifted to the precipice of collapse.

No one in the media asked why he was traced on the internet like a terrorist, and because sex scandals were top stories in America, nothing was unusual about it dominating the news. Calls for him to resign were being echoed throughout congress as well as his state. But somehow Lou still had core support from the people he helped, and they stuck by him.

Then horror struck!

The Des Plaines library blew up, killing fifty-eight people in his home town. It was the very library Lou educated himself at and one of the only ones remaing in the state. A powerful exploding device did the damage. Who placed it and why the library was targeted was never made clear. Only the H.S.I.U. (Homeland Security Investigation Unit) was allowed to investigate, and they quickly blamed it on the terrorist group Al Zazar.

With Lou still demanding the government to lower the military budget to pay down debt, he was criticized for ignoring terrorism in his own town, and they blamed him for the tragedy. Lou was removed from office in an unprecedented recall by his constituents six months after the bombing. It emotionally devastated him.

He divorced, sold everything and gave his wife $500,000 of his $685,309 total value. He told her to leave the country immediately and get their son a good education in Australia. Later that year the Compatriot party won a large majority in the house and senate, as well as the presidency.

All this occurred only six years ago.

After his son departed for Australia, he took his money and moved to Byron where the houses were cheaper. For the last six years he watched the country fall into chaos and then re-emerge under this oddly constructive tyranny.

Presently his face was buried in his hands against the grimy bus floor. He was on his arms and knees with his head down and ass up.

The bus driver glanced in the mirror and amused himself by swaying the bus left then right. Lou's ass swayed back and forth before he tipped over, falling on his sore hip. The driver grinned. Lou kept covering his face with his hands and a sort of moaning surfaced from his throat. The moans were sporadic, incoherent, hateful words spewing out of him.

People stared. Lou's way of crying was humorously odd, but the sight only slightly amused the preoccupied spectators. For the first time in recent memory, Lou lost all control of his emotions. Dread washed over him, and long repressed feelings overwhelmed him.

When he eventually stopped moaning, the sound of the bus tires humming on the pavement returned to him. He sat up slowly and hugged his knees. Remarkably, he felt no shame for this humiliating public display. His anxiety had finally released his stomach from the queasy hold it secured. He felt oddly at ease. The weight of despair had been lifted. This degrading episode was a moment of catharsis. Now he could see his current situation for what it was . . . no more trying to understand the ambiguous evil nature of the oligarchs. It was time to do what he did best: speak his mind.

Chapter 2

He regained his intellect once the wheel in his head began to turn again.

He looked around, pleasantly surprised he was not the object of everyone's amusement. A woman, six rows back, was looking right at him with pity in her eyes. She seemed to be in her fifties, and her sun-beaten, prematurely-aged face made him look back at her with equal pity. Other than her, nobody else was paying any attention to him anymore.

Slowly he rose to his feet, swaying as he took a few steps forward, discovering seats were scarce. He boldly went to the nearest one available and slickly sat down next to the very man that threw him. The thug had a black bandana on his bald head. He flinched defensively the moment Lou came into his peripheral vision. Lou just sat looking forward calmly as if nothing had happened.

"What the fuck is wrong with you, boot? You want me to toss you like a bitch again?" The large, imposing, bald, black man glared down at him with crazy distant eyes. Their piercing glower and his flaring nostrils on his thick nose terrified Lou, but he didn't show it.

"Relax man," he said calmly.

The man loudly inhaled slowly and deeply while drawing his right fist back, gearing it up for a powerful blow.

Louis raised his forearm, fist clenched in a defensive position. "Come on now, I just want to sit here a sec and talk. Relax, man." Instinctively, Lou readied his body to recoil into the isle so not to fully absorb a lethal blow. His leg muscles twitched in the moment of silence.

"You sure is one crazy fool," the thug growled. Then his arm relaxed, and the crazy glare dissipated as he exhaled. "You got nothing to say to me, boot. You white people fucked this country all up. First them rich folks take our jobs away and give 'em to poor people in shitty countries who work for peanuts. Now they done made all us broke so they can put us back to work for peanuts. It's bullshit, man."

He settled down in his seat and looked back out the window. In the distance they saw the imposing gate guarding the affluent city of Park Ridge.

"Meanwhile, all them rich folk in their fancy houses with their gates and armed guards. Hell, all you whites ain't been nothing but boots marching to make us slaves again."

"Let me tell you, man, I'm no boot," Lou said. "In fact, I fought against them. I was the last independent in congress, but they disgraced me in the media and got me booted out. People are easily fooled you know."

The black man rubbed his chin and frowned, as if he made a rare mistake.

"Actually," Lou continued, "I gotta admit the black community stayed loyal to me, and I still got all their votes in the recall election."

The black man studied the white guy's face and squinted.

Lou's face was rugged with defined features, perhaps handsome to some women, those who would look beyond his receding hairline and the scar over his right eye. Lou was a slender man and did not look very physically fit, but he had an aura of scrappiness to him.

The man looked at his thin, brown and grey hair and into Lou's mild, brown eyes. Something about them was familiar. They exuded honesty, kindness and hardship. "Man, you look kinda familiar," he pondered a moment, rubbing his scrubby chin. "Who was you?" He looked back at the skinny, white dude. A slight smile flashed across his face as his brain produced the memories. "Is you that perverted, Governor, that was sleeping around with all them bitches?"

Lou gave the man an angry look. "Actually I was a Senator here."

The man erupted in laughter, vigorously and uncontrollable.

Perfect time to stick the knife in, if that was my intent, Lou thought.

"You is, ain't you?" The black man's violent image disappeared as Lou watched him continue to laugh in a child-like way. "Yeah, man, you was all over the news some years back." The man was talking and laughing louder as his enthusiasm grew. "Damn that was some five six years ago. They said some nasty things about you, boy, talking about all them porno sites you were slapping your stick too. Shit, how bout that little Mexican bitch's pussy you was scoping." His laugh went to a high pitch crescendo.

Most of the other passengers nearby were now staring.

Lou shook his head in disgust and then yelled. "Yeah, they did some nasty stuff to me, and what you did to me was nasty too. I should be asking what the fuck is wrong with *you.*" Lou said the last part in his tough guy voice with an Italian gangster accent.

"That's it, man, you is one crazy boot. I'm gonna mess you up boy. You ready to cry like a baby again?"

"No way," Lou roared, "that crying thing won't be happening again. I got it all out. I'm ready to stand up and fight for what's right again."

Lou got up, startling the black man. Then he smiled, held out his hand. "My names Lou, and I'm no boot."

There was a momentary pause, making Lou terrified again, but his eyes still appeared defiant and brave.

"Yeah, that's it, man, Lou Rizzie or something." The tension dropped, and both men relaxed. The thug erupted into more laughter, subtle and controllable this time. He eventually stopped and looked up at Lou, who was still standing and extending his arm. The thug grabbed his hand, squeezed tightly and shook it. "My name's Tyrell, and you in my world now so act right, boy." He released Lou's hand and wiped his own on his shirt. "Man, if you spank it with your right hand, I hope you done washed it this morning." He broke into laughter again.

Lou chucked to display sociability. "That's real funny, Tyrell. Now can we talk like adults for a minute?"

"I don't talk much with crazy white dudes," Tyrell replied

callously as his laughter abruptly ceased.

"You see that's what we have to solve. We have to kill the hatred. That's why our class is weak and powerless, because we're divided and dumb."

"Who you calling dumb, boot?" Tyrell snapped.

"All of us who buy into the hate. Listen, some white people believe the majority of our tax money was being wasted on welfare for poor, lazy, black people who don't want work. Truth is, it was being wasted on everything they did: war, bail outs, homeland security, drug enforcement. Every government program was corrupt and running up debt while taxes on upper-class citizens decreased. Our government failed us because we, the people, failed to change it. Now we're living in the aftermath of the consequences. We should have done something long ago when they started outsourcing jobs to maximize profits. Instead of having small local business we got unrestricted monopoly capitalism. Wages and jobs shrunk, and towns became devastated. I'll bet the best paying job in your town was drug dealer. A lot of black communities were hit hard by recession and they inevitably became violent. Therefore, the white conception is blacks are lazy and violent." He drew a short breath, relieved Tyrell was still allowing him to speak. *The first hurdle is to get them to listen.*

Lou was trying to engage eye contact. "So conversely, I completely understand why blacks resent whites. But I know if we lived in a better society, fair and rightly governed by honest people, we would all get along just fine."

Tyrell squinted and inhaled deeply.

Lou continued, "Middle class whites always thought they had it better than poor black folks sponging off welfare. Well, not no more. We're all equal now. We're all broke. We represent eighty percent of this nation, and we're still divided by race. The only way we can win is to unite." He looked around as if he said a contentious word too loud.

"Unite to win what? Ain't nothing to win anymore," Tyrell said surprisingly somber.

"To take back our country from the wealthy plutocrats, make our government by, of, and for the people again."

"Yeah, what you gonna do against the mighty G? They in

charge of the po-lice and the army. Look around you, boy. They ain't stupid. They got the game rigged, fool." Tyrell sounded as sarcastic as possible.

Lou heaved a sigh. "There's one thing that still exists in this dying democracy: elections."

"Man you *is* a fool if you think they ain't got that rigged. Damn, boy, they been rigging that shit for fifty years, and it don't even matter who wins. Both sides are the same. Shit, there ain't been nobody worth voting for since you."

Tyrell chuckled at Lou's display of ignorance, and Lou admired Tyrell for knowing the truth.

"Maybe I'll run again. They can rig a close election, but they can't steel a landslide, and if they did, wouldn't that cause the people to finally revolt?" Again, Lou felt uneasy the moment he said the last word. Tyrell seemed a bit edgy too; his eyes grew wide the moment the words were spoken.

"Man," Tyrell spoke quieter now, "I like your enthusiasm, even if you is crazy. But most people nowadays, they don't even know how or where to vote."

Lou was shaken with sudden paranoia from his last remark. His eyes searched the bus for a monitoring device. There was the standard overhead camera in the front of the bus mounted to the roof and parallel to the driver. That was to be expected, but surely it couldn't monitor much sound, certainly not a voice this far away, *could it?*

They drove down the empty highway exit ramp and accelerated down the empty road toward the service city. Lou and Tyrell were silent for some time. The bus turned on to Congress Boulevard, and the road went under the old abandoned Chicago post office.

Tyrell was looking out the window. "Man, look at this shit," he said sounding disgusted.

All along the way you could see vacated neighborhoods. Once thriving middle and lower class areas now were eerie and desolate. Buildings seemed dilapidated and dirty. Some were sound, sturdy structures, but the windows were broken, and graffiti covered most every building in many different colors, most with black paint. A variety of symbols, words and slogans could be seen; some artistically beautiful, but all their vague meanings bleak. However, the vacated neighborhoods were not completely empty.

Tyrell noticed something. "Lookie here," he said, nudging Lou.

Lou leaning forward to see out the window. A shaggy human figure in the distance wearing a sweat stained tee shirt and raggedy jeans was crossing the street, looking over at the bus. A look of shock crossed the man's grimy face, and he darted off.

Scavies, they were being called. The ones who did not want to register for the government action plan or join the military. They would rather fend for themselves living a scavenger's life.

They were not frightened by the lack of medical care, despite people dying from a new disease that can strike anyone at any age. This horrible disease was not unlike an extreme case of asthma. The bronchial tubes swell dramatically and the airways in the lungs become so constricted, the victim eventually dies with the agony of slow suffocation. The government publicly asserted over the last year that once someone joins the G.A. plan, he would receive the vaccine. It was an extra incentive for people to enroll and not add to the scavie population. This made Lou suspicious of what the horrible truth could be. The government never publicly released any credible or helpful information so the public had no way of knowing how to prevent acquiring this horrible disease. It was never officially given a name, but most of the common folk called it the strangler disease. Lou guessed it was deadly toxins in the air.

The scavies distrusted the Compatriot party. Many of them also believed the government was behind the outbreak.

To survive, scavies ate pigeons, rats, fish, and the more crafty hunters could catch rabbits, squirrels, and deer.

The government admitted there could be a few hundred scavies in the outskirts of Service City, Chicago, and that they would be apprehended. However, it was rumored there may be more of them than the government wanted to admit.

A thought occurred to Louis. *The scavies are the last truly free Americans. I wonder, could they ever become organized?*

"Man I'd be one of those people too," Tyrell said after the

scavie ran off, "but I don't wanna die from that strangler disease. Every time I cough I think I got it."

"I know what you mean; nobody even knows how you get it. The government has silenced the entire medical community and cut us off from the rest of the world. I happen to know..." Lou stopped in mid sentence and looked up at the camera.

"What man," Tyrell demanded.

"Nothing." Lou spoke quietly "We'll have to talk somewhere more private."

Tyrell nodded, feeling a sort of kinship with Lou, something that was quite surprising to him. This white guy was different from everyone else. It seemed as if he was above the turmoil with a higher knowledge, and Tyrell no longer felt the hatred that most white people evoked in him.

The bus rolled on without a stop.

The massive depression did help in one way; years ago traffic was so bad that city people spent a huge amount of their lives in traffic jams. Now the streets were virtually empty. Government and military vehicles were all that roamed the roads with the exception of rich folks tooling around in expensive sports cars or limousines. This transformation happened rapidly, all during the last six years.

The unregulated greed driven only by short term financial gain, with careless disregard to the future, had been doing damage for decades.

Presently, the bus was relatively quiet. Everyone was nervous with anticipation of the forthcoming life-changing event. The bus was driving down Ogden Avenue, Garfield Park, near down town. The city had suddenly come to life. They passed a busy hospital. People were out roaming everywhere, some walking, some standing and chatting.

It seemed overcrowded to Lou, coming from his small town. It looked like a street fest. People were congregating everywhere. They dressed primarily in similar clothes; dark blue was the main color, and all the jackets and pants were clearly manufactured at the same textile mill.

Condominium buildings lined the streets. There were sturdy, older buildings that at one time people paid hundreds of thousands of dollars per unit for, and newer ones: plain with basic architecture, made epically for the Government Action Plan.

Everyone on the bus was looking out the windows. The bus driver's voice pierced the tense air. "This is 915, Northwest route arriving. Where should I go, fifteen sixty one still?"

"No, check that, 915," the voice from the radio speaker replied, "The processors are set up next door. We're filling up fifteen sixty-three today."

"Affirmative," the driver replied.

Lou closed his eyes and wished, *Please let us get one of the old well-crafted buildings. These new ones are so crappy and cheap looking.*

He immediately felt stupid for wishing that because that ensured him of getting a new prefabricated building, for he was convinced that whatever he wished for, he wouldn't get. Hence, his credo was, *don't count on what you wish for*, his modification of, *be careful what you wish for*. He reasoned with himself in his endeavors by creating a new credo: *do your best and never give up, but in no way wish or pray for that is the duty of the inactive*.

The bus passed a well-constructed, older condominium building with elegant brown and red brick patterns, complete with iron railed balconies. It was originally intended for upper class yuppie couples with two incomes and no kids. They paid a high price to live so close to downtown. The bus pulled in front of the one next door, a newer building just as high, basically identical in size but very plain, no balconies or bricks, just a plain framework and brown vinyl siding to match the older buildings' brown bricks.

The bus driver parked in front and stretched his arms over his head. After heaving a loud moan at full stretch, he pulled the handle and opened the door.

Through the window, Lou saw people sitting behind folding tables on the lawn near the front entrance. They were all wearing identical grey uniforms. Each person seated had a laptop computer on the table in front of him.

A tall, burly uniformed man with a G.A. badge over his right, muscular, chest and a bolt blaster visibly holstered on his belt, stepped into the bus and looked back at all the insecure faces. "Okay ladies and gentleman, exit the bus and come over to the processor's tables. Please line up in front of one of the receptionists in an orderly fashion so we can get you all registered and assigned to a unit." He stepped out of the bus, followed by the driver. People slowly began to stand.

"Damn, man, I should of got on the bus last week like I was suppose to," said Tyrell as he stood. "I'd probably be in that brick building next door."

"Yeah. probably Tyrell, but then you would have never met me." Lou flashed him a slight smile and headed up the isle.

Everyone began lining up. With ten processors and forty-six new arrivals, the lines were four to five people deep. Lou was last in line. It was about ten minutes till the four people in front of him were finished.

"Name," the middle-aged, female asked.

"Louis Rizzo, that's r-i-z-z-o." In seconds the computer produced his profile.

The lady mulled over the information. "Hmmm, maybe I got this wrong. Are you Louis Rizzo, 936 Rock River Road, Byron Illinois?"

"That's right," Lou replied.

She leaned over to the man to her right and quietly spoke. "This can't be right, can it? Look at his employment history. He's classified as upper class." She turned her laptop so he could view it.

"Check with Officer Zipp. He'll probably just update his status. He's obviously not upper class anymore." He looked at Lou with a smug smile.

She adjusted her laptop and examined it again. "Okay, sir, if you could just hang on a minute, we'll get you set up right away." She got up and walked to the front of the yard where the G.A. officer was positioned. As she talked to the officer, he gave her a puzzled look. They both walked back together. The processor sat in front of her computer while the officer bent at the waist peering over her shoulder. Something drew his attention. He moved closer to the screen, placing his hand on the table. After a moment, he stood straight and looked down at Lou.

Lou was five foot ten and figured the huge man to be around six foot five or so. The burley man had a pudgy face, thick black hair parted to the side and wooly eyebrows that rested closely over his dark eyes.

"Excuse us for the delay, Mr. Rizzo, we just need to update your profile." His voice was deep and authoritative. "I see your last employment was for the government, an elected official no less." He raised his eyebrows, acting impressed.

"Yeah," replied Lou.

The quiet uncomfortable pause insisted Lou say something more.

"Hey, that's okay about the delay. I have plenty of time, my friend." He stepped closer and extended his hand over the table. "I'm Lou, nice to meet you Mr.…."

The burley man looked down at him puzzled and made no movement to shake Lou's hand. "You can just call me officer. See the badge, sir?"

Lou looked at the badge, which was about eye level to him. The officer seemed about thirty years old and displayed military mannerisms. Lou was forty-eight years old and looked every year of it.

The officer never moved to shake Lou's hand and stared blankly down at him for a moment.

"Yeah, of course, officer, that's fine," he said lowering his arm. "I just…you know, wanted to meet you on a personal level."

The officer seemed shocked, displaying a frown. Then he turned his head slightly as if considering his next move carefully. Shaking off the impulsive reaction this comment would warrant, his expression suddenly warmed.

"Alright Lou, I'm G.A.T.E. Captain, Edward Zipp." Lou took a closer look at his badge. The words Government Action was across the top, Captain, in the middle, and below it, in smaller letters, was Team Enforcement.

Gate, that's a clever acronym, Lou thought.

"Now then, you were last employed by the government and making enough money to be classified as upper class, but you haven't filed taxes for the last six years. So what have you been doing?"

Louis squinted and turned his gaze upward, appearing to be in deep thought. "Well sir, I haven't filed taxes because I haven't earned anything for six years. I held out in Byron as long as I could, and now I'm broke." He shrugged his shoulders and raised his palm to the air. "So here I am. I'm ready to work for a fair wage. You think I can be a G.A.T.E. Captain like you? I got good references."

Captain Zipp snickered at the outrageous comment. "You'll have a job placement interview tomorrow. First, you need to get moved in." He looked down at the woman and softly patted her back. "Go ahead and check him in and then you can update his file."

"Yes sir," she answered and opened a lockbox next to her on the table. She took out a dark blue object that fit neatly in the palm of her hand. With a flick of her thumb, she flipped it open. It was a keyphone. She held it sideways and slid the top edge through a magnetic scanner/transmitter module that was connected to the computer. She slid it through once and the phone lit up. Then it made a quiet beep. Bringing it closer to her face, she looked at the display screen of the phone. As soon as the phone finished starting up, she held down a button until the phone beeped again. She turned back to the computer, made a few clicks and hit the enter key. Next, she slid the top of the phone through the scanner again and looked at the display screen of the phone to make sure it received the information.

"Okay, Mr. Rizzo, here's your keyphone. It's important you don't lose this. You slide the top of it here through scanners." She touched the top of the phone. "It will unlock your door and can be used like a credit card to buy things. Right now your account holds a balance of negative eighty because you're charged for the phone, but you won't be charged interest for that."

"How nice," Lou said derisively.

She went on, unfazed. "You're approved to charge up to two thousand dollars on your account, and your interest rate will be only eighteen percent for this year." She smiled looking up at him.

He just stared at her, stupified.

"This, of course, is your phone too. Your phone number is your building number ,followed by your unit number, which is three-fourteen." She folded up the phone and handed it to him. "Now, what was your moving pod number?"

"Ah, what was it?" he slapped his head trying to jar his memory. "My short term memory isn't what it used to be. Just give me a sec, hon." He rubbed his chin for a moment, then blurted out, "fifty-nine."

She typed on the laptop and waited for the information to process.

"Okay, your pod will be here today at three fifteen. You'll get a courtesy call on your phone when it arrives, and you have until five to unload it. "There's a tutorial you are obligated to watch that will automatically run once you turn on your unit's computer for the first time. It explains things you need to know." She smiled at him. "Have a nice day, Mr. Rizzo."

Lou studied the phone in his hand and started walking away without a word.

Officer Zipp began walking after him. "Hey Governor," he wrongly called, "I'm monitoring unloading hours today so I'll see you later."

A chill passed down Lou's spine as he imagined his laptop being confiscated by this boot kisser. "Boy, they give you the important jobs, huh?" he replied over his shoulder without stopping.

Lou climbed the veranda steps and walked through the front door. The lobby had a sophisticated look to it, though somewhat dreary: all plainly colored in light and darker shades of gray. Off to each side were the stairways. All the floors were covered in durable, short, grey carpet. Ahead were the elevators where six people were standing around, waiting for them to return. In the middle of the lobby was a directory screen. A man who was looking at it strolled toward the elevators, leaving the area empty.

Lou walked up to it. It was a sleek computer monitor, large in width and length but amazingly thin. It listed all eighty units, floor by floor. The building was ten stories high with eight units on every floor. Along the side of the directory screen ran the names of the residents listed in alphabetical order with the unit number next to them. There were only thirty-six names so far, and Lou's was already up there with the number 314 after it. He went to the west stairway and quickly ran up, two stairs at a time.

He ascended to the third floor. Short of breath he walked down the hall, and found unit 314. He flipped open his keyphone and slid the top through the magnetic scanner over the door handle, and the bolt unlocked. He entered the room and was surprised to see it was cozier compared to what he expected. The same grey carpet from the hall covered the inside floor too. It was a one-room studio, about three hundred square feet. The back wall, the exterior one, had two windows. The front wall had a shelf connected to it, waist high. On it was a monitor, also built into the wall so there were no visible cords, save the one that ran from the bottom of the screen to a mouse, which was sitting on top of a mouse pad. There was no keyboard. It's unlikely many people here would care since writing had become uncommon. (Creative and non-fiction writing was already a dying art when the government prohibited independent journalism. They avowed that the Freedom Forever Network would report the news honestly, and independent journalism was divisive and unhelpful to the effort of uniting the country.)

The room was empty except for a plastic chair in front of the computer table and the complementary twin size bed frame and box spring.

The left wall was the kitchen area and the bathroom.

He sat in the plastic chair and slid in close to the monitor. There was no power button anywhere, just a plain square screen with a scanner built into the side and two speaker slots on the bottom. Across the top, on the black plastic frame, was the brand name, Technotron. The middle of the first letter "o" was clear plastic that could be a power light indicator, but Lou first thought of a camera lens. He rubbed his thumb over it. The screen remained blank. Then he touched the mouse, and the monitor turned on. There were a few boxes he could click. They were labeled, (Freedom Forever Network), (Freedom Airways), and

(Personal account). The one on top that was blinking said (new user Tutorial). He clicked it and then clicked the volume icon at the bottom and turned it to full.

"Welcome to your new G.A. home," a pleasant female voice announced. She went on to explain how wonderfully the G.A. plan is working and all about how America is manufacturing its own goods at home now.

"America will be a strong, self-sufficient nation with no unemployment and no homelessness. The destructive and unfair politics of the past are over. When the Compatriot party was elected overwhelmingly by the people, they took action, government action! Now all the country's problems are being solved in the most practical ways."

Lou got up and walked toward the kitchen sink, trying to momentarily block out the propaganda the tutorial woman was spewing. It disgusted him deeply because it sounded so sincere. It almost made him feel fondness for the Compatriot party.

He could hear the voice babble on while he opened the water faucet and bent over to sip it and rinse his mouth. The water tasted fine, "Ah, good old Lake Michigan. They can't pollute you enough to taste bad," he said aloud. As the tutorial lady continued, his mind drifted to the thought of Officer Zipp watching him unload his pod.

Being filled with rare books and dvds, his curiosity would lead to him finding his laptop.

Suddenly he froze with his mouth wide open, and a chill passed down his spine. The same feeling he got every time he discovered he'd made a stupid mistake. *Oh my God! I forgot about the satellite link disk!*

The precious illegal disk was still in the disk drive of the laptop. He intended to hide it somewhere clever, and it slipped his mind. Realizing it was in the worst possible place made him overload with paranoia and self-loathing. Surely his laptop would be inspected and perhaps confiscated. That was predictable. It would hurt to lose his laptop, but he could overcome that. However, if that disk is found he would be a prisoner for life.

A familiar feeling came over him. It was intense self-hatred.

He hated his weaknesses, forgetfulness being the most annoying. It's an uncontrollable weakness with no bliss. At least with his other weaknesses there's an upside, short term, pleasant high, or sexual stimulation. But simply forgetting something so critical was just plain stupidity.

His self-hatred intensified, causing blood to rush to his head, making him feel light-headed. He fell to the floor carefully, using his hands and knees to absorb his weight. Rolling onto his butt and heels, he buried his head between his knees and wrapped his arms around his legs.

He reasoned with himself. *Come on, it's no big deal. I can outsmart that big goon. The laptop is squeezed between the mattress and the wall. Ill just eject the disk without anyone seeing and hide it in my pants.*

He lay back on the floor, stretching his arms over his head, fully extending his limbs. His sore back emitted a flurry of cracking sounds.

As he gazed up at the ceiling, the tutorial woman began to explain the job placement interview process that was soon to come.

Stress was why he could forget something so important. Giving up his peaceful home where he lived leisurely for the last six years caused him to have awful anxiety for weeks prior to this day.

How will he live in this hectic environment, return to a forty hour work week? He felt like his life officially reached the beginning of the closing chapter. Optimism was hard to spiritually construct. He relaxed his body, closed his eyes, and tried to meditate. The tutorial voice and worry faded.

Sixteen minutes later he got up, feeling composed and mentally in control again. He walked to the window and looked at his new view. No longer would he see the beautiful trees, the serene Rock River and the abundant wildlife. That was the only thing he still loved about his country, the land itself, the beautiful wild.

The side of the building next door was his view now. As he hung his head and sighed, something caught his eye. Quickly peering into the third floor window next door, he saw the figure of a large-breasted, attractive woman in a tee shirt walk into view and sit down. She carelessly set her bed and dresser on each side of the window and from Lou's unit, he had a clear view of her sitting on her bed.

He grinned slightly. *Maybe I'll have a pleasant view after all,* he thought.

Chapter 3

Lou spent time surfing the governmentally controlled internet. People could not communicate with one another or post anything on the web anymore. Most people didn't even have a keyboard. The entire web was shut down for a year during the chaos of the collapse, and it emerged as a government information service when the G.A. plan was passed. The only technological way to communicate was with your keyphone, and it only reached people within your service city region. Lou often marveled in horror how brilliantly the media owners kept the people strategically divided for decades before the collapse. Now it was flawless. He was convinced this was planned long ago, and every horrible decision made by his government was part of an evil, unchallenged plan. It sounded so crazy when he talked about it, like he was a conspiracy nut, but being a student of history, he knew the awful truth always sounds crazier than fiction because it is. It's just too hard for most people to imagine the depth of men's greed when they're already obscenely rich and powerful. The only challenge ever given to the plutocrats, in *his* lifetime, he gave himself. That was a proud legacy for him even if he achieved nothing else.

Still, he knew he had to shout to the people once more, even if it is again vain. Only then could he die believing he did all he could. That's why he sent away his son and remained in this land of experimental tyranny. That is also why he is presently exposing himself to the Freedom Forever Network. *You have to know what the people are being told and expose the lies.* He forced himself to view the propaganda and became fascinated.

Time passed unnoticed until his keyphone rang at 3:15.

"Hello," he answered in a monotonous voice.

"Mr. Rizzo, your moving pod has arrived. You have until 5:00 p.m. to unload," a woman's voice announced.

He got up, unbuttoned his pants and pulled them partly down. Pulling up his underwear, he folded over the elastic waistband of his briefs, making his underwear tighter. He quickly headed out, taking the elevator this time and exiting through the rear door of the building. There were 20 pods lined up in a row along the side of the alleyway. The Pod carrier trucks just park behind the building and unload the pods as they slide off one by one on a retractable ramp that extends from the side of the truck to the ground.

People were already beginning to unload, while G.A. officers looked on.

He walked along the row looking at the numbers till three from the end. He came to pod fifty-nine.

There were six uniformed men in blue and one captain in gray. Lou didn't bother to look at any of them directly, attempting to be inconspicuous.

"You don't have to have all your stuff moved up to your unit by five; just get it out of the pod by then," he heard the deep voice of Captain Zipp explaining to a new arrival.

Lou never turned to look and unlatched the pod door. He opened it, feeling the familiar uneasiness in his stomach that occurred when he was nervous. His political achievements were only attained by his public speaking, and this weakness would awaken to do battle every time he was about to give a speech. Throughout his adult life, he was plagued by nervousness, but he audaciously conquered it every time. He opened the pod door. Moving swiftly, he took out the first thing in his way: a desk chair. He set it down a little too quickly, and it rolled a foot before the wheels tangled in the grass. Just as the chair crashed to the ground, he inadvertently looked toward Officer Zipp, who looked back at the same moment.

Zipp looked Lou in the eyes and frowned. Lou's expression was wide-eyed shock momentarily. Then he smiled and nodded. "Take it easy down there, Governor!"

Lou carried on in a frenzy, pulling out bags of clothes and boxes of books while observing the officer in his peripheral vision. He removed the last box, clearing the way so he could move the mattress and get at the laptop.

As he went back in the pod, he sensed Zipp was finishing up his conversation by the way he spoke louder. "No one is going to steel your crappy stuff. We're here watching. Now get moving."

Knowing time was short, he pushed the mattress forward a foot, leaned it out toward him, and balanced it on his thigh while he bent over and grabbed the laptop with both hands. Keeping it out of sight behind the mattress, he opened it and struggled to hit the power button.

"I swear, some people can't follow the easiest directions," The voice was close and approaching fast. The computer powered up, and Lou nearly dropped it as he fumbled for the tiny eject button. Just as the disk slid out, a shadow darkened his view.

"How's it going, Governor?" Zipp asked.

"Fine, I guess," Lou quickly responded from behind the mattress. He grabbed the edges of the disk and yanked it out. Pushing the mattress out with his shoulder, he closed the laptop. Just as he snapped the computer shut and placed it on the floor, he cried out, "Ah, my Goddamn back is killing me." He stood upright and grabbed at his back with both hands. The mattress fell against the wall as his fingers lifted up the back of his shirt. Pretending to massage his lower back, he pushed the disk up against his spine and slid it down into his underwear, lodging it against the top of his buttocks. "Some huge thug roughed me up on the bus this morning and threw me out of my seat. Now my back is all out of whack again. You think you could just help me pull this thing out?"

A moment of silence as the officer stared at him. Lou brought his arms forward and stretched them over his head, showing his hands were empty.

"Sorry Governor, I really can't," Zip said with a chuckle. "We're not movers, you know. Now come on out here. You gotta pull it from this side, or it'll get stuck on the grass. A man of your intelligence couldn't figure that out, huh? You haven't done much moving, I'll bet."

"That's not true. I used to move my stuff before I became Senator."

"Hey, that's too bad you got roughed up. The bus driver

told me about it. It was that big black guy, I heard."

Lou nodded as he got out.

"You can file a complaint against him, you know." Lou felt the Officer looking him over.

"Maybe I will. Hey, why are you calling me Governor when I served in the senate?"

"The senate, yeah, don't Governors serve in the senate?" Officer Zipp seemed confused. He knew very little about his government, like most citizens. He just followed orders to subsist.

He sees the world through tunnel vision.

"No, senators serve in the senate, I was senator, and I got booted out before my first term was over."

"Senator huh...whatever, I like the sound of governor, so get use to it." Lou grabbed the front of the mattress and pulled it slowly out.

"Anyway, just get the stuff out of the pod. We gotta take a look at everything. Then you can take your time getting it up to your unit. You can ask someone to help you with the big stuff. Then you help them; that's how it works around here."

The mattress was halfway out, and the laptop tipped over and crashed against the plastic floor.

"Oh boy, that didn't sound good. You breaking stuff now, Governor?"

Lou stopped pulling.

"It's alright; keep pulling. Whatever it was, it already fell," Zipp gazed in the pod. Once Lou pulled out the mattress, Zipp walked in. "It's an old laptop computer," he erupted. He picked it up and stared at it. "This is something we have to take. You're not allowed to have this, you know. You got a computer in your unit already."

"Well, I don't use it for much," said Lou. "I was addicted to this online video game called War Wager. I was really good at it." He grinned and shook his head, "Man, I used to love beating the shit out of people in that game."

The genius of the program on the satellite disk currently stuck to his ass was its camouflage. While Lou was linked to the world internet committing treason, it would appear to homeland security internet monitors that he was playing an online video game at the War Wager website. The only suspicion they could have is over the many hours he spent there.

"Yeah, I heard of it," replied Zipp. The rich kids play it. I didn't think anyone outside the gated cities played," he said, giving Lou a strange look.

"Well, I guess it's no big deal," Lou said, sounding ambivalent. "I guess I was wasting too much time with that game anyway. But hey, they damn well better pay me for it. It's got to be worth a few hundred at least. You gonna just rob a fellow citizen? That things an antique, man."

"I'll get back to you on that, Governor." He walked away staring at the computer and tilting it from side to side.

Lou was sad to see his computer carried away but warm with relief that the disk was safe for the moment. He went in the pod, intending to move the disk to the front of his underwear. Just as he grabbed at the back of his pants, he looked out the door. A gate officer was standing in view of him, just staring at him with his arms crossed. Lou grabbed a box and brought it out.

In a little while he had all his things out and aligned neatly in front of the pod. The whole time the gate cop watched him and the Hispanic man with the pod next door. Lou got a feeling the little Hispanic guy was glancing at his stuff and intentionally setting his things closer to it.

"Hey man," Lou called to him, "can we start bringing our stuff up?"

"No man, didn't they tell you?" The little man pointed to the cop. "You got to wait for these guys to look at your stuff, man."

The search team was still checking some woman's belongings three pods down.

"Why are they so Goddamn slow?" Lou blew through his lips and looked at the staring cop. "Watch where you put your stuff so we don't get confused, alright buddy," he said to the Hispanic man. The little man moved away without a reply. Lou went to the box labeled as the *sin bin* in black marker. He pulled out his smoking pouch and filled his pipe with sweet tobacco. As he lit his pipe, he unthinkingly began squatting to sit on a box full of books. The disk began to bend on his ass. Loosing his balance, he dropped his pipe before he steadied himself and stood back up clumsily, turning to see if anyone noticed. Surprisingly, someone did! A new gate officer was approaching fast and staring right at him. Lou massaged his back and grimaced, as if in pain. This grey shirt officer was a slender man in his forties with grayish dark hair that was cut short. The man was similar to Lou. They had the same build and similar age, but this man had a dangerous look to him. His evil gaze pierced Lou's bluffing eyes as he walked up.

"Mr. Rizzo, we need your Internet password so we can log on to your Freedom Forever Network account." The man spoke with a lowered brow. His fists were clinched, and his forearm muscles flexed.

"Why would you need that? I'm sure you can log on with a universal password the government uses," Lou said, holding his hands skyward in bewilderment.

"I see," the man said. He stood next to Lou and put his arm around his shoulder. "Show me what you got in the pod," he said and forced Lou to walk to the door. The officer released him and stood right behind him.

"Open it," the officer ordered.

"Its empty," Lou said as he opened the door.

The officer swiftly grabbed the door with his left hand. With his right he grabbed the back of Lou's neck, striking it hard enough for him to see a flash of white. He forced him into the pod and gave a mighty push. Lou stumbled forward a few steps, and the cop shut the door.

"What the hell, man!" said Lou turning with his fists up in defense. He faced the cop and saw a bolt blaster aimed right at his head. The cop used his free hand and smacked Lou on the side of his skull. For a second, Lou thought he had been zapped and let out a whimper.

"When a G.A.T.E. officer asks you a question, you don't answer with another question. Now what's the password?" The officer spoke low but ever so serious.

Lou was immediately at the mercy of this cop and believed he would kill him without a thought. *He would just leave my body in the pod till everyone left and then dump me in the river. No one would know or care.*

"Cow pie y," said Lou. He couldn't blurt it out fast enough.

"Don't fuck with me, man," the officer's voice growing louder.

"C-o-w-p-i-e-y, I swear to God."

The officer holstered the weapon, took out a pad and pen from his breast pocket, and wrote it down. He then replaced the pad and pen. "It better work, old man," he warned while rubbing his hands together. "The search team is gonna go through every inch of your stuff out there, and I'm gonna search you right now. So if you got something on you, you best tell me right now."

Lou's vision blurred, and blood rushed to his head, but he remained calm somehow.

"I got nothing to hide officer," Lou said, his voice cracking.

"Alright, hold your arms out like this," said the cop while demonstrating. Lou held out his arms, and the cop began patting him down. He went from his armpits to his back, right to his buttocks. The cop breezed over his ass cheeks, feeling the pockets but not quite laying a finger on the disk. He patted down his legs and ankles, then felt his front pockets. "Take that keyphone out of there and drop it on the floor." Lou pulled it out and dropped it. "Now unbutton and drop those pants." Lou made an expression of outrage, and the cop put his hand on his bolt blaster. Without a word, Lou opened his pants and pulled them down to his ankles. Once the cop looked at his backside, he would see the round shape on his ass, and his legacy would end.

The cop walked up to him and grabbed the waistband of his underwear. He pulled it out and looked down at his crotch, taking a thorough look. Then, without a word, he stormed out the door, leaving Lou with his thoughts.

Holy shit, that was close. Either that guy is queer, or they really suspect me of something. And he sure didn't look like a sissy. Oh man, am I stupid. I'm gonna end up in the penitentiary plant.

He stood there for a minute before gathering his composure. He shifted the disk to the front of his underwear and pulled up his pants. Then he leisurely staggered out. He picked his pipe off the ground and replaced it in the *sin bin*.

Did the sin bin seem light? I thought I brought five bottles of whiskey.

Moments later the search team was going through his stuff. They emptied every box that Lou took so much time packing. The team was surprised to see so many books and videos.

The cop in charge of the search team suddenly gazed at Lou. "What you going to do with all this junk, old boy," he said scowling, "open up a book store? I don't think many people round here care much for reading." He was a stocky, dark-haired cop.

"Reading is an exercise for the mind, young man," said Lou, smiling. "I'd hate to go through life without something to read."

The cop just stared at him for a moment as if in awe. Then he went back to pulling out books and looking at the covers.

"If you see something you want to read, let me know," said Lou. "If it's not one of my favorites, I'll let you have it."

The cop ignored him.

The team was franticly flipping through the pages of every book and opening every disk case. Lou just stood by the pod trying to act natural.

The guys opening the disk cases were fascinated. "Damn, look at how old some of these are," one of them said.

"Are they movies?" asked another.

"No, they're called documentaries," the oldest one said. "Shit like that was made years ago, but they didn't make much money."

He inspected the back of the case he was holding and read a few lines. "Documentaries are supposed to be true stories. Some of these are what you call docudramas. I heard most of them were just liberal-commie bullshit."

Now the whole team and the officers were looking over the documentaries.

"Look at this one. He's not allowed to have stuff about this era," the fat, dark-haired team member said.

Lou recognized the cover. It was a documentary about 1969, mostly concerning protesting that occurred over the

Vietnam War and the last American revolutionaries called The Weather Underground.

"I know he ain't supposed to have that one," the elder member said. "All of these are probably considered illicit material. I didn't think shit like this still existed." He stood up to speak eye level with the cop. "The only place you could find shit like this was at the library, and that was years ago. You know we had one of the last in the country here in Illinois, the Des Plaines Library. That's the one that blew up seven or eight years ago. Any of you kids remember that?"

None of them replied.

The gate cop pulled out his radio communicator and held it to his mouth. "Captain, can you come to pod 59?" The captain was busy with Lou's computer, which was linked to the van's central processing unit. The data was being instantly analyzed.

"This better be important," he muttered.

Moments later, Zipp climbed out of the back of the G.A.T.E. van at the end of the alley and walked over. He squatted and looked at some of the documentaries spread along the grass.

After a few minutes, he walked over to Lou. "Hey Governor," he said, greeting him with a smile, "you got a lot of controversial stuff here. We're supposed to confiscate this kind of material, you know." He spoke sternly.

"They're just old documentaries," Lou snapped. "Why you gotta take them away? Are your bosses trying to dispose of the past? Think about it. Is that not frightening to you?"

"We follow orders," Zipp roared. "That's why things run smooth now, all because we all follow our orders. We don't try to make sense of them."

His loud tone caused everyone around to look at them.

Zipp cleared his throat and calmed himself, "Now, concerning your laptop, you're right. You spent a lot of time, in fact most of your online time, at the War Wager website. God, you must have really been addicted to that game." His tone grew milder now. "I hate to say it, but we have to keep the laptop." His eyes seemed apologetic. "But hey, you can still play War Wager from your unit. I hear you just have to upgrade your internet subscription."

Lou frowned and shook his head.

"I'll tell you what," Zipp continued, "we have to take away all these documentary videos. The government doesn't want people seeing old, political propaganda stuff when we need to unite behind the compatriots to get through these hard times, but I'll let you keep all your books. Hell, no one reads anymore so I can't see any harm in it," he said sounding magnanimous.

Lou remained cool, knowing to argue would be useless. "Gotta do what ya gotta do, I guess, but shouldn't I get some money for the computer? I mean, shouldn't they have to reimburse me?"

"Hey man," replied Zipp, "ask not what your government can give you; ask what you should give your government."

The horrible botching of John F. Kennedy's old quote from his inauguration speech made Lou's face wrinkle up in disgust.

Officer Zipp noticed and it made him feel intellectually inferior to this bust out of a man. "See ya later, Governor," he said, looking Lou in the eyes and spitting before walking off. He gave some orders to the other cops, and they began to take away his documentaries.

"Alright, start getting your shit up to your unit," a cop finally told him. The team moved to the next person and began to check the Hispanic man's stuff.

Lou packed his books back into the boxes and moved his stuff up as quickly as he could, just placing things anywhere. He took out the disk and hid it the best he could.

On the second trip out he noticed the officer looking at some bottles the Hispanic man had boxed. The labels looked familiar. He went to his *sin bin* and opened it. There were three bottles of whiskey now, not five.

That sneaky little shit, Lou thought. The Hispanic man moved and was now standing beside the office to block Lou's view.

He went about his business moving things up and then checking if anything else had been stolen.

Everything he could carry was now in his unit. Only his mattress and dresser were left.

"Hey Buddy," Lou called to the Hispanic man, "if you can help me with my dresser here, I'll give you a hand with yours."

The man looked somewhat worried but smiled before saying, "I don't know, man. I was going to help this guy." He glanced toward the person in the lot next to him, now just noticing she was actually a short-haired, unattractive, middle-aged, plump lady, "Ah, the lady over here," he corrected.

Lou walked over and held out his hand. "My name's Lou," he said smiling

"Oh, okay," he said, sounding awkward like he had never been introduced to anyone before. Taking Lou's hand, he said, "I'm Hector Ramos, good to meet you, man."

Hector was a small man, about five foot four and thin. His shiny dark hair was greased back, and he had a thin mustache.

Hector gave in and helped Lou move. He didn't speak much, and Lou only asked him a few questions. Lou found out hector was from Des Plaines too and worked for a landscaping corporation that serviced homes in the gated city. He didn't say why he lost his job, but Lou would have bet good money he got caught steeling something. Hector may have been small and thin, but he had strength and seemed less strained with the heavy dresser than Lou. He was obviously no stranger to physical labor.

They carried Hector's stuff to his unit and when they finished, Hector shook Lou's hand. "Okay, later man," he said to Lou and suddenly hurried off.

Lou followed him. Once they got outside the building, he cornered him.

"Listen Hector, Those bottles of whiskey you stole from me are very expensive and…"

"I don't know what you talking about, man. You calling me a thief?" interrupted Hector. He threw back his shoulders ready to fight.

"Give it up, Hector. I'm not a stupid man, not the type you want to mess with either, and I'm sure you don't want me to tell my buddy, Captain Zipp you're a thief."

Hector exhaled and remained silent.

"Now just relax and listen. I have a deal for you. You can keep the whiskey and help yourself to any of my stuff, and I'll even pay you ten percent of my income for six months if you can get me something."

A momentary silence occurred as Hector contemplated, Lou stared at him with contempt, and Hector surrendered.

"Okay, what you want me to get you, man?" he asked, sounding defeated.

"You see that police van, with all that stuff in it?" Lou motioned with his head being inconspicuous. All the confiscated stuff, mostly Lou's was put into the back of the van.

Hector nodded.

"They got my laptop computer in there, and it's very important to me. If you can get it for me, you will have a friend for life plus all that I mentioned."

"I don't know, man. That won't be easy," Hector said, shaking his head. Then he smiled. "But for you, I will try."

"Good." Lou looked around before continuing, "Hector, treat this with the utmost respect. This is more important than you will ever know. It has to seem like a random theft, so take some other things too if you can."

With a nod Hector walked away.

Lou was about to walk back to his unit when the plump, unattractive lady from the lot next to Hector's came trotting up to him. "Mister, Mister, excuse me," she called franticly, "can you please help me carry up some of my things?"

Lou looked over at her things left to carry, noticing there were still lots of big items. He blew through his lips and considered running away. "Of course I can help you, my dear," he said with a smile.

He spent most of the next hour helping the lady move her stuff with sore arms and legs. He kept his eye on the gate van each time they came out for more. On their last trip he saw that all the cops were standing at the front of the van. It was the perfect time to swipe something.

Hector was in the alley, smoking and talking with two other Hispanic men. Lou caught Hector's eyes and motioned his head toward the van then immediately went up to his unit.

At his first moment of solitude, depression weighed down on him like gravity had suddenly doubled. He lumbered to the *sin bin* and had a few shots of whiskey straight out of the bottle. He felt like a dog must feel when it was away from its cozy home and thrown into a kennel with other unwanted and abused dogs. He passed out at midnight without getting much unpacking done.

Chapter 4

The sound of a keyphone woke Lou the next morning. He continued to lay with no intention of moving until the fourth annoying ring tone. When he realized the severity of his new situation, he leaped out of bed and moved toward the sound. Boxes and books still cluttered the studio floor, and he stumbled twice. His mind was groggy from drinking whiskey and water last night without eating. He wasn't used to being up this early.

Grabbing the keyphone from under a book, he flipped it open with his thumb, trying to sound cheerful and said, "Hello."

"Mr. Rizzo, you have a job placement meeting at 8:30 this morning. You need to be at the conference room in your building, first floor, room 100."

"Who do I ask…"

Click. the call was disconnected before he could finish.

He closed the keyphone and checked the time. *Seven fifty, Jeez, it must be years since I was up this early.*

He plopped back into his twin size bed. In ten minutes his hunger convinced him to get up and see what he could get for breakfast. Taking some time to find clothes, his tooth brush and mouthwash amidst the clutter, he cleaned up and left twelve minutes later.

Across the street were the restaurants and shops. They were all government owned and unnamed. There were only symbols in front to identify the shop. The grocery store had a picture of an egg carton, a gallon of milk, and a pork chop sticking out the top of a grocery bag.

The first restaurant he passed had a picture of a chicken leg in front of a wine glass. The next one had a frying pan with an egg in it. He went in.

He ordered breakfast number three, a ham and egg sandwich, hash browns, and coffee. He went deeper into debt with a swipe of his keyphone at the cash register. His balance read -$86.50.

Sitting by himself at a table in the corner, he ate while observing busy people getting breakfast and obediently heading off to work, all accepting their prearranged lives.

He took just enough time sipping his coffee to make it to room 100 at 8:30. The room had a glass door. He could see a woman sitting behind a desk. He walked in and stood before her silently.

Looking up at his face for a moment, she looked back down. "Name, please?" she grumbled.

"Louis Rizzo."

Without even looking up again, she pressed a button on her phone system.

A pale, blond woman stood up from her desk and walked up to him. She had plain, unrevealing, government, grey slacks and a blouse on. She had a nice slender body and pretty face.

Lou smiled at her.

"Mr. Rizzo, please follow me." They made their way back to her desk. "Please have a seat," she ordered. Lou smiled again. This time she smiled ever so slightly and looked down at her desk while flicking her blond hair away from her pale neck.

"I see from your background you have had two occupations in your life. Before you were an elected official you were a painter." She glanced up.

"Yes, I've done way too much painting in my life," he complained.

She grinned and went on, "and you're forty-eight years old."

"No, that can't be right," he interrupted. "I'm in the best shape of my life." Razing his eyebrows now, "You wouldn't believe how energetic I am."

She gave him a silly look and plopped her forearms on the table. "I'm looking at your year of birth. It was forty-eight years ago, and you're allowed to do construction or painting labor until you're sixty-five."

"That's out of the question," Lou roared and slapped his

leg, "I will never paint again. Do you know how much I loath that work? I can't do it. I *won't* do it." He sounded frantic. "Please, I really can't. Get me into law enforcement. I could be a great G.A. officer. I'm healthy, fit and smart, I mean obedient." His eyes were pleading. "Please, I'd be so grateful."

She was mesmerized by his eyes momentarily. Then she shook her head as if to snap herself out of it and suddenly became cold. "I'm sorry, sir." This is what you're best qualified for, and we are in need of qualified painters. The only other thing for you is assembly line work. You want that instead?"

"That's the best you can do for me!" He stood up angrily. "You just gonna let my talent go to waste on an assembly line! What a great computer system! You're telling me a man of my intelligence only qualifies for that?"

The woman remained silent and shocked.

Lou noticed everyone in the conference room was looking at him. "Fine, send me to the assembly line. It's better than sniffing paint again."

"Alright then, you'll start tomorrow." She sounded harsh. "All your information will be on your personal account within the hour. Good day, Mr. Rizzo."

Silence again, save Lou's heavy breathing. Lou heaved a sigh and rubbed his eyes. "This is all very disheartening," he moaned and moved closer to her desk, "I don't like being crammed into this city. I miss the country, and I'm cranky." He leaned over and put his hand on her desk. "Still, it was nice to meet such a beautiful woman like you. I feel like I've seen you before. You really are stunning, my dear."

She slowly leaned back while looking at him and softly smiled. "Well, it was quite unusual meeting you, Mr. Rizzo. Normally people don't complain about getting a job outside the factories. I hope you're happy with your choice. now goodbye, sir." She looked back down.

"Please call me Lou. What's your name, dear?"

She looked up, appearing annoyed. "It's Stephanie, and I'm very busy, Lou."

"I understand, Stephanie. Why don't you just put me down for that painting gig, and maybe you'll let me take you out for a nice dinner sometime. They tell me I have plenty of credit on my keyphone."

Stephanie unexpectedly laughed out loud, a rare sound in room 100. "Don't get carried away now. You know I'm fifteen years younger than you, but I'm glad you changed your mind. Your job info will be available in an hour. Goodbye, Lou."She looked back down to her monitor, this time smiling.

"Till we meet again," Lou said, giving her a bow and walked out.

He went back to his unit and finished unpacking and alphabetizing books while listing to his monitor.

American Airwaves was on for a bit until he was sick to his stomach from the ridiculous program that was on. It was a show that was trying to prove that America was destined to become the perfect society with the perfect government, and this could have only been achieved by the grace of God delivering the Compatriot Party and their bold leader, President Bud Burns. The concept was disturbing to Lou, but it was that handsomely rugged face, the perfect black hair, and the polished voice of President Burns that he could no longer tolerate.

The man appeared so honest and kind, but so few people knew every word he spoke was carefully crafted propaganda from the plutocratic scripture of population control.

He switched over to Freedom Forever Network. It was sure to be just as bias, but at least for the moment the face of Bud Burns was gone.

He continued organizing the room while the local news came on.

The news was a sham, nothing more then a half-hour of positive government morale building, totally devoid from real news, save the local crime report that just came on.

"Yesterday a G.A. police van was burglarized around the fifteen sixty-three building."

Hearing this Lou turned and walked to the monitor and sat in the plastic chair. A stunningly, beautiful anchor woman reported,

"A number of confiscated items were taken." They

switched to a live shot that had been recorded earlier, a parking lot outside a police station. A police team was standing around G.A. vans. One officer was standing with a news reporter, another beautiful female. Lou couldn't take his eyes off her.

"Captain, what was the total value of the stolen merchandise?" she asked.

"I can't, you know, I-I-I just" he stuttered. The man was clearly upset and familiar to Lou. It was Captain Zipp! "We can't even put a value on it right now. One of the items was an old laptop computer that may have contained important information we needed to analyze. We urge all citizens to help us retrieve this item and get the thief off the street. If you know or see anything that leads to the arrest of the criminal involved, there is a two thousand dollar reward. As everyone should know, just dial g-a-t-e on your keyphone to report anything. I'm confident we will get this guy quickly because none of our fine citizens will tolerate thieves living among them."

Lou was suddenly overwhelmed with fear. *Two thousand dollar reward! Damn, they haven't forgotten me! I blew it again! Why did I ask that little Mexican to swipe it?*

Indeed they did suspect the last independent senator who opposed the system. His name was an immediate red flag to the supervisors.

Lou's mind turned to Hector. *Oh God, they're going to catch Hector, and he'll tell them that I asked him to do it. I'm a marked man already.* A crazy, impulsive thought hit him. *Do I have to kill him?*

His mind continued to race, this time turning to the disk. Yesterday he hid it in the closet under the carpet. He sliced the corners of the carpet six inches each way and put the disk under it, then tucked the carpet back under the baseboards. His mind, now growing paranoid, thought of the glowing "o" in the top of the monitor. *If that is a camera, did someone see me on my knees in the closet?* The closet was in view of the supposed camera eye, but only a side view. It could only have seen Lou's feet and buttocks sticking out but not the inside of the closet. He slapped his face with his hands and rubbed. Suddenly he realized someone could be watching him right now, through the tiny "o" that he was sitting right in front of. *Could they read my distress?* He stretched his arms and yawned, trying to act natural.

The next moment loud knocking made his heart jolt. *It's Hector leading them to me, I know it.* He walked to the door and opened it.

It was Captain Zipp and the officer that made Lou pull his pants down yesterday.

"Hey Governor, sorry to intrude, but we have to talk about something. Can we come in?" asked Zipp. Lou stepped aside.

The officers came in, eyes searching assiduously until their gaze both ended up on the monitor.

"Maybe you heard already on the news, someone went right in to our police van and stole some stuff." Zipp looked Lou in the eyes now. "This is very rare. We haven't had much crime here at all. Hell, that's why we didn't even lock the rear door. Anyway, one of the things taken was your laptop." He moved closer, looking sympathetic. "I'm sure you understand that you were named as a suspect since it was your computer, so we have to search your unit." Zipp nodded to the officer, who then began searching. Ironically, the first place he went to was the closet.

"This is unbelievable. Somebody swipes my computer, and I get the blame for it," said Lou. "I don't care. Search as much as you want. I have nothing to hide." He sighed. "Whatever, after finding out I have to do painting again, things can't get any worse for me."

"You had your job placement meeting, huh?" asked Zipp.

Lou turned to watch his closet being emptied out by the cop he despised. "So Captain, what's you partner's name? I've had the pleasure of seeing him twice now." He leaned in toward Zipp and whispered, "I don't think he likes me."

"That's Officer O'Malley. he's a good man he just demands respect."

"Don't we all?" Lou quietly retorted. He was being very cool, despite feeling faint. He kept expecting Officer O'Malley to start tugging up the corner of the carpet.

He had to get off his feet. Heading for the plastic chair,

he said, "Well, knock yourselves out, boys. I have to look at my work schedule." *Get your vile face out of my closet, O'Malley,* went through his mind as he sat. His breathing was short and irregular, causing lightheadedness.

Finally, O'Malley emerged from the closet. Now both cops were searching through his room. Lou rubbed his chin on his shoulder to give him a peripheral view of them every ten seconds or so. He noticed how thoroughly they went over every possible hiding spot. Now that he calmed down, he was able to read the information on his personal account. He was scheduled for a physical and to receive his vaccinations next week. He scrolled down to his employment details. It gave in-depth information about his work schedule. At the bottom it stated he would be charged for his work uniforms, but what really frightened him was the line that said "board blue bus 47 at 7:50 a.m. in front of the building."

I'll never be able to get up at seven a.m.

Officer Zipp walked over by him and looked at the monitor over his shoulder. "Painter, huh? That's not bad. Maybe you'll like that more than being the governor."

Lou didn't feel it was worth it to correct him about being a senator anymore. He harbored hope that Zipp might still have a free thinking brain, but now he was convinced he's just a brainwashed yes-man.

"Listen, Lou." He walked to the side of him demanding eye contact. "Personally, I don't think you're involved in this robbery, but if I'm wrong, and you get this thing back from a co-conspirator or even by chance, dial g-a-t-e immediately and ask for me. Anyone in possession of your computer, including yourself, is breaking the law and will serve hard time at Penitentiary Plant." His eyes were stern with a hint of sincerity.

"Wow, my old piece-of-shit laptop must be real important to you guys. Did you see some porn on there that you liked or something?" Lou heaved a sarcastic laugh.

It must have triggered Captain Zipp's quick temper. He approached Lou at once, got right in his face and spoke boisterously. "We don't give a damn about your computer and whatever's on it. You're a bug, a disgraced politician who became a worthless bum just like all those other democrats."

Lou was not shaken. *Should I bother to tell this idiot I'm an independent,* Lou thought and smirked ever so slightly.

"We love to put people in jail. This government doesn't waste money incarcerating criminals with tax dollars. Things are different now. Our prisoners work twelve hours a day, manufacturing things for three hots and a cot. Someone will be arrested over this, trust me," Zipp nodded his head a few times in a berating way.

"Hey, I know all about the prison plants, it was a response to losing cheap foreign labor," Lou said, causing Officer Zipp to scowl. "It's not a terrible idea, provided everyone there is undeniably guilty and they're treated humanely." He scratched his face. Looking upward, he added, "But I'll bet that's not the case."

Zipp got in his face again. "If you're involved in this, you can find out first hand how they're treated." He motioned to O'Malley, and they walked to the door. Zipp walked out first.

Just before leaving O'Malley looked over his shoulder."See you around, peek-a-boo Lou." Both cops laughed.

That gave Lou a chill down his spine, evoking unwanted memories. This visit was frightening for him, but he felt stronger and more confident in dealing with G.A.T.E. cops now.

He paced his room nervously that night, wondering if Hector would stop by. Hopelessness weighed down on him, and the feeling of time being wasted was depressing him. The worst feeling was the loneliness. He missed encounters with his maid, Lena, terribly. She wasn't the greatest conversationalist, but she listened and tried to learn from him, and he enjoyed enlightening her, that, and she was great in bed.

He brought out his portable digital audio player with built in speakers, turned it on and propped open his door with a shoe, hoping someone might like what they hear and come visit.

No one did, so he walked over to the shops across the street and had dinner alone. Then he charged some groceries to his account and went home.

After some hours of surfing the Freedom Forever network, he picked out a book and read himself to sleep.

He had an awful night trying to sleep, which wasn't too uncommon for Lou, but this night was especially bad. He kept waking every twenty minutes to toss and turn, sometimes forgetting where he was. Then a dreadful feeling would wash over him each time he remembered he wasn't in Byron anymore.

The dominating subconscious and conscious thought was the laptop. The secondary thought was starting a mundane new job tomorrow as a foreign invasion and possible nuclear war loomed.

It had been been three days now since he had contact with Tony Swan on the internet.

Chapter 5

His keyphone alerted him at 7:20 a.m., thirty minutes before he needed to be on the work bus. Despite feeling groggy, he immediately rose, happy to have officially ended the torturous night. He heated a pot of water, made some instant coffee and oatmeal, but his stomach was not satisfied so he fried up two eggs and toasted bread. The groceries he bought last night seemed awfully expensive, but he was glad he stocked up. His long breakfast left him pressed for time so he washed up and dressed quickly. He grabbed his keyphone, glanced at the time (7:48), and hurried out.

There were three blue buses in front of the building. Some people were boarding them, and some were standing around looking confused.

After checking the numbers and finding none were marked 47, he joined the ranks of the confused people. He turned back toward the front of the building and noticed a short slender man leaning against the wall, arms crossed. It was Hector. Anxiety butterflies fluttered in his stomach as he scanned the area, looking to see if any G.A. officers were present. There were two out front, but they seemed preoccupied. He put his hands in his pockets and whistled an old sad tune as he walked toward him.

When he was halfway there, Hector noticed Lou approaching and displayed a fuming scowl. Lou's expression became one of bewilderment, and he almost stopped in his tracks. He continued toward him with no acknowledgement and stopped a few feet away. With his back still turned to Hector he crossed his arms, turned his head toward his left shoulder, and spoke out of the corner of his mouth. "When can we talk, my friend," Lou said, barely moving his lips.

A new bus was now pulling up to the curb. Hector walked forward toward the street.

"You got me in some deep shit, man. You gonna pay. If I go down, you go down too, man," he whispered as he slowly walked. Looking back at Lou, still frowning, he said "Unit 246, eight o'clock. Be there, man."

Lou was taken aback by Hector's demeanor, but he was sure he would be there tonight. He watched Hector board the bus that just arrived. It wasn't Lou's bus.

Moments later, blue bus, 47 pulled up. He waited a minute to see who else was boarding. Five others did, and then he got on.

"Name," the driver asked while looking at the computer monitor next to him.

"Lou Rizzo," he replied and stood still while the driver scrolled to find his name.

"Have a seat, sir."

He walked to the back of the nearly full bus, smiling and nodding at the gazing eyes along the way.

There were only men on the bus, engaging in small talk as they drove. The ride seemed pleasantly quiet. You could barely hear the hum of the engine.

He realized it was a hydrogen fuel cell engine and shook his head. Lou had advocated for the use of hydrogen his whole political life, knowing that the technology was repressed by the oil barons.

Lou looked over to the portly, grey-bearded man in the seat next to him. "Hey, do you know what kind of engine is in this bus?"

The man rubbed his beard a moment and pondered. "It sure does sound smooth, don't it? It's gotta be one of those gas-electric hybrid engines, I have to say." He shot a smirk and a nod to Lou, expressing confidence in his answer.

"Nope, it's a hydrogen fuel cell engine. I learned all about them years ago."

Lou had a pleasant bus ride. Everyone within ear distance listened to him talk about how he advocated for the use of hydrogen fuel cells. He even briefly touched on the reign of the oil barons, and no one interrupted.

The bus pulled into the American Painters Team (A.P.T)

warehouse parking lot. Everyone got off the bus and was standing around while a big bellied man dressed in blue, holding a clip board looked people over, waiting for everyone to get off.

"Good morning, gentlemen. I'm Bob Fortune, A.P.T. Manager. Most of you will be working as trainees for the next two weeks doing work at the new government housing units. First, we'll all go inside and assign your lockers and uniforms so lets try to do this as quickly as possible. Then we can get you all out to the job site." He looked back to the clip board. "I'm looking for Kevin O'Morgan and Louis Rizzo. You guys, come with me. The rest of you go in through the bay door there, and the warehouse supervisor will get you started."

The men walked off, leaving the three men. O'Morgan was a tall, Irish looking man with light brown, short, curly hair. He, unlike most of the other younger men on the bus, looked to be Lou's age.

"Let me guess. You're Rizzo and you're O'Morgan," Bob pointed correctly. "Follow me to my office," he said and walked off. He was a heavy man but shorter than Lou and was clean shaven with neatly styled black hair.

As they followed him to the office, Lou noticed that Bob's rear end was abnormally large. He snickered to Kevin like a little school kid. Kevin didn't seem amused.

They entered the warehouse and went into the small office where Bob plopped into his large leather chair behind his desk. The leather padding produced a farting noise as his huge buttocks made impact.

"Well gentleman, it says here you both have over ten years of painting experience," Bob said, while looking at the computer monitor on his desk.

"Yeah, I ran my own painting company for about fifteen years before moving on to better things," Lou injected.

Kevin O'Morgan looked at him angularly as if he was being upstaged.

"That's good. We're really hurting for a good residential crew manager. We've had some complaints about our residential work in the gated city, so we need pros who can do the jobs right and take care of these whiney rich folks. You guys know how to do those decorative finishes?" He was looking at Lou. He began to nod when Kevin spoke up.

"I can do any faux finish. I used to specialize in it. I swear I used to get complemented on all my jobs, and I could please even the rich Jews in the north shore area." He moved closer to the desk excitedly, "I swear I ran the most efficient crew back then. I worked for Masterpiece painting. We were like the biggest..."

"Okay, okay, that's great," Bob interrupted. "We're giving you a crew, and we'll see how you do for awhile." He looked at the monitor and made a few mouse moves and clicks. "Okay, go see the warehouse supervisor and tell him your name. You're the new manager of team eight. You'll be spraying and back rolling new G.A. housing units. We'll see how many you can crank out in a day. I think Teddy is your right hand man on that team so he'll help you get adjusted." Bob Fortune stood up and reached his hand out "Good luck, Kevin. I'm sure you're going to be a great manager."

Kevin looked dumbfounded as he shook Bob's hand. "Thanks," he muttered, sounding confused. Not being able to think of anything more to say he walked slowly out. Bob remained quiet until they could see Kevin outside, walking past the window on the way to the warehouse. He grinned at Lou.

"Those guys who like to brag and talk shit all the time are usually the biggest hacks, you know that."

"That's the truth," Lou replied laughing.

Bob's phone rang and he held up one finger to Lou then answered it.

Lou was impressed by Bob Fortune. He could tell he was a smart guy and well suited for the position. *Fat guys were usually better suited for office work.* Bob sounded curt on the phone and ended the call abruptly. He turned his attention right back to Lou.

"So you have experience working for rich people, right? I mean you ran your own company, so you must have been doing estimates and dealing directly with the customer."

"Of course," Lou said confidently. "I did a lot of work for people in Park Ridge before they gated it off. I know how to handle them."

"Good," Bob said smiling. "I'm going to put you in charge of a residential crew. It pays a little better than doing G.A. housing work, but you got to please the customer. That's your goal. Were getting inundated with complaints, and we have to turn that around. You do a good job, and I'll make sure you get a raise fast."

Bob stared at Lou, waiting for his agreement.

Lou scratched his head. "Well, I guess I could use the pay. I'm in debt already. Hey, if I really kick ass on the job, you think I can make enough to buy a house in Park Ridge?"

They both Laughed. Bob stood up, and they shook hands. "Please, just do a good job, Louis. I'm counting on you. Now go see the warehouse supervisor." He sat back down and started to update Lou's information in the computer system.

"Thanks, Bob. May you have lasting good fortune,"

Bob Fortune chuckled as Lou left. As he walked to the Warehouse, he was amazed he would be working inside the gated city, just the place he wanted to observe and would never have been able to get into any other way.

He walked through the overhead door and saw an entrance way to the left marked **locker room** in big black letters. To the right were rows of painting equipment: ladders, sprayers, and tools. The warehouse was full of men. They were coming out of the locker room dressed in painter's whites with the letters A.P.T. on the front or their shirts. On the back was a logo, a bald eagle in flight with a paint brush in one claw and a paint can in the other.

He turned around and saw the warehouse supervisor station where a man stood behind the counter with a computer monitor in front of him. There were five men waiting to talk to him. Lou lined up just as the supervisor finished with Kevin, who walked off toward the locker room with his head down.

Lou practiced his mindful-breathing technique while he waited in line. One of the many books he owned and read during his time in Byron was written by a prestigious Buddhist monk at the beginning of the century. He didn't particularly like much of the book since he did not subscribe to any religion, but he respected the monk's viewpoint on life whole heartedly. He learned to meditate and occasionally live in the present moment, mindfully, by letting go of his regrets and anxieties. It helped his health tremendously, though he was still a novice and anger, hatred and despair still affected him, but he was improving.

Minutes later, Lou stood face to face with the supervisor. He was slightly shorter than Lou with dark hair and a mustache. His brown eyes were alert with a devious look to them.

"How's it going, man? I'm Louis Rizzo," Lou said with a smile and a nod.

He began to type on the keyboard while looking at his monitor. "Okay, just give me a sec to get your info. Hey, you're going to be a residential manager, I see." He chuckle sarcastically. "That's cool, man; I mean, I wish you good luck and all." He looked at Lou and forced a smile, "I'm Mike Parilla. If you need anything for your job site, let me know, and I'll get it for you." He reached out his hand. "Give me your keyphone so I can update it." Lou handed it to him and Mike gave it a swipe through the scanner and looked at it. He handed it back to Lou, the screen flashed UPDATING. "Give it a moment to update before you close it. All your work information is on it. Just go to the job icon and hit it. Once you scan it through your home computer, your personal profile will be updated and online. If you need something, call me. Just hit the contacts icon and press Warehouse supervisor, but avoid making me deliver stuff if you can help it, please."

The keyphone beeped when it finished updating.

"Go to your locker and get changed. Then come back here. I'll introduce you to your new crew and show you the contract for the job you'll be taking over."

Lou nodded and walked off. He hit the job icon on his keyphone and got his locker number. There was a stack of four uniforms still in the plastic, all thirty two inch waists. He opened one, dressed quickly, and reported back to Mike.

"Well that was quick," Mike said. He walked out from behind the counter. "follow me."

They walked out to the parking lot and went to a van parked in a slot labeled number three. There were three men standing around chatting.

"Listen up, guys," Mike addressed the men. "This is Louis, your new manager. He's an old pro so we better see some improvements with this team."

"Louis, this is Tom, Freddy and Scott. Scott here is your right hand man and will help you figure things out. You got the contract, Scott?" Scott opened the van, grabbed a folder off the passenger seat, and gave it to Mike. He handed it to Lou.

"They started this job a few days ago, and I got nothing but complaints so we canned the manager. Now it's up to you to save this job."

Lou opened it up and glanced at the contract.

"Alright get going, guys, I'll call the lady and tell her you're on your way." Mike walked back to the warehouse while the crew stared silently at Lou.

"Who does the driving?" Lou asked.

"I should drive. I'm the best driver here," Freddy bellowed then scowled at Scott.

"Don't listen to him. I do the driving," Scott declared.

"Yeah, he does the driving alright," said Freddy. "Last week he almost put us in a ditch because he swerved for no reason. He gets all stupid behind the wheel. I'd be a much safer driver."

Lou looked at Scott. He was bigger and taller than Lou, maybe six foot four and had a stark white complexion. His lengthy, straight, light brown hair was messily held back out of his eyes by a red head band. His eyes were light brown, laid back and distant. Lou recognized them as stoner eyes.

He turned to Freddy. He was shorter than Lou with a similar build. His hair was dark brown and neatly styled. His green eyes were present and demanding, symbolizing an aggressive, intolerant type A personality.

"Alright Freddy, you drive," Lou said.

Tom broke out in a mocking laugh which made Scott frown.

"The right hand man is supposed to drive. I always do the driving," Scott pleaded.

"Get in the back, Scott, so we can talk on the way," Lou

said and climbed in the passenger side of the van.

After they all got in, Scott held his arm out and dangled the keys over Freddy's shoulder and dropped them. "You don't know how to handle this van. You better drive mellow, dude."

Freddy grabbed the keys off the seat. "Okay Scott, I'll drive mellow just like you," he mocked in a slowwitted voice.

They drove off and headed down the quiet highway.

Lou didn't ask Scott about the job. He just looked at the contract while the others eagerly asked him questions about his past.

Tom slumped in the back. He had blond hair and blue eyes and seemed to be the youngest of them. Before he closed his tired looking eyes, he asked only one question. "So Louis, you ever been to the gated city?"

"Call me Lou. I worked in that area twenty years ago, but I never saw the city since they enclosed it."

They spent ten minutes talking about the city when Lou noticed the glimmering gate. As they got closer, a chill ran down his spine when he contemplated the enormity of the huge gate. It rose about twelve feet high. A concrete base supported the corrugated metal fencing that towered out of it. The structure looked impossible to climb, yet three wires ran across the top of the fence, no doubt electrical in case someone *did* manage to scale it somehow.

He silently stared in horror as they drove to the service entrance checkpoint. Armed guards stood outside, giving the appearance of a volatile war zone checkpoint, the kind Lou had only seen in video footage. The guards watched them as they pulled up to the entrance booth window.

"Hey, the painters are here. Halleluiah," the window guard said sarcastically and handed a wireless scanner to Freddy. He took out his keyphone and scanned it, then handed it over to Lou who took a moment to pull out his phone then scanned it the wrong way. Finally, he managed to scan it correctly and passed it back to Scott. Once the guard got it back he looked at his monitor and said, "I see the new guy's name is Louis Rizzo." He made a few mouse clicks. "Alright he's in the system." Gazing in to Lou's eyes, he said, "You be on your best behavior in this town."

The entrance gate began to open.

"Now get to work, you hacks."

Freddy drove off.

As they drove down Greenwood Avenue, Lou was stunned by the beauty of the city. The landscape that surrounded each mansion was beautifully designed and maintained. As they got deeper into town, to the north Lou saw a large open area devoid of trees.

"That seems like a waste of space," said Lou. "I'm surprised they're not building there."

Once they got into town, Tom seemed more awake. "That's where the underground arena is," he said, "The dude at the burger joint told us. He said it's huge and like everyone in the whole town will be able to fit in it."

"What the hell is an underground arena for?" Lou said puzzled.

"Who knows man. Rich people are weird," said Scott.

Presently, they were passing a country club, one of three in the town.

Lou felt deep envious rage as he looked at the rich people golfing on the beautiful golf course. His desire to play never left him, even after all those years of being unable to. "Look at these Goddamn rich people golfing. I'll bet none of them can even break a hundred."

The crew laughed, despite not understanding anything about golf, which was exclusive to the rich.

As they pulled into the driveway of the mansion, Lou's stomach ached from the disgust he felt. He wished he was in Australia playing golf with his son. The crew got out of the van while Lou closed his eyes and took slow deep breaths to calm down.

They walked up to the front door together. Scott rang the bell, and a butler answered. He looked at them with disgust, shook his head and blew through his lips. He held open the door and stood aside.

Freddy walked in first. "How's it going, James? You seem happy to see us."

"I'll inform Mrs. Newman you're here. She wants a

word with your foreman." James, the butler, closed the door and walked off.

"You're going to love her," Scott said and led Lou to the great room where the job had been started.

Lou looked around, surprised to see how messy they had left the job site and how poorly the ceiling cut line looked on the one wall they had completed. "Jeez, you guys, this is a mess. First thing I want you guys to do is clean up the job site up. Pick up all the tools, shake the drops, sweep up, and set up a station against this wall with a clean drop cloth."

They all looked at him blankly.

"Clean up *before* we get started?" asked Tom. "That don't make no sense."

"Just do it, Goddamn it!" Lou yelled, creating an echo and making them flinch.

That got them moving.

Lou opened up his folder to look over the contract.

Minutes later, he heard the click of heels rapidly approaching. He turned to the entrance and saw a grey haired, slender woman in fancy clothes walking toward him. As she drew near, he could tell she was in her sixties and was wearing lots of make up and perfume.

Lou walked toward her smiling.

"I take it you're the new foreman." Her voice was angry and condescending.

"Yes, Madam, I'm Louis Riz…"

"I'm sick to death of you low life painters," she said abruptly, cutting him off. "My daughter's graduation party is next Saturday, and what have they done so far besides make a mess? There's dust everywhere. Just look at my furniture; it's covered in dust." She held out her arm pointing toward the middle of the room where her furniture was pushed together and only partially covered with plastic. "Why wouldn't they cover it properly? That couch is an antique. It's worth more than all your yearly income combined. I came in here to inspect last night and nearly killed myself tripping over all the junk lying around." Her voice was hateful and frantic. She walked farther into the room to point at the mess but noticed the three workers had picked most of it up and were organizing the room better.

"Mrs. Newman, I'm not here to make excuses for the last manager's incompetence. I'm here to make you happy," Lou said, staring her in the eyes.

She folded her arms and took a deep breath. "First off, you're going to see this job move along quickly and neatly now, and I promise to do whatever it takes to make you completely satisfied."

Lou walked toward the furniture, held back some plastic, and rubbed his hand over some couch fabric. "This is absolutely a magnificent set. How's this sound? When we're done, I'm going to have the wood polished and shampoo the fabric with an industrial cleaner," he said walking back to her.

"You'd better, and I'm not paying for that," she cackled.

"Of course not. Also, I've been looking over the job here, and I love this color. It's a great choice. It flows so well with your beautiful marble floor, but can you imagine if we use an accent color on this wall here with the fireplace?" He held out his arm toward the back wall, and she seemed interested.

"Just a few shades darker, it would bring out the character in this room. Plus I'll highlight your crown molding up there in high gloss white instead of just doing it in the flat ceiling white - no extra charge. This is just between me and you. My boss doesn't need to know. If you're happy, just let him know I did a good job for you."

She stared at him silently for a moment and then shook her head. "Fine," she blurted, "just make sure you do everything you said." She walked up close to him and looked into his eyes. Lowering her eyebrows, she displayed a piercing scowl and added, "And it better look good. I don't want to see a speck of dust anywhere." Still looking him in the eyes, she released her scowl, making her look almost sympathetic for a moment. "You do that, and I'll personally write your stupid boss a letter of recommendation for you." Just before turning away she almost seemed to smile.

"You can count on me, and if you have any questions or concerns, just come directly to me." Lou said as she walked away.

He walked over to the crew. They were all staring at him now.

"Way to smooth things out, chief," said Scott.

"I think that old bitch almost smiled at you," Freddy added.

"Yeah, whatever," Lou replied, "I did what I had to do. and now we got a shit load of more work."

Under Lou's guidance the crew began to work more sensibly. He found out Freddy was quicker getting up and down the ladders and had him do the high brush work. The less agile Scott did the low work while Tom rolled out the walls behind them. Lou took time to show each of them the best painting technique for the jobs they were doing. Freddy tried to resist instruction, claming he could work a brush better than anyone. But Lou had a way with people and words. His leadership could dismantle even the most arrogant egos.

They took a half hour lunch, contrary to the hour they were used to taking. The crew complained, saying they deserved to milk the clock by taking an extra half hour for lunch.

"That's bullshit," Lou replied, "You don't even deserve a job if you can't do the work right. When you're doing good work and you're ahead of schedule, you can milk the clock a little. We need to be hard working Americans, not slackers." After that they all put in a productive afternoon. They left the job site tidy and organized at five.

As they were walking to the front door, Lou was lagging twenty feet behind the others. The front door opened just as the crew got to the front foyer, and a young lady walked in. She brightened the room as the inflowing sunlight highlighted her gorgeous blond hair. Startled, when she saw three sweaty, lower-class painters staring at her, she flinched.

"Oh, Hi guys," she said and giggled.

"Hi."

"How are you?"

"Hey."

They each responded differently.

She smiled, then lowered her eyes and walked past them.

Lou noticed all three men turn at once to have a look at her backside. This was predictable because she was wearing tight red shorts that hugged her shapely, lightly tanned thighs just inches below her firm buttocks.

As she walked toward Lou with her eyes down she did something he did not expect. She looked up, straight in to his eyes and smiled.

Lou's heart fluttered as he was instantly staggered by her beauty. Just as she was about to pass him, he regained his wits enough to speak. "Are you the college grad?" he asked smiling.

"Yeah," she said giggling, "that would be me." She had a natural, unprejudiced persona, unlike her prudish mother.

"Well, congratulations. We're going to be here painting the next few days making the great room look beautiful in time for your party."

"Yeah, thanks. My mom is making such a big deal about it." She beamed her green eyes directly at Lou's.

Her gaze was friendly and irresistible. He wanted to embrace her and kiss her moist dainty lips.

"Do you mind if I ask what you majored in?" his voice cracking slightly.

"Of course not. I majored in business."

"Really? Wow, that's very cool." He continued feeling awkward. "Well, if you need any outside advice, you can come to me. I ran a successful business for almost twenty years before I got in to politics and won an election."

"No way! You went in to politics? You do kind of look familiar to me." She studied his face more.

"Yeah, I get that a lot. I use to be a popular man in this state, despite being virtually blocked out of the media." He smirked. "Well, until they wanted to destroy my reputation. Then I was all over the media."

Her eyebrows lifted. Her mouth suddenly opened and she let out a small gasp. Then she was silent for a moment considering her next words carefully. "Yes, well you sound very interesting. Maybe we can talk a little tomorrow if you're not too busy. What's your name?" she asked to confirm it was really him.

"Lou Rizzo," he said, sensing she already knew that.

"You were a senator. Oh, my God, and now your painting our house," she laughed with excitement. "That's so bizarre."

Suddenly she stopped laughing as she came to realize she was making light of a sad situation. "I'm sorry for my reaction, Mr. Rizzo. It's just that I know a little about you. In fact, you came up in a conversation with some of my friends just a few days ago." Now she felt worse realizing that could be taken the wrong way. "We were talking about your warnings of an economic crisis, not...you know, that, aaa..." she sounded uncomfortable.

"So you were talking about my unheeded warnings and not the sex scandals they used to disgrace me."

She nodded nervously.

He smiled putting, her at ease. "Thank you, that's wonderful to hear that someone remembers me for the right reasons."

She sensed no sarcasm by the sincerity in those mild brown eyes. Coming as a total surprise, she became somewhat nervous in his presence. After all, a few of her more radical friends were socially sympathetic to the lower class and considered Louis Rizzo a very significant man.

He was the last true voice of the common people, the last independent, the final voice to oppose the money driven governmental system.

"What time do you take lunch, Mr. Rizzo?" she asked coolly.

"High noon exactly, and please call me Lou."

"Sure, and you can call me Melanie. I'll stop by the great room at noon, and we can have lunch in the kitchen. I'll have the chef make us some sandwiches, and we can talk."

"Sounds great, Melanie. Talk to you tomorrow." He smiled and nodded as she did the same. They both walked away in opposite directions.

The front door was left open and the crew stood nearby where they could eavesdrop. Scott poked his head in. Once he saw Lou approaching, they all quickly walked toward the van. Lou locked the door and closed it behind him. The crew was standing around the van staring at him as he quickly opened the passenger side door.

"Let's go. I'm starving," Lou said, climbing in.

Freddy drove off.

They were all silent for three blocks before Tom blurted out. "Man, I can't believe that chick was talking to you.

Lou smiled and looked back at him. "Talking to me, shit. I got her to have lunch with me tomorrow." Lou laughed, prompting the rest of them to break out in laughter.

"Damn, you're pretty smooth, Lou," Freddy said.

Scott was sitting behind him and patted his shoulder. "Hey, is that shit true about you being the senator?" Scott asked.

"*A* senator, not *the* senator. You know each state has two, right Scott?" Lou looked at each of the men and blew through his lips in disgrace. "Do any of you guys know anything about our government?"

All three men were silent,

"Do any of you guys even vote?"

Scott finally spoke up. "Yeah, I vote. I voted for all compatriots in the last election. Anything is better than voting for a republican or democrat, and I thought Bud Burns was going to kick some ass as president."

"I wouldn't waste my time voting," Tom said. "Everything is bullshit. I bet they don't even count the votes."

"Yeah, it's all a bunch of bullshit," Freddy said. "What's the difference who wins? they're all a bunch of rich crooks."

"Thanks to decades of American apathy, that's all true," said Lou, "but all you guys are forgetting that the government is supposed to work for us. They should fear us. Our government became destructive to its originally intended goals long ago. It is the right and duty of the people to alter or abolish it and to institute new government to secure our safety and happiness. That's stated in the Declaration of Independence."

"The decoration of *what*?" asked Tom.

Lou just scowled at him for a moment and actually felt like smacking him across the head. "The people had every right to overthrow our government, ever since the start of the century. That's when election tampering became apparent and the presidential election was stolen. In fact, the Supreme Court decided not to have a recount and gave the election to the neo-conservatives. There should have been a revolution that day...

Anyway; you know it's bad when every politician was spending millions of dollars to get elected for a job that pays a couple hundred thousand a year. Everything became profit driven and an honest man couldn't get elected to government without being rich and taking money from the plutocrats. I was the last middle class citizen ever to win an election without taking any dirty money. I was blacked out of the media and still won, all by word of mouth and dedicated people working on my campaign for free."

"Damn, you really did all that?" said Tom, "That's pretty impressive."

"Yeah, I did all that, and it took them over five years to get rid of me."

"Who got rid of you?" asked Freddy, "The republicans, cause you were a democrat, right?"

"Fuck no," yelled Lou, "I was an independent. The two major parties became a duopoly long ago. That's why every four to eight years the majority party gets voted out by the people and the other party would take over, but nothing ever changes for the common people because only the upper-class is represented. Corporate control of the media was the biggest reason we lived in a secret plutocracy. Giant corporations were spending billions for commercial time on every media outlet. They, in effect, became owners of the public airways, and a business can't speak ill of their clients. All news stories were put through a corporate friendly filter. So this cabal of billionaires, in accord with the ruling administration, determined what stories get reported, how to spin it and what gets ignored. So these egotistical elites with their insatiable greed have been in control of how the people view the world."

"That's how they convinced people that the best economy is when money trickles down from the top, not from the bottom up, and that profits should be maximized off everything, including healthcare, and American jobs should be sent overseas for lower labor costs. We could never get a majority to revolt because the media kept the nation divided by pretending we were either republicans or democrats."

"So I guess because of that divide," he said while rubbing his chin and looking upward as if just figuring something out, "and the drudgery of the necessitous lifestyle most of us had, the people never united and did their duty to revolt."

The crew was silent, but Tom and Freddy were nodding as if they understood and agreed.

It was Scott who finally spoke for all of them by saying, "I gotta admit, I don't understand everything you said, but I know you're right. The government sucks, but why waste time thinking about it? You can't change anything."

Lou exhaled deeply and ran his hand over his head with an irritated expression. "Yeah, you're right, Scott. You can't do anything," he said in a queer voice. "I mean, you're only a tax paying citizen. If not the citizens then who, Scott? Tell me who is going to change things."

Lou stared at him so irately Scott felt intimidated and remained silent. "You guys all feel that way? Cause you're not alone. I've heard that shit my whole life. That's why we have what we have. You know what they do in France when the government acts unfairly? They protest. Their government fears the people. Here the people fear the government."

"I heard France is a shit hole, and they pay like so much in taxes," Tom said.

"Yeah, that's exactly what they tell ya!" Lou yelled. "What they don't tell you is the taxes they pay are used to benefit the whole society. Here they taxed the shit out of us and did very little to benefit the working class. Our country fell behind in equality to every other civilized country."

"That would be great if we could stage a huge protest," Freddy bleared.

"You'd never get enough people together," said Scott. "Most people think the government is finally doing some good now."

"We have to get the people united for the sake of the future," Lou said, sounding very serious. "A protest won't do it either. We need a revolution. It has to begin somewhere, and it starts here with the four of us. Are you guys with me? We have to transform this country before it's too late."

Lou looked at each of the men who seemed indifferent, but they all nodded at him like they were placating a child.

"I know some secrets I could get in trouble for knowing," he said and shot them all a cold look. "I'm gonna tell you guys everything I know because we have to be able to trust each other. I'm about to trust you guys with my life here. Now, are we in this together?" First he looked to Freddy, whose eyes were on the road.

"Yeah, you can trust me, man," he said looking over.

Next Lou looked at Tom who was seated behind Freddy.

"Yeah man, I'm in. You can trust me," he blurted out and smiled.

Lou turned to his left and stared over his shoulder at Scott, sitting behind him.

Scott pondered a moment and frowned. "Yeah you can trust me chief, but about this revolution stuff, I'm like all for it, but I got to tell you I don't want to do anything that might jeopardize my life or get me tossed in jail."

"You little bitch," Freddy blurted. "What makes your loser life too important to risk? You think you're so much better than us, huh?"

Tom Laughed mockingly.

"Alright ,take it easy," Lou shouted."It's a very reasonable response. I've only known you guys for one day, but I can tell we're all good people here. No one has to do anything they don't want to. Scott, I believe I can trust you. I know you would never turn me in…Am I right?"

"Of course, chief, I would never rat you out."

They were just reaching the edge of town now.

"Alright then, after we get through the checkpoint, I'm going to let you guys in on a secret that will blow your minds."

They pulled up to the checkpoint, and a guard walked up to the driver's side. He peered in to the van, his eyes searching assiduously. Then he had them scan their keyphones and logged what time they departed the city. The gate lifted, and Freddy drove away. They were a mile away before anyone spoke.

"So what's the big secret, Lou?" Freddy asked. Lou suddenly became paranoid. He had yet to discuss this with any other American.

"You think they bugged this van?" he whispered, looking

closer at the instrument panel. "You know, I'm sure they have our computer monitors bugged."

"Come on, man, they aren't going to bug and monitor every painting van," said Freddy. "They would die of boredom. Now give us the story."

"This might not totally shock you, but everything you hear in the news is bullshit, and I mean everything. The reason the president declared isolation from the world is because the rest of the world cut us off. The world is pissed at us for fucking up the economy. They formed a World United Nations and asked us to abide by world market regulations. We refused. Then they wanted us to pay restitution in food and water to countries we shot up and ones we owe trillions to. We refused. So then they asked us to ban nuclear weapons along with the rest of the world and we refused again. Then they issued a trade embargo against us until we agree to the W.U.N. treaty." He paused letting it sink in their lazy minds. "You understand what I'm saying here? The rest of the civilized world has agreed that we are the biggest threat to peace and prosperity and the nation most likely to cause a nuclear holocaust. Now they have a formidable coalition headed by China to oppose us. You know what this means? We can be invaded at any moment, and if there's a war, it will involve nukes."

The men seemed skeptical. He went on to explain everything in detail. He answered every question they had except one.

"How do you know all this?" Lou wasn't ready to reveal his secret yet.

"I can't tell you guys yet," he told them. "There's an investigation going on, and after it blows over, I'll reveal my secret."

They weren't sure if Lou was a quack or a genius, but they were amused by him. Freddy pulled in to the A.P.T. parking lot and parked.

"Now you guys know the urgency for a revolution," Lou said before opening the door. "I'll see you guys tomorrow."

"See you tomorrow, chief," they replied, and the work day officially ended.

As the quiet hydrogen powered bus got closer to his building, Lou's mind turned to the meeting with Hector tonight. He didn't want to be distracted his first day on the job so he avoided thinking about it all day. Now he envisioned how things might go and the possible dangers.

The bus pulled in front of building 1563, and he got out feeling stiffness in his legs after his first day of physical labor in over a decade.

People were standing in front of the building conversing. Lou walked to the nearest restaurant and purchased a substandard meal. He ate alone by the window and casually looked out at all the people.

It was pleasant to see People out in the street just chatting for their amusement. This sort of behavior use to be an abnormality. His generation and his father's generation lived in a consumption based society where People were occupied at every moment, working to pay off their bills all day for six days a week, and in their precious free time they had professional sports, television shows, movies, or the internet to feed them mindless amusement. He just discovered this new system produced something positive. People were actually engaging each other face-to-face in their community, not just by e-mailing and texting.

He finished his meal and walked back to his building. As he was about to head up to his unit, he suddenly recognized a voice. He turned to its direction. A group of five black men were talking out front. They claimed the area on the grass between the sidewalk and the street.

"Man, I told that old boy I was going to smack him upside the head," the largest one was saying. It was clearly Tyrell.

Suddenly an idea dawned upon him. He quickly jogged across the street to the cash machine. His haste was in vein because when he got to the bank of America there were two people waiting to use it before him. He waited tensely as the person using the machine seemed to be moving in slow motion. He restrained himself from yelling out, "Hurry up, Goddamn it."

Finally it was his turn. He swiped his keyphone through the sensor and pushed the withdraw option. With one more touch of his finger, he withdrew the maximum amount, eight hundred dollars, and went deeper into debt. Lou never made a cash advance on credit in his life, but he felt it was necessary. The decision was made easier knowing that he would never pay it off, not just because they would bleed him with interest rates, but he knew this system must not, could not, and would not stand. He put six hundred in his back pocket and one hundred in each of his front pockets. Now he could hear awful dance music spilling out of a night club a few doors down as he briskly walked back toward his building.

A woman, who was standing out in front of the bar, caught his eye. Her face was somewhat unattractive, and she smiled at him.

"You need a date, honey?" she asked, just as he was about to cross the street.

For a moment, Lou was distracted from his plan. He stopped in his tracks, turned to her and looked at her body, paying close attention to her legs. She had cut off the pants legs on her standard American made blue jeans, making them short shorts. Her exposed thighs appealed to him at once, becoming almost hypnotic. She had the standard blue tee shirt with the sleeves cut off along with the bottom half of the shirt. He finally raised his eyes from her legs to her exposed stomach, and there was some excess fat hanging over her waist band, not uncommon for the lower class Americans who consumed all processed food, which had become increasingly saturated with fat calories and excitotoxins.

Not a good fashion design for that belly, he thought. Suddenly he became less distracted.

"Maybe another time, honey, I'm in a hurry right now," He said and walked across the street. Lou was heading right toward the group of black men when one of them saw him approaching. He stared right into Lou's eyes and began moving his body and arms like a half dance, half fighting display. This frightened Lou, making him lower his eyes and veer away from the group. He didn't look back in their direction until he was well behind them and near the front of his building.

He considered abandoning his plan. After all, Tyrell

despised white people, perhaps rightfully so, for their idiotic voting record. Surely all five of the group felt the same way and would love to take out some of their aggression by roughing him up.

I can't let fear discourage me from my ideas.

Slowly, he began to approach the group again. As he grew closer, one of the men in the group, a furry headed man, shorter than Tyrell but just as stocky with tattoos all over his arms, looked toward him.

"Man, look at this boot walking up to our space like he looking for something," he said, waving his hands.

Lou shuddered, thinking the thug was addressing him but saw he was staring down a young white man walking by to his left.

"You looking for something, boot?"

"No, man," the white guy replied.

"Then get the fuck out of our domain, bitch," the furry tattooed man said and gave the white guy a push. The group laughed as the white guy scurried away.

Lou stood behind Tyrell and hesitated until he was done laughing. "Hey Tyrell, can I talk to you a sec?" Lou said, his voice cracking.

Tyrell didn't hear but the furry tattooed guy did.

"Hey Tyrell, some slimy little boot is calling for you. Wanna play bitch slap the whitey with him?" He stared down Lou.

Tyrell whipped around to face Lou. He had a wild, dangerous expression.

The furry tattooed man began to walk toward him, seemingly with intent to strike.

Tyrell grabbed him by the arm just as he was passing him. "Hold up, man, I know this dude. He ain't no boot."

"What? He sure look like one to me," the furry man said.

"I said hold up. Did I stutter, fool?" Tyrell shouted. He was clearly the dominant one.

He smiled at Lou, "What up, old boy?"

"How ya doing, Tyrell? I could use your help, and I was

wondering if you wanted to work for me…you know, make some extra cash."

"Work for you? Doing what? You ain't got no money. If you did, you wouldn't be here."

Lou pulled out a hundred dollar bill. "This is yours just for one hour of work tonight. I need you to be my body guard. I gotta meet someone and pick up something important, and I'm worried they might try to intimidate me or something."

"You want me to be your body guard?" he replied in a comical voice, making the idea sound stupid. Then he fell silent as all eyes were upon him. He spoke seriously now, "I guess you really are a smart dude since you knew I would be the best choice."

Lou smiled and nodded.

"So this is a one day job, huh? Cause if not, you better have a whole bunch of those c-notes."

"How much money you got on you, boot?" the furry tattooed man said. "You got a c-note for each of us, boy?"

Tyrell frowned at the man. "Chill, Devon," he ordered.

"All I have is this one bill. I took out a cash advance on credit. They say I have a two thousand dollar limit." Lou surged his shoulders.

"Alright man, I got your back tonight for a c-note - one hour. When we do this?"

"Meet me out front here at ten to eight. I'm supposed to meet this Mexican guy at eight sharp. This is serious shit, Tyrell!" He spoke like a leader and made eye contact with all of the five men, "It involves illegal shit on my end, but I think you might believe me when I say it's for a good cause, a cause I hope we all fight for together."

After a moment of silence it seemed as if they were all intrigued by this different, audacious white man until Tyrell brought them back to reality by laughing. "Whatever, man. Give me the money, and I'll meet you later."

"Don't you think I should pay you when we're finished? I mean, what if you don't show up and keep my money?"

"Well, you just gonna have to trust me, boy? Ain't you supposed to trust your bodyguard?"

Lou nodded. "You're right." He handed him the bill without apprehension. "When you show up at 7:50, I'll give you another hundred for down payment on the next job," he said to add an incentive to show up.

Tyrell nodded and pocketed the money. Lou walked away and went right up to his unit. He had an hour and a half before the meeting so he took a nap.

Chapter 6

He had dosed off for the last half hour before waking up at 7:40. The physical demands of the day had drained him more than he wanted to admit to himself. Now, pressed for time, he got up, went to the kitchen area, and splashed his face with cold water.

He made a cup of instant coffee, and while drinking it, he strolled to the window to see if the attractive woman from the building next door was parading herself in front of the window. No such luck.

He walked outside to the front of the building. The sun was just setting, but the overcast skies made it seem later. The sounds of people's voices and bass overtones from the bar across the street filled the air.

After a few minutes, he checked his keyphone: 7:53, still no Tyrell.

Lou already started accepting that he would be alone for this meeting and out a hundred bucks when, to his delight, he saw a dark imposing figure crossing the street. He must have been at the bar. He noticed that ten yards behind Tyrell was another black man. He could already see the furry afro, and his delight faded. Tyrell saw Lou from a distance and walked right up to him.

"What up, man? Am I right on time?"

"Close enough," Lou answered and turned his eyes to the man approaching.

"Oh yeah, this is Deron. He gonna tag along, you know, watch my back."

"How you doing, Deron?" Lou said, stepping around Tyrell and holding out his hand.

Deron extended out his tattooed arm and shook Lou's hand. "I'm alright," he said, oddly sounding shy.

"Okay, here's the story." Lou began. "I told this guy to

steal my laptop computer from the G.A. police van, and I would pay him to return it to me. Apparently, he got it, and now the heat is on, and we have to meet him at unit 246."

"Aw shit, man," Deron blurted, "that's the thing they been talking about in the news."

"Yep," said Lou, "and it's not going to look good if I bring both you guys with me."

"That's cool, man," Tyrell said, "Deron can watch from a distance, like down the hall or whatever." He grabbed Deron around the neck in a friendly headlock. "He's interested, man. I told him who you was."

After being freed from the headlock, Deron popped his head up smiling. "Yeah man, you were the last person I ever voted for. Me and my momma went out to vote for you in that crazy recall election." His joy faded, and his face saddened. "She dead now, wasn't even that old. She couldn't get no medicine. Goddamn pills was twelve bucks a piece, and that was with the state discount for poor people."

"It's unbelievable there wasn't a revolution just over healthcare," said Lou looking sympathetically in Devon's eyes, "I'm sorry about your momma."

Devon frowned then nodded.

"Okay, let's do this," said Lou. Hopefully, it will be the easiest money you ever made, Tyrell." Lou began walking in the building and noticed Tyrell hadn't moved. He turned back to face him and looked at him puzzled.

"Ain't you forgetting something, my man?" he said. Lou shrugged his shoulders. "You suppose to give me another hundred, remember?"

"Aw shit, come on, man. Fine, I'll go deeper in debt for you." Lou dug out another hundred dollar bill, handed it to him and walked in the building. This time Tyrell followed.

"Man, don't make it sound like that," Tyrell was saying as they climbed the stairway to the second floor. "I ain't trying to tap your credit. Hell, maybe I'd of done it for fifty, you the fool who made the deal."

They entered the hall, walking slowly. They passed 240.

"Its cool, man," Lou said in a quiet voice. Forget about

the money, and just get your mind right for this."

They stood in front of 246. Lou motioned for Tyrell to stand off to the side, out of the peephole view. Then he knocked. Lou's senses heightened. He felt floor vibrations from the footsteps approaching the door. It was definitely not Hector, judging by the vibrations, but somebody much heavier. The peephole darkened for a moment. Then the door slowly opened.

Lou was staring at a portly Hispanic man. His expression read annoyance mixed with resentment.

"Hey, how you doing? is Hector here?"

The Man's expression never changed. "You Lou?" he grunted.

"Yes, I'm Lou and you are?" Lou held up his hand in offering.

The man didn't reach out or speak; he simply opened the door further and swung his head cooly over his right shoulder, motioning Lou to come in.

Lou looked to Tyrell and did his own head signal and walked in. The man began closing the door. It stopped abruptly when it hit Tyrell's broad shoulder. The portly Mexican man recoiled.

"This is my good buddy, Tyrell. We go everywhere together," Lou said once they were both inside.

Hector was sitting at the kitchen table. He got up quickly. "You suppose to come alone, man!" he yelled.

"Really? You didn't mention that. Oh well," Lou said calmly. He walked closer with Tyrell following, "So what's going on?"

Hector looked at Tyrell for a moment, then refocused on Lou and frowned. "Man, you tell me to cop this thing, and I do like you say. Now the whole police force is looking for me. Miguel was sick today, and he say to me, they search people's rooms while we're at work. I can tell they searched my room. They probably searched your room too. Good thing I hide it here, man." Lou walked toward the front corner of the kitchen and held his finger up to his lips, commanding silence.

"Hey you got anything to drink here?" he said as he grabbed the end of the table and dragged it a few feet closer to the front. "Come on over here, boys. Let's have a drink."

Hector and Tyrell came over, but the portly Mexican man stood by the door staring dumbly.

Lou lowered his voice and said, "Let's talk over here, away from the front of the computer monitor. Did you guys notice in the middle of the trademark at the top? It looks like a camera lens is in the O?"

Both men just shook their heads.

"Well I did, so let's stay out of sight," Lou said, keeping his voice low. "So you got it hidden here, huh? Nice job."

"Yeah, I got it alright," said Hector, "but I didn't know how bad it was going to be. So here is the deal, man. The cops say it's a two thousand dollar reward for helping them find it, so you have to match that. I want two g's, a thousand for me and a thousand for Derwin since he stashed it."

The portly man by the door looked over, hearing his name.

Lou exhaled deeply. "Okay, get Derwin over here."

Hector motioned with his hand and Hector slowly walked over to them.

"Listen, you guys did a great job getting and hiding this. With this laptop, I, unlike any other citizen, can be in touch with the outside world. Listen up now. Everything you hear and see is bullshit. Our government is lying to us, and the rest of the world is fed up with them. These distorted fools that are running our country refuse to acknowledge or obey the World's United Nations, and the rest of the world views us as a threat to humanity. We could be invaded tomorrow, and every ordinary citizen wouldn't even know why." One at a time Lou engaged eye contact with all three of them.

"No way, man. No one would ever mess with the U.S.," Hector said.

"Not just one country, Hector, all of them! The world is united by their fear and hatred of our country. It's up to us, we the people, to overthrow this government and form a just one. If we fail, there will be a foreign invasion. Trust me. In fact, I suspect our crazy leaders are already planning for nuclear war, and guys like us won't survive it." His eyes were wide, beaming his famous look of intensity.

He was gifted at making people listen, relate and believe. He took a deep breath and exhaled. He was getting the feeling that he could still connect with people no matter how out of touch with reality they were. "This is not only the most important time in our country's history but also for the future of mankind, and it's up to us to take action."

Hector and Tyrell were both wide-eyed with shock as they considered the possibility that Lou was correct. Somehow it seemed plausible, but they each harbored hopes he was crazy. Derwin looked detached, perhaps not understanding or paying attention.

"You're part of this now, and we have to spread the word." Lou dug in his back pocket and inconspicuously used his fingers to separate three bills from the six and pulled them out. "Here's a hundred for you and a hundred for Derwin and here's another one for the trouble. Now I have to figure out how to get it out of here and hide it somewhere safe. Go get the thing, Hector." He turned to Darwin. "Can I use one of your pillow cases? I got an..."

"No fuckin' way, man!" Hector stood and yelled. "I want two g's, or I'm keeping it."

"Shhh," Lou commanded, "keep quiet. Didn't you hear anything I said? This is more important than money unless you're like them. They hold money above all. You're not like them, are you?"

Hector seemed to ponder for a moment then went back to business. "You say you were going to give me ten percent of your pay for two months. I want a payout of two g's now, or I give it to someone else." Lou looked at Tyrell, trying to read his expression.

"Listen Hector, I can't play games here. Go get the Goddamn computer now, or Tyrell here is going to put you in a painful headlock and cut off your air. I'll try to get you more money, but you're part of the revolution now so quit being so fuckin' greedy."

Hector stood in silence, frowning.

Tyrell, who now felt somewhat guilty for taking two

hundred from Lou already, walked up behind Hector and began breathing heavy like he was summoning his strength. Hector nodded to Derwin who then went to the kitchen sink and opened the cabinet under it. He got down on his knees and struggled for something in the back. He pulled something out and walked over. Derwin placed the laptop on the kitchen table.

Lou stared it for a moment, feeling both joy and fear interweave in his mind.

"If any of you guys don't believe me, I'd be happy to show you the real news of the world to prove it. I have an amazing program on a disk that allows me to access the world internet through the local internet. It looks like I'm playing an internet video game with a bunch of rich kids to anyone spying on me. First we need to figure out where we can bring this thing. It's got to be somewhere safe and still close enough so my Wi-Fi antenna and router can access the building's network. The next problem is if I sign on to my F.F.N. account, they will know it's me and know I have my laptop. I have to start a new account under someone else's name that lives in this building."

A thought immediately occurred to him. "Hey Derwin, how often do you use the internet?" he asked smiling.

Derwin looked nervous and wide-eyed now.

"I don't want to be involved," he replied. "I'm not going to end up in the prison plant working twelve hours a day like you are."

"Aw, come on now, Derwin, you have to be involved. We're fighting for our lives, and now you know the truth. You can't just ignore it. I don't even see how you could get in trouble. If they bust me, just say you didn't know I stole your identity." Lou looked over to Hector who seemed to be drifting away, getting ready to leave.

"That reminds me, Hector," his voice rose saying the name. "You guys are now part of the revolution so I'm sure you won't be thinking about turning me in to the G.A. police to collect a big reward. It wouldn't be worth it because before you get to spend the money, Tyrell here will find you and crush your head like a grape."

Hector and Derwin looked at Tyrell who crossed his arms

and gave them an evil look.

"I just want us to be clear on this. The only way this can work is if we trust each other."

Lou opened up the laptop and pressed the power button. As soon as the operating system booted up, he clicked on the F.F.N. icon. He then deleted his screen name and clicked on "new member."

"Okay Derwin, spell your last name for me."

Derwin sucked his lower lip and rubbed his messy dark hair.

"Come on, man, we all in this together," Tyrell said to him in a friendly tone. Hector sat down at the kitchen table and looked up at Derwin silently.

"Its Vazquez v-a-z-q-u-e-z."

Lou typed in the name and hit enter.

"What's your F.F.N. password?"

"I don't have one. I didn't even go on the stupid internet yet. Why should I? It's like you say, all bullshit…right?"

"Right you are, my friend, but you're going to have to make one up and set up an account on your computer. Think of a password that you'll remember, and it's got to have at least six letters or numbers."

"Hey, how about d-u-m-b-a-s-s?" Hector said, causing him and Tyrell to chuckle.

Lou smiled at the display of comradery.

Derwin seemed to be in deep thought the following moment. "I want it to be m-y-j-e-s-s-i-c-a," he said as his face grew long, and his eyes moistened.

"Okay, that's good." Lou typed it in. "Who may I ask is Jessica?"

"She was the girl for me. I never love anyone else like I did her." Derwin looked to the ground, hiding his remorseful gaze.

Lou assumed he would say how she tragically died.

"But she didn't want to be with me, and I never see her again."

Despite the lack of a tragic death, this made Lou feel deep pity for Derwin. To have loved someone you lost is still a wonderful experience while it lasted, but to have loved someone who doesn't love you back is far more regrettable.

"Yeah, that's a killer. I know how that can feel," Lou said.

He successfully logged on to the F.F.N. network then quickly logged off and shut down the computer. There were only nine minutes of power left in the charge, and his charger was somewhere in his unit.

"Okay, now you got to go over to your computer and set up you account with the same password." Lou watched him do it from the kitchen, staying out of sight from the tiny lens. Derwin finished and logged on. He observed the suppressed American internet for the first time in his life with no real interest.

"We have to get this somewhere safe, and nobody's unit is safe," Lou said.

After moments of silence Tyrell spoke up.

"There ain't nobody who goes in the basement except the maintenance man. Maybe you can hide it somewhere down there."

"That's a good idea. You've been down there, huh?"

"Naw man, I ain't been down there. Deron told me about it. He and Willy went down there to get cranked."

"Alright, you guys, lead me down there. Deron can look out ahead of me, and you look out behind me. We got to be very careful..."

A loud knock at the door silenced him as his heart pumped hard against his chest. The knock startled everyone in the room. They looked at each other stupidly with open mouths for one frozen moment. Lou snatched up the laptop and awkwardly began to put it in the cabinet under the sink again.

Tyrell and Derwin began to walk to the door. Tyrell got there first and looked through the peep hole.

Lou closed the cabinet door and turned to Tyrell, still displaying panic. Tyrell walked back by Lou and whispered, "It's another Mexican dude."

"Aw damn, man!" Hector hollered, "I forgot about Miguel. I told him to come by and pretend he want to buy it."

"Goddamn it, Hector. Get rid of him," Lou ordered.

At that moment Derwin opened the door.

A slender Hispanic man, wearing a red bandanna around his forehead and a tee shirt with the sleeves cut off, entered. Though his attire was that of the younger crowd, he looked to be in his thirties.

"Hey Holmes," he said to Derwin. "Hector, what's happening? You still got that thing, man?" Hector walked quickly over to him.

"No Miguel, forget about it, man. I'll talk to you later about it. Now go."

"You don't understand, Holmes. I really got this buzz cut dude who wants to buy it, and he's willing to pay large, Holmes."

Lou dashed out from the kitchen, startling everyone in the room and stood right in front of Miguel.

"Don't mess around now, man, Hector told us about the plan you guys had. Now tell me the truth. Did you really tell someone about this?"

Miguel pushed Lou back three steps with both his arms. "Get the fuck out of my face, bitch!" he yelled.

Tyrell walked up to them quickly, and Miguel's expression changed to fear.

"Who you calling bitch, fool? I hope you ain't talking to my boy here."

Hector pushed forward and got in between them. "Let's relax, dudes. Miguel, tell him the truth now. This is serious. I'm not trying to get more money anymore."

"Damn man, I'm serious. I swear this dude was asking around if anyone knew who had the stolen laptop, so I said I might know, and how much you willing to pay, and this boy said he'll pay two thousand or more if he has to. He just wants the thing really bad."

Lou slapped the top of his head and rubbed it as he grinded his teeth. "Jesus Christ, Hector, for a thief you're one dumb son of a bitch. Why would you tell this guy anything?" He frowned intensely. Then, turning to Tyrell, he said, "We're gonna have company."

"No man, this dude's cool," Miguel said. "He really

wants to buy the thing. He said he's a writer and needs something to work on."

"Where's he waiting for you now?" Lou asked.

"He's down stairs in the lobby. What's your problem, man?"

"I'll bet you don't even think he followed you up here to see what unit you went into, do you? You Goddamn idiot." His voice was low but reprimanding. "Did you know stealing is a crime if it's committed by anyone who isn't a member of the government? Did you even care that you could get your buddy, Hector here, thrown in prison just because you're trying to get a finder's fee pay out?" He looked over the others in the room. "You people have to realize money means nothing. We can only gain power by uniting. Money is their power. Unity is our power and our only chance."

None of the others could think of a word to say. They all silently watched Lou frantically move around the room looking at everything. He stopped at the window, lifted it open and examined the screen. It was a permanent screen that could not be removed. He dashed into the kitchen and fired through Derwin's utensil bin until he found a steak knife. He went back to the group and huddled them in close.

"Derwin, go stand right in front of the monitor and block the lens with your body."

Once Derwin was in place, Lou said, "Come here, Hector," and led him to the window.

"As fast as you can, without running, go out there and stand right under this window. I'm going to drop it down to you, so please catch it. Just stash it in the bushes the best you can until we can move it somewhere safe tonight."

Hector looked nervous.

"No way, Holmes," said Miguel. "Hector will drop it. He can't catch, man. Let me do it."

"Keep your voice down," Lou ordered. "You're staying right here."

"Deron can catch, man. He ain't ever dropped a pass in basketball," Tyrell said. Lou felt a moment of doubt, like everyone was just out to steal from him. He found comfort considering that he would rather have Deron steal his laptop than have the G.A.T.E. get it.

"All right Hector, listen, on your way down if you see a black guy with a furry afro and tattoos all over his arms, his name is Deron. Tell him you're doing something for Lou and you need his help. Then have him catch it."

Looking nervous, Hector nodded but remained still.

"Go man, hurry, I got a feeling they'll be here any second."

Hector got moving, quietly opened the door, and left.

"Say man."

They heard a voice calling to Hector from down the hall. Lou ran over to the door, opened it ever so slightly, and put his ear to the crack.

"You know that guy in the unit you just came out of? You know the dude with the red bandanna?" It was definitely a Caucasian voice trying to sound Hispanic.

"Aaaa, yeah man," replied Hector. "He'll be coming out soon, man. I got to run over to my unit real quick, and I'm coming right back," He walked past the man.

"Hey, hold on a second!"

"I'll be right back, man." Hector sprinted away.

Lou closed the door quietly and locked it. He ran over to the window and cut the screen along the bottom edge and a couple inches up along each side. He ran back to the kitchen, dropped the knife in the sink, and opened the cabinet underneath. He pulled out the laptop and stood up, clutching it against his chest. Calling out to Tyrell and Miguel, he said, "You guys get over there, sit at the kitchen table and pretend you're arm wrestling or something. Make small talk and act natural."

All three men moved toward the kitchen.

"Not you, Derwin. Get your ass back there." Once Derwin's wide body blocked the computer's lens, he rushed to the window, first taking a look to see if Hector was in position yet. He was nowhere in sight, just a staggering man looking like he had a few too many beers at the bar and could puke at any moment. Lou slid the left side of the laptop into the slit he cut at the bottom of the screen. The side with the disk drive was on the right, and he was getting the feeling he may be dropping it with no one to catch it in a moment. At least it probably wouldn't fall on the disk drive side.

If it falls in the bush just right, maybe there's a slight chance it will survive the fall, was his doubtful thought.

He pushed it a quarter of the way through, causing the screen to slightly rip higher on each side. There he stood sweating, holding the computer on a sixty degree angle ready to release it, like dropping a package into a mail box chute. He kept his eyes looking out the window. The noise of an engine approaching made him look toward the front street. He saw a blue and white gate van pass through his field of vision. He knew it was stopping in front of this building, judging by the brake lights and the downshifting engine.

"Come on, Hector," he muttered.

Just then three slow heavy knocks rang out. At once, everyone had the same impulse to look toward the door.

Lou and Derwin's eyes met. Lou silently mouthed the word WAIT to him, then one last look for Hector.

Knock, Knock, Knock, "Hey, it's me, open up." The voice sounded like a white guy attempting to sound Mexican. Bang! bang! bang! The knocking was hard and fast without stopping now.

Lou eased it out the window, now only grasping the end of it in his long, thin fingers and extending his arm as far out the window as he could. One last look toward the back of the building, and just before he dropped it to the hard ground, a man emerged from around the corner. He could see a furry afro!

"Who is it, for Christ sake?" Lou called out.

The pounding at the door stopped. "Open up!" the voice yelled, and the pounding began again.

Lou could no longer see Deron from this angle and assumed he would be under the window in three, two, one, he let it go... Without even looking down to see what happened, he tugged down on the screen and tried to straighten it the best he could and closed the window quietly.

"Get the door," he said under his breath to Derwin. He hurried over to the kitchen table, sat down across from Miguel on Tyrell's side, and put his arm on the table. "Come on, I'll kick your ass."

The moment Derwin turned the doorknob, it was forced open and in popped a light skinned, Caucasian man with a buzz cut. He was armed with a bolt blaster.

"What you guys got over there?" He rushed over to the kitchen table. Seeing nothing, he quickly surveyed the rest of the room.

"Where's the laptop, gentleman?" he said pointing his weapon at them. The men looked at each other. Miguel was about to open his mouth when Lou blurted out.

"What the hell are you talking about? Who the fuck are you anyway? You come here to arm wrestle the champ or something? I got twenty says you don't last twenty seconds with my boy here."

"Look, I know its here, Okay. This guy here with the bandanna said he could sell it to me if the price was right. So where is it?" He directed his question to Miguel as he pointed the bolt blaster at his head.

"Oh, sorry man," Miguel replied, "he no have it. I was bullshitting, Holmes."

"So that's how it's going to be, huh?" the man said, pulling out his keyphone with his free hand. He pressed a button and held it to his ear. "Alright," he said into the mouth hole, "not yet, but its here."

Eight seconds later, three G.A. officers barged in with bolt blasters drawn. In one second they were aimed at each of the four men at the table.

"Nobody move!" one of them shouted.

"Is this your unit?" buzz cut asked while moving closer to Derwin.

"Yes, please don't shoot. I did nothing wrong," Derwin bawled while sitting in the desk chair.

"Tell me where the laptop is and you'll save yourself a lot of pain," buzz cut demanded.

"I don't know what you mean, I swear," Derwin sniveled, tears in full flow now.

"We're going to have to search the place," Buzz cut man

said, turning to the other cops. "Get up, maggot!" he yelled to Derwin.

Once Derwin got up, he grabbed him by the back of the neck and pushed him to the center of the room. "Get on the ground you filthy spick," he yelled and kicked the back of one of his knees making Derwin go down quickly.

Lou stood up. "Hey asshole, treat him with respect. He's a working class American citizen just like you."

Now the other Officers moved in. One came up behind Lou and violently wrapped his arm around his neck in a tight headlock, cutting of Lou's air. Lou didn't resist. Having knowledge of how bolt blasters worked, he was extremely fearful of them, even if they were only set to stun.

Tyrell got up at once, startling the officers as they saw the full size of him. "Let him go, man! You're choking him!" He grabbed the cop's arm that was around Lou's neck and pried it off easily.

Just as Lou drew in a breath of air, he heard a zap.

"Aaarrggghhh," Tyrell's scream was cut short, and his body convulsed as electricity shocked his system. He fell forward on the table, his body weight instantly breaking it as he crashed to the ground.

"My, oh my, he's a big one," one of the officers said and laughed.

Lou and Miguel didn't move or speak.

The officers ordered them to sit on the ground in the middle of the room while two of them struggled to drag Tyrell's unconscious body over there.

While one officer stood over the men with his bolt blaster drawn, the others began to search the room intensely.

Lou concentrated on remaining calm by considering the positive side. Both Derwin and Miguel denied knowing anything about the computer, and Tyrell bravely stuck up for him.

Derwin's unit was becoming a mess; they were throwing things out of the closet and onto the floor. Then they began emptying all of his kitchen cabinets. This went on for ten minutes before the officers had searched every inch of the unit.

The cops gathered outside the front door.

"Its definitely not here. Way to go, Billy," A tall officer said to the buzz cut man.

"Screw you, Lowes," Billy snapped. "We're close. That's the guy who owned the thing. You know he's involved."

"It makes you wonder what the hell is so important about this thing," said Lowes. "The chief says it's our highest priority, even with all this other shit going on with the Scavies."

"Yeah, I mean who gives a shit about an old laptop?" a shorter officer said.

"Don't you guys get it," Billy said. "That guy in there is a spy or terrorist or something, and I think there's some important shit on his computer."

"I doubt that guy's a spy," said Lowes. "I mean, come on, non-domestic communications have been shut off for five years now."

"Maybe he's a domestic terrorist. No, I bet he's a revolutionary," the short cop said.

"A revolutionary is a terrorist, you idiot. Now let's go have a word with this guy," Billy said then walked back in.

"Were supposed to wait for Captain Zipp," the short guy said to Lowes.

Lowes just shrugged his shoulders and walked in.

Billy stood before Lou, looking down at him with evil eyes. "So why are you here? you must want to get your laptop back real bad. Are you a spy, old man?"

Lou scowled right back at him after hearing old man. "I don't know what you're talking about, but I'm here to hang out. Derwin's my friend. I met him through my friend, Hector, who was my pod neighbor when we unloaded. And Tyrell here is a friend that I met on the bus coming out to this oppressive place. We're hanging out and making friends! And you gentlemen electrocuted one of my friends. Don't you think you should treat your fellow citizens with respect?"

"No, but I think I should treat you to a bruised skull." Billy, being an undercover cop, had no club on him, so he walked over to Officer Lowes and pulled his bash club off his belt. Lowes flinched but let Billy take the club and looked amused as he watched Billy walk back toward Lou, lightly smacking his palm with the club and smiling precariously.

Lou covered his head with his arms and went into a fetal position before Billy was even close enough to strike him.

"Don't do this. We're all working class Americans here," pleaded Lou. "We have to stick together. Don't be a puppet for the greedy bastards who ruined our country. We're on the same side, man." Lou could only see the man's shoes from his cowardly position.

"Don't give me any of that pathetic liberal talk! That shit ruined our country and brought us to this!" Billy yelled down to him.

"How can that be when this country hasn't lived under any sort of liberal values for over forty years? Don't buy in to their lies, officer."

Whap! The club came down, striking Lou's shoulder blade and his right hand, which was covering the back of his neck.

He let out a yelp as the pain raged in the back of his hand.

Tyrell moaned as he began to regain consciousness.

"Don't tell me what I can't buy in to, scum bag." His eyes moved to Tyrell, "Hey, your big black buddy's waking up just in time to see you get bashed."

Billy raised the club again. This time he intended to hit Lou's thigh.

"Hey, Captain," Lowes and the shorter officer said at the same time.

Billy lowered the club and looked over to see Captain Zipp walk in with a Mexican man in handcuffs. Billy smiled and nodded to Zipp.

"Hey Billy, is this the guy that ran off?"

Lou recognized the voice and sat up. He saw Captain Zipp and Hector in cuffs and let out a deep breath.

"Yeah, that's him, Captain. The things not in this room, but they must know where it is, and look who's here," he said, pointing at Lou.

"What happened to the black guy?" Zipp asked, making no acknowledgement to Lou.

"Oh, him, we had to shock him because he tried to attack Lowes."

Zipp seemed to be in thought. After a moment of silence he spoke. "Okay, we're going to question them right here, one at a time. You two take every one out in the hall and watch them. Me and Billy will question them here starting with that skinny Mexican with the red bandanna."

"Alright, you guys, lets go," said Lowes as he and the short cop escorted Lou, Derwin and Hector out. They took the cuffs off Hector and ordered the men to sit against the wall.

Moments later, Zipp and Billy came out, each with one of Tyrell's arms over their shoulders, helping him to walk. They backed him against the wall and let him go. He slid down until he was sitting with his legs bent in front of him.

"Damn man, what the hell happened? I feel like a bus hit me," he said rubbing his eyes.

"They shocked you. I'm sorry, Tyrell. Thanks for sticking up for me."

"Damn boy, what kind of shit you get me into here?"

Everyone was quiet now.

Lou was thinking about what they must be asking Miguel. *Please let them all deny knowing anything.*

"Can I ask you guys a question?" Lou said to Lowes and the short cop.

"Sure, as long as you're polite," the short guy said.

"Okay, I'm going to use a hypothetical scenario, and you guys each give me your answer, if you please."

They all seemed interested.

"Imagine there's a big protest going on where the lower class people were demanding representation and threatening to overthrow the government. In response the government ordered you to suppress the uprising by using extreme measures. Would you start shooting the people or would you join them?"

"I'd do whatever I'm told," Lowes said quickly. "If they want me to shoot down a bunch of lowlifes, fine with me."

"Okay, that's an honest answer. So you would never question an order they give you under any circumstances?"

"If I did, I wouldn't deserve to be a G.A. officer," Lowes proudly stated.

"What about you? Would you shoot American citizens because you're ordered to by your wealthy superiors?"

"You can't ask a question like that. That's hypothetical bullshit," the short guy replied. "I ain't answering that. I think you should just keep quiet until the Capitan talks to you."

"Fine, I'll shut up as long as you consider that when there's good reason to overthrow a government, **you,** the police and the military members will be the deciding factor. The country's fate is in the heart and minds of our soldiers and cops." Lou cleared his throat. "So please stay open minded if the time comes." He was choked up from Lowes' callous response, causing him to lose faith momentarily.

"You see, I told you he was a revolutionary," the short cop said.

"Yeah, well he's going to end up in the penitentiary plant," Lowes replied. "Most people love the compatriot party, and those who don't soon disappear."

"The Scavies haven't disappeared," Lou muttered.

Derwin's eyes were growing increasingly worried as he listened. "I'm not with him. I swear I know nothing about this guy," he blurted.

"Relax, Derwin, we did nothing wrong," Hector said, pleasantly surprising Lou.

The next few minutes were quiet with the exception of Tyrell moaning and complaining of a headache. Then the door opened and out walked Miguel followed by Billy.

"Let him go," he ordered and looked down at Derwin. "Get up boy, you're next."

Nine minutes later they released Derwin and told him to stay away from his apartment for the next hour. They brought in Hector next. Several minutes later they released Hector and brought in Tyrell. It was a longer wait when the door opened again and Tyrell groggily walked out.

"Get up, old man," Billy said. Lou walked in and was ordered to sit in the desk chair while Captain Zipp stood over him, staring coldly.

"I though I could trust you, governor." He smacked his own head. "I forgot, never trust a politician." He leaned closer, towering over Lou who was slouching . "So what did you do with it, Rizzo? We know you're in on this; everyone admitted it."

"Look," began Lou, "I guess you guys know I'm opposed to the government and for good reason. We all should be united in taking back our government, but I got to tell you, Captain, I would never do anything that could get me put away in the prison plant, believe me. I don't give a damn about that laptop, and I haven't seen it since you took it away," he said acting sincere.

"So now you're friends with the black guy that kicked your ass on the bus, huh? Well, he spilled the beans on you. We got a lot of info on you. Everyone said you know where it is." Zipp took a deep breath and leaned closer to Lou. "Just tell us where it is, and we can be done with this."

Lou felt a distinct possibility that Zipp was lying. He knew the trick.

"Jeez, you must have beaten a false confession out of them. I hear the old Chicago cops were the masters of that."

Billy twitched with rage and moved closer to Lou with clinched fists.

"Relax, Billy," Zipp ordered and turned back to Lou. "Get out of here, Governor."

Billy looked puzzled and frowned.

Lou got up and walked away.

Billy slammed the door shut. "Why the hell did you let him go?" he erupted, "I could have got all the info out of him in five minutes if you let me."

"That's not the smart way, Billy. He wouldn't say shit. He's got a strong will. First we let him go and watch his every move. Then when he leads us to the thing, we bring him in. The agent on this case told me to let him go and wait for him to reveal whatever he's planning before we torture him."

Billy would never question the orders of a government agent, so he pushed Zipp no further. He just nodded in agreement.

Lou went right to his unit and stayed there the rest of the night.

Chapter 7

At 7:20 the next morning Lou's keyphone woke him from another night of broken sleep. It had been four days now since he had contact with the outside world. This morning felt different to him. He felt hopelessness weighing down on him from the agonizing thought of all these people unable to comprehend the need to unite and revolt. They were overworked, underpaid, and had no chance of prosperity, but it was better than the brutal anarchy that preceded the G.A. plan. They were grateful to be part of a working society and didn't know the dangerous choices their leaders were making with the world.

He decided none of that mattered anymore. The end was nearing. Something will change for better or worse and he vowed to do his part the best he could. He washed up and ate.

Standing in front of his building, waiting for blue bus 47, he carefully observed everybody standing around.

They're watching me now. I'm sure someone here is an undercover cop.

He slithered around the corner of the building and began looking through the bushes in a nonchalant way.
He walked all the way to the back, checking every bush - nothing.

He looked again as he walked back to the front - still nothing.

Blue bus 47 was pulling up. It seemed he wouldn't find out what happened to the laptop until he runs in to Tyrell and Deron again. He walked toward the bus with his head lowered. Suddenly a body in his peripheral vision bumped violently in to him.

"Man, watch where you going, fool." It was a black man, unfamiliar to Lou.

"You watch where you're going. You blame others for all your mistakes?"

The man leaned in close, making Lou flinch in defense.

"You Lou?" the man whispered.

Lou nodded.

"You know a dude named Deron?"

Lou nodded again.

"He wants me to tell you the thing is in the dumpster." The man walked off quickly and casually.

Lou did the same thinking, *Deron is one smart dude. Oh shit, what if the garbage collection is today?*

He turned back and suddenly sprinted back to the building, taking the steps three at a time up to his floor. He dashed down the hallway, scanned his keyphone on the lock, and entered his room. He opened the closet door and got down on his knees, removing the disk from under the carpet. He stood up inside the closet and slid it into his underwear.

Not taking time to find the charger, he dashed off and made it out front before bus 47 pulled away. He got on the bus, gasping for breath and took his seat. A moment later the driver pulled away.

He sat quietly for three minutes and devised a plan. The rest of the ride he did what he did best: got people fired up.

"How do you guys feel about the billionaires buying our government and bankrupting our country?"

People gasped at his outburst early on.

"How do you feel about losing our rights and being fed government controlled media all our lives? Don't you think it's time to restore our democracy and open communications with the world again?"

Some men were shouting, some in silent shock, but all were amused.

He went on ranting about the government's injustice toward the lower class, and then he always explained the way to fix things, making everything sound so obvious: wisely directed, fair taxes, to provide the essential common things all people must have equal rights to for a strong, fair society.

He had a way of breaking things down to their simplest form and explaining the purpose of a true democratic government.

Toward the end of the ride, everyone was politically awakened. Lou was standing in the isle so everyone could hear him.

"We are the ones who can make the change. We are the work force, and they can't live without us. We, the people, have to join together. We need to let the government know we're sick of them fucking up our country and cutting us off from the world, and we're not going to take it anymore."

Some of the men yelled and Lou had to quiet them to make his announcement. "Listen everyone, spread the word. I'm holding a rally tonight. Get all the workers we can to join us tonight at seven in front of my building, fifteen sixty-three." He stared right at the front overhead camera now. "I'm Lou Rizzo, and if they take me away, I want you guys to demand my release. It's our most important right as Americans to have the right to protest, and it is our duty to overthrow an unjust government. Don't let them silence us this time."

That comment made some of the people a little uneasy, as reality set in and they considered the enormity of really opposing the government.

The bus driver opened the door and looked at Lou like he was insane. He just smiled at him as he got off the bus.

The crew was assembled and set to go minutes later. Lou checked the back of the van first. A collection of tools and drop clothes littered the floor. He pulled the disk out of his pants and stashed it in the corner under a shelf then covered it with a bag of rags.

He opened the driver's side door and said, "Let me drive, Freddy."

Freddy scowled but got out almost immediately and went to the passenger side.

"I need you guys to kick ass today because I have some things to do, and I won't be able to help much." He drove off, and after the first turn almost at once Freddy and Scott yelled.

"You're going the wrong way!"

Tom had his eyes closed trying to take a final nap before

work.

"I know…I have to go back to my building real quick. Tell me if you see anyone following us."

Their faces displayed nervousness as they looked at the road behind them.

"Hey Lou, we don't want to get into any trouble here," Scott said.

"The whole fuckin' country is in trouble, Scott. I'm not doing this for fun, you know."

He drove all the way back to building 1563, tuned around the corner, and went into the alley.

"Anyone tailing us?" asked Lou.

Tom and Scott shook their heads.

He pulled up behind the dumpster allocated to his building.

"When I get out, Freddy, climb over to the driver's side and take off as soon as I get back in, you hear." He jumped out, quickly looked around and scampered over to the dumpster. He flipped open the lid and looked in.

Of course, it couldn't be just sitting there in plain sight. That would be too easy. Nothing is ever easy for me.

After turning his head to get a deep breath of air he climbed in the foul smelling dumpster, half filled with garbage. His left arm fell against something damp and greasy the moment he landed. To the front of him were small white things, maybe it was rice, but once he saw them moving, it confirmed they were maggots. Flies circled his head as he was nearly overwhelmed by repulsion. Gathering himself, he swished his arm over the top layer of garbage - nothing but squishy disgusting trash. He moved over to the other side thinking that it would be just his luck to get this maggoty shit all over him for nothing. He began sifting through the garbage on the other side, and he needed a breath. A pungent smell of rotting fish assaulted his nose and nausea arose, but a second later he felt something solid and sleek. He grabbed it with two hands and pulled it up. There it was, full of coffee grounds and some sticky, syrup-like substance, but it appeared to be intact. He waded his way through dozens of people's rubbish, back to the front edge and poked his head out.

Satisfied it was safe, he climbed out, holding the laptop in his left hand and clumsily fell to the ground. Staggering to the back of the van, he opened the rear door, jumped in and swung the door shut.

"Go man. Get to the job." he implored, sounding like he was crying.

"Are you alright, man?" Tom asked. His tired, reddened eyes looked concerned.

"No, I'm not alright, man. I'm gonna fuckin' puke." He set down the computer and pulled his shirt off. He began wiping his face with a painter's rag that was near him in a hysterical way.

"Are there any maggots on me? Look." He turned his hairy back to them and franticly began wiping his body with the rag.

"Relax man, I don't see any maggots on you," said Scott, "just some dark greasy stuff on your arm. Use the hand cleaner on the shelf there."

Lou took a deep breath and let it out slowly, calming himself. He grabbed the tub of hand cleaner and rubbed it all over his arms. "Is anyone following us? did anyone see me?" His voice was back to normal.

"No, I don't think so," said Scott. "What was that all about?"

"Yeah man, what you got there?" Tom asked.

"Remember you guys asked me how I knew so much about world affairs, but I wouldn't tell you? Well, this is how I do it. I use my trusty old laptop computer and a secret program that allows me to tap the world internet."

After he wiped the hand cleaner off, he shook his shirt out and put it back on. "Jeez, I'm gonna talk to that gorgeous girl today, and I smell like garbage." He rubbed hand cleaner on his shirt to cover the smell.

Scott and tom stared as Lou buried the laptop under some drop cloths. He climbed over the back seats and into the front passenger seat with some difficulty and groans brought on by his sore back.

"So we're transporting an illegal object right now, huh?" said Freddy.

"I can't believe that I'm not being followed. They're watching me," said Lou, "but don't worry about it. You all can just claim ignorance. That should be easy for you guys to pull off. Just make sure you all don't forget me when they haul me in."

They asked Lou questions right up until they neared the Park Ridge checkpoint, at which time they were silent. The checkpoint guard looked in at the crew and handed them the scanner, and then he traumatized them by walking to the back of the van and opened up the back door. Lou became light-headed. The guard did a quick look around, shuffled some tool buckets and drop clothes but did not discover the laptop. He walked back to the front and leaned in Freddy's window, took back the scanner, and glanced at it.

"You hacks are running late again. Get moving," he ordered and stepped back.

They drove down the streets of the gated city while Lou kept looking back to see if anyone was following them.

Inside the city of the rich were other vehicles on the road: fancy cars with hybrid or hydrogen engines and some vintage cars that still had gas engines and owners willing and to pay $28.50 per gallon of gas. They pulled in to the Newman's driveway and were let in by the butler. Ten minutes later they were all hard at work.

It was just after ten when Lou called the crew together. As they drew close, he looked into each of their eyes, his own beaming with intensity.

"I gotta go out and use that thing in the van, It may be the last chance I get to talk to my contact."

The other three men's expressions changed to suspicion and Scott suddenly gasped.

"Yeah, I know how you all must feel, but get over it. We're the good guys. Now I need someone to stand outside the van to keep a look out for me." He glanced at Scott who looked terrified, "I think Scott is way too freaked out so it's between you guys."

Tom and Freddy looked at each other.

"You can go, man," Tom said.

"No, it's cool if you wanna go - go ahead; it beats painting," Freddy insisted. There response disheartened Lou.

"Come on, you guys, Step up. Freddy, don't you wanna help the cause?"

Freddy looked up to the ceiling and squinted in a moment of self-evaluation. "Yeah, lets do it. I'll help you out, Lou."

"Alright, you two get back to work, and if the old hag pops her head in and starts asking where I am, just say I went to get something out of the van. Come on Freddy, we'll bring those drop cloths and shake them outside."

They walked out to the van, arms filled with drops, and dumped them on the ground behind the van. They grabbed each drop cloth by the ends and shook the dust out of them, holding their breath as the dust lingered in the calm warm air. Lou looked around for surveillance devices. His eyes focused on a device way atop an electric pole across the street.

"Stand right by the door here," he whispered. "I'm gonna keep it slightly open so you can see and hear this and tell everyone I'm not full of shit.

Just warn me if anyone is pulling up. Say 'cow pie' to warn me."

He climbed in the back and left the door three inches open. Quickly pulling the laptop out from under the drops, he opened it and hit power. He set it in a position where Freddy could see it from a side angle. The charge indicator said only nine minutes of power left, and he groaned. He clicked on the F.F.N. icon and then pulled the disk out from under the bag of rags in the corner. After putting the disk into the disk drive, he raised the modified Wi-Fi antenna, clicked on Derwin's user name and entered the password m-y-j-e-s-s-i-c-a. He had no problem getting a signal from here.

Once he logged on, he deleted all the first time user messages, went right to the war wager website and entered the disk code that would run his program and route him into the nearest satellite link. This process usually took two to three minutes. Lou wiped the sweat from his brow.

Freddy peaked in. "All this so you can play a damn game," he whispered.

"It takes a few minutes to link up with a satellite," Lou replied.

It took two minutes forty-eight seconds to link, which seemed excruciatingly long while he watched the charge indicator diminish to six minutes. Finally the screen changed to the World Wide Web welcome sight.

"I'm in," Lou whispered out to Freddy, who stopped folding drops and peaked in. "Look at this headline, Freddy." He pointed at a headline that read *U.S. Government refuses to acknowledge W.U.N. despite threat of invasion.* "That's how they conduct foreign relations. Nice, huh? We're heading for nuclear war."

Freddy's attention on the headline was recklessly deep.

"Hey man, keep an eye on the street," Lou cautioned. "I'm gonna try my contact before my charge runs out." He clicked on the instant message icon and entered (deputyp.m-t.swan) on the address line. He quickly typed (get me Tony Swan immediately, this is Indy1 from America, I HAVE ONLY FIVE MINUTES!) in the message line and hit send.

Twenty nine agonizing seconds passed before a message returned. (We are contacting him now. He's at parliament house having another late night. Hang in there Indy1. It's good to hear from you, mate. Switch on camera mode). Lou clicked on the camera mode option and a lean Australian face came into view, one of Tony Swan's many assistants. Lou recognized him but didn't remember his name. He turned on his web cam, and the Australian gazed at Lou's face then looked strangely at the surroundings.

Another message appeared, (They're rushing him to a computer now. Can you switch to live audio, or is it unsafe.)

Lou clicked the live audio link icon. "Can you hear me?" he said quietly near the microphone hole.

"Sure can, mate. I'm switching over to him now." The Australian voice was clear and loud, getting Freddy's full attention again.

No email or instant messaging existed in America

anymore because people were not allowed to connect with each other on the Freedom Forever Network.

Lou lowered the volume slightly. The screen changed, and now it was a middle-aged woman. She immediately got up and moved away. A moment later Tony Swan, the deputy Prime Minister of Australia, sat down, wide-eyed with concern. His normally neat blond hair was untidy and tangled, and his deep blue eyes were squinted and showed stress.

"Louie, I was worried sick about you. Are you safe, mate?" he said.

"This may be our last time to talk for awhile, Tony. They're looking for my computer, and I'm gonna have to hide it."

Tony nodded. "Yes, of course, I understand. So how are you making out? Have you engaged with the people? Can they be rallied, or are they hopeless?"

"Too soon to tell," Lou interrupted sharply. "I'm sorry we can't chitchat, but I only have three and a half minutes of power. Can you update me real quick on the W.U.N.'s plans?"

"Yes, I see, there is so much that happened since we last talked. First thing you must know is that China will present the rationale for invading America to the W.U.N. some time this week. The expectation is for it to be unanimously approved, and the number of countries who will join the coalition could be huge."

"Oh jeez…already? You said it wouldn't be till next year!" Lou spoke loudly hoping Freddy was comprehending this.

"Yes, well it seems that the absence of America's wheat, grain, soybean, and corn on the world market has been devastating to countries that used to import from the U.S., especially now with the drought in Africa, and the Middle Eastern countries that have been devastated by floods. They are experiencing massive food shortages. The W.U.N. feels it's pointless to wait any longer. The American government must be overthrown, and a resonable one must emerge as soon as possible," Tony said somberly.

"For Christ's sake. have they considered the nuclear implications? These crazy bastards won't hesitate. I have reason to believe they're making massive nuclear shelters for the upper class. They're calling them underground arenas."

Tony shook his head. "Oh dear God!" he said, "I'll never know how the most malevolent people got total control of your country," he said sounding chastising.

"You know that they gained total control of all the media," said Lou. "They create how the people view the world and made us stupid. It could have happened to any powerful nation. Even you Aussies would be subdued by it."

"Louis, you're a dear friend and brilliant man, but we Australians would never have let our government get that out of hand, and I don't think people as immoral as your leaders would ever win an election here."

"Tony, I would love to discuss this with you some day while we drink stout beer together, but I got a minute and a half here. Is there anything else I need to know," Lou said sounding flustered.

"Yes, indeed there is, Louie. This is information that you must die before ever giving up, you understand?"

Lou nodded.

"Do I have your word it's safe to tell you this information, and no one else can hear me?"

Lou stretched his left arm out toward the open door and fluttered his hand at Freddy, attempting to make him go away, without ever moving his eyes from the camera. For the most part, Lou never told a lie (save a few harmless ones to better his chances of getting women in bed,). He despised people who lied.

He should try to explain to Tony that his laptop was in the custody of the G.A. authorities for a short time before a little Mexican man stole it back for him, and that one of his co-workers might be within earshot right now. That would be the truth. He should explain his predicament and perhaps not receive this information. But there was no time to explain! The computer would soon shut down. He couldn't risk not hearing this secret information. The curiosity alone would kill him. He simply had to hear this.

"Yes, you have my word. Hurry up and tell me," Lou answered.

"Alright then, listen mate, the British have sent a small elite militia, six men in all. They snuck into America from Ontario, Canada, crossing Lake Superior in a top secret, portable, underwater vessel. They are armed with a highly advanced rocket launcher, and they have five rockets that can pierce nearly any material. Once it penetrates a wall, it explodes and omits toxic gas. They landed in Wisconsin at the Ottawa National forest. This was over a month ago, and they trekked their way south, all the way to the outskirts of Chicago."

"Thank you, Louie for information you gave us about the government moving out of Washington. It was confirmed. They did indeed move to Rosemont, Illinois. I assume the team is not too far from you now. They're in an abandoned town called Crystal Lake, and they set up an outpost where they've been recruiting renegade Americans that are living in the wild. What do you Yanks call them? Scurvies or something."

"Scavies," Lou corrected.

"Yes, scavies. Well, the Brits will be carrying out their mission soon enough. I'm sure you can guess what it is. You know, try to cut the head off the snake with one blow."

"Yeah, kill the leaders," Lou said.

"If the objectives are met and the head is severed, perhaps your government can be overthrown, but it's all up to these Scavies and whatever people you can get. Someone will have to gain control quickly and take over as acting president. If you can get people behind you somehow, it should be you to take command. Many of us know you as someone who can be trusted to make the right decisions, unlike anyone in your current government, and the W.U.N. will fully support you. Unfortunately, they wont wait long. If this doesn't work, there will be a land invasion soon after. I'm certain of this, Louis." Tony Swan's face displayed somberness mixed with sympathy.

"I'm almost out of power, Tony," Lou said, speaking fast.

"I understand, and I'll do my best, but they're probably gonna lock me up soon. Do you know when they will attack?"

"The Brits are being very careful and won't tell us the

exact day. Perhaps they are not sure yet, but I'm sure it will be within a week."

The computer was counting down the last fifteen seconds of power.

"It's about to shut down, Tony."

"Be careful, my friend. We're praying for you, mate."

"Yeah, well I hope that praying shit works because this is way too fast, Tony. It takes months to rally people, not days. I'm not happy you can't hold this off longer and-"

The computer shut down, fully drained of power.

Lou looked out at Freddy who was listening in. "Were you listening in the whole time?" Lou snapped.

Freddy shrugged his shoulders. "I got bits and pieces."

"We can't tell any-"

Suddenly a car raced up the street, silencing him. It slowed down just before the driveway and turned in quickly.

Lou's heart pounded against his chest. He slammed the laptop closed, slid a drop cloth over it, and climbed out casually. He closed the door and helped Freddy fold the next drop cloth. Not even looking at the car, they acted perfectly natural.

Moments later, the passenger's door opened. Lou glanced over, holding his breath. It was Melanie Newman, and she was looking radiant once again. She waved to the driver, a reckless looking, blond haired young man. The car backed out and left.

As she approached Lou on her way to the front door she spoke. "Hey Louis, are you still gonna have lunch with me?"

"Of course. I've been looking forward to it all day, Melanie."

"Great." She looked at her watch, "I'll see you in an hour then." She turned and trotted to the front door, not taking notice of Lou's pale complexion and sweaty forehead.

Lou dropped his end of the drop cloth, held his hands out before him. Watching them tremble, he shook his head and exhaled deeply.

He picked up half the stack of drop cloths that Freddy piled and set them in the back of the van. Then he pulled out the laptop and put it in between the stack, making sure it could not be seen. He picked up the stack, slammed the van door shut with his butt, and walked to the door.

"Get the door for me, Freddy," he yelled over his shoulder.

They walked back to the great room and Lou set down his pile by the sliding door that led to the back patio. He looked up at the work, or lack there of, that Scott and Tom did while he was outside and said, "Hey Tom, maybe you should stop cutting in the wall up there since you're supposed to do the crown in semi gloss first."

"Oh shit, I forgot. Sorry dude," Tom responded.

"Just fix it!" Lou yelled and walked out the patio door. He surveyed the large back yard and looked along the brick wall of the house, paying close attention to the shrubs and the air conditioning unit.

He walked back inside the house and turned to Freddy. "Freddy, come here." When Freddy got closer, he said, "I want you to see where I'm gonna hide this." He grabbed the laptop, holding it against his chest, and went out the door, followed by Freddy. He trotted twenty feet down along side the wall. He slid in between some bushes and walked up to the large air conditioning unit on the back of the house. Bending over, he reached back and slid the laptop into the narrow space behind it and the wall. It seemed like a decent place to stash it because the large eves overhead would protect it from the rain, and it was unlikely anyone would find it there. He slithered his way back through the bushes and came back to Freddy.

"Remember, it's behind that A.C. unit. In case something happens to me, you can bring it somewhere safe when we finish this job."

Freddy nodded but was silent as they walked back in.

Lou immediately assessed the job and quickly planned how to better attack it since this morning seemed somewhat unproductive. Freddy and Tom did the brush work while Scott and Lou rolled the twenty-foot wall. Lou did the top ten feet with the long extension pole, and Scott rolled in the lower ten feet.

Scott and Tom were bursting with curiosity and bombarding Freddy with questions. Freddy told them about the ominous headline but didn't want to say much more and demanded they shut up about it. He seemed irritated and didn't speak for most of an hour, nor did Lou except to give a few orders.

Suddenly Freddy quickly climbed down his ladder, his feet slamming hard upon each rung, catching everyone's attention. He set down his paint can and turned to Lou. "Why the fuck are we working so hard! I mean, if we're gonna be nuked cause our government is a bunch of childish pricks, why the hell am I busting my ass for some rich bitch?"

Lou's eyes were wide. His jaw dropped as Freddy's voice echoed through the room. His first reaction was fear because he thought Freddy was about to attack him.

"Its okay, Freddy. Take it easy. I can see your point," Lou answered calmly. He rested the end of the extension pole on the ground like a giant twelve-foot staff and thought carefully how to answer. "Because we need to do a good job here and continue to get jobs in this town. It's not time to throw down our tools and revolt just yet. We have to prove our worth in the meantime. People can't go on strike if they're shitty workers. You have to prove you're valuable if you expect to win anything."

Everyone was silent for a moment, waiting for Freddy's reaction.

"I guess I'll accept that for now," he finally said, "but I'm not busting my ass anymore. I'll work as hard as slouchy Scott over there."

"Screw you, Freddy. I work pretty hard," Scott replied.

They all worked at a casual pace from that point on.

Noon came, unnoticed, until five minutes later when Lou saw the lovely young blond standing by the entrance, watching him work.

He smiled and waved to her.

"Ok guys, break for lunch. It's five after so get back to work at thirty five after if I'm not back yet."

He walked over to Melanie, smiling. "Hi," he said as he neared her, "I'm glad lunch is finally here."

"I was talking to my friend about you." She sounded excited, "He couldn't believe you were painting my house. Come on, lets get something to eat." She seemed so bubbly, Lou thought she was going to take him by the hand, but she walked in front and he followed.

That was fine with him because back here he could watch her gorgeous backside moving so gracefully and seductively ahead of him. Her perfect rump, fitted so tightly in her light grey khakis, was such a glorious sight, he became lightheaded.

She looked over her shoulder and caught him gazing at her ass.

Lou became aware of his genitals expanding and became nervous.

"I'll have Lowell make us something good. He's an awesome chef," she said, slowing up to walk side by side with him.

They walked through the immaculate foyer, through the west hallway, beautifully decorated with fine art, and came to the kitchen's swinging door. She opened it halfway and suddenly stopped.

Lou's momentum caused him to bump into her, and the second he was against her body was immensely arousing. She began to back away slowly. Lou did the same, sensing a change in plan.

"Melanie, is that you?" The old bag's voice carried out from the kitchen.

She turned back to Lou still holding the door, looking somewhat embarrassed. "How would you like to go out for lunch?" she asked.

Lou just smiled and nodded, thinking, *honey you could get me to do anything for you if I could just have sex with you once.* He backed away from the door, hoping the old lady didn't see him.

"What on earth do you do with your time?" Mrs. Newman yelled. "Did you even set up an interview with Mr. Hutton yet? I haven't seen you in two days. It's ungodly, the hours you keep."

The old bag's voice was so irritating to Lou's ears, he came out of his lovesick trance immediately.

"Okay mom, we can talk tonight. I promise I won't go out until we do," Melanie shouted and backed away, letting the door swing back.

"What? Where are you going?" Mrs. Newman screeched.

"To call Mr. Hutton!" Melanie shouted.

She snickered as she trotted away and grabbed Lou by the hand. They trotted down the hall, giggling like kids. They reached the foyer and quickly walked to the front door. He could hear his crew talking in the great room. Their voices were muffled from here, but the profanities were audible. He felt like running in there and yelling, "Keep it down and watch your language, you idiots," but he certainly didn't want to leave her side. Once they got outside Lou shut the front door.

"Sorry about that," she immediately apologized. "I didn't expect to see my mother in there."

"Oh, that's okay. Anything we do is fine with me," Lou said grinning from ear to ear.

"Come on, I'll take you to Carlucci's. Do you like Italian food?"

"Sure."

He followed her toward the garage doors. It was a three car garage with three separate doors. She went to the middle one and entered a four digit code. The door began to rise. He was face-to-face with her as they waited for it to fully rise.

"I'd love to treat you to Carlucci's, but I don't think I'm dressed appropriately, do you?" he said.

She looked him up and down. "You look fine to me," she answered with a smile. "But you're right. Carlucci's might not agree. Don't worry, I know just the place. Are burgers Okay with you?"

"That sounds great. I'm just delighted to have lunch with you," Lou said and felt like a corny fool immediately after.

"Come on, hop in," she said. She opened the driver side door of her red sports car and got in. When Lou got in she had the center compartment open and was moving the contents around, searching for something.

"Damn, my keyphone must be upstairs. I was hoping I left it in my car. I have to run up and grab it really quick, Okay?"

Lou hated the idea of her leaving him here alone. "No, you don't need it!" he insisted, "I have plenty of cash. You don't need to charge anything on your keyphone. Lunch is on me. Let's just go."

She looked him in the eyes silently for a moment, then smiled and started up the car.

The quiet, smooth sound of the engine (a gas-electric hybrid that was running all on electric now), impressed Lou. She pulled out of the garage and through the driveway. Once she hit the street, she accelerated hard. The force pushed them against their seats.

Instead of watching the road, Lou took the opportunity to lower his gaze to her lap and eyed her thighs. Once she began to slow down, he forced himself to stop gawking at her legs.

"This is a great car," he said. "I wish they made more of these available around the turn of the century. The technology was sure there, but the oil tycoons wouldn't allow a dip in their huge profits, even as they became aware we had reached peak oil production worldwide."

"Oh, my god, I've heard that!" she shouted, looking over, and patting him on the leg. "Tony, that guy who dropped me off today, told me how big oil influence even slowed the advancement of hydrogen fuel cell technology. He's the guy that brought you up a few days ago. His Dad was a democrat and a self-made millionaire that grew up poor."

Lou's mind was clouded, being overwhelmed by his strong physical attraction to her, but he maintained a conversation. "Tony's right. He sounds like one smart dude to me."

They continued to talk the whole ride. Lou explained the powerful hold the largest corporations held on the government due to private campaign donations and how it adversely affected the country for the last sixty years and led to this.

Melanie asked questions and displayed deep interest in his answers, knowing full well that most people in this town would consider them left wing conspiracy theories.

They pulled in to a pleasant looking restaurant named Paradise Burgers, parked and went in.

Lou noticed people staring at him immediately, but it only made him feel proudly out of place. He never felt embarrassed of himself in his entire adult life. He wasn't embarrassed to be a dirty looking painter, and he wasn't embarrassed as a senator when the pornography scandals hit the media. His attitude was what's so bad about admiring female bodies in action. I'm a senator not a Catholic Priest.

The restaurant had a Hawaiian theme to it. The walls had palm trees, sand and blue ocean painted on them. A decent lunch crowd was there, and most of the people were young. Some of the young men, who were wearing tailored shirts and fine silk trousers, were frowning with disgust, as if to be thinking, *How obscene for a dirty worker man to be here with her.*

Lou walked with a cool smirk as if to be saying, *Ha, look at these prissy rich boys. They'll never know want or need, and they'll never learn how to cherish anything.*

They were seated by a young, dark haired, female hostess that had an admirable working class look to her brown eyes.

They glanced at the menus, and a bus boy brought them water, making Lou think about something.

"Do all these people with the low wage, servant jobs commute here like I do? Or do they live inside the city somewhere?" he asked her.

"There's a section on the north side of town where the lower class people live," she answered grimly.

"Do you know anything about the underground arena being built?" Lou suddenly blurted, "Do people talk about it around here?"

Melanie was startled by the question. Her reaction was more like a woman being interrogated. She looked around at her surroundings, checking for eavesdroppers.

Lou noticed but didn't bat an eye. His intense stare demanded an answer from her.

She could only look at his eyes for a moment before dropping her gaze back to the menu. "I don't know. It's for performances, and it also acts as a shelter for severe weather events," she submitted.

"I wonder if they think a hurricane can develop over Lake Michigan," he said. "Actually, I think there was a funnel cloud spotted around here once, but I'm pretty sure very few, if any, tornados ever touch down this close to the big city. No, I got

a feeling it's a bomb shelter. I bet it's quite an exquisite one too."
Before she had time to respond, the waitress approached.

"Are you ready to order?" she asked with a fake smile.

Melanie ordered the cheeseburger in paradise with a side of mixed fruit. Lou asked to have the same and was looking forward to getting fresh fruit since only French fries were available as a side dish in the service city.

After the waitress left, they were silent for a bit. Melanie had changed her mood, and it was clearly expressed in her eyes. It reminded Lou of other first dates, when halfway through the night the woman's mood changes from something he said and he knew he wouldn't be getting laid.

"Is something wrong, Melanie?" he finally said.

"Oh no, I'm fine," she replied.

Lou just stared silently waiting for her to say more.

She hesitantly looked back up to him, her eyes now moist. "I was so looking forward to this. You're like some cult hero to Tony, and I didn't even ask him if he wanted to join us. I wanted to have lunch with you alone. I feel so selfish. You and Tony would have had a great discussion about that damn thing if I let him come along to meet you. He's so much smarter than me, and I hate to talk about that...that thing being built."

Hearing this, Lou felt arousal from below again. *Maybe I still have a chance.*

"Hey, believe me, I'm extremely happy it's just the two of us right now. I hope this doesn't make you feel uneasy, but I find you to be the most beautiful, enchanting woman I ever laid eyes on." She seemed to perk up and smiled slightly, then wiped her eyes with her cloth napkin.

"Let's have a nice lunch," he said. "We'll talk about anything you want, and when we get back in your car I'll tell you something about our government that you can tell Tony. It's something being withheld from all of us."

That ominous pre-curser frightened her a bit but his personality put her at ease, and they conversed cheerfully throughout lunch.

She focused the conversation on Lou's amazing run for the senate and seemed thrilled to hear all about it.

Lou found himself enjoying reminiscing about how he went up against the Washington insiders, their corporate masters and their procured media. He talked about how he held rally after rally, none of which were covered by the news, and talked to everyone he could and how he knew what to say to get people's attention right away and how to describe why it mattered for them to vote for him.

The enjoyment of reminiscing faded when he explained how it all ended. He included his divorce and separation from his son, ending his story with irony. Illinois was a state that did not allow recall elections to remove an elected official, but Lou fought the entrenched Illinois democrats to get it on a referendum so the people could vote on it, and it passed. He hoped they could remove the corrupt governor for their first recall election. As it turned out, he was the first and only politician to be removed that way.

He paid the bill, deciding to charge it on his keyphone and was shocked to see their burgers were eighteen bucks apiece.

They got back in her car.

"I hope I didn't keep you away from your work for too long," she said.

"No, my crew will understand. I'm out with a gorgeous girl. They're all jealous, but they won't report me. It's a code among men."

She giggled.

"Actually, I was wondering if we could take a drive before I got back to work, if you don't mind."

She looked at him suspiciously for a moment. "Sure, I don't mind. You have something to tell me, right?"

"Yep, if you're sure you want to hear it. Can you drive me by the north side where the servant class lives while we talk?"

"Yeah, I guess. There's much nicer things to see but whatever turns you on." She put the car in drive and sped off. With the windows halfway down her blond hair fluttered behind her and her posture highlighted her breasts.

This time he stared at her, not caring if she noticed and thought, *Whatever turns me on huh? I wish she meant it.*

"Alright, you sure you wanna know what's really going

on? Remember what they say, ignorance is bliss," he said, finally looking forward again.

"Just tell me, and don't be so dramatic!"

He told her alright, about everything the government was hiding, how the rest of the world was united against us and even *how* he knows. He was surprised over her calm reactions, thinking perhaps she didn't believe him.

Presently, they were driving through the southeast section of town. Lou gazed at the servant class quarters. Three floor apartment buildings lined the block, all identical. A nicely maintained park and playground were across the street.

"Stop here for a sec!" he shouted.

She did and he just gazed out the window silently. There were young kids playing in the park and ladies watching over them, some playing with toddlers.

"What is it? why did we stop here?"

He didn't reply.

"Lou?"

He slowly turned his head toward her. She was stunned to see his eyes tearing.

"That's something I haven't seen in a long time," he said, wiping his eyes with his sleeves. "The entire time I was in Byron I didn't see any kids, and now where they have us living I've yet to see one child. I always got along with children the best. No one who is destitute wants to have kids." He heaved a sob that he played off as a chough. "They've been planning for a population decline all along. They finally got everything they could from us, so now they're creating a private utopia. The wealthy will survive, along with just enough servants to maintain the fields." He put his face in his hands and leaned forward, fighting desperately not to despair.

As Melanie drove off, Lou whipped his head toward the side window to get one final view of the children. Once they were out of sight, he looked over to her. She was staring forward sternly.

"I'm sorry if this seems trivial to you." He felt the need to explain why he was so emotional, "I just figured out their end game. It's quite a moment for me, you know."

"I don't think it's trivial," she replied. "I think it's terrible that you have to live like this." Now *she* was beginning to sob. "I'm going to take you to see Mr. Mediate. That's Tony's dad. He's a city councilman. I'm gonna demand he get you a job inside the city so you can live here." She seemed serious. Her actions showed she was driving somewhere with intent.

"Melanie, I'm flattered you would do that for me. It really makes me feel good, but I can't let you do it."

"It's not a problem. Mr. Mediate can pull strings. I'm sure he can arrange it."

"I can't live here," he said, causing her to look at him queerly.

"Why the hell wouldn't you want to? You're not safe out there," she implored.

"Cause the people I fight for are out there."

She fell silent, wondering if he is really this admirable or just too blind to know what's best for himself.

"Fine then," she said after some time, "I'm sure a guy like you won't change his mind, so I won't try. I guess I better take you back now," she said seeming sad.

"Before you do, can you drive me by the entrance of the underground arena." She looked at him suspiciously again so he added, "I just want to see how far along they are."

She didn't answer but made a left turn at the next street. They didn't talk much after that. Lou asked her about her plans for the future, but she didn't seem too interested in talking much anymore.

They approached a driveway that descended into a wide tunnel that went underground.

"Well, here's the north entrance. We're not allowed to go down there, so, as you can see, there isn't much for you to look at."

He looked at her with pleading eyes. "Could you please just wait for me for five minutes so I can run down there real quick?"

She sighed and rubbed her forehead. "Alright, but they won't let you in, and if they arrest you, I'm going to leave."

"Thanks," he said, got out and trotted down the driveway that became a tunnel.

He guessed he descended about 200 feet. At the bottom was an overhead door for vehicles to go through and side doors for people walking. All were closed. Two guards sat in a booth. They got up and stood in front when they saw Lou trotting up to them. Both looked surprised.

"Where the heck do you think you're going, old boy?" one said in a southern accent.

"Hey guys, I just got to run in there real quick and get Ricky Barns. His mother is very sick. She had a stroke and may not have much time left," Lou said acting somewhat frantic.

"Well, call his Goddamn keyphone, you fool," the other guy said with the indigenous Chicago accent.

"I can't; I don't have his number," Lou replied, "His sister is depending on me to get him. Don't make me look like an incompetent fool to her. I know right where he's working. It will take me two minutes. Come on. I've worked down there before, for Christ's sake."

"Look, we have our orders: no one enters that doesn't have work clearance," the local guard said.

"Fine, then you got to tell him for me. Just let me get your name so if he doesn't get the message, he'll know who to blame," Lou said and squinted to read his badge.

The two guards looked at each other, and the southerner shrugged his shoulders. Then he squinted at Lou. "Why don't you just call the sister on your dang phone and get the number? Ain't you got any sense, old boy?"

"I know you're right, man, but the sister is at her mom's bedside while she watches her fading away. She told me to do this, and I can't call her now. I'm trying to get this chick. She's good looking, man. I don't want her to know I'm a senseless fuck up. Please help me out, cuz," Lou said, hoping to get the southerner to empathize with him.

Then, after exhaling loudly, he picked something up and stepped out of the booth. He handed it to Lou. "Here, put this tracer in your pocket. We gonna be watching where you go so get in and get out cause if we got to go in and fetch your ass, you going to be in a world of trouble, old boy."

"I know, man. It won't take long. Thanks, cuz." The guard opened a door and held it for Lou. The moment he entered, he walked quickly, almost trotting.

He observed the great structure in awe, first noticing that the ceiling was a series of curved quarter circles, one after another. He deduced they dug it out with drilling techniques they use to dig subway tunnels. Digging next to each preceding tunnel, they overlapped each one to make the shelter wider and wider. Through out the ceiling were complex ventilation systems, each eight feet by ten in size and spread out every fifty feet or so.

He had to stop to get a better view of one and theorized how it worked. They must draw in surface air through the intake ducts that go up to the surface and into the large grey boxes which must be multi-chambered air sterilization systems to remove bio chemical gasses and radioactive particles.

He could have left now, having his suspicions already confirmed and his question answered, but he explored further. All along the far north wall was two levels of doors. Stairs ran up to the second level walkway every fifty feet. The entire wall had hundreds of doors. They must be sleeping quarters but surely not enough for the entire gated city, which had a population of thirty-six thousand.

When he got further in, he saw the back wall was also filled with doors, and workers were busy framing more units. Apparently a few thousand people would get their own quarters and the rest would sleep on cots.

Just like the society they prefer outside will be like that in here too. Some people deserve better treatment.

He explored to the south, amazed by the size of the place, at least a few hundred thousand square feet, he guessed. Now he could see designated areas were being completed. The furthest looked like a command center. Next to that was the large generator which was complete and running. Next to that looked like a mess hall area, and workers were stocking shelves at present, while fork lifts were busy moving crates in.

He continued down the south wall where a large stage was almost completed.

Suddenly he began to feel queasy. He thought about what it may be like to be killed in a nuclear strike. Death may come in an instant, or it may come slowly in the aftermath, depending on the location. He bent over and grabbed his knees to stabilize himself. He felt like his expensive burger might come up at any second.

"Hey buddy, you okay over there?" a worker who noticed him said.

"No," Lou replied in a nauseous voice. He stood straight and turned to the worker and yelled, "None of us are okay!"

He trotted off with one hand holding his stomach, trying to get back to the entrance where he came in. He was trying to fight the feeling that all was lost and war was inevitable.

If they are spending so much money and effort to build these enormous shelters, they won't settle for anything short of nuclear war...Come on, Lou, don't think like that. Its not over yet.

He got to the doors, took a deep breath, and pushed them open. Both guards were looking at him.

He pulled the tracer out of his pocket and handed it to the nearest one. "Thanks guys. Take it easy." He continued walking.

"Hold on, we have to scan your keyphone to record that you were here," the other guard yelled.

Without stopping or even slowing his pace, Lou turned around, walking backwards now. "Okay, I'll grab it out of the car and be right back."

The guards were silent momentarily while Lou turned back and quickened his pace. Halfway up the drive, footsteps echoed, boots on the concrete walking quickly in pursuit.

"Hold up, old boy, where are you parked?" the southern guard yelled.

"It's right out here. I'll grab it real quick. Just hold on a sec," he said.

Then he sprinted up the driveway as fast as he could. He heard the guard shout something, but Lou was practically deaf as he used all his might to run.

Once he reached the top, he looked over to his right, then to his left and saw Melanie's car fifty yards down the street pulled on to the side. He sprinted toward her car, impressed by his own speed but disgusted to know he couldn't keep this up for very long. He reached her passenger side door and tried to open it, but it was locked.

"Come on, come on," he cried while knocking. Once the lock clicked, he opened it, got in, and said, "Get out of here… go!"

She fired up the engine, put it in drive, and pulled slowly away.

"Hey, where the fuck are you going!" the Chicago guard yelled.

She glanced in the mirror, saw the guard running after the car, and slowed down.

"What the hell are you doing? Go!" Lou yelled.

"Oh, my God, you're gonna get me in so much trouble," she said and accelerated.

Lou was still trying to catch his breath as his heart pounded rapidly. "Damn, I should have kept in better shape," he muttered.

As she drove back to the house, he talked about what he saw down there.

Melanie showed only faint interest. The fun and interesting lunch she planned with this significant man had turned into a depressing event.

Lou could tell she was gloomy now, and he would not be having sex with her and would probably never see her again. Through the years, the women that he went out with (before, during and after his marriage) always seemed to take the attitude that nothing can change in the country so it's best to ignore it and carry on. Lou couldn't ignore it and he would end up depressing women with his political rants, hence, he would never get a second date. So he learned that if he ever wanted to have sex again, he would have to act ignorant and only speak about mundane, unimportant things or just hire a prostitute.

When they got back, she parked the car in front and looked over to him.

"Thanks for lunch. It was nice talking to you," she said.

"It was my pleasure. Do you think we can exchange

phone numbers?" he asked without hesitation. She seemed to hesitate for a moment then smiled.

"Sure, you can call my phone, and your number will be under my missed calls so I can put you in my contacts list." After she gave him the number, and he memorized it, he programmed it in and called her keyphone. Then they said goodbye.

He got out, and she pulled away without looking back.

When he entered the great room, the crew stared at him. He observed their lack of production and shook his head but did it with a smile.

Working together the rest of the day, they finished all the walls with two coats. All day they discussed the tragic decisions made by the government that were uncontested by the people. Lou seemed motivated, giving amusement to the crew. They became closer friends through stimulating conversation. The rest of the work day passed quickly. They cleaned up and left the mansion.

On the way home Lou asked for all their phone numbers and programmed each into his contacts list.

"Its time to stand up to this government," he said as he finished. There was a moment of uncomfortable silence. Lou lowered his eyebrows.

"Lou, are you like a spy for a foreign country or some-thing?" Scott asked.

Freddy turned back and scowled at Scott.

"Hmmm, I guess in a way I am," Lou quickly responded. "I'm risking my life to stand against my own country's govern-ment. I hope you understand I'm doing the right thing. You know, I was in that underground arena today. It's definately a bomb shelter, and we're not invited to take shelter there when they provoke war." He turned to look at Scott and added, "So instead of calling me a spy, I think true patriot fits better. Make up your mind. Are you on my side or the government's?"

"You went down there," Tom blurted. "Why didn't you tell us?"

"My mind is still in the coping process. I almost lost it down there. I mean I already guessed what they were building, but actually seeing it and having my suspicions confirmed really affected me. It was like this flood of emotions washed over me. I felt sick and almost puked." Lou hung his head.

"If they're building a bomb shelter, how come nobody told us about it?" Scott sarcastically blurted. "I mean, with all the guys working on it, they would be blabbing all about it."

"Not *if,* you asshole, it *is* a bomb shelter. I saw it. Now quit implying I'm a liar!" Lou yelled and turned to stare down Scott with fuming eyes. "The workers live right there in town. They have a section of apartment buildings on the southeast side. I saw it with my own eyes. The workers never leave the city, so how can they blab about it to us?"

Lou looked up while squinting, grabbing a thought that just entered his mind. "You know it is a smart idea to have people working close to where they live. We have to commute the farthest since we live in the service city and work in the gated city."

"Well, shit!" Tom shouted. "Why don't we get to live there? Do they got their own painters in town?"

"I don't know," replied Lou. "They probably don't want us painters living in their fancy city because they know we're all subversive, degenerate boozers." He chuckled to himself, and then they all laughed. "What we need to do is unite the people and overthrow the government, and the only way to do that without violence is if I run for president and win, but we don't have time for that. We need to rally the people now."

"Well, no one is running for president," said Scott. "Didn't you see the news last night?"

"No, I was busy last night."

"Well, you missed President Burns's speech. He said that all three branches of government agreed to suspend elections this year."

"What? Are you serious?" Lou yelled. "Oh, my God, they actually ended the last remnant of democracy."

"Yeah," Scott confirmed, "he said things are going well and a change now might set us back at a crucial time in our country's history. It was a good speech."

"Wow, I hope people are outraged. You guys are outraged, right?"

"I am," answered Tom, "but there wasn't anyone different to vote for anyways."

Lou was quiet for the rest of the ride, in deep thought. When they were pulling into the A.P.T. parking lot, Lou looked them over.

"You guys have to meet me in front of building fifteen sixty-three at seven o'clock tonight. Please be there. I'm staging a rally, so get everyone you can to come." He got out of the van, not waiting for a response and went straight to the warehouse supervisor's window to talk to Mike Parilla.

"Hey, how's it going? Lou right?" Mike asked.

"Yeah, how you doing, Mike? I was wondering if I could get something to use for a few days."

"Sure," Mike replied, smiling, "I hear your crew is getting through that Newman job okay. That's awesome. I thought no one would be able to please that old bag. Bob Fortune's ecstatic. What you need, bro?"

"I need a bullhorn, and I'd like to take it with me now."

"What the hell you need a bullhorn for? We only use them on big, new construction jobs," Mike said, looking puzzled.

"I need it for our country, Mike. I'm going to hold political rallies, and I need it to talk to the people. I'm going to run for president."

Mike looked at him queerly for a moment. Then he burst out in laughter.

"That's a good one. Now, do you really need a bullhorn, or is this all a big joke?" Mike was now seeming a little perturbed.

Lou leaned in close. "Mike, look at my eyes. Can you tell I'm not joking? We have to stand up to this government now before they get us killed. The rest of the world hates us and wants to attack and overthrow our leaders. Listen, I know it sounds crazy right now, but I know what I'm talking about. I used to be a senator."

Mike looked puzzled.

"Please Mike, I need this. I'm going to talk to the people tonight in front of my building, fifteen sixty-three. I want you to be there. Now, will you do this for me or not?"

Mike stared silently at him for a moment, trying to

determine if Lou was insane by looking deep into his eyes.

"Hold on a minute," said Mike. "I'll be right back," He walked off.

Lou assumed Mike was going to get the manager, Bob Fortune. He didn't care. His attitude was it's time to speak truth to power, come what may.

A few minutes later, Mike came back with a green nylon bag and handed it to him.

"Bring it back when you're done and try not to let Bob see you walking with it onto the bus. He'll freak out if he knows someone is taking home a tool from the warehouse."

Lou looked in the bag and saw a bullhorn. "Thanks, Mike, I hope you'll be at the rally and join us in standing up to them."

"Yeah, sure, this should be interesting," Mike said quietly, looking around to make sure no one could hear him, "but you're up against enormous odds, you know."

"If all of us are united, they're the ones up against enormous odds, my friend," Lou said and walked away.

He got on the bus holding the nylon bag close to his body, shifting it from his front to side, being inconspicuous in front of Bob's office window and the bus driver. He sat next to a grey haired, middle-aged painter and placed the green bag on his lap. As the other painters nearby looked at him in interest, he gave himself confidence by thinking, *This is no accident I'm sitting here with a bullhorn on my lap. I'm probably the most capable man among these people to do this. Louis Rizzo, America's greatest rabble rouser, time to do what we're best at, old sport.*

Lou looked at everyone around him, making eye contact and smiling. "Hey, you guys, its Friday so no excuses," he announced. "I want everyone to meet me in front of building fifteen sixty-three tonight at seven o'clock." His voice was loud enough for everyone to hear. "Bring beer if you want. I'll break out my whiskey and get some tunes going, but everyone has to come. And tell everyone you know to come too. We're holding a rally. We need to talk about the government. Maybe they should ask the people what they think before they suspend elections. Maybe someone else should run for president, an honest man. If you're not ready to give up our democracy, be there tonight!"

Lou again surveyed the staring faces, all of them looking shocked with open mouths that remained silent. "I'm not kidding, you guys, everyone better show up."

`He went on to explain how it will be fun, like a big party, while coolly slipping in the political implications. When he got off the bus in front of his building, his feeling was that everyone would show up, and he allowed only positive thoughts inundate his mind.

It was now 5:40. He had an hour and twenty minutes to get set up. First, he went over to the restaurant and had dinner. Most every option available came on a bun with French fries. This time he went with the turkey burger. On his way out, he told everyone eating there to meet across the street at seven.

He walked back to his unit, belching up fiery burps and fearing his heartburn is requiring a higher level of attention.

Ever since I started eating this fast food here, my esophagus has been burning. I'll bet at my physical next Wednesday they'll fix me up with some pills for a nominal fee. Then I can keep eating their shit food, pain free.

When he got back to his unit, after filling himself a cold glass of ice water, he began to look for the things he needed. First, a duffel bag, then he put two of his three remaining bottles of whiskey in it, four shot glasses, a towel and the bullhorn. He set it near the door and grabbed his portable digital audio player. It was made over thirty years ago and still sounded great. It also had five megabytes of memory filled with his favorite music, vintage music, some of which was over eighty years old and none under thirty years old. There had been no good music made for the last thirty years in Lou's opinion as music was solely manufactured for profit, and distinctive creativity was ignored until it died.

He flipped up the handle and set it next to the duffle bag. He checked the time: 6:20.

After six minutes of frustrated searching, he found a notebook and a pen in one of his boxes. He sat on his bed and made notes for the next thirty-five minutes about what he would talk about. At five to seven he grabbed his things and went out front.

There were a few people sitting on the front veranda where Lou planned on setting up. He set his things down right next to them.

"How's it going, people? Do you mind if I set up here? I'm holding a rally."

They looked at him oddly for a moment. Then one of them spoke.

"What's that thing you got there?"

"That's my digital audio player. I'll bet you don't see many of these. It's over thirty years old, and it has hundreds of great, old rock and roll songs on it."

They seemed fascinated by the machine and took interest in what he was doing. One of them asked what a rally was. When he explained his intentions, they seemed somewhat keyed up.

"Does anyone know what I can use for a table to set this stuff on?" asked Lou.

"I think they got some of those folding tables in the basement storage room," a middle aged white guy with grey and black hair said. "I'm Carl, head carpenter on these government housing units." He extended his hand.

"Hi Carl, I'm Lou. Head carpenter, huh? That's cool. I do painting."

They shook hands.

"Yeah, I framed out this building we're living in. I never thought I'd be living in it a year later. Hell, I'm from Crystal Lake. I'm a small town guy, you know. Don't like this concrete jungle shit. Give me the trees and prairie land."

"I know exactly what you mean," said Lou. "I was living out in Byron, right on the Rock River. It was so beautiful there."

"Let's get this man a table," Carl said to a guy next to him, "He's a small town boy like me." Lou smiled and looked out at the people standing around commiserating. Only seventeen he counted, but seconds later he noticed more people walking over from down the block.

When Carl and his friend returned, they opened up the folding table for him.

"Thanks, guys," Lou said and put his bag and music player on it.

He opened the duffel bag and took everything out.Then he uncapped a bottle of whiskey and poured a shot. Afterwards he turned on his music player and searched the music library for the song he wanted. He picked up the bullhorn and locked the trigger so it would stay on without having to hold it. He held it up to his mouth and licked his lips.

"I drink to the American citizens who are ready to do our duty and restore our democracy." His voice ripped through the area, and everyone standing around looked at him. He picked up the glass and downed the whiskey. "Ahhhh, that's good stuff. Now who wants to drink to democracy?" His amplified voice got their attention, and then he put the bullhorn next to the speakers of the music player and hit play.

"**Power to the People, power to the people, power to the people, power to the people right on,**" John Lennon's voice rang out across the area. "**You say you want a revolution, we better get it on right away.**"

The song never sounded so good to Lou. He inched up the already high volume as his skin broke out in goose bumps.

He certainly had their attention now. People began moving closer to the veranda.

One guy yelled "I'll drink to democracy."

Lou filled him a shot, and then another man wanted one, then another. This continued until the bottle was gone so Lou opened the other.

A crowd was gathering, drawn to the sound of real music. Lou saw some of the painters from the bus were showing up with drinks in hand. People inside the building began filing out into the front yard, and a group of black men was forming in front of the veranda. Tyrell and Deron were among them. The song ended. It was set on random play, and a slow song came on. Lou skipped it, and next was The Who.

"**People try to put us down .... Talking bout my generation .... Just because we get around .... Talking bout me generation......**"

The people began to stir, tapping their feet, bouncing

their heads, and despite the distorted, high pitched tone from the bullhorn, the band sounded great. After so many years of only hearing over produced commercial music, this lost art of true rock and roll sounded bizarre to most of the people, and it appealed to all of them.

By the sidewalk a few G.A. officers got together. They stared at Lou in amusement and talked. People were coming out of the neighboring buildings and the bar across the street.

Lou figured he better start talking soon. He scanned over the faces in front of the building. Freddy, Tom, or Scott were nowhere to be seen.

Jeez, I couldn't even get the guys on my painting crew to be here.

He felt the old familiar queasy stomach feeling as nervousness emerged.

The hell with those idiots! There's a nice crowd here. I could care less if they don't show up.

He summoned anger, effectively defeating the nervousness and leaned over the table. He was about to open his notebook but instead made a fist and punched it. He aggressively grabbed the bullhorn off the table and lowered the music. For a moment he stood still, holding the bullhorn down by his waste. Looking like a gunslinger getting ready to draw, he lifted the bullhorn to his mouth and addressed the crowd.

"Can I have everybody's attention please? My fellow Americans, I have an announcement to make. Can I please have everyone's attention?"

Most of them were now giving their attention, and some began moving closer to the veranda.

"Ladies and gentlemen, I would like to inform you that we are all making history at this moment. This, I believe, is the first political rally in twelve years."

A smattering of applause broke out.

"Forgive me for not knowing for sure, but as you know, our government and the billionaires it represents control our media, and all factual information from the past and present is absent from our society. But I do know rallies like this died. For a long time now politicians don't even have to see us. They don't look us in the eyes and shake a few hands. They have no contact with us. They live in gated cities among their fellow money hoarders. It's nice for them too. Believe me, I've been inside one. They live a nice leisurely lifestyle, safe from all us peons. Our country is a two-class society, rich and poor, and they cut us off from the world."

"I'm certain that the last political rally ever held in Illinois was twelve years ago cause I was there. An Independent candidate was running for the senate. He was an ordinary working class guy who educated himself at his local library, which doesn't exist anymore. It got blown up, along with the belief that cities need a public library. This man educated himself because he couldn't afford some prissy rich boy college like all the other senators from the good old boy fraternity. He was blacked out of the media, and the only way he could be heard was public rallies like this. But you know what people? They couldn't silence us. You know why? Because we're given the freedom of speech and the right to public assembly in America. It was earned by people who fought for America's independence. We used that right twelve years ago, and that guy won the election."

Lou paused and the crowd was completely silent.

"Maybe we all haven't noticed how fast our rights have been fading away, along with our voices. It's gotten to the point that the most important factor in our democracy was taken away yesterday, the right to vote. They decided that things are so good for them that another election would be a waste of time so they suspended elections, expecting no objection from the docile and easily controlled working poor people." He scratched his head. "It makes sense too since nobody is ever worth voting for. You need millions of bucks to buy a seat in the house and millions more to buy a senate seat. Plus you have to be approved by the money hoarders to get their money. That's why no one represents us. We've lost our voice, and our economy was destroyed! Well, I'm here to tell you that what has been lost must be retrieved. It's time for all of us to unite. We're not whites, blacks, Hispanics, Asians, old or young. We're all working class American citizens, and its time to stand up and take back our country before its too late. This is our duty and our generation's calling."

Lou paused for a moment hoping to hear a roar but getting only a smattering of applause. But at least no one was walking away, and most eyes were upon him.

"That Independent senator who the people elected twelve years ago went to the senate and spoke out about what we had to do to save our middle class and our economy. He was a pest to the economic royalists who spent their whole lives taking everything they could from us."

"Our country should have a government that tries to protect all its citizens by collecting taxes by percentage of income and providing medical care, quality education, dignified retirement and protection .... not just protection from criminals or foreign enemies but from domestic enemies like the billionaires who destroyed all our economic regulations that could protect us. Instead we had recession and depressions and all the wealth concentrated to the few. Then they sold our future with debt and profited off war while we paid for a behemoth industrial military complex. Generations before us should have taken back our government, but still there has been no revolution."

A rumbling rose from the crowd.

"Since the people didn't act, they bankrupted our nation and destroyed our quality of life while isolating us from the world."

He licked his lips letting the facts soak in.

"Now that we hit rock bottom and millions of us have died, we need to take a new direction fast, my friends. We need to do things only a new president with a majority of the American people behind him can do. If we fail to act, this tyrannical government, led by good old double B., will continue to isolate us and provoke world war. This I am certain of, but don't worry for good old Bud Burns and his class. They have cozy bomb shelters in their fancy cities and a strong military with enough nukes to make unimaginable horror. This is all very hard to think about, but it is the truth, and this is what they are hiding from us. We are truly isolated, my friends, not just from the outside world, but from our own fellow workers in the rest of the country. That's why it's so easy for them to keep information from us. Well, I am the bringer of truth, and each of you must spread it." He pointed at some of the shocked faces.

"At that rally twelve years ago I believed that we could turn the tide and save our country from economic downfall. But the money hoarders used their phony media to disgrace him. They ignored his initiatives that could have saved our country from this ruin and they decided to smear him every day in the media until he went away. What was it? Oh ya, they said he liked to look at sexy women. What a crime, huh. Does anyone remember this guy? It was only about seven years ago"

Some people began to laugh.

"Peek a boo Lou," someone bellowed and set more of them off laughing.

Lou snorted and slapped his knee."Yeah, buddy, that's right…peek a boo Lou. How could he have been right about our economy if he liked to admire a woman's body?"

The crowd seemed to loosen up and came to life. Many of them remembered the stories about him in the news.

"That's great you remember the sex stories, but I hope you also remember that everything he predicted has come true, and because we didn't make the change then so many of us perished."

"But it's not over. We're still in grave danger. You may not know it because we are cut off from real information, but our leaders have not only destroyed our economy, but also our relations with the rest of the world, and if we can't change our government, the rest of the world that is united against us will invade our land to try to destroy our leaders for us. That won't be pretty with all the nuclear bombs flying everywhere."

"That Independent senator, the last independent ever to speak in congress, is me, Louis Rizzo, and I'm willing to represent you again." He paused, looking out at the faces, "We need to replace the president with me. The only way I can do this is if we all work together and never give up."

A buzz went through the crowd and a commotion began to rise. Suddenly a low round of applause broke out. Then it gained momentum, and everyone began applauding; except the group of G.A. officers. They looked confused. One began talking on his radio.

"Here's what we got to do. Demand they give us TV time so we can get our word out to the rest of the working class people in every other service city in America. Let them know it's time to stand united and take our country back. We can't allow these greedy, sociopaths called the compatriots to make one more decision for our country. Yeah, I said it. The compatriots are bad. They're all just republicans in disguise. Do you all remember the republicans and how destructive and deceptive they were along with their clones, the democrats? Well, they formed the compatriot party and just pretended to be different. It's basically the same people. The new boss is the same as the old boss."

He fell silent as did the crowd until some one shouted."So what do we do?"

"I'll tell you what we do. We make our demands!" Lou shouted. "So how do we get our demands met, you're wondering? We have to be aware that we are the workers, and they need us... because American workers get the job done right. We're the best working people in the world when we're treated right."

"When the government stopped protecting us, every corporation sent our jobs overseas for cheaper labor, but they still needed us to consume and drive the economy so we all used credit cards, and the banks juice us to death. Well, their evil plan finally collapsed. Those behemoth corporations couldn't get foreign workers for dirt cheap anymore. Now they need us to do it all."

This seemed to strike a chord in the people. Some were shouting out in agreement now.

"And we will continue to work if our demands are met." He wagged his finger at the crowd. "But if not, nobody works, and I mean nobody. We shut down this city till we're given our constitutional rights."

That immediately sent the G.A. officers walking up to the veranda. Lou saw this and spoke more quickly now. "I'm willing and prepaid to lead, but they will try to silence me. It looks like they're coming for me already. Stand with me. Don't let them lock me up for using our constitutional rights. Demand our freedom." His voice rose like a general preparing his troops for battle. The eight cops made their way to the steps and began closing in.

"If we are to save our country, we have to act now. If they deny us our voice, then we have to physically throw them out, and if we are to achieve that, the military and police must be on our side."

Lou began backing away and pointed at them. "You cops! You're working class people just like the rest of us. You must stand with the people not the money hoarders who have ruined this country."

The cops were nearing now, and one of them was holding out his hand.

"Come on now buddy, give me the bullhorn," he said and pulled out his Billy club with his other hand.

"Officers, you mustn't allow them to use you against us anymore. People don't let them silence us."

The cop sprung forward and ripped the bullhorn out of his hand. Another grabbed him by the arm and twisted it behind his back and shoved his torso down on the folding table.

"Leave him alone!" a man yelled.

"Let him speak! you bastards!" yelled another.

Tyrell and his gang moved up to the stairs. "Let him go! He ain't done nothing wrong!" he yelled, catching their attention.

The cops looked to where the deep voice came from and saw the gang of eight black men. They all drew their bolt blasters at once, except the one holding down Lou who now began handcuffing him.

"This man is being arrested for disturbing the peace. This is government property, and amplified sound is a violation," the head officer announced loudly.

"We pay rent here! He should be able to talk if we want him to!" yelled a large white guy.

"Yeah, that's right, man! We all pay rent here!" Deron yelled.

Lou was pulled upright by the back of his shirt collar, grimacing as his shoulder pained him. "We're taking this guy in.

He'll be issued a citation, and he will be released. That's standard procedure we must follow."

"You don't have to do anything," said Lou. "You're all employees of the government, not slaves. We all have to unite. You're one of us." Lou spoke loud enough for many people to hear.

The head officer walked up to him and whispered. "You better keep your mouth shut, boy." He turned to the crowd, "Clear out of the way, people!" he yelled, and they began walking to the street with Lou in the middle.

"Are they going to let all you cops in the bomb shelter when they incite a nuclear war?" yelled Lou.

The posse stopped because the head officer froze in his tracks and walked back to Lou. He was a tall, bulky and imposing man, presently frowning down upon Lou.

"Spread the word! No work till we're heard!" Lou yelled as loud as he could, kind of singing the words.

The crowd erupted in shouts and cheers.

Lou smiled at the large cop.

Whap! The butt end of his Billy club landed right in Lou's gut. The air was forced from his lungs, and he let out a heaving sound. He began to fall forward, but the cop escorting him held up his body.

The crowd gasped and pushed forward. All the cops, being in a circular position, held out their bolt blasters.

"Everyone, get back or you will be shocked and arrested!" yelled the head cop. Those in the crowd who saw the bolt blasters being pointed at them moved back, pushing against the people behind them while the cops slowly moved toward the street again.

"What you have to hit him for? Afraid to let him speak?" a woman's voice cried out, and the crowd erupted again. Some yelled, "Let him go!" and a chant broke out as the cops got him closer to their destination of the G.A. van.

"Let him go! Let him go! Let him go!" The chant gained momentum. Some People from farther back that were out of harm's way pushed forward.

"Get back!" four officers yelled in unison. The sound

of electric charges rang out, instantly followed by cries of pain. Four men fell to the ground, and everyone near the cops pushed away with all their might. The cops quickened the pace, and moments later, two of them lifted Lou under his shoulders and tossed him into the back of the van. Six cops jumped in with him and slammed the door. The other two, the driver and the head officer, got in front. The van sped away.

All the officers in back breathed a sigh of relief. One shook his head and yelled, "Damn! That was a close one!" They laughed, all in agreement. The cops sat on the benches that ran along each side of the van, three on each side. Lou lay sideways on the ground, his hands cuffed behind his back, trying to regulate his breathing.

The van made a quick right turn, causing him to roll onto his stomach and knock up against a cop's boots. Pain flared in his shoulder again.

"Get away from me, maggot!" the cop said as he pushed Lou away with his boot. Lou rolled onto his side and pulled his knees up to stabilize himself.

"Do you guys honestly feel good about the way you're treating me?" he said, his voice sounding forced and weak.

"Hell yes," the guard on the left end said. "You almost got us in a world of trouble, boy. We had to blast some people back there."

"Yeah, come to think of it. we're treating you way too kind," the middle cop on the right side said. He was a big Irish looking bully with auburn hair.

He rose from the bench and pulled his Billy club from his belt.

"Don't do it, Duffy. Just sit down," a dark haired cop on the other side said.

Duffy frowned at him, then...whap! He smacked the back of Lou's thigh .... not a killer blow, just a routine smack to the meaty part of the leg. However, Lou's thin legs were not very meaty, and he cried out in pain as the club caught some bone. Duffy scowled at the man across from him as he sat.

"Don't tell me what to do Frank," Duffy groaned.

Lou glanced at Frank, a man in his twenties with thick brown hair. His eyes showed thoughtfulness with a hint of venerability, unlike most cops whose eyes seem callous and apathetic.

"Did you guys hear what I was saying back there?" Lou grumbled, "You have to choose sides. Are you with the people or the tyrants?" Lou tried to look at every cop, one at a time, waiting for a reply. No one spoke, but Duffy chuckled sarcastically.

A minute later the van stopped, the door opened and the cops jumped out. Two of them pulled Lou out and helped him stand.

He was thrown in the van at dusk. Now it was dark under the overcast sky. He was roughly escorted in to the G.A.T.E. station by his pal, Duffy.

"Put 'em in the holding cell, Duff," the head cop said.

"Sure thing, Lieutenant Herzog," Duffy replied, squeezing Lou's arm painfully tight.

"Please Lieutenant," Lou implored, "not Duffy, I think he's a sadist."

Frank and the cop next to him laughed.

"This guy's a fuckin' riot," Duffy said. "I better lock him up quick before he makes us laugh to death and escapes." Duffy shook Lou by the arm causing him to groan.

Lieutenant Herzog looked at Lou then back to Duffy. Somewhere in his stern blue eyes Lou saw a faint glowing, a fragment of decency that still flickered.

"Oh shit, you know what, Duff," Herzog said. "You guys better get back on the beet, see how things are settling down." He looked over to Frank. "Frank, you lock him up, then help me with filing."

Duffy blew through his lips in protest. "Whatever," he bellowed. "Can I at least take a piss and get a cup of coffee after all that shit we just went through?"

"Yeah, sure, all you guys take five in the break room," replied Herzog, and everyone walked away except Lou and Frank.

"Well, let's get you situated," Frank said, escorting Lou through the double doors to the left. They entered a large processing room where about twenty chairs lined up facing the back wall like it was a movie screen. The wall was made of brick on the bottom four feet and bulletproof glass to the ceiling. A lone woman was on duty, sitting behind the supervisor's window in the middle. She looked at them when the doors opened and sprang up at once. She walked to the door at the corner of the room and came through it eagerly.

"Hey Frank, did you apprehend yourself a dangerous criminal tonight?" Her tone read intrigue mixed with sarcasm.

"Hey Sara," said Frank with a smile, "you won't believe this, but we were nearly trapped in the middle of an angry mob. This guy almost started a riot."

"I know, I heard about it," Sara said in a high sweet voice. "Betty from dispatch told me. They were all watching it on the street camera monitors. This is the guy that started it, huh?" She was a small brunette with plain, delicate features. Her deep brown eyes were wide with interest.

Frank escorted Lou to the processing window built into the middle of the back wall.

"You got any needles or sharp objects in your pockets?" Frank asked.

Lou shook his head and Frank dug into his front pocket.

"Hey, shouldn't you let Sara do this?" said Lou while grinning at Sara.

Frank dug out his keyphone and his wad of money and placed it into the slot under the processing window.

"Yeah, this is the little rabble rouser," Frank answered Sara, "I tell you, it got pretty nasty out there. I'm talking some hairy shit. Bolts were fired! I'm just relieved we got the hell out of there without any more trouble."

"Jeez," said Sara, "what did this guy say to get that kind of reaction?"

"Sara ,my dear," Lou said, "I merely tried to hold a public rally and announce my intention to replace the president, but they bum rushed me, beat me, cuffed me, and carried me off, leaving my digital music player for anyone to take." Lou had raised his voice in anger. "That thing's absolutely priceless to me!"

"No, that's not true," Frank contested, "He did more than that. He was telling people not to go to work. Anyone in the holding cell?"

"Yeah, a few drunks," Sara replied.

"He's paraphrasing, Sara," said Lou as Frank dragged him toward the holding cell. "I said if our demands aren't met, we must all refuse to work until we're heard. That means you guys too. It's our duty as American citizens to defend our rights."

Frank looked through the window of the holding room door, opened it and pushed Lou in. He turned and faced the cop.

"Turn around. I'll take those handcuffs off," Frank said sounding kinder. "You know, I was kind of stunned when I heard they were suspending elections last night, but hey, what can you do, man? They say it would be stupid to waste time campaigning during this crucial period. You can't argue with that. We're isolated from the world, man."

After the cuffs were removed, Lou turned around and faced him again. "If decent men and women were leading our country, we wouldn't be isolated. This definitely is a crucial period. The rest of the world doesn't like us, and we stand at the brink of war. We need to have cooler heads in charge. I hope you'll stand on the people's side, Frank ... you and every good cop and soldier."

Frank gave him an intriguing glance and shut the door.

Lou looked down at the three intoxicated men sitting on benches ... two Latinos and one young white guy covered in tattoos. "Are you guys willing to fight for our democracy?" he said.

They looked at him blankly with blood shot eyes.

Lou started to lecture them about revolution and saving the country. He estimated the inebriated men to have the mental capacity of an eight year old child, and that may be too kind of an estimate. But he spoke to them as if they were bright, coherent men. He diligently tried to enlighten them. He knew large populations of working class Americans were equally undereducated.

An hour passed before the drunks were annoyed and tired.

"Can you shut up now?" one of them grumbled.

After a few minutes of silence, a sudden claustrophobic feeling rushed over Lou. Being locked up was one of his greatest fears, and now that he was forced to shut up, his mind dangerously raced. He paced the room, over and over, in a circle. Like a wired junkie in the paranoia stage, he kept looking out the window every time he passed the door. *How long are they going to leave me in here? This is bullshit. Why wouldn't they be talking to me by now? Alright man, just calm down.*

He exhaled deeply and began to control his breathing. The benches were completely occupied now that the three drunks were sprawled out and snoring. He walked around the room one more time and glanced out the window. After taking one more step, he doubled back and put his face up to the glass. His heart palpitated as he gasped! He saw a man, who looked very distressed, being escorted through the processing room, heading to the exit. Lou didn't recognize him instantly without his painting clothes on, but it was clearly Freddy. Instantly, he got a head rush and felt faint. Stumbling to the back wall, he leaned on it and collapsed to the ground in despair.

The same thoughts kept repeating in his mind. *Freddy knows where I hid the computer. Shit, Freddy knows everything! Why am I so Goddamn dumb?*

After his breath returned to him he thought about what happened. *No wonder why my crew wasn't there tonight. They were all hauled in and interrogated.* His mind raced for some time, perhaps hours as he tried to work things out and prepare himself for the worst.

Finally he laid flat on his back and stretched out on the cold floor. Staring up at the ceiling, listening to the drunk's snore, he somehow dozed off.

Twenty minutes passed, and he woke up with the back of his head aching from being on the hard floor. He was filled with anger for being left there so long. One of the drunks was using his dirty jacket for a pillow, but now he had turned and was only on the corner of it. Lou painfully crawled over and gently yanked it away, causing the drunk to moan and stop snoring momentarily. Lou folded it up, placed it on the ground and laid the back of his head on it. He slept more, but he continued to wake every twenty minutes or so to shift his sore body.

Chapter 8

The moment the door opened Lou woke abruptly. He sat up feeling pain shooting through his back. He winced and felt even worse pain in his shoulder.

"Let's go, you booze hounds, on your feet," the chubby morning shift officer said.

The drunks slowly got to their feet, one looking confused being unable to find his jacket. Lou threw it to him and got to his feet. The men began walking out, and Lou followed them with squinted eyes, trying to appear to be a drunk with a hangover.

Just as he was about to walk through the door, the officer put his hand against Lou's chest and pushed him back. "Not you, Mr. President. You get back there and sit down. We're still working on your charges," the chubby cop said grinning.

"I've been here all night!" cried Lou. "I slept on the Goddamn floor and my back is killing me now. You have no right to hold me this long."

The officer just slammed the door shut.

Lou sat on a bench, trying to relax his racing mind but could not dispel his anxiety. He kept picturing how Freddy's face looked. Lou only caught a glimpse of it, but his mind could summon every detail of his strained expression, perhaps embellishing a bit, he wasn't sure. His anxiety worsened when his thoughts inevitably arrived at suicide.

I'm fucking helpless. Even if I wanted to kill myself, I have no way to do it. What am I gonna do? Strangle myself with my shoe laces? He looked down to his shoes and blew through his lips. *Hang myself with those mangled laces? That's almost funny.* He felt totally helpless with no way out and searched his mind for ways to die. *If I really wanna be an ultimate, shit head, quitter, only one chance for that...death by cop.*

With that shred of hope, he was able to calm down.

It was another two hours before the door opened again. This time it was a large, imposing, dark figure that walked in.

"Well, well, well, Governor … you just couldn't behave, could you?" Captain Zipp was staring down at him.

"I did behave, Captain."I behaved like a man who cares about his country. I wish you and every other cop could understand that. What side will you be on in a revolt, the people's side or the money hoarder's side?"

Captain Zipp reached down and pulled Lou up by the arm. "You're not gonna be the one asking the questions around here," he warned. "Now let's get moving. Some people want to talk to you."

He escorted him out the door, down the hallway and into a white room with a table, four chairs, two doors, and an outside window that was slightly open. Above the main door was a camera pointing down at him.

"Have a seat, Mr. Rizzo. We'll be with you soon. You want some coffee and a pastry?" he said, sounding very formal now. Lou nodded. "That door behind you is a bathroom. Go ahead and use it." He walked out, and the door automatically locked. Moments later an armed female guard walked in with black coffee and some coffee cake. She put it in front of him, smiled, and walked out.

"How about some cream and sugar?" Lou yelled as she closed the door.

He used the bathroom, devoured the coffee cake, and sipped his black coffee.

The door opened again and in walked Officer Zipp with two men in grey business suits. Lou hated business suits and refused to wear one his entire life. "When I see a white man in a business suit, I know that man is gonna try to con me," he used to say, and his experiences proved him to be right.

The men in suits sat down across from him while Zipp remained standing.

"Now then, Mr. Rizzo, you want to tell us where your laptop computer is?" Zipp asked, staring down at him.

"Humm, I would guess it's somewhere in this station by now," Lou said.

They looked at each other surprised.

"That's a good guess. Are you surprised it's not still behind Mrs. Newman's central air unit?" said Zipp.

"Not really," Lou replied calmly. "You guys sure made a big deal about it. I knew you all were competent enough to get it if you wanted it that bad." He looked up at them somberly now. "Seriously, the computer means nothing to me. What's important is what we're going to do to stop this destructive government."

"You really should be concerned with your laptop," one of the men in suits said. He was a blond haired, blue-eyed man with the aura of pretension.

"We have testimony from multiple sources that you were committing crimes against your country, such as treason," the other suited man said. He also had blond hair, just a little darker, and his eyes were green, but their features were quite similar.

Lou looked at the two men with angry eyes. "Jesus Christ, please tell me you didn't hurt anyone," Lou pleaded.

"No one gets hurt, if they tell the truth, but if they don't, we do whatever it takes to get the information," the green-eyed guy said.

"Within the confines of the law, of course," blue-eyed guy added and smiled.

Lou looked down and rubbed his forehead while moaning. "Did you guys torture my painting crew?" Lou asked now, peering at them through his fingers.

They looked at each other seemingly surprised at Lou's powers of deduction.

"Scott and Thomas were very cooperative after one volt session," blue-eyed guy said. "We had to use a little tough love with Fredric."

Lou blew through his lips and shook his head.

"The point is, Louis," he continued, "that we have enough material evidence and video testimony to give you the death sentence for betraying your country; however, if you agree to our terms and fully cooperate with us, your life can be spared."

"Who the fuck are you guys anyway!" Lou shouted. "You don't even introduce yourselves to me. It's like you don't consider me a fellow citizen. Just because your job is solely about following orders, you still have to realize you're dealing with human beings, your fellow citizens."

They were all frowning at him now.

"Fair enough, Mr. Rizzo," said blue-eyed guy, "I'm Agent Dieter Parrish, and this is Agent Joe Gerbuls. Captain Zipp, I believe, you already know."

"Yeah, me and Zipp go way back." Lou looked up to the six and a half footer. "Why the hell did you have to bring them all in here and scare the shit out of them? I mean why didn't you just haul me in if you knew I had it."

"We're told you would have never confessed that you had a foreign contact no matter what methods we could employ," Agent Parrish said.

"So we questioned the people that you were with yesterday and got the evidence we wanted before we brought you in," Agent Gerbuls said. "We weren't gonna bring you in till today, but you managed to get yourself arrested yesterday," he added.

"So who was the genius who said I wouldn't have confessed?" asked Lou. "One of my old political rivals, I'm guessing. But it's kind of hard to narrow down since most of them were my enemies." There was a moment of silence so Lou continued. "He's dead wrong whoever it is. I have nothing to hide from you. All I want is to be honest with the American people about what I know is going on in the world and find out if they want a change of course."

They were all giving him their attention and let him continue uninterrupted.

"If we're going to change this government's suicidal course, you're the Americans that matter most. Will you guys mindlessly follow their orders or stand up for democracy and optimism for a prosperous future? There may soon come a time where police and military people must decide whether to obey when ordered to shoot their own citizens. Your individual choices will determine our future."

"Thank you for that little speech, Mr. Rizzo," said Parrish. "A little dramatic for my taste, but still well delivered. Now if I may interject, we'll get down to our terms. Captain, bring in exhibit A please."

Zipp lifted his radio to his mouth. "Bring it in," he said.

A moment later another female guard brought in the laptop and handed it to Zipp. Right before exiting she glanced at Lou in wide-eyed wonderment.

Captain Zipp opened it and set it in front of Lou. After a moment of close inspection he found the power button and hit it. The computer came to life. He gazed at his old familiar display theme, the blue partly cloudy sky meeting the green pasture. He already knew what they were going to ask him to do.

"I see you charged my computer I'll bet it was no easy task to find a charger to fit it. This things ancient, but if you treat things right it will last. Democracy parallels that notion."

"Yes, it's fully charged," Parrish said. "Now if you would be so kind, please show us how you attain satellite linkage."

"Honestly guys, I was just bullshitting everyone. I can't really link to the world wide web. I just made stuff up, but I'll bet it's probably all true. You guys have to agree our government has totally fucked up and put us all at risk." Lou felt his cheek muscles and biceps twitch as his intuition assumed pain was forthcoming.

Zipp began walking up to him, and his senses heightened. Something caught his ear, a distant murmuring. It was coming from outside. He looked behind him to the window. It was open about three inches, allowing in some air and sound.

Zipp towered over him. Lou held his breath as Zipp bent and turned the laptop slightly so agents Parrish and Gerbuls could see the screen. Then he grabbed the back of Lou's chair, turned it left, and dragged it a foot, easily hauling Lou's weight with one arm. Then he swiftly drew his bolt blaster and pointed it between Lou's eyes, half a foot away. When his finger touched the trigger, the blaster charged, emitting a low hum. If one is staring into the business end of a bolt blaster, at this close range, he can see the tiny blue electrical current that illuminates the tip. Knowing how liberally cops choose to employ it, he stared at it, mesmerized by fear.

Then he cried out. "This is bullshit! Get me a lawyer! To treat a citizen like this is criminal!"

"No, Mr. Rizzo, this is all totally legal," yelled Gerbuls as he stood. "Perhaps you're unaware of the N.T.T. act President Burns singed into law. The No Tolerance for Terrorists act basically allows us to do anything necessary to extract information from a dangerous terrorist."

"Yes, and you can imagine how wide ranging the definition of terrorist is," added Parrish, "so I suggest you just do as you're told, Mr. Rizzo."

"I'm counting to five, and then I blast you with a level two shock to start with. You'll be smelling the smoke from your brain frying," Zipp said, "One, two, three-"

"Okay, take it easy. I'll do whatever you want. Just get that thing out of my face," Lou said and clicked the F.F.N. icon. "Actually I want you guys to see this. I'll bet none of you guys have access to international news, well maybe Deter and Joe since they're special agents, they might have some inside information, but I guarantee you, Captain, you don't know any more than anyone living in those G.A. buildings because you work too closely with the public."

Agent Gerbuls leaned on the table with his hands. "Shut the hell up, peek a boo Lou," he bellowed. "No one wants to hear your socialist shit. Bud Burns' administration is saving us from the mess your ideology of appeasement brought us."

"Wow, now I'm getting to know the real Joe," said Lou, "and your grip on reality is lost." Lou was about to say more but he heard something from outside again that caught his attention. It sounded like an amplified voice but much too faint to be sure. Gerbuls just scowled at him, so Lou got busy.

He logged on to F.F.N. under his name rather than Derwin's and went to the War wager site. "This is where I connect from. I just enter my code, and the program routes me to the nearest satellite link."

"Proceed," Deter said. Lou entered the code and the program engaged.

"Its searching now. It takes a few minutes," said Lou.

Moments of silence passed. Zipp finally holstered his bolt blaster. The two agents were just staring at the computer screen, and Lou was gazing upward trying to listen to the still undefinable noises from outside.

"Here we go. It linked up," Lou announced.

"Captain Zipp, can you stand outside and make sure nobody disturbs us for the next five minutes please?" Agent Parrish ordered.

"No," Lou yelled, "hang on Captain; you have to at least read some headlines from the world wide web before they kick you out."

Zipp stood still, frowning, then batted an eye toward the agents, who he did feel were a couple of pompous assholes. He defiantly walked toward Lou and began bending to get a closer look.

"Captain, outside! That's an order!" special Agent Deter Parrish shouted.

"Understood sir," Zipp replied, "but I have to check on the suspect's condition first." Remaining calm and cool, he grabbed Lou's wrist in his hand and pretended to be examining his heartbeat while he looked at the screen. He saw the world news headlines, and his eyes widened.

"This is the real shit here," Lou said to him. "Look at this one." (**Coalition grows, Invasion of U.S seemingly inevitable**).

"Our fuckin' government is gonna get us killed." Zipp had a look of shock on his face. He just stared, mouth open, eyes wide.

Agent Gerbuls put his hand in his coat pocket and fished around.

"These agents work for the elite class so I assume they already know what's going on," Lou told him, "but our deranged government brilliantly managed to hide this from all of us working stiffs. I say brilliantly, but it's just down right evil to the core."

"You were told to shut up, you pain in the ass," Gerbuls yelled and sprang toward him. With a swift move, he held his fist out in front of Lou's face and pressed a trigger with his thumb. A mist splashed onto his face. He instantly recoiled and franticly wiped his face with his hands.

"What the fuck," he cried.

The drug contained in the mist was dubbed (terminal bliss), not by the scientists who created it, but by the doctors who have seen how the awful effects can cause permanent brain damage to almost half of the people it was tested on. It was actually a synthetic neurotoxin that alters specific electrochemical signals in the brain and by blocking neurotransmitters. After the initial shock when the brain overloads, the user will black out for a moment and wake up in a total carefree bliss. Memories are scrambled and sometimes altered.

"You stupid prick. You got some of that shit on me," Zipp yelled and stormed out of the room, slamming the door.

"Goddamn it, Joe, now I have to run after him. He saw the world headlines," Agent Parrish stood up.

"Forget him, Deter; we'll handle him later. Now let's do this."

Lou felt a warm tingly sensation where the mist hit his skin, not painful but uncomfortable. His face was scrunched up. His eyes squinted, and he couldn't release muscle tension. His face didn't itch, but he had to rub it frantically, and in doing so, he made it worse. With great difficulty, he forced his hands away from his face and panicked to find his vision was blurry as he tried to look up at his assailer. He saw two figures standing in front of him completely blurred and unidentifiable. He tried to focus, but it got worse. He began to see faces on the figures, terrible, hideous and deformed faces. Dreadful fear and paranoia washed over him as he realized he had been drugged in a heavy way. As he slipped into delirium, his mind raced.

It's just that easy for them. If they want to silence you, they just drug you and cause you to lose your mind. No one will listen to an insane person. They've destroyed my mind. It's all over for me now.

Despair grew in his mind until he was sure it was about to break. It felt like he was falling off a cliff and bracing for the deadly impact. He did fall, right off the chair, onto the floor and blacked out.

It was forty seconds Lou was unconscious, but when he awoke, he was unaware he even passed out. He stood and sat back in the chair as if nothing happened, and to him nothing had because he didn't remember anything in chronological order now. He was now in a calming, blissful, dreamlike daze. His sight had cleared, but he didn't remember it was blurry moments earlier. Now he had no worries, no fear, no paranoia and no regrets. Everybody was passive, and the two men in the room must be friends. He realized there was no need for anger or hate. Everyone was part of a harmonious race of men. He smiled while looking around the room.

"Hey Lou, how you doing buddy?" Agent Gerbuls said in a voice you would use to talk to a small child.

"Wonderful, this chair is so comfortable, it just fits me perfectly. Everything fits. I don't have to worry. I think everyone knows the truth. Do you think everything's gonna be alright now Denny?" He said, while looking up at Gerbuls' clean shaven face.

He was seeing a very different face in his altered mind. He was seeing the kind, elderly face of Dennis Nader, his old campaign manager. Denny was a democratic Illinois house representative for six consecutive terms until he denounced his own party and declared himself an independent. He lost the next election to a democrat since most Illinois voters just punched an all democratic ticket. Years later he attended a Rizzo rally and was impressed by the speech Lou gave. He met Lou that day and offered his assistance. Lou truthfully told him how much he admired him and made him campaign manager. Denny was in his mid-seventies and didn't want much responsibility so his only job was to give advice when Lou needed guidance. Lou respected Dennis Nader immensely, and talking with him was therapeutic in times of self doubt. No other man's advice did he respect more than old Denny Nader.

Lou was seeing the grey haired old man standing before him and thought nothing strange about it, even though Denny died during Lou's second year in the senate, ten years ago now. All he knew is he was pleased he was here. Everything was going to be alright now. The struggle was over, the dream achieved.

I can finally truly relax. Tears trickled down his face. He had never felt so happy. *No man has ever felt so happy.*

"You're right Lou, everything is going to be alright now."

Gerbuls was still talking like Lou was a child. "You did a great job too, never gave up."

Lou smiled, nodded his head and continued to bounce it as if in rhythm to music.

Agent Parrish chuckled at the sight of the once quick witted Lou looking so silly now.

"You just got to do one more thing, buddy," said Gerbuls

That annoyed Lou, like a child being called home when he was in the middle of having a grand old time. "Aw, I don't want to do anything. Just let me relax now," he pleaded.

"Look, the computer is right there in front of you," Gerbuls said softly, "Just contact our foreign friend and ask him when they're planning to invade. Then tell him everything's okay now."

"Contact who?" Lou said, sounding puzzled.

"You know who. We should tell him everything's ok, right?"

"Tony?" Lou said, just coming to realize his old friend indeed should know everything was okay now.

Tony will be worried.

"Yes, of course, Tony. Contact him now," Gerbuls said, then looked at Parrish who began to write in his note pad.

Lou looked at the laptop in front of him and squinted at it. Finally, he put his finger on the mouse pad and slowly navigated the arrow to (Instant Message) and clicked. Both agents were standing behind him now, interested to see what address he would type in.

"Humm," Lou looked up to the ceiling, "what did I want to tell him now? I'm not really sure what to say."

Agent Gerbuls walked in front of him again. "We have to ask him when they're planning to invade and where. Then tell him everything's good. The people won," he said, sounding like a hypnotist.

"Yeah, the people know," Lou said and actually just began to hear the sound of a crowd of people chanting something. The sound leaked in through the window and now that his ears were focused on it, he began to hear it louder.

Agent Parrish heard it too. He squinted and tilted his head trying to listen closer. "What the fuck is that?" he said and walked to the window.

After hearing it repeat over and over, they could make out the words. "Spread the word! No work till we're heard!" a crowd was chanting.

This enhanced Lou's dreamlike consciousness. He perceived the people were chanting for him, and they were in reality too. It made him feel dominant now in his drug induced contentment.

Agent Parrish closed the window and walked back to the table. "Okay Lou, let's do this."

Lou blew through his lips, producing a mocking sound. "I'll do things the way I see fit. You're just an adviser, Denny. I love ya, but don't ever order me. After all I did for this country, I deserve a cool drink. I'm gonna fix me up some rum and orange juice on ice and kick back, maybe watch one of my documentaries." He stood up, swayed a bit and began walking toward the door. In his mind he was going home to his first house in Des Plaines, a suburb just north of Chicago where he lived with his wife and son until they divorced.

Agent Gerbuls sprang forward. "Sure Lou, just hang on a second. Don't forget you're here to meet someone." He gently grabbed him by the shoulders and turned him away from the door. "Have a seat. We'll get you a cold drink."

Lou looked Gerbuls in the eyes. His own pupils were huge dark disks leaving just a narrow ring of brown. This face was new to him, but the idea crept through his mind that it could be his son, aged ten years since he last saw him. After pondering profound thoughts, he smiled.

"I'm glad you're working for me, kid," said Lou. "With all that's been going on, I forgot who I'm meeting."

Gerbuls escorted him back to his seat, trying to think of something and not having any luck.

"You're here to see a woman that wanted to meet you," Agent parish said and nodded to Gerbuls. Just hearing the word woman added nervous excitement to Lou's condition.

Gerbuls walked up to Parrish and whispered. "Good

thinking, I'll be right back. Keep him occupied." Then he left the room. Lou began babbling about crazy theories he had about women and recalled some perverted old jokes. Parrish was doing his best to sound interested and encouraged him to continue.

"Hey kid, you know why women have to suffer through their period every month? Cause the bitches deserve it." Lou nearly fell off his chair and continued cracking himself up for the next eight minutes.

Finally, the door opened and a woman entered the room holding two glasses full with orange liquid and ice. Their eyes met, and Lou's stomach fluttered. She had dark black hair and submissive brown eyes that appealed to him at once. She wore a grey skirt down to her knees and a matching blouse with the top three buttons undone. As she set the drinks down on the table, he had only one thing on his mind

Oh, look at that smooth pale skin. I'll bet it feels so soft. I wanna kiss her neck and get her breathing heavy.

"Hi, I'm Teresa Gorgie. It's nice to meet you." She extended her arm, dangling her dainty hand.

He caressed her fingers, staring like her hand was a holy relic and began rubbing her palm with his finger. She shook his hand and pulled away.

"Thanks, likewise," he replied, forgetting to introduce himself. She sat in the chair next to him and pushed a glass toward him. Lou licked his lips and reached for the cold drink. As he sipped, she adjusted the laptop so the monitor was angled directly toward the camera above the door.

"That's a good mix," he said and gulped some more. "Try some."

She brought her glass to her lips and sipped. Lou stared at her moistened lips as she took some more, this time moaning as she swallowed. "Wow!" she exclaimed. "That tastes so good. I never had orange juice with rum before, but I love it." Giggling, she brushed her hand through her silky, black hair, pushing it away from her gorgeous neck.

They awkwardly made small talk about drinks until he suddenly got on the subject about how he was a good musician and used to be a great golfer before the depression hit. Feeling threatened by her youth, he explained how important it is to stay physically fit and how much energy he still has at his age.

"You would be surprised how energetic I am," he said, smiling and winked.

She giggled a lot, and after that comment she nudged her chair closer. Crossing her legs, she bumped her calf up against Lou's right thigh, and it rested there for a moment. He felt tingles go up his leg and directly to his genitals. She crossed her arms and leaned forward a bit giving Lou a peek of her cleavage. Deep, strong sexual desire flooded his mind, and blood flowed to his growing shaft. He cleared his throat and reached down to his crotch to make a much needed adjustment. He snickered oddly, wanting to speak but finding it difficult to think of what to say.

Terminal bliss caused the brain to only focus on the present moment. Memory is convoluted and irrelevant, and in this state of mind, Lou's sex drive was bordering uncontrollable. This drug would have been the most popular ever if coming down from it wasn't so dangerous to the brain.

"You know," he tried to remember her name but couldn't though it was on the tip of his tongue, "I got to come right out and tell you that I'm like incredibly attracted to you. I'm sorry if I'm acting odd and all. I'm just stunned by your beauty ... and I can't believe I'm saying this."

"Oh, that's so sweet," she said, leaning forward and placing her hand on his upper thigh.

Animalistic impulses nearly caused him to embrace her and begin kissing her now. If she allowed it, great, but if not, he would grab her arms, force her to the ground and begin humping her.

No, rape is bad ... can't be doing that.

He wasn't sure why rape was bad at the moment, but he managed to restrain himself for now. He tried to remember how to ask a girl out on a date.

"Do you think sometime maybe you could come with me out? I mean go out with me?" His perspiration increased. Sweat beads were forming and dripping off his forehead.

"Sure, I'd love to," she said. "In fact, we can go back to my room for awhile." She smiled then turned her head toward the door, or the camera above it. "Just as soon as you do that thing with the computer," she added.

"Really?" Lou rejoiced! "Oh that's so great. I would love to spend more time with you. Please take me to your room." He leaned in and placed his hand on her thigh, giving it a tender squeeze.

"Okay, but," she sniffled and glanced at the camera again, "first contact Tony, and we can go."

He took his hands away, sat up and scooted closer to the computer. He tried to remember what he had to tell Tony and why but didn't want to ask and look like a fool to his dream girl. He moved the arrow to the instant message address line and clicked. He looked down at the keyboard, had to squint and blink a few times to focus on the letters. Trying to remember the address he needed to type seemed impossible at first.

Who did she say to contact again? Tony, yeah, that's right.

Then the address appeared in his mind like he had taken a file from a catalog. He typed in (duputyp.m-t.swan) in the address line and wrote (Indy1 to tony). He held his finger suspended over the button before hitting send, looked up and squinted. He had no idea what to say and looked in her eyes.

"You're so stunning my dear that I've forgotten what I need to tell the good man." Her eyes were still beautiful but not joyful anymore.

After a moment she quickly turned her gaze to the computer. "Ask when the war is starting and tell him everything's good now." He didn't notice she was acting uneasy. Now her eyes were watery and uncertain.

"That's right." he clicked on send, "I'm gonna say when's the war starting and I'm okay."

Twenty seconds later a message came back (I'll have him in a jiff. Switch on mic and cam). He clicked the microphone and camera icons, pushed back from the table and faced her.

"It takes a few minutes for them to get him to a computer. The sooner the better. I can't wait to be done. God, you're so lovely."

Lou continued to babble about her beauty but shyly

avoided her gaze, not noticing the tears.

Tony's face appeared while Lou was looking at her chest.

"Louie, glad we're speaking again so soon, mate. How's it going?" The Australian's voice startled Lou. When he looked up to the screen, Tony Snow squinted and studied Lou's eyes.

"It's going great..." He paused. Again a name eluded him, "my friend."

Tony was silent, still looking oddly at Lou's eyes.

"Ah, listen, I have to go. I have a date with a beautiful woman." He glanced over to Teresa and smiled. "I just wanted to say I'm doing fine, and what time's the war on. I mean when is the war starting?"

Tony's heart sunk. A lump welled up in his throat, but he composed himself enough to answer. "There will be no war. Your leaders refuse to agree to the chemical and nuclear weapons ban, and W.U.N. leaders would never risk that scale of immoral human suffering." Tony's voice was sad and serious. "Louie, where are you right now? Do you remember how you got there?"

Lou looked puzzled for a moment, like the question should be considered, but sex was still in the forefront of his diluted mind.

"I don't know. Listen Tony, can we talk later? I have a date, and I don't want to keep her waiting." He looked at Teresa, smiling, but this time her eyes were squinted, and her mouth puckered. Now she didn't look so attractive.

What happened to her? Even a beautiful woman looks ugly when she's crying. Oh my God, she's crying, he finally realized.

"What's wrong, sweetie?" he asked with deep concern.

She broke out in a high pitched cry. Lou moved closer, intending to embrace her, but she jumped to her feet and ran to the door.

Just as she was grabbing the doorknob, Lou leaped up and dashed toward her, yelling, "No, please don't leave me!" he cried, struggling to remember her name.

She ran out of the room, leaving the door open. Lou was going to catch her. He felt an adrenalin surge and knew he could move fast. He took four steeps in full stride.

Just as he got through the door, a thick arm grabbed him around the torso, instantly stopping his progress. He tried to pull away with all his force and almost did, but the man with the thick arm was behind him now and used his other arm to put him in a headlock. Lou finally remembered a name.

"Teresaaaaaaaaaaaaaa!" He yelled so loudly, it pained his throat.

He was thrown to the ground, his chest and face making first impact, and the guard put his knee on his back applying most of his two hundred and thirty pounds while he cuffed him. Lou continued to struggle the whole time, yelling "Noooooo!" He took a punch to the back of the head but felt no physical pain, only the anguish of her leaving.

Agent Gerbuls walked into the room, stepping over Lou's legs in front of the doorway. He went right up to the laptop and sat in front of it.

"Well, well, well, Tony Snow, the deputy Prime Minister of Australia, associates with an American spy. How immoral," he said.

"Listen, whoever you are," Tony said sounding stern, "I demand to speak with your superior. If Louis comes to any harm, there will be serious consequences. I will personally take this matter up with your president."

"I see, so this guy is a close friend of yours, and you care about his well being, ay mate," said Gerbuls, poorly mocking an Australian accent.

"This is a very serious matter!" Tony yelled, slamming his fist on the desk. "I have an offer to make with your country for his release, and if you hurt him before I can negotiate with your president, you will be personally responsible."

"Sorry mate," Gerbuls replied, "maybe you haven't noticed, but my country doesn't negotiate with terrorists, and we kill people for treason, and now we have proof that the W.U.N. had a spy working for them." He slammed the laptop shut. Then he sat back and broke into loud, maniacal laughter.

Two officers picked up Lou, grabbing him at the arm

pits. They dragged him down a hall and opened the huge security door leading to the cells.

Lou was sobbing hysterically and trashing his head from side to side, hoping to wake himself if this was all a nightmare.

They went through the door and into a hallway with five cells on each side. One guard opened the door to the third cell on the right. The other removed the handcuffs, then pushed him. Lou fell to the floor. The guard slammed the door shut. Lou curled into a fetal position and bawled, not because he would be put to death, but because he lost the girl.

As he bawled and trashed around on the floor, the dreadful feeling of unrequited sexual desire agonized him so intensely, he had to escape the pain. He got to his hands and knees and stared at the floor in silence for a moment. Letting out a mighty roar with all his strength, he slammed his own head to the concrete floor. Blackness...

Chapter 9

The crew inside the red white and blue American Airways Television van was surprised to see a group of forty to fifty people chanting outside the G.A.T.E. station. They were there to report the capture of a dangerous American terrorist, plotting against his own country.

"What the hell are all these people doing here?" Frank, the portly driver said.

"I don't know," replied Keith Colman, the handsome young local news reporter from Park Ridge.

"I ain't ever seen people form a mob like that. Are we gonna get this Keith?" asked Tim the tall, slender, blond haired cameraman.

"We're here to report on this spy guy; that's it," replied Keith while he combed his auburn hair. "You know how much grief we get if we report anything on our own. I don't need more of that shit. They have plenty of reporters ready to take my job."

Tim, sitting across from him, frowned and crossed his arms. "Whatever, momma's boy, I'm at least getting some shots of them."

The TV van parked in front of the station, and the crew began to unload while Keith went inside to find out who he would be interviewing.

The group of protesters moved closer to the van.

"We want to spread the word to the whole country: no work till we're heard," A white, middle aged man with black and grey hair yelled. It was Carl Mazola from the rally. The guy who fetched and helped set up the folding table for Lou.

"You can't just end elections in America. We want Rizzo to run for president," another yelled.

"Relax people," said Frank in his throaty fat man voice,

"we're here to cover something else, not your little gathering you got going here."

"It's called a protest," yelled Carl.

"You damn well better cover this." a black man's voice shouted. He moved to the front, "Or your lead story's gonna be about a TV crew being beaten to death." It was Tyrell making the threat.

Tim and frank looked nervously at each other as the crowd began to yell and move closer.

"Okay, okay, we'll do a quick report. Who wants to be the spokesman?" said Tim, who always was a quick thinker and level headed.

"I'll do it," said Carl.

Tim turned on the camera and placed it on his shoulder. "Set up the microphone, Frank, and interview this guy."

Frank labored to hook it up and stood in front of the camera to do a sound check. Tim lifted his thumb and hit record.

Frank moved over to Carl and looked into the camera. "We're here at the north side gate station where a group of protesters have gathered. Sir, can you tell us why you're protesting?"

Frank's voice was unprofessional, but his delivery was adequate. "We're here to demand elections be restored. The working class will not give up our right to vote and surrender to a dictatorship. We have a candidate qualified to run for president, and his name is Louis Rizzo. He was apprehended last night for giving a speech, and we want him released. We demand our voices be heard across the country to the entire working class. We will refuse to work if democracy is not restored." Carl was an excellent spokesman for his first time. "Spread the word. No work till we're heard," he said, and the crowd cheered loudly and then began chanting it.

Tim slowly panned over the crowd, thinking how great a story this was. He returned the camera to Frank.

"From the north side this is Frank Muso reporting."

"You better broadcast that," Carl said.

"Tubby, over there, ain't even a real reporter!" yelled Tyrell. "We want a real interview."

Frank frowned.

"No, no, I recorded it. Frank was fine. It was all good," Tim pleaded.

Just then the doors of the station flew open and G.A. officers came trotting out. Lieutenant Herzog and Captain Zipp were among the first ones.

The cops spread out along the front of the building.

Keith Coleman popped out and shouted to Tim. "Get your asses in here!"

Tim and Frank quickly lumbered into the building.

Herzog stood forward and spoke loudly to the crowd. "The law states you have the right to protest but only in designated protest areas no closer than two hundred feet of a government building. So we need everyone to move back across the street please. You must remain on the north side of Van Buren."

Everyone stood motionless for a moment in the breezy morning air. Forty-nine working citizens and eighteen officers stood silent just absorbing this extraordinary moment in their lives.

"We want you to free Lou!" Tyrell yelled, breaking the moment.

"Yeah, Lou did nothing wrong!" Carl shouted, and the crowd rumbled.

"Mr. Rizzo is a spy," Lieutenant Herzog proclaimed. "He confessed that he maintained illegal contact to a foreign government for years. He will be charged today, and bail will be set. Now please everybody start moving back, or we will use force."

"That's bullshit! You're framing him!" someone yelled.

The crowd grumbled.

"Everyone, move back now. This is your last warning," Herzog ordered.

The crowd stood firm and continued to grumble.

"Let's move in," Herzog said to his men and pulled his Billy club with his left hand and his bolt blaster with his right.

Every officer did the same, and they began moving toward the crowd yelling at them to get back across the street.

Most people got a look at the approaching electric shock guns and moved back quickly enough to avoid pain. Others were not so lucky. If they chose to stand their ground, they got whacked with a club. If that didn't get them running, or if they defended themselves, they were immediately zapped.

Chapter 10

As his eyes slowly opened, the glossy white cinder block walls came into focus. Lying on his chest, the left side of his face was in a puddle of blood. His eyes were facing the back wall. There was a toilet in the corner, a small sink next to it, and a small bed against the side wall. Lou was confused and frightened. His primal instinct told him he must get water and comfort or die. He needed to move, had to get water, but it would be a mighty test of his will to move there. First, with great difficulty, he moved his right hand over to his head to have a feel. Whimpering when he touched the protruding burse on his swollen forehead, he felt the skin of dried blood. Slowly rolling onto his back, he looked directly into the ceiling light. The brightness burned his eyes, but he continued to stare into it like he did the sun on the G.A. bus. His sight clouded. The ceiling pulsated with his heart beat, and suddenly the light expanded, opening up to infinity. He felt like his sprit was departing, and he welcomed it. He wanted to float away, into the glowing expanding light and be done with this haggard body, this torturous life.

Let it be over ... no more disappointment. I want it all just to end.

He was coming down from the most intense synthetic drug ever used on a human brain, and during this period the mind can be permanently damaged. Lou was presently heading down the path to severe neurosis. Coming down was the exact opposite of the high: intense despair and depression that can break the mind. Lou began drowning in self-pity, mostly over what would seem childish, like his looks.

I'm too fuckin' ugly. My whole life I could never get the hot girls. It was always something: too skinny, too poor, too nice, or too Goddamn political. I never achieved anything in my life. All that work for nothing. My life sucks. I hate being poor. That's

*why politicians take bribes and don't give a shit about the people,
because getting rich is the only way to be happy, and you gotta be
a greedy crook to be that rich, so I'm shit out of luck with these
stupid, Goddamn, morals. I eventually lose at everything. I'm sick
of losing. I'm sick of fighting for regular people. It's hopeless. I
tried. What else could I do? Now just let me fuckin' die. End the
misery, please.*

His eyes fluttered, and his head rolled to the side. He was
just on the verge of letting himself drift into unconsciousness. As
his eyes fluttered, his last vision was of the toilet and sink. They
shut. The end was a moment away.

Water, I gave up on water. He wrinkled his chin, flexing
his face muscles as hard as he could. *Am I that much of a loser?
I can't even try to get water...No!*

He opened his eyes and judged how he could make it
to the sink. At first he turned onto his side and nudged his torso
forward and then his butt and legs. He did it five times and could
only budge a few feet, but his determination grew. Now that his
mind had an objective, his despair lightened. He pushed his torso
up with his arms and pulled one knee forward, then the other.
On all fours now, he slowly began to crawl toward the toilet.
This was just what he needed to fight off the final effects of the
neurotoxin. The last few feet were difficult but he made it. He
crossed his arms on the toilet seat and rested his head on them.
Hitting his burse on his arm caused a jolt of pain. He readjusted
the top of his head on his arms and was staring into the toilet
bowl.

*That bowl actually looks pretty clean ... no skid marks
down there, and the water is clear. Could I possibly...*

He reached up with his right hand and flushed. As the
water drained and began to fill up again, he stuck his hand in
and gingerly splashed his face and head. He cupped his hand,
scooped water, and sipped it. The cold water on his forehead
soothed the pain slightly, and he continued to splash it for the
next minute. Peering up at the sink, he was like a mountain
climber halfway through his ascent staring up at the peak. He
fought off the temptation to let himself fall to the floor, reached
up and grabbed the side of the sink. After a series of grunts and

groans, he eventually rose to his feet. Leaning over the sink, he opened the faucet, put his lips under the running water, and got a proper drink. Some strength returned, and he managed to take his shirt off without falling. He took one more sip of water and held his shirt under, giving it a good soak. He didn't attempt to wring it out, knowing that would waste too much energy.

He stumbled over to the bed and collapsed onto it as gently as possible. Painfully turning onto his back, he then folded up the wet shirt a few times and gently placed it on the lump protruding from his forehead. This thin squeaky prison bed felt cozy after being on the ground so long. He relaxed his mind and recalled memories from his life like he was picking up files that were scattered on the ground and returning them to the file cabinet in his brain, trying to get them in order.

In each memory he didn't view himself in self-pity and depression anymore. He looked at his life with anger and rage. He wished he was more assertive and aggressive. He soon realized that wasn't all. He also wished he was meaner and more callous.

Compassion for those who are worse off than me was my greatest inspiration and my biggest weakness. Well, No more! No more stupid, altruistic, superhero shit...

When the neurotoxin wears off, his mind would not be broken, but it would be forever changed **and serve him for ill or good on the next life-changing decision he will make.**

Fuck everyone . . . no more Mr. nice guy.

Chapter 11

Captain Zipp stood off to the side while Agent Gerbuls and Lieutenant Herzog answered questions being asked by roving reporter, Keith Colman. Herzog explained how Louis Rizzo was trying to incite a riot before they arrested him. Then Gerbuls talked about Lou's alleged confession that he was a spy and that he demonstrated how he used his laptop to divulge secret information to terrorists.

The information was vague but adequate. The public should be convinced that a significant arrest was made and homeland security was on their game.

After the interview, Zipp approached Gerbuls. "Agent Gerbuls, I'd like a word with you."

"Later, Captain, I got to make some calls." He walked right past.

Zipp followed. When he caught up, he grabbed his shoulder and turned him back. "Just a minute here!" he shouted, "you may have higher authority, but I'm entitled to conduct how this station is run." Zipp was firm, despite Gerbuls' furious expression.

Gerbuls exhaled deeply and shut his eyes for a moment. "Alright, Captain, one minute. Now what the fuck is so important?"

Zipp ran his palm over his head and grinded his teeth. "I want to get him over to the medical ward," he muttered.

"Who? Rizzo?" Gerbuls screeched. "What the hell for?"

"You soaked the guy's face with terminal bliss, nearly got it up my nose too. Then you put him through a traumatic event and shoved him in an isolation cell. The guy must be going batty by now. I want to get him out of there and over to the med ward."

"What the fuck do you care?" Gerbuls said with a stunned

expression. "The guy is done for, and he was batty to begin with anyway. Just keep him locked up tonight. We don't want to take any chances. We'll be transporting him tomorrow."

"What's the difference? He'll be locked up in the med ward. Nobody is ever gonna escape under my watch."

Their eyes were locked as they were silent for a moment. Zipp's stare was unwavering. A pivotal moment in time awaited one man's uncaring response.

"Whatever," Gerbuls finally blurted. "I don't give a shit where you put him, as long as you bring him directly to us for transfer tomorrow. You fuck something up, you're done for. You got it Zipp?"

"Yeah, I got it," he replied smugly.

"Fine, I'm going to the clubs tonight, maybe find me a naughty, rich girl or two and live it up for a while. I would suggest you do the same cause tougher times may be right around the corner, but you just got yourself a double shift cause you're gonna stay here all night until we take him tomorrow." Gerbuls walked away while Zipp stood still for a moment.

Chapter 12

Eventually Lou fell asleep. The same self-loathing was in his subconscious.

I'm sick of that nice guy, No more. Let there be blood!

He woke less than an hour later, and the bed didn't feel comfortable anymore. The once cool, wet shirt on his forehead was now warm.

Just as he was making adjustments, attempting to make himself more comfortable, the door opened. Two armed guards walked in and stood off to the side and then Captain Zipp entered.

"Rizzo, you awake?"

Lou slowly took the shirt off his head and looked to see who it was.

"What did you bastards do to me?" he said groggily.

"Are you alright? How do you feel?" Zipp asked, moving closer, getting a better look at his head.

"I feel like a truck hit me, and I'm going in-fuckin'-sane.. How do you people live with yourselves?"

"We're going to take you to the medical ward and get you fixed up. Put your shirt on."

"Eat shit. My shirt is soaking wet," he replied and weakly threw the shirt toward him. It plopped to the floor well short.

Zipp knew he was in weak condition and this new nasty attitude might be a consequence of the synthetic neurotoxin. He actually enjoyed, maybe even admired, Lou's sharp personality and felt a sadness, considering it was probably gone for good. He felt anger toward those Goddamn pompous agents and knew using the neurotoxin was unnecessary.

"Get a wheelchair and a gown," ordered Zipp, and one guard rushed off. He walked over to Lou. "Can you sit up? Let me give you a hand." After a moment, Lou took hold of Zipp's outstretched hand and allowed to be pulled upright. Lou swung his feet off the bed and sat hunched forward.

"The government agents are planning on taking you somewhere tomorrow." He looked toward the other guard and spoke quietly to Lou. "You really got those people riled up at your little rally. I got to say that's pretty impressive, governor. Some of 'em even came out here to protest your arrest."

Full memory returned like a flash of light, causing his head to jolt backwards. Now he remembered how one of those sleazy agents sprayed his face with something just before everything went crazy. Vividly he could picture the girl, and he remembered how she left after getting him to contact Tony. Lou closed his eyes for a moment.

Oh God, I gave them Tony.

Then he remembered Zipp seeing the world internet. "You were there; you saw the world news headlines. You know what I was fighting for is righteous." Lou looked up to Zipp's eyes, squinting because his head ached.

Zipp tightened his lips and nodded once.

"Don't you agree that we need to overthrow this government?"

"Some things get beyond repair," Zipp replied. "The government is too powerful to challenge now."

"Not if the people were united against them, including the cops and soldiers," Lou said, but not with his usually vigor. It sounded like a platitude now.

The guard returned with the wheelchair.

Zipp picked up the hospital gown off the seat. "Here, stick your arms in," he said, holding open the gown. Lou put it on, and Zipp helped him into the wheelchair.

Lou's head was slumped, and his back was hunched as they wheeled him to the medical ward. Not a word was spoken. When they entered the ward, the door automatically shut and locked. Only an authorized keyphone could open it.

"Hey Doctor Coleman." Zipp spoke in the intercom to a doctor sitting in an isolated security room behind a desk. "You wanna check this guy out. I think he's in serious need of an ice pack."

The doctor came out and walked over. "Violent offender?" he asked quietly.

"He's a dangerous spy, apparently, but a bunch of people yelling out front of the building think he's a revolutionary."

The doctor squinted at Zipp.

"He's harmless," Zipp said, smiling and then whispered something that Lou only understood a few words of, but he knew it had to do with the drug they gave him.

"Put him there," the doctor said and pointed to the first bed.

The ward was relatively small. There were eight beds and only one other patient was there lying in the last one. A black man with a puffy face was sleeping. It looked as if he had been beaten.

The guard wheeled Lou to the first bed. "Get in," he ordered, offering no assistance.

Lou placed his hands on the bed and slowly climbed on like an elderly person. He lay back, closed his eyes and exhaled deeply.

It was a few minutes later when the doctor came over to him. "Ouch, that's a big bump you got on your head."

Lou opened his eyes and looked at the doctor. He was a blond haired, green eyed, fair skinned man with black rimmed glasses and looked to be in his mid thirties.

"Lift your head. I want you to take this." He held out a small paper cup with a pill in it and a glass of water in the other hand.

Lou looked at him suspiciously and didn't move.

"I know what they did to you. It must have been hell on your brain. You can trust me though. I treat the sick, and I take my job seriously. If they want to beat you or drug you, it won't be in here." The doctor had a high, nerdy, unassuming voice.

Lou raised his head and opened his jaw. The doctor dumped the pill from the cup to his mouth and handed him the water. Lou drank, swallowed the pill, and lay back down. The doctor held open his eye and shined a light in it, then the other. He asked a few questions and checked his blood pressure and heart rate. He left and returned with a cold pack.

"Put this on your bump and get some rest."

The cold pack felt good on his forehead and he fell asleep twenty minutes later.

Chapter 13

As soon as the News van pulled in front of the of the American Airways Chicago station, Keith Coleman turned his head back to Tim, the camera man.

"Do the editing and finish up for me, okay Timmy?" he said. "I got to get over to the Park West."

This, of course, Tim expected. Keith almost never went to the editing room and almost always left early.

"Yeah, why not, I never have anywhere to go." Tim continued to stare out the window, never even looking over as he replied.

"Thanks," Keith said as he opened the door and dashed off.

Frank got out of the driver's seat and walked to the back, opened the doors, and started to unload the footage.

"That was quite a day, huh Timmy," said Frank.

"Yeah that was pretty wild for a bit there," Tim replied, "but I think we handled that mob pretty good. Still, I'm glad those cops came out when they did."

Frank laughed hard enough to cause his large gut to jiggle. "I'm a decent reporter, ain't I? We don't even need that selfish prick anymore." Chuckling, he handed Tim the footage. "You need me to do anything ,Timmy?"

"No, I got it, Frank. Get on over to the pub."

"Okay, I know we ain't supposed to talk about that rally thing, but they can't expect me not to tell everyone at the pub. I'll catch you later."

"Alright," Tim replied and headed inside to the editing room.

A few people said hi to him as he walked past the reception area and down the hall to the editing room.

"Hey Tim, how the hell are ya?" Burney, the old white

haired editor said the moment Tim walked into the room.

"Hey Burn, I had a wild day. How you doing?" Tim said, holding out the tape for him.

Burney grabbed the tape and slid it into the editing machine. "I'm ok . . . boring today. None of the local shit I did this morning is going to be aired, but I hear you got a big story." He hit *play,* and Frank interviewing Carl with the protesters played. Burney looked at it and broke out in a gurgling cackle. "You got Frankie doing interviews now?" he jested.

A thought occurred to Tim just now, and being upset with Keith for never doing his own editing caused him to like the idea too much for his own good.

Burney was a kind old guy, not dumb but overly trusting, someone he could easily deceive.

"Yeah, he looks pretty funny but he did alright," replied Tim. "I mean, he had to do it. Keith was too chicken shit to get that close to the mob. He sat in the police station while Frankie did it."

Burney stared at Tim with his mouth wide open. "You're not going to believe this but we're using this interview in the segment," proclaimed Tim.

"Well I'll be dammed," said Burney. "That is hard to believe. They're gonna let the whole country see fat Frankie. That's a fuckin' riot."

"Yeah, so let's run this interview with Frank first and then Keith's interview with the agent and the cop next. I'll help Gloria with the narrative because there's been a change, and Keith took off already."

He knew this act of defiance could cost him his job, but he was a recipient of his rich father's inheritance, and he owned a large home in Park Ridge. He needed this job to pay property taxes and live an upper class lifestyle, but he wasn't afraid to defy orders, and he wouldn't accept he was a slave to his job like most everyone else on the crest of affluence did. He was bursting inside with the exhilaration of defying the higher ups. When questioned, he would just play dumb and say he thought this side of the story was supposed to be shown. He smiled proudly to his fortitude.

Chapter 14

Lou awoke and was struck with the horrible, sinking feeling of not knowing where he was. Remembering he was in custody made the seriousness and severity of his situation sink in for the first time. Like a wave hitting his body, he suddenly felt vulnerable, defenseless, and hungry. He let out a moan and closed his eyes tightly, and tears began to form.

I'm either gonna be killed for treason or be locked in the penitentiary plant for the rest of my life.

He was about to bawl and then suddenly realizing he may not be alone. He swallowed the lump in his throat and cut it off. He lifted his head to look around. The room was dim now. The main lights were off, and only the light in the security office was on. It had a large glass window in the wall, and Lou could see a man sitting behind a desk looking up at a TV mounted on the wall. It was not the doctor from earlier; this guy had dark hair. Lou figured it was late, maybe 1: 00 a.m. or so, and the doctors changed shifts.

He looked the other way and saw the puffy faced black guy was still lying in his bed. He shifted his body to a different position while Lou was looking at him. He began to realize he wouldn't be able to sleep anymore and wished he had never woken up.

Tossing from side to side for twenty minutes, afraid of his own thoughts, Lou's ears buzzed from the haunting silence. Once in a while he would hear a strange sound he couldn't identify. After a few more times, he noticed it was the guy in the office laughing at something he was watching on the TV, He became angry at this man for enjoying himself while his own life was devastated. He had violent thoughts of bashing the man's head with a baseball bat while yelling, "What's funny now, asshole?"

He wanted to smash the laughing man's skull and felt like he could do it too.

Then he realized that he had detested violence his entire life. He even hated killing bugs and would go to the trouble of capturing spiders in a container and tossing them outside instead of killing them. Furthermore, he never had violent thoughts.

He tried to sleep, now focusing on how much he hated being rejected by women throughout his life, and if he had another chance he would force himself upon them violently and have his way with them . . . like girls from his younger days that rejected him, right up to the dark haired bitch that got him so excited while he was drugged and ran out after she got him to contacted Tony.

Goddamn her! What was her name? oh yeah, Teresa. That Bitch!

He could picture her seductive brown eyes and her glossy black hair against her smooth light skin. His genitals tingled, and he involuntarily put his hand in his pants. He gripped himself and found he was almost fully erect. He imagined how he would rip her clothes off and force himself in her, and in this fantasy she actually likes it, despite his vicious manner.

For a moment he stopped stroking and looked over to the table next to his bed, hoping to see a towel or at least a napkin. He didn't, only a cup of water.

Fuck it. These ain't my sheets, he thought and continued to fantasize.

He was enjoying a brief time of pleasure in an awful situation until his concentration was suddenly interrupted when he heard a sound at the door. He quickly and instinctively took his hand out, laid it to his side, and pretended to be asleep . . . like a teenage boy almost being caught playing with himself by a parent.

The door finally opened, not abruptly but slowly as if the person was being clandestine. A person entered and closed the door quietly. Lou felt the person looking at him in the moment of silence. He wanted to open his eyes but dared not. He only lifted one eyelid ever so slightly. With blurred vision, he saw a slender figure that walked over to the office door. The person tapped with a fingernail three times on the door's window.

Moments later the door buzzed. The person opened it and entered the office. The buzzer woke up the black man who sat up and looked toward the office. Lou looked too and saw that the doctor sitting behind his desk was smiling and talking to the person who entered. It was a female. He could tell by the body and long dark hair. She was wearing blue slacks and a black blouse. She was carrying a clipboard, and when she reached the front of the desk, she dropped it in front of the doctor. He continued to look at her talking, and then he smiled widely. Finally, he looked down at the clipboard.

In that moment the woman swiftly reached into her back pocket, pulled something out, and pointed it at the doctor. An electric bolt brightened the room and made contact with the doctor's head. His body jolted, and he let out a yell that could be slightly heard by Lou. Then his head fell forward onto the desk, now motionless.

"What the hell be going on in there?" the black guy said and swung his feet off the bed. Lou glanced at him with a surprised look but didn't speak. When he looked back to the office the woman already opened the door. She left it ajar and was walking swiftly to him.

"Louis," she called.

"Yes," he answered.

"I'm going to get you out of here if I can. They're going to kill you if I don't."

Stunned, Lou just stared at her with his mouth open. It was Teresa!

"Wow, this is amazing. I was just thinking about you," he finally said.

"I'm sure it wasn't good after what I did to you. I felt awful about it. That's partly why I'm risking my life to get you out of here. Come on, we have to move quick." She looked around on the ground for his shoes. Lou buttoned his pants and swung his feet off the bed. She grabbed his shoes and plopped them by his feet.

"I'm coming too, man," the black guy said and got up.

Teresa pulled the bolt blaster out of her pocket and aimed it at him.

Lou could tell she intended to fire without hesitation. She was graceful under pressure. Her eyes were intense but cool. She obviously had police training. Lou thought she probably was a star student too.

"Hold up," Lou said, standing abruptly. He teetered a little, feeling weak and light headed. Teresa glanced at him, wondering why she should hold up.

Lou wondered himself. His whole life he tried to fight injustice and violence. Even as a youngster he was the one who always jumped between young antagonists and tried to break up every fight while every other kid was trying to encourage it. It was a thankless job too. When he did prevent fights, all the other kids were upset they didn't get to see two kids try to bludgeon each other, and of course, the would-be fighters never thanked him because that would appear weak. But sometimes he could read a look in their eyes that said, *Thanks, dude. I really didn't want to fight.* Although their words said, "I would have kicked his ass if you didn't get in the way."

"Listen, buddy," he said to the black man, "you don't need to get zapped. It hurts man."

"Come on, man. Please let me get out of here," the black man pleaded.

"We don't know if you're a violent person. If you get out and start murdering people, it will be our fault." Lou explained.

"No, man, I swear to God. I'm here cause I was growing dope out on my balcony. They caught me selling it. I swear I ain't no killer. I get beat up by the guards all the time. They say cause I'm slacking, but I hate working on that damn assembly line. Man, my brain get tired doing that same old stuff all day, Come on man, please."

The typical Louis Rizzo response was to show compassion, but in that moment he realized something was missing. He responded the way he did in life because he cares about the well being of others, without prejudice. He was a bonafide altruist. But it was not there now. He realized he didn't care if she shocked this guy. In fact, he wanted her to do it. Three is a crowd, and he wanted to be alone with her.

"Just sit back down on your bed," he said, "I swear to God we'll leave the door open for you. I'll stick the pillow between the door and the jam so it doesn't shut." The black man sat back down without hesitation, which made Lou respect his intelligence.

"You have to swear that you'll wait a couple of minutes for us to get out before you go, alright? And be smart about it," Lou instructed. "That Doctor is out cold in the office, and the door is open. Maybe he's got something useful. Maybe you can fit in his clothes so you look less conspicuous. "Lou put his foot up on the bed and tied his shoe, then the other. He tucked his hospital gown into his pants.

"Man, you all better leave that door open," the black guy said.

"We will; just give us time to get out first. If you come creeping up behind us, she's gonna zap you."

The black guy nodded.

"My name's Lou Rizzo. If you get out, talk about me. Spread my name. I'm starting a revolution, and you're in it, okay, my man?"

Again the man nodded, looking mystified.

"What's your name?" Lou asked.

"Jamaal Brown," he answered.

Lou turned to Teresa and shrugged. "I trust him. Let's go. Show me the way to freedom." He grabbed a pillow and walked toward the door.

She took a few steeps and turned back to Jamaal.

"Listen," she said to him, "after you wait for us to clear the building, creep down to the end of the hallway and on the left is the elevator area. Make sure no one is around. Go past the elevators, and the door on the left is the stairway. Go down three levels to the lobby and sneak out the emergency exit door. The handle says *alarm will sound if opened*, but it won't cause it's been disengaged. Just wait here a few minutes, or you'll blow it for all of us. Got it?"

She could hardly believe she was going to leave this man

conscious. She was a split second away from blasting him before Lou spoke up. Now she was giving him the escape route. This was only the second time she ever witnessed an act of sympathy by a man. The first happened earlier that very night, and it helped convinc her to sacrifice her comfortable lifestyle for Louis Rizzo. She knew he would be killed, and she knew it was unjustifiable. She knew of Lou's political history and understood he could be the last activist in a country of numb conformists. In addition, she didn't want to admit it, but the way he looked at her earlier made her feel exalted and desirable. He had run after her and screamed her name at the top of his lungs and it affected her deeply.

"Yeah, momma, thank you. You a good lady, and you a good man too, Lou Rezzo," he said, smiling and nodding.

"Rizzo," Lou corrected.

Teresa got her keyphone out of her front pocket and slid it through the scanner. As she opened the door, Lou looked up at the security camera.

"They can see everything we're doing," he told her.

"The surveillance man is out cold," she whispered. "As long as no one goes in the surveillance room in the next few minutes, we're fine." Holding the door partly open, she looked down the hallway. "Stay close," she said and started off.

Lou set the pillow down to keep the door open and followed closely. They crept down to the end of the hallway. Lou kept looking back to make sure Jamaal didn't run after them. The elevator area was clear so they set out to the stairway door. Just then the elevator light went on, and they could hear it arriving at their floor. Lou froze, wondering if they should run forward or back.

Teresa grabbed his wrist and ran forward. She opened the stairway door and pulled him through. Then she held the door from slamming and shut it quietly just as the elevator opened.

Two guards flew out of the elevator and ran down the hall with bolt blasters in hand. Luckily, they didn't look toward the stairway door where they would have seen Teresa's head through the window.

"Oh God, they found the surveillance guy. Hurry up." She started running down the stairs.

Adrenalin allowed Lou to keep up with her, jumping down three steps at a time and thinking, *Poor Jamaal will be back on the assembly line tomorrow.* Two flights down Lou heard a door open from above and the sound of boots quickly running down the stairs.

As they reached main floor, they heard someone yell, "They're in the stairway!"

On the main floor, Teresa slowed slightly to check her pockets. She pulled out some keys. "We have to try to make it to my car." Without even checking if the coast was clear, she flung open the stairway door.

They ran out and only ten feet away was the emergency exit. She pushed it open, and the alarm didn't go off. They were outside running through the parking lot, Lou trying his best to keep up.

"Here it is! jump in!" she yelled as they got to a small, grey, gas-electric hybrid car.

"Freeze, or I'll shoot!" a voice shouted from across the parking lot just as Lou was opening the door.

He looked back to see a cop standing outside the emergency exit door with a bolt blaster aimed at him. He heard the man fire and an electric bolt flashed out toward him. Luckily, he was already in the process of lowering himself into the car so it missed high. He could hear the crackle of electricity pass over his head.

Teresa started the quiet engine and drove off immediately.

"I'm sorry they found out so quickly. We're never going to be able to outrun them in this thing. Do you want to try or just surrender?"

"You risked everything and got us this far," replied Lou. "Now punch it!"

She tore out of the lot and into the dark street. Lou turned back to look out the rear window and saw the police lights turn on. He lowered his side window and looked at the side of the road. The road had a narrow, gravel shoulder then dropped off into a drainage ravine. Beyond the ravine was a forest.

"Turn you lights off," he said.

"What? It's completely dark on this road," she said sounding frantic. "I can't turn them off anyway because they go on automatically."

"Put it in neutral, and turn the car off. Hurry!" he demanded. Looking back, he saw the cop car was just about to pull out of the parking lot and onto the road behind them. She seemed reluctant. "Do it now!" he yelled.

She popped the car in neutral and shut off the engine. Now they were coasting down the road in complete darkness.

"Now ease off to the right side of the road and into the ravine, and please try not to flip us. What ever you do, don't hit the breaks, or they'll see the break lights. Just coast to a stop."

She looked over to him with an expression of terror. Then she exhaled deeply and began coasting toward the ravine.

The police car was rapidly accelerating now that it was on Pulaski Avenue.

Teresa was getting over too slowly, apprehensive about entering the drop off.

"Get down there now!" Lou yelled.

She gasped and hit the slope. The car tilted severely to a forty degree angle as they entered the ravine, and she shrieked. It felt as if they were about to flip just before the right side tires hit the bottom and she was able to level out the car. They were still coasting at thirty miles per hour, and the car shook violently, riding over the rough terrain. They began to slow down and the shaking diminished.

"Hopefully, they think we turned at the next intersection," Lou said quietly.

The cop car was approaching. They could hear the engine racing at full acceleration and shift into overdrive. Lou held his breath and hoped for luck hard enough to give him a head rush. The car raced past them so fast they felt the wind pass over the ravine.

Lou reached up to the dome light and smashed the plastic cover a few times until it broke loose. Then he took out the light bulb so it would not shine when they opened the door.

"We have to go on foot now," he said, putting his hand on her arm. "If they don't locate the car for awhile, we may get a big enough head start to find somewhere to hide."

She was trembling as she nodded.

"Come on, we got to move fast. They may be turning around already." He opened his door. "Don't forget your bolt blaster," he said as he climbed out.

He waited for her at the front of the car and grabbed her hand once she arrived. They hit the incline running, Lou pulling her as he aggressively climbed. When they made it to the top, they scurried into the forest preserve.

Noticing how good her soft hand felt in his made terror momentarily take a back seat to desire. They trudged through the forest at a quick pace until Lou stumbled over a fallen branch. Visibility was nearly nonexistent in the forest on this cloudy moonless night. Lou was leading the way with his right hand waving in front of him defensively.

"This forest preserve can't be very wide," whispered Lou. "I think this is La Bagh woods. Once we get through to the other side, we'll find somewhere to hide. It's all abandoned areas."

"I heard it's extremely dangerous out there," she said. "They say the scavies will cut your throat just to take the clothes off your back."

"That's why I reminded you to grab your bolt blaster."

Minutes passed as they made their way through the woods not speaking except for Lou occasionally saying, "Watch it," or "stay low," as they dodged limbs and fallen branches.

"I think we're almost through. The trees are thinning out a little,"

Just as he said that, they heard a helicopter in the distance.

As they made it to the end of the forest the sound was growing closer. They looked out at Cicero Avenue, still under cover of the trees.

"They probably found the car so they'll be searching the woods any minute." He tried to determine if they should make a break now or wait for the helicopter to pass. "Come on, we'll walk along the edge of the woods until the helicopter passes. At least we'll know where it is before we run out and leave ourselves exposed." They only made it twenty yards before the helicopter was over them, confirming he made the right decision. The search light scanned the street in front of them and then moved up to the edge of the forest. Lou hid behind a tree and pulled Teresa right in front of him so they were both out of sight. As the light shined right on the tree they were behind, he held her tightly, pulling her firmly against his body.

He felt more vivacious in that moment than ever in his life as fright-induced adrenalin mixed with sexual desire. When the light passed, Lou reluctantly released her and peered out. The helicopter had passed and was still heading away from them.

He was contemplating his next move when his ears picked up the sound of racing car engines from the north. Instantly, he made the decision to move. Pulling Teresa by the hand, they sprinted toward the road.

Lou had not felt the adrenalin charge and excitement like this since he was a teenager running from the cops after he and some other rebellious friends had just thrown potatoes at a cop car.

They darted across the street. On the other side was an old abandoned high school. They were now running through the large parking lot.

They were still fifty feet away, and they were completely exposed, sprinting through the parking lot toward the building.

The dilapidated school looked haunted and foreboding, yet they desperately needed to reach it.

The air thumping sound of the helicopter blades softly returned. With each ungainly stride, the sound grew louder. The helicopter was coming right over the school. It was not yet in sight, but Lou knew it was going to be a photo finish whether they could get to cover before it spotted them.

"Come on! Fast as you can!" he cried, dropped her hand and went in to a sprint. For the final ten yards, the spotlight was on the ground illuminating the area they had occupied just two seconds ago. Just as he stepped under the cover of the school's side entrance veranda, the helicopter was right overhead. Lou turned and caught Teresa by the arm just as she got under. He scurried to the back corner, pulling her up against him and pushing his back against the brick as if they could sink into the wall. The spotlight moved about, coming a few feet under the overhang nearly exposing them.

After it moved on, he released her and ventured out a few steps to check if any cars were coming.

"Listen...I'm deeply moved that you broke me out. I mean, knowing that you gave up your career and risked everything for me, it's just beyond words to express my gratitude." He took a deep breath feeling awkward about what he was about to ask. "Now that we're both fugitives, I was wondering if you'd stay with me. You know...if we manage to get away." She just stared so he shyly prattled on. "I mean if you're not planning on going your own way, or whatever."

At that moment only her response mattered to him and the way she silently gazed at him with her soft brown eyes made him ripe with anticipation.

Finally, she moved forward and stood right up against him. "I was planning on staying with you from the start," she whispered and put her hands on the sides of his slim waist, "so if you're planning on leaving me behind, you'll have to run off on me when I'm sleeping." She was looking up at his face, her stunningly submissive brown eyes gazing in a way he would never forget. The danger surrounding them was lost in her gaze. He put his arms around her and felt her body heat rise, as did his sprit.

Chapter 15

Agent Joe Gerbuls was sipping his martini at the bar, listening to the attractive, young, blond haired woman next to him try to explain why she hated having to go through the Park Ridge checkpoint every night when she went home.

"Those filthy guards undressing me with their eyes . . . one of them had the nerve to ask me out once," she explained.

They were at the popular lounge Park West on the north side of Service City, Chicago. It was the part of town where the upper class hung out. The city powered a few blocks of lounges, restaurants, fancy shops, and the American Airways television station was located there.

She was boring him to death. He hated how prudish she was, but he knew he had a chance to get her into bed. She seemed impressed that he was a government secret agent man. He even showed her his badge to prove it.

As she continued to bore him, he looked closer at a man at the end of the bar who was talking to two elegantly dressed women. Gerbuls realized he knew this man; it was the TV reporter who interviewed him earlier, Keith Colman.

Suddenly, Keith stood up and called to the bartender. "Hey Henry, turn it up! My story's coming on!" he yelled.

Gerbuls turned his attention to the TV when the bartender turned it louder.

A fat unlikely looking reporter was standing in front of a crowd of people. *"We're here at the north side gate station where a group of protesters have gathered. Sir, can you tell us why you're protesting?"* the fat man asked.

"What the fuck is this!" Keith yelled. "What the fuck is he doing on TV?"

"We're here to demand that elections be restored," a

middle aged protester answered. *"The working class will not give up the right to vote and surrender to a dictatorship. We have a candidate qualified to run for president. His name is Louis Rizzo. He was apprehended last night for giving a speech, and we want him released."*

Gerbuls was stunned. His entire mood changed. He knew this must be a mistake. He stood with his hands behind his head, breathing deeply untill Frankie signed off.

"From S.C., Chicago's north side, this is Frank Muso reporting."

Seeing that report set off Keith Colman in a tirade. "I'm gonna kill that Timmy!" he yelled. "How could that son of a bitch do this to me? He's dead. He's fuckin' dead." He buried his head in his hands and dropped it on to the bar, making a knock. "Jesus Christ, I'm fuckin' through. What am I gonna tell Mr. Daily?" he muttered through his hands.

Then, realizing his own voice was on the TV, he couldn't help but to look up and watch.

"Now that's a good looking news reporter," he said. "They wouldn't fire me. I'm too damn good."

Realizing that wasn't true, he dropped his head back into his hands and plopped it on the bar again. "Oh God, I'm gonna get all the blame for this. Oh God, Oh God, Oh God."

It sounded like he was crying. The glamorous women walked away from him.

Gerbuls knew there would be consequences for that ill-mannered act by the news network, but he saw no way he could share any blame. He wasn't involved with news monitoring. He still had every intention to get this blond in bed, but he wanted to speak with Colman.

"Hey, let's talk to this guy for a minute, come on," said Gerbuls, involving her so she didn't take offense.

They walked over to Keith who was just picking his head off the bar. His watery eyes searched for his scotch and soda. He grabbed it off the bar and gulped it down.

"Another drink, Henry!" he yelled to the bartender, then noticed Gerbuls walking up. "Hey, I know you. You were the last interview of my career," he said in despair.

"How the hell did this happen?" Gerbuls asked, "you're the only one who could have authorized that to be shown, right?"

"I have my cameraman do stuff for me. He has my authority to authorize, but he went fuckin' nuts. I didn't tell him to show that. My orders was just to interview you guys. He fucked me big time. I never thought he would do anything like this."

Just then, Gerbuls' keyphone vibrated in his front pocket. He held his hand up to Keith. "Hold on, I got a call. It's probably about this." He took out his keyphone, "Gerbuls," he answered.

Keith saw the color wash off the man's face as he stood there silently with the phone pressed to his ear. His mouth dropped, and he remained silent for a moment. "Yes, I'm still here," he finally said calmly. "If you're fuckin' with me, Parrish, end it now. It's not funny." Silence again. Color returned to his face, but now it was red and his expression was fury.

"No, no, no, not me. *You're* gonna call the chief and tell him what happened. You got the details. I'm going down to the station and kick some ass. How the hell could this guy escape? I'll tell you what; he must have had inside help. I'm gonna tear that big Zipp head a new asshole." He ended the call, returned his keyphone to his pocket, turned and trotted off, never even looking back to Keith or the blond.

After they watched Gerbuls leave the bar, they looked at each other.

"Can I get you a drink?" Keith said to her.

Chapter 16

L ou was utterly determined to escape. Yes, he still
wanted to save the country after the British rocket
attack, but he always wanted to be with a woman that truly
inspired him, and by all early indications, Teresa was that woman.
His brain, in the heat of the moment, acted with acute acumen.

He released her and went to the school door, despite
knowing it would be locked. The door had to be opened from the
inside. He looked over to the left side glass wall panels. There
were four, five-by-five foot glass panels that made up the eight
foot wall on each side of the door.

Near the corner they were hiding in, the upper glass panel
was cracked, but the glass remained intact. Just as he moved
toward it, he caught headlights in his peripheral vision. Not even
bothering to turn and judge how far away the cop car was, he
positioned himself in front of the window, took two steps and
gave it a leaping side kick driving his leg through the target. It
was a karate move he had not performed in decades. A piece of
the window fell out and broke inside the school's hall as he fell to
the concrete. Perhaps it was adrenalin or the pill the doctor gave
him, but he was feeling no pain.

"Wait by the door," he commanded and knocked out the
remaining piece of glass with his elbow.

"Oh my god, they're coming this way," Teresa cried.

Not wasting a moment to look back, he put his hands
on the window ledge and jumped. Straining, he got his torso up
on the ledge. Pushing himself through the window, he fell to
the floor, tucking his head at impact and rolling off his shoulder
blade.

A shard of glass remained in the frame where the palm of
his left hand pushed off, but he saved himself head injury. Sitting
up immediately, he looked at his palm.

"Aw shit," he yelped. The glass shard was still stuck in it. He grabbed it with the other hand and yanked it out with a grimace. The bump on his forehead began to throb with his heartbeat. He made a fist with his bloody left hand, got up at once, ran to the door, and pushed the bar.

Teresa popped in looking terrified.

"Hurry," his voice cracked as he yelled and dashed off.

Looking back as they ran, he saw the police car speeding through the parking lot right toward the entrance. The car screeched to a stop.

Flashlights shined into the building just as they turned the corner.

Lou's fist was damp with blood. He looked into class rooms as they ran past.

He suddenly stopped halfway down the hall, and drops of blood spattered to the floor. Outside the window of the class-room, he saw foliage.

"Here," he said and entered the classroom. He ran to a window and grabbed the handle, turned it and pushed. The windows were set on an eight inch wide ledge along the exterior brick wall. The bottom pushed out about a foot and a half. The top hinged out, so it was definitely going to be a tight squeeze. "Quick, climb on the ledge and slide out the window. When you fall to the ground, stay down."

She lay out on the ledge, put her head through the window, and began to slither out.

They heard Glass shatter in the distance. Cops were entering the building.

"Hurry," he whispered. He put his knee on the ledge and held her legs, helping to slide them through the opening. She plopped to the ground, and Lou began to go through. His shoulder scraped hard on the narrow top, but once he forced it through, he quickly slithered to the ground. Popping back up immediately, he pushed the window closed, doing it gradually so it didn't squeak. He squatted back down and pointed to the evergreen bushes about eight feet down from them. They both crawled toward them. Lou was watching her buttocks as she went, nearly salivating. They got between the wall of the school and a row of thick evergreens.

"I can't stop shaking. Can we hide here awhile and rest," she whispered.

"No, they're searching the school now, and it won't be long till they find us here." He looked down to his hand and opened it, "I left a trail of blood."

She saw the bloody hand and gasped. Grabbing his wrist and pulling it toward her face, she inspected it. She pulled the bottom of his hospital gown out of his pants and lifted it to her mouth. With a bite and a pull she ripped a hole in it and ripped off a strip. He held his hand out while she tightly bandaged it and tied a knot.

"Thank you," he whispered.

He poked his head out from behind the bush and surveyed the surroundings. Suddenly the cops turned their flashlights into the classroom they just came out of. Lou pulled his head back in. The window creaked as it opened.

"Look, this is a fresh blood smeared on the ledge here," a cop said, "They climbed out this window."

"Damn, they must be skinny," the other cop remarked.

Neither cop could have fit out the window so they shined their flashlights on the ground outside.

Lou motioned to Teresa to move to the other end of the row of bushes. He squeezed by her and popped his head out.

Suddenly the window shattered, making them both flinch. The cops cleared out the panel with their Billy clubs.

"Follow me," Lou commanded and scurried off, staying between the school's wall and the row of bushes. They hurried to the corner.

He looked behind them and saw a cop jump out of the broken window and stumble clumsily into the bushes. They turned the corner and ran along the east wall, the cops now in pursuit. He peaked around the corner. Right in front of the side entrance veranda the police car was still running with the lights on. It appeared to be empty.

"Bet they don't expect us to circle back and steal their car. Come on!"

He darted toward the car. Teresa followed like a track

sprinter. He ran around the back of the car, opened the driver's side door and climbed in. Once Teresa jumped in, he floored it in reverse, all the way through the parking lot before stopping and shifting to drive. He gunned it again when they reached the street, hitting eighty miles per hour in seconds. They flew past Foster Avenue, and the cop lights in the distance appeared in the rear view mirror. Every intersection was dark, no street lights or traffic lights. Power had been completely shut off in the abandoned areas for years.

"I don't feel safe in this car, Louis," Teresa said. She was pale white as Lou sped dangerously fast.

"We're not safe," replied Lou. "Once those cops radio in about us swiping their car, they'll use the G.P.S. system and know exactly where we are."

That made Lou think about something. *How'd they know we were at that school so fast? We could have come out of those woods anywhere.*

"Do you have your keyphone on you?" he asked.

"Yes," she answered, feeling her thigh over her front pocket to verify.

"They're tracking us with your keyphone. Toss it out the window."

"No, my keyphone is turned off." She pulled it out to make sure it was off. "I know for a fact they can't trace it when it's off. I've been involved in surveillance activities trust me," she assured him.

"Your bolt blaster is government issued, right? It must be because they outlawed all private gun ownership." She didn't speak since he answered his own question. "They may have a tracking device in your bolt blaster. They stay charged for two years, right? So it's always on. That's why they knew where we were so fast."

He whipped a right turn at Irving Park Avenue. She had her eyes closed tightly and was holding her breath.

"Oh God," she shrieked, "we're gonna be defenseless without it. Should I toss it out the window?"

"No, they can track the car anyways. I got an idea. Rip off another strip of my gown."

She immediately did without question as he took turns indiscriminately at high speeds to avoid pursuit. Just as she finished ripping off the strip, Lou stopped in the dead center of the street, in front of some run-down abandoned apartment buildings, and put the car in park.

"Run in that building and hide the bolt blaster somewhere."

He opened his door and kneeled on the street, still leaning his top half in the car and began to tie one end of the strip to the bottom of the steering wheel.

"I'm not going in that building alone," she cried.

"I'll be right here. If you see someone, just run back out to me. Please hurry." She summoned the courage needed, opened the door and ran off.

Lou tied the other end around the seat adjuster control stick directly under it and made it tight. He tested if he could turn the steering wheel and was satisfied that the strip would hold it steady. In the front yard he saw large rocks on the ground all laid in a row in front of the evergreens that lined the front of the run-down apartment building. He ran over and picked up a rock with both hands. While he was lumbering back to the car, Teresa darted out of the building.

"Come over on my side and stay back," he told her. He squatted down and placed the rock on the driver's side floor. With his left hand, he held down the break while shifting the car into drive with his right. Then with his right, he slid the rock up to the gas pedal. Holding it above, he readied himself. Common sense told him this had to be done fast. He let it fall onto the accelerator and fell backwards as fast as he could.

The car raced straight down the street. Lou watched it go down the middle of the road with pride.

"Come on," he said and grabbed her hand. He led her to a nearby building on the other side of the street.

As they ran up to the entrance, he suddenly veered to the side, reached under the evergreens, and grabbed a baseball sized rock in his hand. This would be his defense if there happened to be a scavie with a violent personality in the building. They ran to the door and entered the dusty hallway as a cop car sped by.

They ran to the stairway, and he led her up to the third floor of the six-unit apartment building. Every door was unlatched because they had all been kicked in. Lou entered the front unit cautiously. The building was dark, but their eyes were adjusted. They moved slowly through the clutter toward the front wall windows. The place had been deserted long ago, but junk still littered the room. He knelt below the windows and pulled her arm down toward him. She knelt down, and he put an arm over her shoulders as they leaned against the wall.

"Shouldn't we be running as far away from here as we can?" she whispered.

"That's what they'll think we did. They'll find the car wherever it crashes down the road and the bolt blaster across the street, and hopefully they'll never suspect we would be right here watching them bust into the building across the street. If they don't go into that building, we'll know the bolt blaster is safe and we can get it tomorrow."

"And what if they find it and start searching every building on the block, including this one?" she asked.

"Then we hide and hope for the best," he said and rubbed her back. "Now, you gotta tell me how you managed to get me out all by yourself. That was amazing."

"Actually, I had some help. In fact, Ed basically planned it all out. I just had to execute," she said seeming humble.

"What?" Lou blurted. "Who's Ed?"

"Edward Zipp . . . he's a gate Captain. You must know him. He said you showed him world news headlines. He said that was evidence that we're being lied to, and that you're right to challenge the government."

He shook his head and blew through his lips.

"Captain Zipp . . . well, I'll be damned. Is he gonna get caught for this?"

"I don't know, but he'll catch hell for an inmate escaping at out station."

"So how did it all work?"

"I approached Ed and asked if I could speak to him alone. I told him how awful I felt about what they made me do to you and how much I hated those government agents. Ed agreed and said they were pompous bastards, and they didn't need to use that neurotoxin on you. He told me about what you said and what he saw on your computer, and we both agreed that you're a good man for opposing the government. Ed said they would, no doubt, dispose of you before too many people heard your message. It seemed so sad that your life would end like this. He said it would be a terrible day for America if the last independent was killed. I told him I wished I could get you out of here, and if I could I would." She took a breath and shook her head. "I thought he might suspend me till you were gone, but Edward must like you because he agreed."

Lou was amazed and had to fight back tears thinking about old Zipp head.

"He told me to come back at midnight in uniform. When I did, he had it all planned out. He disengaged the emergency exit alarm and told me to shock the surveillance guy. Then go up to the medical ward, shock the night physician, and get you out. But since they will identify me as soon as they wake up, I would be a fugitive and have to live with that for the rest of my life. But hopefully, no one would ever figure out he was involved." She sighed, "I guess it didn't go quite as planned, but we haven't been caught yet." She forced a smile.

"Well, that Zipp is alright," said Lou. "I never would have guessed he-"

The sound of cars racing up the street made him go silent. He turned to the window and raised his head to see. Two cop cars stopped out front. His stomach tightened. Just as he predicted, they got out of the cars, pulled out their bolt blasters and rushed into the building across the street. Teresa peeked out to see.

"You were right," she said, "They were tracking us. Thank God you're a smart man."

The comment made him feel good, but he began to worry that their current place of hiding might not be the right idea. Two more police cars pulled up, making it eight cops on the scene now.

Teresa grew uneasy too, feeling vulnerable being this close. "God, they're out in full force looking for us. You sure they won't check this building?" she asked.

"They'll figure out that we purposely left your bolt blaster in that building because we knew they were tracking us, and they'll instinctively assume we're trying to get as far away from here as we can. I think we're safe for now . . . unless they have a really smart cop in charge who thinks outside the box." They looked at each other wide-eyed. "Stay here and keep an eye out. I'm gonna look for a hiding place."

Lou was not unfamiliar with this style of three flat apartment building. He spent many years of his life living in apartments, moving from one to another each time the rent was raised.

He wasn't looking for a place to hide, a closet would be the only place, and they always check them first, but more of an object to hide with. He walked to the bathroom first. The darkness was almost total, but his eyes were sharp. He could see there were holes punched into the drywall in front of him and pieces of broken mirror in the sink and toilet. The back wall had its drywall totally ripped out.

He decided to pee in the sink and kicked a broken sheet of drywall on the ground as he relieved himself. When he finished, he picked up the large piece of drywall and placed it in the bathtub, one side in the tub and the top resting against the wall. He climbed up on the tub ledge, lifted up the side of the drywall and got under it. It was a possible hiding spot that might work. It would be tight with two people, but Lou certainly didn't mind that.

He reached into the sink, being careful not to cut his hand on broken glass, and grabbed a handful of dark soot-like substance his pee had moistened. He started throwing debris on top of the broken drywall he had placed in the tub. After the third time reaching into the sink, he had a handful of damp and slimy material that had a strong mildew and urine aroma. He took a few scoops, placing it higher up on the drywall and patted it down. Then he wiped his hands over the top edge of it and finished wiping them on his pants. He wished dearly for a jar of hand sanitizer at that moment. He sprinkled drywall dust and fragments from the floor onto the mucky substance which stuck to it. This would hopefully give the appearance that it had been lying there for some time and not recently disturbed.

He maneuvered back to her as a helicopter passed over the building, then moving away, urgently searching in another direction.

"You wanna use the toilet?" he whispered. "We may have to stay in a tight space for awhile so maybe you better go now. I'll keep watch."

"Oh God, what's that horrible smell?" she said, wrinkling her nose.

"Sorry, my dear, but we're gonna have to deal with that for awhile."

She looked to be on the verge of tears.

"Don't worry, I'll find us somewhere nice to live someday, but it may be tough for a while." He smiled and helped her up. "The bathroom's over there." He pointed. "You better hurry up."

With her hand held out in front of her like she was blindfolded, she found her way to the bathroom, quickly unbuttoned, and hovered her rump a few inches over the toilet.

Lou turned his attention back to the street, cautiously peaking out through the window. It appeared as if the cops were just given orders and springing into action now. Blood rushed to his head when he saw two cops barge into the apartment building next door to the one where they planted the Bolt blaster.

Oh shit, how could I be so fuckin' stupid!

They were pairing up, and each group was taking a different building.

Suddenly a creak from three floors down rang out. Someone opened the main entrance door!

His heart pumping hard, he sprang up and moved swiftly to the bathroom.

Teresa was still in mid stream when Lou popped in. She gasped.

He put his finger to his mouth, shushing her, and then he turned to the tub.

She finished with added force. He gave her only a fleeting moment to pull up her pants before he turned back to her.

"They're in the building," he whispered and motioned for her to come toward the tub. He pulled the broken drywall sheet away from the wall.

"Get under there fast, and be extremely quiet."

She looked completely befuddled and wasn't immediately sure where he wanted her to go.

Surely not behind that filthy sheet of drywall into that nasty tub.

Bang!

They both jumped, gasping in unison. It was the sound of a door being flung open and striking the wall in a room beneath them.

"Hurry up and make room for me." Holding out the drywall with his right hand, he used his left to grab her under the arm and help her balance as she stepped onto the tub wall and then into the tub behind the drywall. She squatted down into the tub and tried to lie down. Lou got up on the tub wall and put his right foot into the tub, almost stepping on her. He managed to kneel with one knee between her legs and one outside her left leg. He lowered himself slowly while resting the drywall back against the wall. He was right on top of her now. He shifted onto his hip so he wouldn't be crushing her, shaking the drywall in the process. They were cheek to cheek. Her ear was touching his lips and vice versa.

"We have to be silent," he whispered ever so quietly.

He realized how sexually aroused he would have been if he weren't so frightened and so painfully uncomfortable. His legs were bent backwards, and his bad knee was chastising him for putting it in this position.

They were as silent as possible, and now they could hear cops walking around in the building . . . then voices, only murmurs of two men. They were coming from the second floor. Their footsteps ascending the staircase was terrifying. Soon one of them entered the apartment and began walking around the living room. Lou heard the closet door squeak. The footsteps stopped for a lengthy moment.

Yeah, that bastard is sure checking every inch of that closet, he thought.

Footsteps moved again. He was sure they would be heading to the bathroom now, but he was wrong. They went to the bedrooms first.

The cop took some time looking around the bedroom. Lou found himself becoming less nervous and more impatient. Every minute he had to stay scrunched up like this was increasing agony, and he was sure Teresa was uncomfortable as well.

Minutes later, the footsteps approached, coming to search the bathroom last.

They could hear the man standing by the doorway, breathing while he shined his flashlight around the bathroom. He walked in and began inspecting every inch. Lou and Teresa sensed he was looking right at the tub now. Light crept over the back corner of the drywall. The small hiding place they occupied brightened when the light passed on to the front of the drywall near their heads. They could hear the fingers fall onto the top of the drywall, grabbing it.

Damn, we're busted. He decided then to surrender rather that fight and risk death. *Not with Teresa here, just surrender.*

The hand reached over the edge, squeezed and pulled back the drywall a few inches. Suddenly, the hand released it, and the drywall fell back against the wall.

"Ewww," the cop grunted. They could hear him rub his fingers together.

He had placed his thumb in some of the urine soot Lou had smeared on it.

The cop raised his hand near his nose and took a whiff. "That's fuckin' disgusting," he said to himself.

Sudden anger arose in the cop. He stepped back and kicked the sheet of drywall hard.

Teresa let out a quiet, involuntary gasp the same time the drywall sheet cracked.

Fortunately, it did not fall backwards and expose them; it sagged forward, resting lower against the wall and on Lou's shoulder. They didn't move an inch. Now the cop kicked the side of the sink. They could hear it coming away from its wall mounts, drywall ripping and the old water pipe pulling. Again, the cop gave it a forward kick, pushing through with the bottom of his boot. The sink fell away from the wall, hitting the floor with a great thundering crash.

"Hey, you got something!" the cop from across the hall

yelled and ran over to his apartment.

The angry cop walked out of the bathroom to greet the other. "Yeah, I got something . . . nasty smelling shit on my hand. Can I wipe it off on your jacket?"

"What's with the racket? You see something?" said the other cop.

"Naw, I'm just kicking shit around. This sucks. I already put in a full day, and they want me to do a double shift for this shit . . . looking around nasty old buildings for some idiots that must be miles away by now."

"Hey man, you better change your attitude. We got more to do on this block, and I don't want to be hearing you whining like a little bitch for the next hour. You done in here?"

"Yeah," angry cop answered.

Their boots made a loud racket as they descended the stairway. To Lou it was like the sound of a victory ovation. The feeling of relief was like warm water washing over his tense body.

Once they heard the entrance door swing open and shut, Lou pushed the broken drywall sheet off of them. He stood trying not to lean on her too much, and then he reached his hand down and helped her to her feet.

"That was a close call," he whispered.

"What now?" she said, not looking much relieved.

The triumphant relief of evading the cops faded from the forefront of his mind in an instant as this new dilemma gained supremacy.

What now? That's a damn good question. What do I tell her? I don't know myself. Okay, just start with the basics.

"Well, first thing is our basic needs: food and water. Finding shelter is easy enough. There's tons of abandoned buildings and houses, just no running water or electric. I'd like to stay local and be near Rosemont because something is going to happen."

He kept the British militia a secret.

She lowered her eyebrows, looking away from him. He knew what she was thinking and could empathize with her uncertainty.

He was wrong, however; she was thinking about how she envisioned their lives to be before she even broke him out. She dreamed they would run off to the country and find a nice abandoned house on a lake. He would hunt for meat, and they would grow fresh vegetables in the summer and store food for the winter. She would make their home cozy and learn to cook over a fire. They would live off the land like the early settlers and be content, existing every day to be with each other for as long as fate allowed.

Now, she realized that was a fairytale. She felt she had made a big mistake running away with this man. He was a man with a mission, not a romantic that wants to spend his life with her. She felt childishly naïve. Her body trembled, and she had to fight back tears because she suddenly felt embarrassed to be there with him.

"Don't worry, we're gonna be fine. We'll stay here till dawn. Then we'll find water and decide what to do next." He was trying to sound wise and confident.

"We don't even have a weapon," she said as they got out of the tub and went back under the windows in the living room.

"The Doctor never needed a weapon," he said.

"Who?" she asked, once they sat down.

"Yes, Who, Doctor Who . . . it was an old, British, science fiction TV show. I have some of the DVDs. The Doctor never carried a weapon, and he had to face many evil savages and aliens. He used his intellect to survive."

Lou laid flat on his back on the dirty carpeted floor, and Teresa lay on her side with her head and arm on his chest. This was the first possible chance he had to try to make love to her. He dearly wanted to but he thought doing it here on this dusty carpet and with no water to clean up with might not be so good. Also he sensed something in her. She seemed to grow colder toward him since he mentioned what to do next. Even now it felt like she was lying on him for necessity and not because she wanted to be near him. He decided not to talk and closed his eyes. If she wanted to make love and initiated it, he would do it wholeheartedly but it seemed doubtful.

Chapter 17
(The Privilege of the Presidency)

President Bud Burns was enjoying the evening. His meeting with Rick Daley, the Illinois senator who suggested using Rosemont as the new capital and was overseeing the whole relocation operation, was conducted at a pool party. They were lounging around the beautiful indoor pool in the luxurious Hilton hotel that was connected to the Rosemont Convention Center. He and Vice President John Paul Morgan were sitting next to each other drinking champagne. Both were in the pool earlier and were still in shorts and shirtless, neither looking odd because they were tanned, healthy, and muscular. Both men were in their late forties. Bud Burns, with his jet black hair, looked ten years younger and was adored by the upscale ladies, and presently there were lots of them walking around, all wearing swimming suits and all of them dying to meet the dazzling, shirtless president.

John Morgan looked good as well. He had blond hair and was taller and bigger than Bud. His muscles were more defined, but he had the face of a privileged rich boy who always got his way. They were two of the richest men in the country, both born into wealth. Their fathers were banking tycoons, but only John looked it, which made him unattractive to some women. Bud looked rugged in his face and demeanor, but perhaps they loved his voice above all.

The meeting with Rick Daily was over. Rick actually had work to do and had already left. Now, like most of his life, Bud was just enjoying himself. He was talking to a stunning young lady, who was sitting at the end of his lounge chair in an almost nonexistent bikini. He was sharing his expensive champagne with her, and as he became tipsier, he wondered if he should give her the thrill of her life and invite her up to his private room.

With the end of commercial media, infidelity of politicians

was again ramped and secretive. Bud was so relaxed he didn't immediately notice his white haired chief of staff, Bill Trump, a man even richer than he and the vice president, was calling to him.

"Mr. President," Trump repeated.

Bud took his eye from the woman and looked up. "What?" he said, sounding annoyed, "What is it, Bill?"

Trump was in a grey suit, jacket and all. The seventy-eight degree pool area temperature made his weathered fifty-eight year old face damp with sweat.

"You have to make a televised statement tonight," Trump informed him.

"We'll, do it tomorrow morning. It's getting late, and I've been drinking," Bud ordered and looked back to the women.

"Mr. President, this is serious. We need this recorded tonight to let the network start commentating on the morning broadcast."

Bud felt like refusing, but he knew Bill would keep pressing. He could tell by his grave expression.

"You'll have to excuse me, honey. I have to do something," he said to the woman and raised his hand to hail his head bodyguard over.

The large bald man in black pants and a tee shirt came over and leaned near to him.

"This is Mario. Just give him your information, and maybe we can get together later and continue our discussion over a fresh bottle of champagne," he said, loud enough for both to hear. Then he followed Bill.

"I'd love to Mr. President," the woman shrieked as he walked away.

"Let me guess," Bud said as they walked, "this is about the protesters being shown on the nightly news, right? I can't see how this could amount to anything, Billy boy. I mean, the guy they were protesting for confessed to treason. They'll forget about him in a week."

Trump led the way to the presidential dressing room. "Mr. President this is a serious situation. We can't let people talk about what they saw at work tomorrow without giving them a presidential statement. Controlling the masses is a serious business, and this is the first incident of dissent for us. It must be squashed fast and not given time to fester."

Bud knew Bill was right. He was always right. He was the brains of the government and the unspoken leader, the man who delivered the orders from the plutocratic cabal.

The presidency was completely reduced to an acting role. Bud was the face of the party, and the party couldn't exist without him and his charisma, but he made no real decisions. Bill Trump told Bud what to do, and that was that.

Once they got to the dressing room, Bud changed into a suit and got his makeup done. An aid held up his speech in front of him while he sat in the chair. Bud was shocked at how candid it was. Some of it was actually based on truth. This would be a monumental speech, and Bud was feeling a little nervous now.

Sixteen minutes later, he was approaching the podium in a room at the Rosemont Convention Center that was replicated to look like the White House press room. He stood in front of it, looking right into the teleprompter, did his patented cool nod to the camera, and began.

"My fellow Americans, I'd like to talk to you about government transparency. I can tell you as president and for the entire majority party, one of our goals is to be open and transparent to the American people. We ended secretive and corrupt government that devastated our country's economy. After decades of disastrous economic policy, perpetrated by both major parties, the economy collapsed. Our party emerged with the promise of immediate action, honest action, sensible action, government action that is saving our country. Our first action was to take care of America first, get our people working and prosperous again.

We dealt with the oil crisis that the rest of the world will be feeling soon. Now that we are out of the World Trade Organization and finally looking out for our own country, we are using our resources wisely by keeping everything local. Each service city serves the city they live in. Our choice was to live in a sustainable way or perish. We took the action needed and the American people proved that we are the most resilient and patriotic people in the world. Now we do everything for ourselves. All of our troops are home, and we no longer engage in foreign affairs. We are totally self-sufficient, and in one decade we will be the most prosperous country in the world with a strong economy and plenty of good jobs that will never be outsourced again. Soon, every citizen will be able to afford a high living standard and be able to invest in a strong free market once again."

He took a scripted momentary pause, lowered his eyebrows and spoke with an elevated sense of uncompromising significance. "My fellow Compatriots recently passed a bill that has suspended elections until our country is past this curial time in our history." He paused for breath. "I want to explain why we have made this unprecedented declaration. First, I support this action because our major online poll shows congress has a high approval rating. Every incumbent congressman and I would likely be reelected. However, the campaign process would be a terrible distraction at this vital time.

"Second, we have weathered the worst economic disaster in our history and under the Government Action Plan we are rebuilding. We're making it through the tough times and restoring the American dream. Any deviation from our plan could destroy all hope of achieving our goals in a decade. Both the senate and the house are working harmoniously to rebuild America. We shouldn't risk any possible changes that could disrupt our progress to prosperity.

"And our third reason is undoubtedly the most important. Although we still have the best military in the world, we remain under the increasing threat of foreign aggression toward us. Some countries have evil leaders with evil intentions that threaten our democracy and our very existence.

"These militaristic states are jealous of our new localized society and are uniting against us, forming a formidable coalition."

His grave stare turned to bold anger, and his voice began to rise. "They see our current situation as one of venerability. They fear that our emerging society under the Government Action Plan will make us the strongest, happiest, healthiest culture in the history of mankind. So they view this moment as their only chance to destroy our liberty and seize our great land and all of its natural resources for their own.

"Let me assure you, we are ready for any challenge, and we will never waver in the face of danger or threats. Our military men and women are the best in the world. Today we have the largest military the U.S. has ever had, and we possess the greatest technological weapons available. Taking care of our military and securing our resources is our highest priority, and they are prepared to defend our great nation. At times such as these, we shouldn't be caught up in campaigns and elections. We are now on high alert."

He paused. His demeanor calmed and his voice lowered.

"After it was reported on the fair and balanced Freedom Forever Network news that a group of people were protesting the suspension of elections, I personally felt responsible to honestly explain why we decided to suspend our most precious right to vote. I will also personally guarantee that if the people want elections, I would overturn our decision because this is a government of the people and for the people. We will conduct an online poll to see how you, the American workers, feel about it. So please vote from your home computer anytime over the next two days. I'm confident you will agree we made the right decision, but it's important that you are included in the process. Thank you, and May God bless America."

He turned and walked away while the camera stayed on him. There would be no questions by reporters, not ever the usual pre-written ones by the administration. Bill Trump was satisfied with the performance and felt certain that would end any controversy over this matter.

The online pole would be eighty-five percent favoring the decision to end elections. That was preordained.

Hours later, Trump was in a sound sleep in his luxurious Hyatt hotel room when his keyphone sounded off, waking him slowly.

He finally reached to the nightstand and fumbled for the keyphone. It was one of the special agents assigned to the Rizzo case. He would have expected Joe Gerbuls, but it was his partner,

Deter Parrish for some reason. Parish informed him of Rizzo's escape, much to his chagrin.

"Jesus Christ, what the hell is wrong with that gate precinct!" he yelled. "Get him back, or kill him. Use that gate precinct and the local national guardsmen. Don't let word get out and create a Goddamn martyr with this guy." He ended the call and did not sleep well the rest of the night.

Chapter 18

L ou floated along the edge of sleep for hours before he finally managed to drift into a light sleep for a short time. It was just before dawn when he woke. Teresa was still sleeping quietly. His ribs were sore where her head rested on his chest. He shifted slightly trying not to wake her, dealing with the discomfort on her behalf. As he lay there, too uncomfortable to sleep, he thought of the coming day, envisioning the pros and cons of each action he was considering. He knew what would be best if he still intended to play American hero and try to save his country, but he sensed Teresa would not be happy.

He tried to decide how to treat her. Would he be stern? Or would he be sympathetic? After all, she did save his life . . . for the time being.

As the dim glow of morning light flowed into the abandoned apartment, he decided to get up. Gently, he moved out from under her and tried to lightly rest her head on the ground, hoping not to wake her. She moaned angrily in her sleep once her head was placed on the dusty floor. Lou was looking out the window and suddenly heard a helicopter in the distance. He could tell it one was moving fast by the way the sound grew so rapidly. The pilot must have been waiting for first light to take off and didn't waste a second the moment it came.

It passed over them and went north. Lou saw it briefly from his window. It wasn't a police helicopter like the one that was searching for them last night. This was a military helicopter, a Blackhawk, armed with missiles. Lou's body quivered the moment he caught a glimpse of it passing over. The powerful rotation of the lethal Blackhawk blades made a frightening, all encompassing, thumping sound.

The floor vibrated from it, waking Teresa prompting her to rise to her knees and look out the window next to him. She startled him by coming into his peripheral vision suddenly. He smiled silently till the sound was quieter before talking.

"That was a military heli-"

BOOM! An explosion shook the ground. Flames rose, brightening the dim, dawn sky.

It was only three blocks away, less than a quarter mile. Both of them turned pale with wide eyes and opened mouths.

"That scared the shit out of me!" Lou finally exclaimed.

Teresa seemed to calm down quickly. "They must have spotted a group of scavies and called in an air strike. It's pretty scary being this close to the explosion," she said with little interest.

"What?" Lou screeched. "You mean killing people is normal procedure?"

She frowned, tilting her head, trying to understand why he seemed so outraged.

She shrugged her shoulders. "When they find out where a group of scavies are hiding, they take them out before they can become dangerous."

Lou felt nauseous, and being hungry and thirsty didn't help, but the thought of people being vaporized because they joined with others for survival sickened him.

"After all the terrible things I know about our government, I think that just sickened me the most!" he said in disgust.

"Yeah, it's pretty bad," she said, "but if you refuse to enroll in the G.A. plan, you're not counted as a citizen and your're breaking the law, so, you know. . . they're knowingly taking the risk. Let's face it; they're savages."

Despite being enraged by her comment, his expression never changed. He was a pro at dealing with people who had inhumane opinions. He believed most decent people with intolerant opinions gained them from unavoidable exposure to propaganda by a pro-war party. Once he calmly explained the rational side, he could sway people's opinions, provided he could get them to empathize. However, he also learned about two out of ten people had no interest or ability to empathize. Lou called them hate heads.

"I don't think people who refuse to surrender their free

will should be punished by death, and I bet they're not anything like we're told."

He knew she wasn't a hate head. It was an incredibly selfless act to free him, but he sensed her idea of a scavey was exactly how the media portrayed them as: desperate, murderous, fiends. She probably even believed the rumor about some of them resorting to cannibalism. She didn't comment, and he decided to let it rest for now.

"Well, we better get started," he said. "I'm pretty sure that road at the corner is Central." He pointed west. "We're on Irving so it's probably less than three miles north to Edgebrook Golf Course. The North Branch Chicago River runs through there."

"Are you sure?" she asked.

"Yeah, I know this area well. I used to play golf at Edgebrook because it was open to the public and the only one I could afford to play when I was a painter. We need a home base, so we'll find a house with a fireplace near the river and find something to boil water in. And then we'll take it from there."

She nodded, and they walked out.

They crept down the stairway as if trying not to disturb a sleeping resident and halted at the front door. Lou opened the door and looked up and down the street. Then he reached for her hand, and they darted out into the morning light. He confirmed the street at the corner was Central, and they began heading north. They didn't walk along the street out in the open; they cut through the back yards of the houses that bordered the east side of the street. They were moderate middle class houses that were occupied less than a decade ago. Now they were abandoned, and the neighborhood seemed eerie.

He helped her climb fences, and they sprinted across intersections where they were the most exposed. They made small talk along the way. He would inquire something about her life, and next she would ask him something about his. They learned a lot about each other, but Lou didn't want to discuss the fact that he had a son and ex-wife who safely escaped to Australia.

One time they had to take cove under some bushes because they heard a helicopter, but it didn't pass directly overhead.

In just under an hour, they made it to the river, unseen.

They walked down a quaint block with large oak trees that bordered the river. The first house Lou spotted with a chimney was a small, brown, wood siding, ranch with vines covering most of the exterior. The lawns were waste high, but some areas were trampled down and eaten away by wildlife, mostly deer and geese.

"This one looks good. Let's check it out," he said.

He walked up the gangway while Teresa trailed behind. Pulling open the screen door, he tried to turn the door knob. It was locked, but the door seemed weak so he gave it a boot with the bottom of his foot.

It took five more kicks until it flung open. Teresa stood behind Lou and put her hand on his shoulder as if she was worried he might disappear. They moved in slowly. The front room was empty and reasonably clean.

There was a rotting smell coming from the kitchen, but it wasn't overwhelming. Teresa came out from behind him and moved to the middle of the room. Lou glanced into the kitchen and saw a dog carcass. It had been stripped to the bone, which would explain why it no longer stunk to high hell in the house; the air had only the remnants of decay. Teresa didn't notice it.

"This isn't so bad, and it has a nice fireplace," she said, circling the room.

She went over to the back wall that had a wooden bench built into it.

Lou noticed a hole was gnawed out of the wood underneath it.

"Look, it has a built in bench too," she said and plopped her butt on it.

"Ahhhhhhhhhh!" She let out a high pitched, ear piercing scream as a group of rats scurried out from under the bench and fled into the closet left of her. She ran at full speed, squealing along the way and jumped into Lou's arms, grabbing him around the neck so he had to hold her off the ground.

"Get me out of here," she said crying, and buried her face into his chest.

He carried her out of the door and had to walk all the way

down the gangway before she let him put her down.

"I'm not going in that house. Find another one," she said still crying.

Lou was actually relieved to learn that even if he couldn't kill a deer or catch a fish to eat, they wouldn't starve as long as he could catch rats. He decided to keep this revelation to himself.

"Okay, but you know I could just plug up the holes and..." he began, half joking.

"I'm not going into that house. Just forget it," she declared. She glowered at him but quickly softened and hugged him. "Please Louis, I can't stand rats. Now lets move on."

He nodded and they walked farther down the block, holding hands.

He spotted another house with a chimney. This one had a red brick exterior.

"This one might be good. You want to wait out here while I check it out?"

She immediately felt like he was trying to fool her. He would go in alone, and if there were any rats, he would scare them away and tell her it was clean.

"I'm not leaving your side," she insisted.

They walked together up the gangway. He stopped in front of the porch and scanned the facade. Something made him nervous about entering this house. Though everything looked still, his instincts told him not to go in.

Man, I wish we had that bolt blaster. Doctor Who was about as fictitious as science fiction could be. This is brutal reality, he thought with a defeated smirk on his face.

He finally began to ascend the concrete stairs slowly and checked the front door. It was locked, and by pushing on it, he could tell he was not going to be able to kick this solid door in. He scurried over to the window and squatted down to have a look inside. The view was obscured by dark yellow curtains that were probably white when they were new. At the bottom of the window, right in the middle, where the two curtain edges met, was a small gap. He peered through it and got a partial view of the living room. It looked dusty and dreary, but it was not empty. He could see an object in the form of a chair that was covered in dingy material resembling clothes and towels. He could see a small portion of another shape. He struggled to identify it. Then suddenly the room brightened, and he could tell it was a pile of wood.

The room darkened again.

Someone just went out the back door.

Lou froze for one full second, deciding what to do. He turned to Teresa, who was standing behind him, hooked her waste, and pulled her to the porch rail.

"Jump over the rail and squat down," he said frantically but quietly.

Lou put his hands on the rail and sprang over it in one hop before Teresa had one leg up. Lou was holding his arms out to her. She jumped to him, and he softened her fall by grabbing her waist. They immediately squatted down and were a few inches lower than the waist high lawn. They heard the footsteps come running out front.

"You move, you die," a chilling, high pitched male voice screeched.

They sank down in the grass a few inches more. Teresa had her chin down against her chest; eyes closed and looked to be praying. Lou was keeping his head up, eyes wide and alert.

"Where d'ay go?" a second voice called from the other side of the house. There was silence for a moment, and then they could hear the footsteps moving again, now walking through the deep grass.

The high voiced man on their side of the porch began approaching. Closer and closer, the footsteps came.

Lou was holding his breath, getting light-headed when a head appeared over the grass . . . a grubby looking face with a light brown beard and shaggy long hair. The man was looking forward, and Lou could see the top of what he was holding: an old wooden, recurved, composite bow. He couldn't see the arrow, but he could tell the string was drawn.

The bowman veered closer but had not looked toward them yet. Closer and closer he came.

Lou filled his lungs with air.

The bowman was only a few feet away when he looked

down at them.

Lou sprang up! With his left hand, he grabbed the arm that was holding the bow. In one quick motion he swung his right arm around the man's neck as he moved behind him. The bowman let go of the arrow, and it fluttered toward the front. Lou had him in a headlock now and was applying all the strength he had to choke him. The bowman dropped the bow and grabbed at Lou's wiry arm. Lou surveyed the other man. He looked similar to the one he was choking but was not armed with a bow and arrow. Instead, he was carrying a machete.

"Run, Teresa! I'll catch up!" he yelled. She obediently sprang up and took off like a gazelle through the deep grass.

The man used all his strength to loosen Lou's grip and then flung his head backwards, crashing into Lou's nose, stinging it intensely. Next, the man flung his right elbow back and buried it in Lou's ribs. That broke him free. The man spun around and faced Lou, ready to fight.

"It's a woman, Scooter. Run her down," he screeched loudly, never taking his eyes off Lou.

Scooter, the machete man, took off after Teresa.

Lou raised his right fist in the air like it was a lethal weapon. "Aaarrrggghhh," he screamed while approaching his rival. The bowman looked up and raised his arms to block. Lou faked the punch and did a front snap kick that connected hard on bowman's left inner thigh. He was intending to hit him in the balls but missed since he never looked down to aim, trying to sell the fake.

The bowman was hurt enough to fall to his knees, and Lou sprinted after Teresa. He was running full force because the machete man was gaining on her fast. He surprised Lou by dropping his machete so he could sprint faster. He seemed frantic with catching her. He was like a hungry cheetah chasing a gazelle, Lou decided he would risk losing pace to pick up the machete. He veered to where it hit the ground, still in full sprint. Catching sight of it, he bent down to grab it.

POW! He was hit by a force that knocked him five feet forward to the ground. A shoulder led, blindside tackle by the bowman partially knocked the wind out of Lou and left them both on the ground. He heard Teresa scream, and it gave him an adrenalin boost. He rolled onto his assailer and used his left elbow to strike the side of his head while he rolled right over him and leaped to his feet.

The bowman jumped to his feet just as quick, and they were again facing each other, again ready to battle. The bowman was unarmed, but he was cackling amusedly on each deep breath he took.

He's actually enjoying this!

"Come on, old boy, try to fool me again," he said, daring Lou to make the first move.

Teresa screamed again prompting Lou to lash out with a left jab and then follow up with a flurry of punches. Some grazed his head but most just hit his arms. The Bowman grabbed Lou's shoulders and spun him a hundred and eighty degrees and threw him to the ground. His cackles grew louder as did his amusement.

Lou got up to a three point stand and launched at him. Bowman braced himself, and they collided together and pushed apart. Lou blocked a wild swing intended for his head and hit the bowman in the gut. Then he pushed him aside and desperately tried to run over to Teresa. The Bowman turned and grabbed hold of Lou's hospital gown just before he got going. As he tried to pull away, the collar pulled tightly against his neck, cutting off his air.

"Where you going, boy? We ain't done yet," the bowman said and kicked Lou's feet out from under him. Then he jumped on his legs and pulled the gown tighter. Lou was immobilized and choking.

Scooter caught Teresa and had her in a headlock as he dragged her back.

"Alright, Joe Bob, let him up," Scooter said. Joe Bob didn't let up, only pulled harder, and Lou was beginning to black out. He could hear Teresa whimpering. Then his vision began to blur and then smothering silence.

"We ought to kill him before Pa gets home," Joe Bob grunted.

"No, don't kill him, please don't," Teresa begged.

"Whoa, I like hearing a woman beg me like that," Joe Bob said and finally let go. He got up off Lou and looked in to Teresa's frightened dark eyes.

"I can't wait to hear you beg some more . . . woo wee! We got us a woman, Scooter."

"Yeah, and she sure is a pretty one too."

Joe Bob grabbed his pocket knife from his back pocket, flipped it open, and then grabbed her away from Scooter.

"I got her. Now go get a couple feet of daddy's rope. Hurry now."

Scooter ran back into the house.

Lou was gasping for air. Once his vision was restored and his breath returned, he rolled to his back and sat up.

"You stay right there, old boy," Joe Bob said, "or this sweet thing here's gonna get blood all over her pretty little skin."

He looked up to see the grubby bearded man holding Teresa's arm behind her back with one hand while the other was against her chest, pulling her backside up against his front. In his hand was a switchblade, and the tip was touching the skin of her neck.

Rage clouded Lou's thoughts for a moment. He drew in a deep breath and allowed his intelligence to return.

The only way out of a bad situation is to think my way out.

"Listen, please don't hurt her. I have a lot to offer. But you must not hurt her. We're valuable people, you understand? She's the wife of the president of the United Stated," Lou said calmly.

Joe Bob squinted and puckered his lips. His gaze was drawn away as Scooter darted out the front door with rope dangling from his hand. He came over to them smiling.

This man looked similar to the other in build, and they both had narrow cheek bones and beady eyes. They must be brothers, he deduced and the one he was fighting was the elder by a few years.

"Alright, old boy, stand up and put your hands behind your back," Joe Bob said as Scooter stood behind Lou. "Tie him up good, Scooter," he ordered.

"Please listen, you guys, you can't harm her," Lou pleaded, putting his hands behind him. "There's a huge reward for her. She's the first lady, for Christ's sake. I kidnapped her from her hotel in Rosemont. If you don't hurt her, you could be millionaires."

Scooter began tying Lou's hands behind his back. Lou squeezed his fists, flexing the muscles to make his lean wrists as thick as possible.

"Hear that, Scooter? We could be millionaires," Joe Bob said and cackled.

Lou tried to judge their intelligence and age. They appeared to be in their early to mid twenties, but it was hard to tell with their grubby beards.

Young and dumb, he deduced.

"I swear to God, it's true. You got to understand how important she is," Lou said, acting anxious. "You mentioned your pa. This is something he should hear. When's he coming back?" Lou winced as the rope painfully tightened when Scooter tugged on the knot.

"Shut your damn mouth, old boy, or she gonna start dripping blood!" Joe Bob yelled.

Scooter grabbed him by the shoulders and stood him up. "Get in the house, old boy," he ordered and began pushing him toward it.

Once they entered the house, the musty air assaulted his nose. Lou looked around at the cluttered front room, his mind searching for ideas.

"You guys, you don't understand how important she is. If you harm her, we're all fuckin' dead!" he yelled.

"I had enough of this old boy," Scooter said. Wham! He put his weight behind a right hook to Lou's head.

Lou saw it coming and rolled with it the moment it hit his head. He flopped to the dusty floor like a sack of potatoes.

Teresa screamed.

Holding his eyes closed, he remained listless, fighting his instinct to find out if another blow was coming.

Teresa was shrieking and crying and calling out, "Louis!"

"Damn! You caught him a good one Scooter. He's out cold," Joe Bob yelled over her crying.

"Didn't feel like that good a one," said Scooter, "but I guess he ain't much for me to knock out." He stuck his chest out, flexing his muscles at Teresa.

"Get some more rope and something to gag her with. She making a racket," Joe Bob commanded.

Lou lay motionless while Teresa begged them.

"Please don't do this!" she said, sobbing as Joe bob forced her down on a pile of blankets. He knelt over her and sat on her chest as he grabbed her arms and held them down. Scooter returned with more rope, cut off a three foot length with his pocketknife, and dropped it next to them.

"Bring that big sittin' log over here and drive some stakes into it," Joe Bob said as he picked up the rope and began tying Teresa's wrists together. Scooter rolled a wide, heavy log behind her head.

Lou had to sneak a peek when he heard hammering. Scooter was driving stakes into the log. He put one in the middle, and one near each end. When he finished, while Joe Bob remained on her chest, Scooter unbuttoned her pants and began pulling them off as Teresa tried to kick him away futilely.

"Woo we," he squealed once he got her panties off. The end of the rope that bound her wrists, Scooter tied to the middle stake, stretching her arms over her head. Then he tied each of her legs separately, just above her knees. He grabbed the rope tied to her left leg and pulled it back, lifting her leg off the ground. Then he tied the end of it to the stake on the left end of the log. When he grabbed the rope tied to her right leg and pulled it toward the right side stake, she began shrieking hysterically. Her knees were over her shoulders, legs spread apart, and her feet dangling in the air as she cried.

Joe Bob went over to the pile of dirty clothes. He returned with a shirt in his hand. He twisted it up, wrapped it over her mouth, then tied the ends behind her head. Her screaming continued but muffled now.

"Lookie here, we done hogtied the first lady," Joe Bob said. They both cackled, making Lou's skin crawl.

He almost tried to get up now and fight them both with his hands tied behind his back.

Wait for the right moment, he reminded himself and felt awful for what Teresa would have to go through.

"Let's lock that dumb old boy in the back room. I don't want any interruptions if he wakes up."

They walked over to him. Joe Bob grabbed his legs while Scooter grabbed him behind his shoulders, and they carried him into the master bedroom. They let him go while his upper body was still a few feet high so he had to let his head crash onto the ground. They stood over him and looked down at him for a moment. Joe Bob kicked him in the side to make sure he was out cold. Lou didn't blink or cringe enough to be suspected of playing possum.

"He ain't dead, is he?" asked Scooter.

"Naw, I can see him breathing," replied Joe Bob. "Come on, we gonna have some fun."

Once Lou heard the door close, he opened his eyes. He wanted to save Teresa from them more than anything ever in his life, but he knew he had to remain calm. His first act was to get his hands from behind his back to the front. He pulled his knees up to his chest, lowered his arms, and pushed his butt between them. The rope pulled hard on his wrists, burning the skin. This was not going to be easy. He was too tense, moving too fast. He had to take a few breaths and calmly exhale all his air. Carefully, he fit his narrow ass between his arms. Then he rolled onto his back and worked his legs painfully through the gap. It took longer than he would have liked, but he finally had his hands in front of him.

He quietly tried the door knob to confirm it was locked. He could hear Teresa's muffled crying, making him feel like he might go mad with rage.

He quickly considered his possibilities.

I'll bet that back door is still unlocked. He scurried over to the window, devising a plan.

It was awkward trying to open the old wooden frame window with his hands tied. It took all his strength, making a scraping noise as he slowly pushed it up. The storm window was jammed. Lou had to wiggle it to jar it loose. Once he got it open, he immediately climbed out the window, arms and head first. His butt scraped against the storm window as he began his descent to the porch floor. Holding out his arms to protect his head, they collapsed at impact, and he rolled with it. There was a thud as his heels hit the wood at the end of his roll. Fortunately, the hillbillies and Teresa were being too loud for them to hear his noisy escape.

Not wasting a moment, he got to his feet and crept down the stairs. He ran to the front yard and over to where Scooter dropped the machete. He found it and placed the handle between his knees, then put the blade between his wrists and began moving his arms up and down, cutting the rope on the sharp blade. He got up with the machete in his hand and tried to stay low while scurrying around the front yard, looking for the arrow Joe Bob released when they first met.

He was worried they might look out the window and see him, but he knew it was unlikely, given their current amusement.

Finally, he found the arrow near the sidewalk, right in front of the house.

It didn't take long to find the bow near the front of the porch where Joe Bob dropped it.

Carrying all three items in one arm, he ran to the back porch and crept up to the door. Through the small, grimy window, he could see the iniquitous men on their knees with their backs turned. Both had their pants pulled down. Teresa's calves and feet were dangling, bouncing in the air. Joe Bob was between her legs, his head bobbing and hips thrusting. Both men were yelping, "Woo wee!" and "Yeah baby!" and much worse vile vulgarity, loud enough to drown out Teresa's crying.

Lou wondered a moment earlier if he was capable of murder. The answer was probably not, but after witnessing this, he could easily massacre both of these men.

He quietly turned the doorknob. It was unlocked, just as he assumed. The scavies had been careless, leaving their weapons lying outside and the back door unlocked. Raping Teresa as soon as possible was all they could think about.

His mind flashed back to when he was in his hospital bed

angrily pleasuring himself just before she walked in. His thoughts about her were not much unlike what these fiends were doing to her now. He pushed it out of his mind and focused his anger.

Quietly opening the door, he crept in and squatted behind the pile of wood. Lou placed the machete on the top of the pile and set the arrow on the string of the bow, still unnoticed.

Presently Scooter was getting irate. "Come on, Joe Bob, it's my turn for awhile now!" he yelled.

"Now don't rush me, boy. Wait yer turn." He reached forward, pulled up her shirt and bra, and slapped her breasts. "Here, play with these babies for awhile," he said while continuing to thrust himself into her.

Lou began to pull the arrow back, aiming it right at Joe Bob's back.

"You know what? She getting kinda dry. Go get the water pan and the squeezie, squirter thing," Joe Bob said.

"The turkey soaker?" Scooter asked.

"Yeah boy, the turkey soaker. We gonna do this right."

They both cackled.

"Alright, but then it's my turn," Scooter said and got up off his knees and pulled his pants up. He turned toward the kitchen. Lou squatted down behind the pile of wood.

He slowly rose when Scooter made it to the kitchen and took aim at Joe Bob again. Suddenly, he had a change of heart. Once the arrow hit his back, if he was lucky enough to shoot straight, Joe Bob would start screaming bloody murder and possibly hurt Teresa.

He lowered the bow and arrow, holding them in his left hand and picked up one of the smaller logs that fit in his right hand. He crept up behind Joe Bob, who was still happily pounding away, unaware of anything but his own gratification. Lou held up the log high in the air, his face wrinkled from intensity as he swiftly swung down the log right into the back of the head. Thump! His body fell forward onto Teresa.

The sight disgusted him. Joe Bob was still inside her. He had to set down the log to pull Joe Bob off her before he could go after Scooter. Once he pushed aside the body, he was overcome by the vision. He froze in time, mesmerized by Teresa's naked, tied up, tempting body. He felt ashamed for finding her so appealing at that moment but couldn't turn away. His eyes were eating it up, his mind imprinting the sexual image.

The next moment he sensed movement and turned toward the kitchen. Scooter was in a throwing motion and suddenly a steel pan was flying at his head. Lou instinctively lifted his free hand and partly blocked the heavy black pan, but the handle flipped around and hit him on the head. Lou fell backwards to the floor, dropping the bow and arrow. Teresa's muffled scream rang out as he hit the floor. Scooter scurried over to the back door. He was about to run out when he spotted the machete on the pile of wood. He sprung over, grabbed it, and hoisted it.

Lou fumbled for the bow and arrow, not sure if he had enough time.

"Aaarrrggghhh!" Scooter let out a battle cry and charged with the machete hoisted high.

Lou set the arrow on the string, got it partly pulled back, and released. The arrow stuck near his left shoulder, barely piercing the skin. Scooter grimaced. He stopped, looked at the arrow, and lowered his arm. The arrow fell to the floor. Scooter scowled and raised the machete again. He yelled even louder and came at him with even more tenacity.

Teresa screamed as she saw Scooter advancing with the machete hoisted high.

Lou dropped the bow and turned his head away from his attacker. The log he whacked Joe Bob with was a few feet away. He lunged for it.

Scooter swung down the machete with both arms, grunting loudly! "Aaarrrggghhh!"

Just before Scooter split his skull open, Lou lifted the log over his face, and the machete stuck into it.

Scooter looked shocked for a moment, puzzled why blood wasn't splattering. Realizing what happened, he tried to pull the machete out of the log. As he pulled, Lou added to the momentum by pushing and smashed the end of the log into Scooter's face. Streams of blood began to plunge from his nose. Lou pulled back the log, smashed it into the side of his head, knocking him to his left.

It felt good to Lou. He wanted to finish him off, couldn't wait to smash his head again.

No smashing.

It wasn't good enough. He wanted to split it. He got to his knees, held the log on the ground with one hand, and pulled the machete free with the other. He moved over to Scooter, kneeling right over him. His arm muscles flexed as he hoisted the machete.

Cut right into his Goddamn skull, he thought while aiming.

But he delayed and looked at Scooter's bloody face for a split second too long. The despicable, cold blooded subspecies he wanted to chop up changed. Now he saw a defenseless, misguided, human being in the prime of his miserable life.

He slowly lowered the blade and reached down to Scooter's neck with his free hand. He grabbed the neck under his chin to confirm if he still had a pulse or not. When he felt the faint heart beat against the tips of his fingers, it made him squeeze tightly. Tighter and tighter, he squeezed. It felt like he could make his head explode if he used both hands and all his angry might to strangle him with. Scooter's face was beet red before his strength wore off. He let go, and Scooter gasped for air.

Not making eye contact with Teresa, he walked to the log behind her. She had closed her eyes the moment Scooter swung the blade down on Lou and just now opened them, astonished to see it was Lou who arose the victor. She heaved a heavy sigh of relief through the dirty shirt over her mouth.

He crashed the machete down on the log, cutting the first rope, freeing her left leg. Two more times, and her limbs were free from bondage.

He went to her as she sat up and untied her hands, and they embraced. She was squeezing him tightly in spasms and crying.

Still holding her firmly, he reached his hands up from her back to her neck and untied the shirt around her mouth. She continued to sob and squeeze him, unable to speak. Lou didn't know what to say for a moment.

"It's over. I'm never gonna let anyone hurt you again,"

he whispered next to her ear.

He wondered if he should say more and struggled with ideas, but that seemed to be enough for now as her body softened in his arms, and her spasms stopped.

Once her sobbing quieted, Lou heard a moan. It was coming from Joe Bob, who was a few feet to the right of them. Teresa gasped as Lou jerked his head around to look.

"I have to tie these bastards up, and then I'll come right back to you."

She didn't let go so he had to pull one of her arms off him.

With two pieces of rope he tied Scooter and Joe Bob's hands behind their backs as best he could. He dragged them to the other side of the room and went so far as to lay them on their side and prop their heads up with clothing from the dirty pile of clothes. Then he picked out two of the least dirty shirts and shook them hard in the air as if that would shake them clean.Then he put them under his arm.

He went back to Teresa, picking her pants and underwear up along the way. He dropped the clothes next to her.

Softly putting his hand on her thigh, he looked into her eyes. "Are you Okay, sweetie?"

She blinked her eyes hard, sending tears to their facial descent.

"Thank you," she whimpered.

He untied the ropes from her legs and used them to tie Scooter and Joe Bob's legs. When he finished he stood over them for a moment, looking down at their defenseless bodies, feeling merciful and victorious.

He really beat them.

Not bad for an old resourceful dog.

He smiled victoriously for a second.

Chapter 19

Lou removed his hospital gown, and they both put on the dingy white shirts he picked out for them. Consoling her for another ten minutes, mostly in silence, he held her to his chest and stroked her hair softly.

The two bound men began to moan as they groggily returned to consciousness.

"I have to work on getting us water and food. You just rest some more, okay?" he said and released her.

"I want to get out of here as soon as we can," she whimpered as he walked off.

He rummaged through the kitchen. There were three backpacks on the ground and various items cluttered around them. Lou deduced they were not here long, and they must be travelers. They had four gallons of water in old plastic milk containers. He grabbed one and took a tiny sip to test it.

A second later he uncontrollably chugged down big gulps until he was satisfied. His belly began to ache, bloated with water.

He brought it out to Teresa, and she drank in small gulps. Then she slowly got to her feet and went in the other room to clean up with the water and Lou's discarded gown to use for a towel.

He grabbed the machete and got another gallon of water out of the kitchen and walked over to Joe Bob and Scooter.

Joe Bob had his eyes open and looked confused. Lou squatted down beside him, pushed his head to the side, and inspected the gash on the back of his head. He poured water on it, patted it with a shirt, and cleaned it the best he could. Joe Bob moaned weakly. Then he cleaned the gash on the side of Scooter's head, which brought him back to consciousness. Now both men were looking at him dumbfounded.

"You guy's got any food stashed around here?" he said to them.

"Untie me, old boy. My head's a hurting," Joe Bob groggily said.

"Dah, sure thing, Joe Bob," Lou said, doing his hillbilly impression, "I mean all ya did is rape my girl and try to kill me. Water under the bridge, right?"

Joe Bob frowned and muttered something incoherent.

"Maybe I will untie you," he said, then picked up the machete and held it up. "Or maybe I'll start hacking into your legs and watch you bleed out. It all depends on the talk we're about to have."

Joe Bob's eyes were wide with fear as he stared at the blade.

Scooter was awake and paying attention. He planned on keeping his mouth shut, just like Joe Bob would have advised; however, this was every man for himself now.

"Now just wait a minute, mister," Scooter said, trying to sound polite, "we didn't mean any harm. I mean, we ain't seen a woman in a long time, you know, and I guess we just went kind of crazy when we saw her."

Lou saw his eyes move to the other side of the room, and he swallowed hard. Teresa had come back into the room.

"I'm awfully sorry, mister. I admit I done wrong, but just so you know, I didn't do anything with your woman. It was just Joe Bob who," he cleared his throat, "you know, done it wit er."

"Shut your mouth, Scooter! We did it together!" Joe Bob shouted and closed his eyes tightly as the pain in his head erupted when he yelled.

"He's right, Scooter. You're in it together, but you do sound remorseful at least. You might get out of this with your legs in tact if you're honest with me."

Scooter looked grateful. Lou moved over to him.

"Now then, you guys got any food stashed?" he asked.

"We ain't got no food," Joe Bob blurted. "Just take some water and be on your way."

Lou rose to his feet, his eyes blazing like a possessed man. He roared as he swung down the machete at Joe Bob's legs.

Teresa shrieked just as Lou veered away from his legs halfway down and struck the floor inches from his feet.

"It's going through your fuckin' ankles next time!" He screamed.

Teresa's heart was racing. She couldn't deal with anymore violent men. Louis looked possessed to her, as animalistic as those brutes looked while they were tying her up and raping her. She was certain Lou was going to cut into the man's legs, the same man that was hammering himself inside her not long ago. She had to get away from these evil men. All men are evil, even Louis. She nudged toward the door.

"Now don't interrupt your brother again," Lou said and pulled the machete out of the floor. Joe Bob looked pale, his defiant expression washed away. Lou went back to Scooter, "well!"

"We got some critter stew in the crock pot, but it doesn't taste too good cold, and we not supposed to light a fire till sundown," said Scooter.

"Critter stew, huh? I ain't even going to ask what kind of critter is in it. Got anything else?"

"We got a few cans of food left, some corn and beans and stuff. They in the duffel bag by the fireplace there."

"Thank you, Scooter. That sounds much better. Teresa, can you get-"

He turned to look at her just as she opened the door and ran.

He got to his feet and dropped the machete. "Teresa!" he yelled as he ran after her.

He was confused by her actions. She was running full speed, trying to get away from him. Lou had to push himself to the limit to gain on her.

As he sprinted after her through the front yard, a noise emerged, quick and unnerving. It was the thumping of helicopter blades, not far in the distance. She was running down the sidewalk. The noise slowed her stride, and they both looked up.

"Teresa, get under that tree!" he yelled, hoping she would go under the willow tree that was not too far in front of her.

She just froze.

Lou caught up to her, grabbed her, pulled her to the tree, and down to the ground under it. She was trying to escape from him.

"Please don't hurt me," she pleaded.

"Teresa it's me. I would never hurt you. Please, snap out of this," he begged. The helicopter was moving right over them now. He held her as tight as he could while she resisted.

Suddenly she broke away from him, stood up and began moving out in the open toward the helicopter. It was going away from them and fortunately didn't see her step out from under the tree.

Lou followed her. He grabbed her by the shoulders and forced her around to look at him in the eyes. "Teresa, please don't do this. I need you to be strong and trust me."

She stared silently for a moment. "You looked like a mad man in there. You were a violent brute, just like them."

He exhaled deeply blowing through his lips. "No Teresa, that was an act. I was trying to scare them so I could get information," he said sounding frustrated, like he was explaining something obvious to a slow child.

She looked away seeming to consider this and then back into his eyes. She saw the compassion in his mild brown eyes that attracted her to him and felt embarrassed. She broke out crying again.

"You've been through a lot. You won't easily forget this horrible day, but you can put all your faith in me. I would do anything to protect you. You're just as important to me as anything in the world. You are part of my mission now. Do you understand?"

He meant every word, but if she didn't understand, he would waste no more time trying to convince her. If her mind was too fragile to get over this trauma, he would have to distance himself from her.

She embraced him. "I'm sorry," she said trembling. Then she looked up at him.

Lou recognized she was herself again.

"Can we get away from here please?"

"Not till I get some information about the dad. I have

a feeling he may be useful to us. You have to face them and be strong. I promise we'll be on our way soon. Come on, we're gonna eat some beans now." He began walking back to the house alone, not looking back for twenty steps.

She was just standing there, looking at him when he turned back.

He gestured for her to come with his arm and then jogged back to the house without another look back.

As soon as he walked through the front door, he saw Joe Bob and Scooter lying on their sides, back to back, trying to untie each other. Lou ran over, grabbed the machete and was about to yell but didn't want Teresa to hear him screaming again at this pivotal point in their relationship. She was making the decision to stay or leave him right at this moment, and if she heard him yelling like a mad man, it might sway her decision.

"Give it up, guys," he calmly said and pushed Joe Bob onto his stomach with his foot.

"What you do? You lead them right to us, boy. They gonna bomb the house now," Joe Bob screeched.

"Relax, they didn't see us. We hid under a tree."

Scooter rolled onto his butt, sat up and looked around, noticing Lou was alone. "I'm awfully sorry your woman ran off on ya, mister."

"I think she's coming back, and call me Lou." He was almost beginning to think Scooter really was remorseful, if that was possible. "Listen, you guys, I was in jail and as good as dead. They arrested me because I wanted to challenge the government, and she broke me out. So we're new to the wild."

"I knew she wasn't the first lady," muttered Joe Bob.

"I just want to talk with you guys. I wanna know how you live." Lou was just looking at Scooter now. "Joe Bob said he wanted to kill me before your pa got home. Tell me about him. When is he gonna be back?"

"Don't you dare tell him, Scooter!" Joe Bob yelled. "He's probably a spy for the pigs." Scooter looked nervous.

"I'm sorry about all that stuff we did mister . . . I mean Lou. He didn't really want to kill you. He wasn't thinking straight, and we didn't kill ya in the end."

"Yeah, that's right. It was me who spared ya, boy," Joe Bob interrupted. "I could have killed ya, and I didn't. Remember that."

"That's true, and I'm thankful," said Lou. "Have you noticed I haven't killed you either?" Then he turned back to Scooter. "Believe me, I'm no spy for the government. They probably consider me public enemy number one. I'm a revolutionary." He smiled. "Now tell me about your pops. I can tell you guys aren't from around here. You're southerners. So why did you travel here?"

"Don't you tell him nothing. We die before we talk," Joe Bob said.

Lou was about to shout and threaten him again, but just then the door slowly opened, and Teresa walked in.

He turned to her, as if he never doubted for a moment she wouldn't come back, and pointed toward the fireplace.

"Teresa, can you go in that duffel bag by the fireplace and find a can of beans and something to open it with? We got to get some food in our bellies before we move on." She glanced uneasily at the grubby men then looked back at Lou and nodded.

He turned back to Scooter. "Why would you die before you tell me about you pa?" They both were silent and Lou squatted down by Scooter. "What would you want to hide from me? It doesn't make sense. You have nothing to fear from me. If anything, maybe I can help."

Scooter licked his dry lips. "I'm real thirsty, Lou. I'll tell you if I can get me some water."

Lou grabbed the container, and Scooter lifted his head. He held it up to his mouth while Scooter took five gulps. Lou put down the water and stared at him, waiting for a response.

"Our daddy's an important man. He second in command for our group, and we on a secret mission. Them cops want to kill him."

"They want to kill all of us, dip shit!" Joe Bob yelled.

"We ain't supposed to talk about it to anyone," Scooter added.

"That's right so keep you mouth shut, boy," ordered Joe Bob.

Lou made crazy eyes and inhaled deeply while lifting the machete. Scooter appeared petrified and looked at Joe Bob.

"Aw hell, Joe Bob, he ain't no pigger. He'd a-had a blaster if-in he was."

Joe Bob exhaled through his lips in defeat. "I reckon so," he muttered.

"You ever heard of the emancipators," asked Scooter.

Lou Pondered. "No, I don't believe I have."

"I have," Teresa said.

Lou turned to see she was standing not far behind them, holding an open can of beans and a plastic spoon.

"They're a resistance group of scavies. They attacked penitentiary plants and freed inmates, and they sometimes sneak into service cities and try to make people come with them into the wild."

"That's right, little lady, and we ain't got many females out here. They all done joined the G.A. plan," Scooter said.

"You savages don't deserve women," she scolded.

"Why have I never heard about this?" Lou broke in.

"It's not something they report in the news, Louis," she said and held up the can to him.

He got up, walked over to her, and she handed him the can.

He began scarfing down large spoonfuls of cold baked beans. "Have some. They're really not bad," he said, handing it back to her. She took a small spoonful and grimaced as she swallowed.

He walked back by them. "So your dad is part of these emancipators or something?"

"We all are, I guess," replied Scooter. "We stay separated because they bomb us if they find groups of us together."

"So where did your pa go?" Lou asked.

"He gone out to meet with the courier to get the orders," he answered.

Lou looked upward, smiling as if in a blissful daze. "So people are opposing the government." He stood up and ran his hands through his thin, brown hair. "And they're organized too."

Now he put his hands over his face and moaned. "This is fuckin' amazing!"

Both men and Teresa were staring at him in wonderment as Lou appeared to weep.

"What's wrong with him?" Joe Bob said mordantly.

After a moment, Lou finally took his hands away from his face and looked at them each silently with watery eyes.

"I've never felt so proud of my fellow Americans," he said in a crackling voice. "When will your pops be back? I have to talk to him."

"About an hour after sundown," answered Scooter.

"You ain't gonna leave us like this till then, are you?" Joe Bob asked. "My arms is going numb already."

"I don't think I can take the risk after what you did to my woman."

"Well, hell boy, we said we're sorry," Joe Bob beseeched. "We promise we won't try nothing. We is trusting that you ain't no pigger. Now you has to trust us."

Lou looked at Teresa.

She looked amazed the fiend would even ask to be set free and was ready to be outraged if Lou even considered it. Lou turned back to the men.

"You boys are going to have to stay like that till we leave. We can't trust your hormones with my woman around. You'll be thinking with your little heads."

It was the longest day of Teresa's life. She stayed in the kitchen with Lou most of the day because he decided it was better to stay indoors, but after not hearing any helicopters for a few hours, they dared to take a walk down by the lake. Lou brought the bow and arrow in case they saw something he could try to kill, and he made Teresa carry the machete.

Once they were away from the house she tried to reason with him. "We should just go," she pleaded. "You heard them say he went to meet a messenger or something. He's probably dead. Remember the explosion this morning? I'll bet the cops found out where they were meeting and bombed them. Who else could it have been?"

Lou felt somewhat naive because he hadn't considered that but he didn't admit it.

"We'll wait awhile after dark, and if he doesn't show up, we'll go."

Teresa accepted it and didn't press him anymore, but it took a strong amount of her willpower.

Lou saw a group of female deer grazing on the golf course, right in the fairway of what use to be the fourteenth hole. With only one arrow, he knew he couldn't have dropped one, but he did take a shot at a rabbit and missed it badly.

They were about to head back to the house when a gift dropped out of the sky. A flock of Canadian geese landed near the river. Lou was able to walk up within twenty feet of them before he easily shot the arrow into a fat one. The bird struggled to fly but couldn't flap its wing with the arrow buried in to its side. It scampered toward the water.

Lou dropped the bow, grabbed the machete out of Teresa's hand, and dashed up to it. He grabbed hold of one of its wings just before it made it to the river. It tried to bite his hand, causing him to drop the machete. He grabbed it by the neck. Pushing the head to the ground, he secured it under his foot. Then he picked up the machete and cut its head off.

Teresa had to turn away as he came galloping toward her, holding it by what remained of the neck.

"Some luck, huh?" he said sounding gleeful. "Now we got something to do while we wait. We can cook this up and have a nice goose dinner. Maybe I can make jerky out of this fat old thing, and we can bring some with us."

They went back into the house. Lou held up the goose to show the brothers.

Nether Lou nor Teresa had any experience with preparing wild game, but Scooter was helpful giving advice when Lou promised to share it with him.

Lou pulled a wide tree stump by them and laid the goose on top of it. Scooter insisted Lou pluck it, and both men seem amused as Lou sweated and swore while he performed the laborious task.

Once dusk came, Lou and Teresa started a small fire with

dry wood, and scooter finally explained how he could burn the goose's difficult pinfeathers off over the fire.

Next he carefully skinned the bird, cutting near the sternum along the wish bone and removed the breasts nicely. After skinning the bird, he cut it in small thin strips and washed it over and over. He moved the crock pot of critter stew and cooked half of them in another pot that he hung over the fire and kept half in a separate pan on top to slow cook and air out enough to make jerky. With no salt, it wouldn't last long, but it would serve as a meal for tomorrow.

Lou left scooter's feet tied but cut the ropes off his wrists so he could eat with his own hands and feed some of the goose to Joe Bob, who Lou insisted remained fully tied.

Only the dim glow from the coals and flame illuminated the room, and being in such darkness with these animals frightened Teresa, but she didn't completely hate the danger. She was free, making her own decisions and as free as a wild animal. Even after the ordeal, she still felt sexy. She was the object of great desire out here in this world of raging male hormones, and Lou was the dominant male who saved her. She began to desire his masculinity.

It was over an hour since nightfall, so she walked over to Lou, who was still chatting with the savage brutes. She hated how well they seemed to be getting along now.

"Louis, its time we head out of here and find a place of our own."

He rose off the stump and walked over to her. "Okay, sweetie, just give me ten minutes, and we'll head out."

She frowned and nudged her head toward the door. "It's been dark long enough," she whispered. "No one is coming. So can we please get out of here now?" Her demeanor convinced Lou she meant business this time.

He nodded and touched her shoulder. "Alright, I'll just let them know we're leaving."

He walked to the men, trying to decide if he would tell them their pa might be dead. "Well guys, we're gonna hit the road I guess." He squatted next to them.

"I thought you was gonna wait for Pa," said Scooter.

"Well, Teresa can't stand being in the same house with you guys, and who can blame her after what you savages did?"

They hung their heads and Lou stood back up.

"Listen, Scooter, you can untie your legs and your brother after we leave. I'm taking the machete and bow, so don't try to track us."

He started walking away and picked up the machete. Teresa was standing by the door holding the duffel bag. Lou turned back to the brothers again. "One more thing guys. . . the cops have been looking for us since last night so be careful. I really hope your pa is okay, but..."

He lowered his head and turned away without finishing. "Let's go," he said to Teresa, and she turned toward the door. She reached for the doorknob. Before she grabbed it, it turned! The door opened as Teresa retreated.

Looking in was a stocky man with grey hair and a grey beard. He had a plump round face and an expression of surprise in his squinted eyes.

Teresa hid behind Lou. The man fumbled in his old, army green, denim jacket pockets and pulled out a pistol.

"Don't you make a fuckin' move, boy," he said, aiming it at Lou.

"It's alright, mister. We're friends. Take it easy," said Lou, raising his hands. The old man looked past Lou and squinted to see in the darkness that his sons were on the floor.

"What the hell did you do to my boys, you son of a bitch?"

"What did we do!" Teresa yelled, stepping out from behind Lou. "Your filthy boys beat him and raped me. Louis should have killed them both when he rescued me, but he spared them."

The man was shocked by her outburst and the sight of a woman. A female voice was so rare in the wild, and she was both beautiful and scolding. His gun hand lowered as he stared at her, feeling like he must respect the female.

"I just wanted to speak with you before we left," Lou said. "As you can see, your boys are okay. I even feed them goose."

"Hey pa," Scooter said and waved.

"Is Joe Bob okay?" the man asked.

"Yeah, he be alright. We just got hit in the head."

Joe Bob remained silent, feeling terribly embarrassed in front of his pa.

"Did you boys hurt this woman like she said?" the man asked.

"Hell pa, we didn't mean to," answered Scooter. "I guess we just went kinda crazy when we saw a woman. I didn't do nothing to her. Joe Bob went first and-"

"Scooter, you son of a bitch!" yelled Joe Bob. "You is one pathetic piece of shit." The grey haired man looked back to Teresa.

"I'm awful sorry for whatever they did to you Miss. My boys ain't had any practice at being respectful to women." He walked closer and whispered. "They had a hard life, and they ain't so right in the head, and their momma ran off when they were young."

Teresa turned her back to him seemingly disgusted. Lou extended his hand to him. "My name's Louis Rizzo. I was arrested for staging a rally last night. They were gonna charge me for treason, but this brave and lovely woman broke me out. Her name's Teresa."

The man looked stunned. "Lord have mercy. You're Lou Rizzo?"

Lou nodded, squinting his eyes.

"I'll be dammed, I just received news about you. Heard you was on the news last night. People were protesting for your release. They say you was gonna run for president." He chuckled. "My name's Gavin Edwards. It's good to meet you." They shook hands.

Teresa seemed puzzled. "That's impossible," she said. "How could you possibly know that? They would never allow a story like that on the news."

"The word is," Gavin replied, "someone who works for the network went against orders and got it aired on the national news."

"How could you get that information out here?" she asked.

"We got contacts in the service cities that communicate with us by using unregistered keyphones, but the G knows we been using 'em. They found two of our spies, and they try to pick up our calls. Anyway, I also got some real bad news. They killed five of our men this morning. I wonder if maybe the cops were looking for *you* and stumbled upon *them*."

"Aw shit," said Lou, shaking his head, "that's horrible. Who were the guys who got killed?"

"Our group leaders. Ain't no way the cops could have known we came up this way already. Our groups stay separated the best we can, and we use couriers to stay informed, but the leaders had to meet face-to-face last night. The house they met in got blown up. Five good men, dead just like that. They're probably gonna increase search parties all over this area and kill anyone they find." Gavin's pudgy face grew long, and his green eyes became somber.

"I guess the mission's off, boys," he said, turning to his sons. "Chuckey's dead, along with the rest of the group leaders."

The room fell silent. Lou felt guilt over the thought of him being the reason people were killed . . . good people, rebellious Americans, and leaders no less.

Finally Scooter broke the silence. "This mean we be heading back to Tupelo, pa?"

"The Bama Boys and the Delphia Diggers are heading out tonight," Gavin replied. "Some guys just started running already, but it's unsafe for everyone to disperse tonight, and I agreed we would stay the night."

"The hell with that! let's get on out a here, pa," Joe Bob said, struggling to sit up.

Gavin walked briskly over to him, his footsteps vibrating the floor. "Goddamn it, boy, when you agree to something, you don't go back on your word."

Joe Bob looked terrified of his father and curled his shoulder up to his face, which was the only defensive move he could make with his hands tied behind his back.

"I don't mean to sound like that, pa," he pleaded. "I'll keep my word, but Chuckey was a good old boy, and now he's dead. Let's get out of here tonight. This thing was a damn suicide mission. Them British fools is gonna get us all killed with this crazy plan."

Gavin grunted, unable to argue with his boy's opinion.

Lou's eyes widened the moment Joe Bob mentioned British fools. He began to consider the significance of blind coincidence.

"Mr. Rizzo, can you please cut lose my boys?" asked Gavin. "They ain't gonna do no harm to you or Teresa ever again. I promise."

Lou immediately nodded, went over to them and used the machete to start cutting the ropes.

"Louis, what are you doing? Stop it!" Teresa shouted.

"Don't worry, Teresa. These boys would never defy their father, and their father's a good man." He looked Gavin in the eyes.

Gavin returned his gaze and nodded.

Once free, both men got to their feet and stretched.

Teresa looked terrified so Lou went over to her and placed his arm around her waist.

Once they finished stretching, Joe Bob punched Scooter in the shoulder, causing him to whimper.

"You a Goddamn rat, Scooter, trying to blame everything on me."

"Now you boys act proper in front of our guests now," Gavin ordered, "and be thankful you ain't dead. Mr. Rizzo had every right to kill ya."

"Just call me Lou. We're all allies here."

"Sure thing, Lou. So you all had something to eat already, huh? Well, I'm starving. I reckon I'm gonna have some critter stew. We can talk while I eat."

"Please, have some of my goose jerky, Gavin. What ya do with it, Teresa?"

She looked at him frowning. "I packed it in the duffel bag. We were gonna take with us." She pointed toward it. "You know, when we leave," she said louder, hinting to him how bad she wanted to get going.

Lou went to the bag and dug through it. He found the

strips of jerky and brought one over to Gavin.

"Well, thank you, Lou," Gavin said and turned to Scooter. "Set us up some sitting logs, boy."

Scooter began picking out tree logs from the pile that were best appropriate for sitting on and set up four in a wide circle. The biggest one that was already out made five.

All four men sat down, leaving Teresa being forced to sit on the only log left, which was the same one she had been tied up to that morning. All four men's voracious eyes were upon her as she finally walked to the log and sat down, heaving a sigh as she did.

"So tell me about this plan and about this group, the emancipators," Lou asked.

"Sure, sure, Scooter, get us some water, and get the whiskey. We can each take a slam," Gavin ordered to his youngest.

"That's our last bottle pa, and it's half empty," Joe Bob reminded him.

"Is that right, Joe Bob? Last time I checked it was half full. Now don't upset me again, boy."

They passed around the bottle of whiskey in the glow of the fire while Gavin described the emancipators and the mission they were about to abandon.

Chapter 20

The group began out of necessity. In order to steal food and supplies from the service cities, they had to work together. They shared everything.

As they became more sophisticated, they began rebellious missions against the government, trying to get people not to join the G.A. plan or quit and live in the wild. When the government began making air strikes against them, they split into groups of eight to ten, and even those groups would split up by day and only meet in designated areas at night. Couriers would deliver messages between the group leaders.

When six British army men arrived out of the blue in Crystal Lake and were planning an attack on the government, the emancipator's leaders met with them and decided to help. Killing members of the government, including the president, they agreed, would be the decisive act for liberty. It was a plan worth the risk of death, all emancipators agreed.

The more Lou heard about the plan, the more it did seem like suicide for the emancipators. They would give some cover to the British when they fled the aftermath of their rocket attack.

Lou assumed that the British wanted to use them to take the blame, so surviving U.S. officials would not suspect foreign involvement. Five groups were making their way to Rosemont, each on separate paths. They were to converge at dam number four, along the Des Plaines River in the forest preserve near the Rosemont Convention Center. Thirty-six brave Americans were going to risk their lives to propel their government into disarray by helping the British with surveillance and giving them cover.

Lou felt great pride for his countrymen, but now, thanks to his escape, all five team leaders were dead. They got together last night to discuss and update the plan now that they were close to Rosemont.

During the search for Lou, the group was silently

discovered when a gate officer on foot noticed thin smoke streams coming out of the chimney where they were gathered. He quietly looked into a window and confirmed five scavies. G.A.T.E. headquarters followed protocol and called in an air strike while they kept surveillance on the house. At first light they were vaporized. Now the British faction would find themselves alone at the Rosemont rendezvous area in two nights.

"They're gonna need some help, you know," Lou said. "At least one group should go and meet them. We can't have British troops attacking our government without Americans there."

Gavin rubbed his beard in silence.

"Do you know how to get to the rendezvous area?" asked Lou.

Joe Bob looked at Lou, scowling and blowing through his lips.

"Well, I ain't ever been around these parts," said Gavin, "and I don't have a map. Chuckey was our guide. I suppose I could find it eventually . . . just a matter of finding the river, I guess."

"I got a suggestion, Gavin," said Lou. "Why don't you lead a team to meet up with the British? I could draw up a map for you. I know this area well, and I know right where dam number four on the Des Plaines River is."

Everyone's eyes widened but Gavin's. He stared at Lou with an unaffected serious expression.

"I would like to lead another team on a separate mission to infiltrate the American Airways Chicago studio and broadcast a message to the people."

"You is out of your mind, boy," Joe Bob proclaimed. "Ain't nobody gonna go with you. You ain't no leader. It's over, and we going home, right pa?"

Gavin ignored him and kept staring at Lou. "Do you believe in God, Lou?" he asked.

Lou shrugged his shoulders. "I believe anything is possible, I guess, but if there really is a God, I don't depend on any help from him."

Gavin frowned.

"Well, we do, and just maybe he sent you here for a reason."

He turned to Joe Bob now. "I believe everybody who ain't rich should know this government has got to be stopped, but there ain't many people ready to fight for their freedom, Joe Bob. That's why we have to do it for them. We got to be the brave ones, and you two have to treat a woman with respect. You understand? I hope the Lord will forgive you for what you done to Teresa. Maybe some day she can forgive you too, but I don't suspect that will come easy."

Both Joe Bob and Scooter looked down to their laps.

Teresa looked at Gavin admirably for the first time.

After a moment of silence, Gavin turned back to Lou. "It ain't gonna be easy, Lou. Like I said, they gonna be a hunting for us now."

"That's true," said Lou, "but my team will move first and create a distraction for you guys to do your job. Can we get enough people together?"

"We're meeting with some people from the other groups one more time before the rest of us disperse. It's tonight before dawn. If you want to come with and try to convince the others to follow your plan, I'll back you up, but I can't guarantee anyone will listen to ya after what happened and all."

"That's fine. One thing I can do is convince people what's right. Are you guys armed?"

"Some of us managed to keep our guns, but ammunition is low, and there ain't no way to get more."

"We can't win any gunfight anyways," said Lou. "We need intelligence, stealth, and camouflage."

"Well, we know camouflage. We all dress in green or military fatigues. A lot of these old boys are veterans, and some of them even mix up soot and mud to paint their faces with. If it's dark out and they in the woods, they're practically invisible. We ain't all dumb hillbillies." He motioned at Joe Bob and Scooter. "You'd be impressed at how good we are."

"I am impressed, immensely," Lou said. "Stealth is the only chance we have. We can't be getting into any shootouts with G.A. cops or national guardsmen. I'm sure some of them are in favor of overthrowing the government, but most of them will follow their orders to the death because they don't think they have a choice. If my message gets out, maybe they will realize they do have a choice."

They spent two hours discussing the idea. Mostly just Lou and Gavin were talking. Scooter and Joe Bob were restless and began pacing around the house, stoking the fire, packing their things and arguing with each other.

Teresa went over to Lou and shared his log. She leaned against him, appearing to be drowsy. Gavin explained that if they were going to gather the remaining emancipists, they would have to be at the rally point before daybreak, around 4:30 a.m., and hope representatives from the other groups didn't already flee.

Lou explained how to get to dam number four in detail, and Teresa knew where the news station was.

"It's by the Park West Lounge on the north side," she explained.

"Well, we better get some rest," Gavin finally admitted. "We can sleep about five and a half hours, and then we got to get to the rally point." He turned to his boys and said, "You got everything packed but the blankets, boys?"

"Yeah pa," Scooter answered.

"Get that blue flashlight out and give it to Lou."

Scooter did as he was told.

Gavin turned to Lou. "You two can take that blanket upstairs so you can be alone. Use the flashlight to get situated, but keep it shielded so it ain't too bright. If there be some piggers looking around out there and they see a light in the window, we all dead."

Lou nodded.

"We'll sleep down here, and I'll wake you around four in the morning."

Lou got up and took Teresa by the hand. He grabbed the blanket Gavin pointed to.

"Thanks, Gavin, see you at four." They walked upstairs as he shined the light through the blanket to keep it dim.

They took turns using the upstairs bathroom, peeing in to the waterless toilet. Teresa chose the smaller of the two upstairs bedrooms because it looked less dusty. After shutting the door, Lou laid out the blanket in the middle of the floor. They nuzzled together and pulled the end of the blanket over them. Lou was on his back and Teresa had her arm, chest, and head resting on his chest. Her breasts felt good against him and immediately sparked sexual desire within him to rise in harmony with the body heat they generated.

He naturally assumed after the horrific event that morning, this was not the time to act on his desires. He fought if off by thinking about the mission.

She lifted her leg and rested it upon his. Slowly she bent it upward until her thigh was up to his groin.

Uncontrollably, he became erect. His pants bulged, and he couldn't avoid picturing how alluring she looked to him earlier, all tied up and nude.

Minutes later, it became unbearable, and he would have to get up and excuse himself. He tried to last as long as he could, but he began breathing deeply, and his hand slid into his underwear to adjust himself. He couldn't help but to squeeze it a few times before he forced his hand back out.

It was only a few minutes later that he reached the point where he had to get up. He exhaled deeply, and just as he began to sit up, she moved her face up to his and gently pressed her lips upon his.

The wonderful feeling caused him to wrap his arm around her back and kiss her harder. She drew back, giving him a push, and he relented with all his willpower, moaning as their lips came apart. Close in the darkness, the dim moonlight streaming in through the windows allowed him to see the beauty of her eyes. They looked at each other for a long moment, neither one turning away.

"Would you still want to make love to me after what happened today?"

"Of course," he said with a chuckle. She frowned, so he caressed her back. "I desire you just as much now as when I first laid eyes on you."

She heaved a sigh of relief and began moving her hand over his chest and stomach in a circular rotation, eventually dipping lower and grazing the tip of his erection.

"I wanna make love to you," she whispered. "I hope this doesn't sound too weird, but I can't have that dreadful man be the last one who was inside me. I need it to be someone I care about."

It did sound weird to him. How could she want sex after being raped.

It must be because I'm so damn irresistible, he amused his ego. *What if Joe Bob gave her some sexually transmitted disease or something? Oh, come on. It's a dream come true. Don't be an idiot.*

Without a word, he kissed her and began to roll on top of her. She pushed him back.

"No, I don't want to be held down," she whispered. "You just lay there and let me be in charge. It will help me get over . . ." She cleared her throat. "You know, the nightmare."

He lay on his back. She unbuttoned his pants and slid them off, then remover her own. She took his erection in her hand and squeezed it, making him throb. His eyelids fluttered, his mouth opened, and his breathing deepened. It seemed as if all his feeling and sensitivity was now condensed into the throbbing inches she carelessly held in her soft hand.

For the first time since he was a teen, he feared he may prematurely ejaculate. He let out a moan, then covered his mouth.

"We better be quiet. I don't want them to hear us and get jealous," he said trembling. This wasn't a night for foreplay. Oral sex wasn't going to happen. They were not at a fancy hotel or even a rundown apartment with a soft bed and a shower. They were in the wild where you had to fill your needs in the most basic ways. She removed her panties and climbed on top of him. After they kissed for a few minutes longer, she guided him into her. Both of them were biting their lips to restrain themselves from moaning too loudly.

Every movement she made was magnificent as he held her waist while she gently bounced up and down and slid back and forth. Nothing else in the world mattered, only the next glorious thrust of pure ecstasy. It felt like his whole life lead up to this moment, like all the hardships he endured was now worth it.

For her it was therapeutic elation. She was afraid she might not be able to orgasm after the ordeal she went through, but now it didn't matter. She had a good man inside her, and it felt wonderful. She was determined not to let the horrendous memory of Joe Bob violating her ruin her sex life. She was a free woman, surviving in the wild, living among savages, and she didn't hate it. She began to flow with her every move.

He felt strong, hard, and dangerous, like his penis was a lethal weapon ready to burst uncontrollably. He held out for minute upon minute, savoring every sensation. Finally, he couldn't hold it any longer and began to push her up to pull out.

"No, keep it inside me," she demanded and thrust down on him. "I won't get pregnant."

He obeyed and exploded in blissful, quiet pleasure. She fell down onto him, and they embraced, still united as he slowly shrunk and eventually slipped out.

Twenty minutes later they fell asleep.

Chapter 21

It was four hours and twenty three minutes later when light knocking on the door woke them in unison. They popped their heads up. Lou fumbled his hand around until he found the flashlight. He brought it under the blanket and turned it on.

"Time to go, you all." Scooters voice called through the door.

Lou felt like calling it all off just so he could sleep in as long as he wanted. He was never a morning person, and he intensely felt like just letting the country go to hell as long as he could sleep more and be with Teresa for every remaining night. He shook his head vigorously and rubbed his eyes.

"Alright, we'll be right down," he announced groggily, Then he whispered to Teresa, "last night was amazing."

She forced a smile, but her eyes displayed distress.

At first it annoyed him.

Why the hell should she seem sad? Didn't she even like it?

Then he began to grasp how much she had been through the day before.

"I never asked you how you feel about this plan," he said. "Truth is, I don't even know if I believe it will work. But one thing I do know is that I don't want you to get hurt. I need you to be safe somewhere so I can be inspired, you know. It's like, when this is done, I want someone to come home to, someone to live for." He felt uncomfortable and corny.

She lowered her eyebrows, making her cute but dangerous frown. "Are you saying you don't want me to come with you?"

"No, of course not." He paused in thought. "Well, actually I guess I am saying that, but only for the mission. I don't want you with me when we're risking our lives. What if you get killed, and I survive? I would lose all motivation to go on living. No, I don't want you risking your life. That's final." He got to his feet and scanned for his clothes. Pulling his underwear and pants on, he felt sticky and unclean. He wanted to take a hot shower immensely. He set the flashlight down by her and left the room without a word. He went to the bathroom with his hands outstretched in the dark and pissed in the dry toilet. When he finished and opened the door, she was standing there.

"You're one selfish son of a bitch," she said.

Lou was stunned. "What?" he stupidly replied.

"You're so concerned about me dying and how hard it would be on you. What about me if you die! What am I suppose to do . . . live with the fuckin' hillbillies? They can all take turns raping me. Thanks a lot, Louis."

She really seemed upset. Lou sensed she was about to hit him with the flashlight so he grabbed and hugged her defensively.

"Teresa, we've been together for one day and two nights, and I've fallen in love with you already. I don't wanna lose you. If I'm gonna risk my life for the American people, I want you to be alive and among them." He held her by the shoulders, away from him now, and looked into her distant brown eyes. "I wasn't going to leave you with a group of horny hillbillies. I was thinking we use your keyphone. I know someone in Park Ridge we could call. Melanie Newman's her name. She could pick you up and hide you at her house. She lives in a mansion with just her and her mother. You can go with her, and I can come and get you when this is all over, win or lose."

Gavin's voice interrupted from downstairs. "Hey there, you two! We best be getting a move on!"

She moved into the bathroom and nudged him out without a word.

The Edwards boys were packed and ready to go when Lou came downstairs.

Scooter held out a can of stewed tomatoes with a plastic fork in it. "Here, we saved you some. Eat a couple and give the rest to your woman."

Lou eagerly swallowed some and found it refreshing.

When Teresa came down, she stopped at the last stair and looked coldly at Scooter and Joe Bob.

Lou walked over to her and held out the can. "Here, they saved us some. Eat the rest."

She reluctantly came off the stair, handed him the flashlight, and took the can. She began to eat, grimacing as she swallowed the last tomato.

"Turn that light off, old boy," said Gavin. "Your eyes need to get used to the dark."

Joe Bob was looking down at the black garments held in his hand. He walked up to Lou only briefly glancing eye contact. "I picked some black shirts out for you two to wear on top so you ain't so noticeable in the dark," he said, extending his hand. Lou took it and then Joe Bob moved in front of Teresa. "Miss, this one's for you," he said.

Teresa didn't move and wouldn't look at him. She looked at Lou, who nodded to her so she quickly snatched the shirt from his hand.

They put on the shirts, and Gavin handed Lou the backpack with the goose jerky and a sheepskin flask filled with water. Lou put it on.

Joe Bob was reunited with his bow and arrow, which was attached to his backpack, and Scooter had his machete. Gavin carried no pack but had his gun and Lou suddenly felt vulnerable.

Gavin opened the door and looked back at each of them. "This is how it begins, five of us setting out, united in a cause to fight for what we know is right. May God watch over us and guide us through the darkness so that we may bring back the light of His holiness."

"Amen," Joe Bob and Scooter said together.

They set out into the night.

As they cleared the front porch steps and the front yard, Teresa never looked back for a final view of the house she would never forget.

They walked along side the Chicago River for awhile. The air was cool and moist. The fresh scent of the trees was invigorating, but Lou's stomach was uneasy with nervousness and hunger. Gavin led the way. Nobody talked, and their footsteps were quiet and steady.

Once they reached the Chicago Northwest railroad tracks, they followed it for a half a mile until they came to Forest Glen woods. They headed back into the forest until they were along side the river again. Not much farther up the river was a clearing where a three foot white birch tree branch had been stuck in the ground.

Gavin stopped and waited for everyone to huddle together.

"This is the rally point. We can all sit down over there and wait to see who shows up."

They sat on a log at the edge of the woods. A fire pit had been made but no coals smoldered. Gavin was sitting with his boys on one end with Lou and Teresa all the way on the other end.

After a few minutes, Gavin got up and came over to them. He squatted in front of them. "Listen Lou, when they come, all I can do is explain your idea. You're going to have to sell the plan and get them to believe you're a strong leader."

"That's what I do, my friend," Lou replied. "Everyone's good at something." Then he began to talk about his time as an independent senator, how corrupt and fixed the system was, and how he still managed to reach people.

Scooter and Joe Bob moved closer, and for ten minutes everyone listened to Lou explain why the American dream collapsed.

Suddenly, without a sound, two men emerged from the south. Lou went silent when he finally noticed them, only ten yards away. Both men were of average height, dressed in dark green, and had black cotton caps on their heads. They reminded Lou of stereotypical cat burglars.

"That you, Edwards?" a man said. He did not have a southern accent and sounded local.

"Yeah, it's me. Who's that? Reilly?" Gavin stood and approached him.

"Yeah," said Reilly. "You and your boys gonna head back south?" He looked at Lou and Teresa. "I don't believe I've ever seen him before, and I know I've never met this woman."

Reilly had thick brown eyebrows and facial hair matching his brown eyes. He looked to be in his late twenties.

"That man there is Louis Rizzo. Next to him is Teresa. She's the one who broke him out of jail."

Lou waved. "Hi, how are ya, Reilly?" he said.

Teresa just nodded.

The other man who was with Reilly walked over to Lou excitedly. He bent down a little to see Lou's face close up. "You're Louis Rizzo?" he asked.

Lou nodded.

"We just got word yesterday that you were in the news. You wanted to run for president, and they arrested you for treason. I can't believe you escaped."

"Yeah, I told him all about the news story," Gavin interrupted.

"I'm Rick Betarelli. Its great to meet you," the man said and shook hands with Lou. Then he moved in front of Teresa, "So you broke him out. That's really impressive. You'd make a great emancipator."

"Thanks, Rick," she said.

He was a strapping young man. When he leaned in close to shake her hand, she saw he had striking blue eyes. She looked over to Lou with a wry smile.

"Listen, you two," Gavin began. "we're not heading back south because we still got work to do. We got a new plan, and we need about sixteen to twenty men to form two new groups. Lou will lead one on a mission to infiltrate the American Airways news station, and I'll lead one to rendezvous with the British."

"You lead! That's insane," Rick said, "If anything, I should lead. I'm younger, stronger, and smarter than old man Edwards."

"Now listen here, boy," Gavin began.

"Just forget it." Reilly cut in. "We don't need a leader because this isn't gonna happen. Choppers will be circling again in about two hours. Man, don't you understand they know we're here. Abort mission. Live to fight another day."

Lou stood up and confronted him. "The fight is now,

Reilly. The British are gonna attack our government. Once that happens, war could break out at any moment. Don't you think we should be there?"

Reilly just stared at him oddly.

"I have to get a message out to the people before that happens. If we can infiltrate the news station and broadcast a message to the people, I can tell them what's really happening. If people listen to me and hear the danger our government has put us in, maybe I can get local workers to converge and protest right outside the Rosemont Convention Center. That will be a perfect distraction before the British attack. After the attack, we can overthrow the government if we have enough people to take over, and I can step in as acting president. The W.U.N. knows of me and will accept my leadership. Then we can stop a nuclear war and begin putting our democracy back together." Lou put his hand on Reilly's shoulder and looked deep into his eyes, "I just want you to understand, it's now or never, Reilly."

Reilly aggressively brushed his hand off. "A lot of the men already died," he said, "and the search party that killed Mike and the rest of the team leaders was probably looking for you and just happened to stumble upon them. They had no reason to be looking for us out here."

"He knows, Reilly. It's not his fault," Gavin said.

Reilly turned to Rick. "What do you think, Rick? You crazy enough to go with them?"

"Yeah, why not. We're here to do a mission. The leaders wouldn't want us to just give up and go home." He looked at Gavin, scowling. "I should lead the team though."

"Alright then," Reilly said, "the rest of our two groups is at a shack with Phil and Pat, about a quarter mile from here. That's six men, if they all agree to help and not including me because I'm not in on this. You got twelve people all together if they all agree. That's about all you can expect. I'm pretty sure everyone else cut out last night."

"Fine, let's get going," said Lou.

Not Much more was said before they set out in a staggered formation. They left the Forest Glen woods, crossed the train tracks and followed them east until they reached the Indian Road woods where they followed the fence along the edge of the trees. A hint of sunlight began to creep over the clear sky, dawn was looming.

All seven of them walked boldly in a group now under the cover of the woods.

Rick was leading and turned back to them. "It's just a block up this way," he said. "We'll stay in the woods and then climb the fence when we get there."

They continued walking as the dawn arrived. The sky was brightening by the minute.

Five minutes later they paused.

Rick was glaring at the house, looking upset.

"That's the shack, the grey one there," Reilly said and pointed. "We'll climb over, two at a time; wait until the pair ahead gets in before the next one goes."

Rick was looking up at the roof of the shack, shaking his head. "Look at these morons," he said in disgust. "There's smoke coming out of the chimney. They must have forgot to put out the coals." He grabbed the fence and began to climb, followed by Reilly.

Just as they reached the top and began to descend the other side, a familiar sound filled their ears. It was the dreaded air thumping sound of helicopter blades! The sound amplified in seconds, traveling at a high speed, approaching fast.

"Take cover!" Lou yelled, snapping everyone out of their frozen shock.

Reilly and Rick took cover under a nearby tree that was fortunately a mature oak. The rest of them scurried away from the fence and found their own trees to take cover under.

"I got to warn them!" Rick yelled.

"Don't move from under this tree! They'll spot you in a heartbeat!" Reilly implored.

"Get out of the house!" Rick stood yelling and suddenly ran out toward the house. "Get out of the house!" he yelled again as he left the cover of the tree and ran out into the street.

The S-80A, multi-mission, black hawk helicopter arrived, immediately firing a screeching missile. Then **boom**! The house exploded. Burning debris shot upward and began raining down.

Rick was thrown back by the blast and fell in the middle of the street.

The black hawk flew over the blast sight, then circled one hundred eighty degrees around, now facing Rick, who was struggling to his hands and knees. The machine guns opened fire and filled him full of bullets so fast Rick couldn't even scream.

The black hawk continued to circle the area, searching for any more defiant Americans to exterminate. Nobody moved a muscle or uttered a word as the killing machine hovered around the area for minutes.

Once it moved farther away, Lou broke cover and ran up to the fence. Reilly was standing with his back against the oak tree with his eyes tightly shut.

"Reilly! Reilly!" Lou called to him.

Reilly finally opened his eyes and looked at Lou.

"We got to get out of here."

Reilly nodded and ran to the fence. He grabbed it, ready to climb.

Lou yelled, "Wait!"

Reilly stopped and looked at him, dumbfounded.

"Did Rick have a gun?" asked Lou.

He nodded, looking stunned.

"Get his gun," Lou ordered.

Reilly shook his head, scowling an evil stare.

"We need it, Reilly. Get his gun. Hurry before it comes back."

Reilly impressed Lou by immediately turning back and running fearlessly out to Rick's bloody corpse. He watched with admiration as Reilly squatted by the body.

Suddenly, the sound of a truck engine emerged from the south end of Indian Road. Reilly looked down the road and saw an army truck was bearing down on him a few short blocks away, and he froze. Lou saw two gate cops, who were keeping the house under surveillance, come charging from around the north side of the burning remains of the house.

"Reilly, cops to your left!" yelled Lou. Reilly grabbed toward Rick's bloody chest and pulled out a pistol as he looked to his left.

The cops aimed their bolt blasters at him, but Reilly was fast and accurate. He hit one cop in the neck and one in the shoulder, dropping them both before they could shoot.

He quickly undid the belt of Rick's shoulder holster and removed it. Holding it by the belt, he put the gun in it, then ran back and pitched it over the fence.

Lou picked up the gun and fastened the holster around his waist and shoulder. Reilly climbed and jumped off the top of the fence falling to the ground. Lou helped him up by the arms and they ran into the woods.

"Follow me!" Lou yelled as he ran to Teresa and grabbed her by the arm.

The group of six ran through the woods like frightened prey.

Lou stood behind a tree to look back. He watched through the foliage. The military truck stopped in front of Rick's body, and guardsmen began to jump out the back.

Lou led the group at a quick pace, west through the woods, back toward the old Edgebrook golf course.

After eight minutes of intense running, they made it to the border of the golf course and climbed a fence. They dashed through the overgrown fairways. Lou was breathing deeply and wearing out fast. Beyond what used to be the thirteenth green, was a hill one had to walk up to get to the next hole. Lou almost didn't make it up the hill. Teresa had to help him. Up there was a wood hut where refreshments used to be sold. The front had a window that opened up and a shelf where the condiments and napkins would be, but it had been boarded up with plywood years ago.

The tree cover was dense, and the grass was thigh high around it. Lou scampered over to the hut, and the others followed.

"We have to hide out here till dark," said Lou. "It's our only chance."

Scooter tried the solid wooden door. It was locked. "Man, let's get out of here. The doors is locked up tight," he said.

"Scooter, give me your machete," Lou ordered. Once he handed it to him, Lou immediately threw it upon the roof.

"What the hell are you doing, boy?" Scooter roared.

"Give me a boost up," Lou said to Joe Bob.

Joe Bob entwined his fingers. Lou put his foot in his hands and got boosted up high enough to grab the end of the flat, tar roof. Lou pulled himself up with difficulty. He had prior knowledge of a skylight in the middle of the roof. He used the machete to pry it up from the already loose casing. Once he got it high enough, he propped it up with the machete. He turned on his side and dangled his legs through. Slowly, he inched his body in. Once he was ready to fall, he grabbed the handle of the machete and fell into the refreshment hut.

He felt his ankle bend inward on impact and rolled with it to the ground as he dropped the machete, barely saving himself from injury. His skinny ankles had been prone to sprains his whole life. He exhaled in relief as he grabbed his ankle and did circles with his foot. He got up and unlocked the door. Once everyone was inside, he locked it, picked up the machete, and went to the east wall that faced the path they walked up. He jammed the tip of the blade into the cedar wall, head high, and began to push and twist it back and forth.

"What are you doing?" Gavin asked quietly.

"I'm making a peephole so we can see if anyone comes up the path."

Once Lou broke through the cedar siding with the tip of the blade, he used Joe Bob's arrow to clear out a peephole. He blew out the dust and peeked through it, satisfied it would give him a good view of the path. He finally relaxed and looked over the faces of his band of rebels, save Reilly, who sat against the back wall with his arms on his knees and his face buried in his hands.

"Someone has to keep an eye out at all times," Lou said, "If they come up that path in small numbers, we have to consider ambushing them. We could drag their bodies in here and take their weapons and clothes. I just wish we had a quiet weapon like a bolt blaster."

All but Reilly stared at him oddly, without response, until Scooter went to the peephole to keep an eye out.

Lou took Teresa's hand, and they went over to the grieving Reilly. They squatted down, one on each side of him.

"Reilly, you Okay?" Lou whispered.

He slowly looked up, glancing at each of them, then keeping his eyes on Teresa, he groaned, "All my friends are dead, every one of them."

"I'm sorry Reilly," said Lou, "but they would want you to fight on, and we need you too. Your country needs you."

"The hell with it. It's your Goddamn fault they're dead." His eyes were tearing, but his gaze at Lou was fierce and hateful.

Lou frowned and looked at Teresa. She gave him a slight wink and put her arm around Reilly's shoulder. Reilly turned his gaze back to her.

"I'm so sorry your friends are gone," she whispered. "You have new friends now, and we need to look after each other."

Lou stood and walked back to the Edwards boys. Gavin handed him a water bottle. He sipped and brought it to Teresa. A jolt of jealousy hit him, seeing her arm was still over Reilly's shoulder, and now his head was leaning on her chest as he sobbed quietly. He handed the bottle to her and lifted his shoulders, his palms faced upward in a (what's this) manor. She frowned at him so he walked away.

"I got a bad feeling here, Lou," said Gavin, "We trapped here."

"Don't worry, the door's locked, and it's unlikely anyone would know there's a skylight on top of this hut that we used to get in."

"How did you know?"

"I use to golf here years ago. I bought hotdogs and beer here. One time I got caught in a lightning storm on this hole so I ran here, and the door was unlocked so I came in for shelter. I remembered that skylight because it was leaking, so I was pretty sure the old thing would be loose and I could jar it open with a machete."

Suddenly they heard a helicopter approaching. Everyone gazed up at the skylight uneasily. They all looked terrified until the sound dissipated.

"We need a plan," Lou said, "They probably split up in

small groups to search for us, so if two or three guardsmen come walking up that path alone we have to be prepared to kill them."

The Edwards boys looked at him strangely.

"What? Don't look at me like that!"

This idea of his was strange to him too, and he didn't realize it could be a side effect of the neurotoxin that altered his psyche from pacifist to potentially murderous.

"I don't want to kill anyone, but this is war. They would shoot us on sight. If we had a way to stun them, we would, but all we have is three guns."

"Yeah, that's true," Gavin said, "and when we fire our guns, all the rest of the troops hear it and come a running."

Lou hung his head. He knew this was true, but he wanted army gear and weapons badly, and killing seemed a small price to ask.

"This is true, Gavin." Lou put his hand on his shoulder. "Every fiber of my being used to be against killing, but something changed in me recently, and I know we may need to kill. This is it; the revolution has begun. They have every intention of killing us. You saw what they did to Rick." He turned to the others. "We'll wait for them to pass, then tell them to freeze and lay down their weapons. If they turn around, we shoot at their heads. Are you guys as good a shooter as Reilly? He took down those two cops like a marksman."

"You ever kill anyone, Lou?" said Gavin, heavy with sarcasm and getting in Lou's face.

"No," Lou replied, "but I was prepared to kill your boys when they were having their way with Teresa." Everyone flinched because Lou's tone was confrontational and loud. Gavin stood his ground.

"I'm grateful you didn't kill my boys, but if you hesitate for a second, you're dead. These are trained killers that will blow your head off. You ever even fire a gun, Mr. Rizzo?"

He had raised his voice high enough to make Lou place his finger on his lips and shush him. Lou suddenly lifted his hands to his head and inhaled deeply. "Okay, forget about ambushing anyone," he said. "We sit tight until dark, and then we head out for the television studio. If something happens to us here, we improvise."

They all silently agreed and eventually sat down. Five would rest while one would keep an eye looking out the peephole. Lou opened the backpack and split up the rest of the goose jerky since it would spoil soon. As they ate and rested, Lou discussed his intentions.

The hope of recruiting more people died with the brave patriots in the house explosion, so splitting into two groups was impossible. Lou said they would have to meet with the British themselves, right after they pull off an improbable rebel takeover of the government owned American Airways television studio. Everyone, including Teresa, seemed pessimistic.

"I know this may sound crazy, but it's all true. Our leaders have decided they will go to war rather than comply with the W.U.N. They have our troops strategically placed around the country prepared for any land invasion. They plan on using nukes and are prepared to get nuked. I know this because they've been digging bomb shelters, and I've been in one. It's in the middle of Park Ridge so I'm sure they've been digging bomb shelters in every gated city and at every military base. The rest of us will probably die in the blasts or during the nuclear winter. You see, they plan on winning a nuclear world war. Each of their gated cities have everything they need to survive, including an underclass to do their labor.

If we can't overthrow these bastards the world population will plunge drastically."

"The British guys said war is close, but are they really gonna use nukes?" asked Gavin.

"You bet they are! That's exactly what they want, to cut the population and just have enough workers to maintain the fields in their private utopia." He paused to look at everyone to see if they adsorbed the gravity of it all. "If the British kill the right people, and the chain of command is disrupted, we have a chance to overthrow the government. A new leader has to take charge immediately. This is critical, or we could plunge into chaos. I'm gonna be that leader. The W.U.N. knows me and will deal with me. Now, first we have to get the people to remember me. The American Airways television station broadcasts local and network feeds. We sneak in, take hostages, and I'll record a quick statement, and we'll order them to broadcast it on national T.V. Then we try to get out before they come and kill us. After that, we go to meet the British at dam number four. It's just five or six miles from the T.V. station."

There was silence for a moment until Joe Bob finally broke it. "Come on now, boy, you know we ain't never gonna get out of there alive. How you gonna be president when you full of holes?"

Lou looked thoughtfully at him. "Good point, Joe Bob. I'm sure everyone was thinking that."

Scooter had abandoned his duty of looking out the peephole for the last half minute and put his head back against the wood to look out again.

"I have a plan how we can get out safely," continued Lou. "Even if it doesn't work, I promise we'll have time to get away. Believe me, I don't wanna die, and I don't want any of you guys to die either. I just need you all to trust in me and believe I would never risk our lives recklessly…"

Suddenly Scooter Jumped back from the wall and slapped Lou's arm with his hand while pressed his finger to his lips to shut him up. "They a coming!" he whispered.

Lou scurried to the peephole. He looked out and saw two national guardsmen walking slowly and quietly up the path, side by side, one looking assiduously north and one south. Lou's heart accelerated at the sight. These were not G.A. officers armed with humane weapons like a bolt blaster and a Billy club; they were ruthlessly trained army men holding assault rifles.

Lou darted away from the wall and over to the group. He waved his fingers to signal every one to follow him to the west wall and then had them lean up against the wall to the left of the door.

"Get your guns out," Lou whispered to Gavin and Reilly who had their own guns. Then he took Rick's former gun out of the shoulder holster and handed it to Joe Bob. "If they break in, I'll get them to walk over to me and you guys sneak up behind them. Order them to drop their weapons. If they don't, shoot them in the head."

Lou ran back to the east wall and looked out the peephole again. Suddenly he realized what he needed for his decoy to work. He ran over to Teresa and grabbed her hand.

"You have to do this with me," he whispered. He stood before the three men holding guns "kill 'em if you have to," he repeated, looking at Reilly, the one he had most confidence in. He led Teresa to the east wall, opposite of the door, and sat down with her. He put his arm around her shoulder and his left leg over her legs with his knee propped up. "If they bust through that door yell, 'please don't shoot; we're not armed,'" he whispered in her ear and felt her body start trembling.

"Check it out," they heard a deep authoritative voice say form outside.

"Yeah," the other replied.

"Wait," the deep voice said and then spoke too quietly for Lou to totally understand, but he thought he made out, "Grass has been trampled," and "I'll cover you."

Fifteen seconds later the door knob jiggled. Lou noticed the look of terror on the faces of Joe Bob, Scooter, and Reilly, but Gavin was staring right back at him, not in terror, but in anger.

Lou remembered Gavin was the one who felt uneasy about hiding here. This was the second time his instincts were wrong about hiding somewhere.

He despaired. *Damn, I'm gonna get everyone killed! I'm not cut out to be a leader. I don't have the instincts.*

Everyone was taking short, silent breaths. Half a minute passed of almost total silence. Only the slight sound of footfalls from outside could be heard.

Another moment passed, and everyone began to relax a bit, feeling like the troops moved on.

Lou and Teresa exhaled with relief at the same time.

Then…**BAM!** A combat boot collided with the door, ripping the bolt halfway through the door jam. Everyone shuddered quietly except for Teresa, who let out an audible gasp.

BAM! The next kick made the door fly open, displaying

a soldier pointing a rifle in. Teresa missed her line and Lou was first to cry out.

"Please don't shoot. We're unarmed."

"Get you arms over your head, now!" The soldier yelled.

They both raised their arms.

"My name's Lou Rizzo. I'm sure your superiors would want you to bring us back alive."

"It's him," the soldier said to the other.

"Is the woman with him?" A deep voice from outside asked.

"Yep, she's here; I got them both covered.

"Get up slowly and walk over to me with you hands over your head."

"I can't walk," Lou said while crying as convincingly as he could. "I busted up my knee real bad jumping down from the skylight. It hurts so fuckin' bad. Please take us back. I'll do whatever they want."

The soldier took a few steps in, his gaze held on them.

"I can't put any weight on it. Please, you gotta help me."

The other soldier lingered at the doorway.

"Get them down on their stomachs and secure their hands. I'll cover you and radio our location."

The first soldier moved closet to Lou and Teresa with his rifle aimed toward their heads. "You heard the man. Lay on your stomachs."

"Alright, alright, please just be careful. My knee popped out real bad," Lou whimpered, while gingerly lowering himself to the floor.

"You too lady, on the floor!" Private Brockman yelled.

"Check the room, McKenzie, and radio in," he said to the soldier at the door without taking his eyes off Lou and Teresa.

Corporal McKenzie took one step in. He glanced carelessly side to side and lowered his rifle without looking behind him and immediately grabbed his radio off his belt and raised it near his mouth.

Just as he pushed the button to speak, Gavin sprang out

from behind the open door and chopped down on the soldier's arm, making him drop the radio and gasp. The soldier turned to his assailant and saw a pistol pointed at his nose. Gavin's messy grey hair and wrinkled round face was a blur in the background.

"Drop the weapon or die," Gavin said calmly. The other soldier turned, swinging his rifle toward Gavin.

Lou sprang up from his position and grabbed the barrel of the rifle with his right hand. Brockmann was shocked at Lou's swift movement, but he was more shocked to see two lean and grubby men dressed in green, pointing pistols right at his head.

"Drop the gun, boy, or we gonna drop bullets in your head," Joe Bob told him.

McKenzie dropped his rifle to the ground, and Brockmann loosened his grip as Lou pulled the assault rifle out of his hands.

"Hands in the air, you two!" Lou yelled once he aimed it at them. They obeyed. "Now get up against the wall." With frightened expressions, they obeyed. "Now take everything off and throw it toward us."

"What?" McKenzie uttered.

"Strip down to your fuckin' underwear! Now!" Lou roared.

They began unhitching their belts. Scooter picked McKenzie's rifle off the floor. All five men were armed and pointing weapons at the two soldiers stripping.

Brockmann was Lou's height and looked young. He was staring at Lou in contempt while unbuttoning his shirt.

"So you are a fuckin' terrorist, huh Rizzo," he said boldly. "Just like they told us, you're a traitor to your own country. Why would anyone want a terrorist like you to be president?"

"One man's terrorist is another man's freedom fighter," answered Lou. "You guys have to know by now our government is leading us to war, right? Notice any new bomb shelter being constructed lately?"

"Yeah, so what," Brockmann said and threw his shirt to the ground. Anger raged in him as he looked over the group. "You're still a disgrace. Look at you with your band of filthy scavies. What do you do, hide out here in the woods and take turns nailing your little bitch over there?"

The rage impulse that had emerged after Lou's exposure to the neurotoxin flared up in his altered psyche. His sight was tinted with red. Thinking dissolved, and only anger remained. He spun the rifle around with his left hand and stepped forward. Lou bent back his arms, cocked his wrists and prepared to smash this asshole's face with the butt of the rifle. He was staring at Brockmann's offensive face and couldn't wait till blood flowed from it. Suddenly another face appeared in front of it.

McKenzie jumped in front of Brockmann and raised his hand to block Lou's advance.

"Wait, wait, just take it easy!" he yelled, holding his hands up to defend.

Lou stopped in his tracks, like a man being called out of hypnosis with a snap of the fingers.

"He doesn't know what he's saying," pleading McKenzie. "Don't hurt him, please. He's just a dumb kid from southern Illinois."

Lou lowered the rifle and took a few deep breaths. He stared down Brockmann with evil eyes.

"Say what you want about me, punk, but don't disrespect my woman. That's the future first lady there. Got it, asshole? Now get those pants off."

Lou walked over and handed his rifle to Teresa. He picked through the army clothes and took off the dirty shirts he was wearing. Then he picked up Brockmann's army shirt and put it on. He took his shoes off and tried on one of Brockmann's boots then took it off. McKenzie's boot was bigger and fit better, though still tight on Lou who had big feet for his size. He laced them up. After that he picked up McKenzie's shirt and brought it to Teresa.

"Here, wear this as an undershirt. It's much cleaner," he said and took back the rifle. He pointed it at the soldiers and said, "Gather up their stuff, boys. They got some nice hunting knives there, and get the ammo too. I want Scooter and Joe Bob to put on their pants and jackets."

They both looked at him strangely.

"I ain't changing my pants," Joe Bob said.

"Look, we need you guys to look like soldiers. You and Scooter are the youngest so...."

"I ain't changing my pants," Joe Bob insisted.

"Goddamn it, Joe Bob!" Lou grunted through clinched teeth. He shook his head and turned to the others. "Fine! Reilly, will you please play army guy with Scooter. You'll be much better than Joe Bob anyway."

Reilly nodded and picked up one of the army jackets. As he put it on, he walked closer to Brockmann.

"You know who the real fuckin' terrorists are?" he said.

Brockmann looked at him silently.

"The people who slaughtered all my friends back there! The bastards who order you guys to kill your fellow Americans in cold blood! The government is the fuckin' terrorists, them and all the troops who follow their orders." Reilly walked away, not waiting for or expecting a response. He took off his pants and put on army pants. He and Scooter looked more like grubby, unshaven, militia men than National Guardsmen, but the uniforms fit them well enough.

Lou handed the assault rifle to Joe Bob and took back the gun. Brandishing it at the soldiers, he approached them, engaging eye contact with McKenzie.

"He's right, you know. The government is and has been a terrorist group for a long time. They're financial terrorists." Lou looked around, making sure everyone was listening. "You know, a law passed in eighteen seventy eight called the Posse Comitatus Act. It was written to prohibit the federal government from using our military to enforce law on its own people, and in two thousand six the government suspended it. They began shredding our constitutional rights and pretending it was all to protect us from terrorism. They knew they would need the military to protect themselves from their own people because their greedy, free market, economic ideology would eventually ruin us, and we would all be pissed, so they made sure they could usher in martial law when the time came."

"That's crazy," said McKenzie. "Maybe some rich, greedy billionaires might be pulling some strings in the government, but why would they want to ruin their own country?"

"Because all they wanted was the maximum profits humanly possible. They had to have no regulations and pay minuscule taxes. So they bought the government for millions and made billions in profits. This went on for decades. Anyone with any knowledge of true economics knew this would crash our economy, and when people are destitute they will work for cheep. It was fine for them because they'll live a long happy life in their gluttonous utopia." He engaged each of them with eye contact. "It was all unnoticed by us because of our hard lives and misinformation in the media, so our bankers had no problem turning us into debt slaves.

"But people in Europe figured out their elected officials were sellouts to the bankers, and they protested. The world could see a new renaissance and peace and equality if these greedy fucks in our country could be overthrown. They don't wanna let go of their power, and now they need to win a nuclear world war to keep it. It say's in the Declaration Of Independence it is our duty as Americans to remove them from office and replace them with a better government that will protect our right to life, liberty and the pursuit of happiness." He looked at the soldiers. "Please consider this when they ask you to kill more Americans like us. You took an oath to protect the American people, and you don't have to follow orders that tell you to harm us. Whether or not we succeed in overthrowing this government is up to you, the cops, and soldiers!"

Both men were respectfully silent.

Lou picked up the radio, holstered his gun, and turned back to them.

"Now, you guys just sit tight for about fifteen minutes. We're going outside for a meeting. If you even poke your heads out the door, we're going shoot them off, so just relax, okay."

"Yeah," McKenzie replied.

"Yeah." Lou mimicked him in a deep voice and continued saying it a few more times, trying to get the impersonation just right. Then he pressed the transmit button. "We're in pursuit of the fugitives. They just passed over Central and are heading east through the woods toward the Eden's." His impersonation was good for a first attempt.

"Affirmative, Corporal," a male voice answered almost immediately, "continue pursuit. We'll set an ambush at Lehigh." Lou turned off the radio.

"Let's go," he said and went outside.

Everyone left the hut while Scooter held the soldiers at gunpoint. Then he slipped out and shut the door. They all followed Lou as he led them west through the forest preserve toward Park Ridge.

Lou looked back a few times to see if Private Brockman and Corporal McKenzie popped out of the hut, but they didn't. He didn't think they would try to track them down unarmed. But after another moment he second guessed himself and stopped dead in his tracks. Gavin stopped beside him and stared. Lou turned to him looking paranoid. "You don't think those soldiers would follow us with no weapons or clothes, do you?"

Gavin rubbed his chin, gazing through the woods from where they came. "They may be unarmed," he said, "but they could put on the shoes and pants we left behind. Who knows? Those jar heads may think they're hot shit and try to hunt us down, but its more likely they'll be heading back to inform their officers what happened."

Lou nodded and tossed the radio in a pile of leaves that had gathered in a low area.

"You bring up the rear," he ordered. "Keep looking back and see if you notice anything. Then I can lead without worrying about what's behind us."

Gavin nodded, and they began jogging again. They trotted side by side for a moment.

"Rick was wrong about you, Gavin. You'd make a great leader." Gavin raised his eyebrows and looked over. "You got the intelligence and the instinct needed to predict your enemy's thoughts."

Lou cleared his throat, finding the next words hard to say, "And you were right back there. We never should have hid in that hut. I could have got us . . ." He cleared his throat again, "you know . . . hurt."

He ran briskly to the front of the group and continued to lead them at a trot for nearly ten minutes, west through the forest preserve. All or them kept a close eye out for soldiers and listened for any sounds.

When he spotted the street at the end of the forest, he huddled up the group.

"That's Milwaukee Avenue. We have to follow it south to Devon and then go west. It's all open road out there . . . no more forest preserves until the Des Plaines River by Rosemont. It's about five miles, and we can't risk traveling open roads till dark." He looked around for any movement from the east, and then looked at all five of them individually. His gaze lingered on Teresa. Everyone was hunched forward toward Lou like he was the quarterback in a six person football huddle. He noticed Teresa had her arm casually resting on Reilly's back. A jealously synapse fired.

She seems awful comfortable with him already.

Lou frowned at her and quickly looked away. He took a deep breath.

"We're gonna have to hide until nightfall. We could head along the edge of the woods that way." He pointed north. "Saint Adalbert's Cemetery isn't far. Maybe we can find somewhere to hide there."

He looked back at Teresa, now with a warm, gentle gaze. He felt stupid for his jealous thoughts and believed it could only signify that he had indeed fallen in love with her.

"Teresa can attest that my last two choices for hideouts got searched, so I think Gavin should lead us from here and find us a safe spot. Me and Teresa will keep an eye out behind us." He grabbed Teresa's right arm and pulled her toward him, making her left arm slip off Reilly's back, which caused her to stumble. "Go on Gavin," he said while Teresa frowned at him.

Gavin set out, followed by Scooter and Joe Bob.

Reilly stood in front of Lou, impeding him.

Lou's heart fluttered as he thought Reilly wanted to kick his ass and steal his girl. He felt weak in the knees like he always did when he thought he may have to fight. That always annoyed him.

When I need to be strong I go weak in the knees. How pathetic.

"I think you should reconsider," Reilly grumbled. "It would be better if I lead."

Lou adjusted his crotch and spit, trying to look tough. "Gavin has good instincts. Let him lead. Now let's move." He walked past him a few steps then turned back, "Come on Teresa."

They walked a few minutes with Reilly bringing up the rear.

A car came suddenly racing down Milwaukee Avenue. Gavin motioned for them all to take cover. A white gate car whizzed past.

They got up and trekked on along the edge of the woods until they came to the eight foot metal link fence that surrounds Saint Adalberts Cemetery.

"Soon as those soldiers are found, they'll be searching all over for us. We have to hide good this time," Lou said, sounding frantic.

"You all look here right now," Gavin said. "See that statue of our Lord out there in the middle of the courtyard?" Everyone looked into the cemetery, and about two hundred yards away they saw the tall monument of Jesus Christ with his arms spread open, towering over a courtyard, but no one spoke. "Well, do you all see it, Goddamn it?" he said louder.

"Yeah," they each replied.

"Good, cause that's where we're all gonna meet about an hour past nightfall. Got it?" Gavin ordered.

"Huh?" Lou grunted, looking puzzled.

"Trust me, Lou, out here we don't hide all together," said Gavin, "and the cemetery is not a good place to hide in the day. We'll split up into three groups of two and cross the road. Find somewhere good to hide as fast as you can: a house, a garage, under a staircase, whatever . . . just hide, and don't breathe or move a muscle until dark."

Lou noticed Teresa was already straying toward the street He set out toward her when Reilly grabbed his arm.

"Look. something's moving over there," he said.

Lou looked back through the woods. He didn't notice the camouflaged men immediately, and then he gasped when he saw a group of soldiers were moving right toward them and not all that far away.

"Shit, they're coming!" Lou said and squatted.

Scooter and Joe Bob ran out of the woods and into the street.

Suddenly, Reilly dashed off and hooked his arm around Teresa's back, leading her out of the woods. They ran hand in hand across the street, never looking back. Lou sprang up to sprint after her, and Gavin grabbed his arm.

"Don't follow them, boy. We go another way."

Lou quickly looked back again. He felt eye contact was made with a soldier, and suddenly they began to run. Lou went weak in the knees.

"Shit, they spotted us," he said. Gavin ran off, and Lou followed.

God, I'm gonna kill that bastard, Reilly, thought Lou as they ran across the street on a different path from where Reilly took Teresa.

They crossed the street and headed into the parking lot of an abandoned restaurant. Gavin's stubby legs weren't built for speed, and Lou found himself slowing up to stay even with him.

The sound of speeding cars emerged as they jumped a fence and landed in a backyard. They jumped through a row of bushes. Gavin's foot got snagged by a branch, and he fell to the ground. Lou stopped, turned back, and grabbed his arm to help him up.

Just then the sound of screeching tires skidded to a stop in the restaurant parking lot.

"Come on," Lou said.

Gavin stumbled to his feet, and they ran toward the back of the two story house. It had a weathered wooded deck on the back that rose four feet off the ground. Along the perimeter, from the deck to the ground, were sheets of lattice. Lou ran to the side of the deck, stopped and squatted down. Just as Gavin squatted by him, the sound of car doors opened and shut.

"You two take that block," they heard a G.A. officer say. They could hear more cars approaching.

Lou grabbed the last four by four foot sheet of lattice

and pulled it off. "Get under there," he whispered to Gavin, who scurried under the porch on all fours. Lou grabbed the back of the lattice with his fingers and backed himself under the porch.

They could hear the fence shake as two cops climbed it and jumped into the yard. Just as they jumped through the bushes Lou, pulled the lattice hard against the posts until the staples dug into the wooden posts enough to stay up. He backed up a few feet, hugged his knees, and held his breath.

Gavin peered through the open spaces between the wooden strips of the lattice, watching the legs of two cops in their blue pants come running through the yard. Lou had his head lowered to his knees and his eyes closed. He was terrified that his hiding spot would be searched once again.

One of the cops bent down to look under the deck. It was dark enough not to notice their dark clothed figures in the corner at a quick glance, which the cop gave and stood back up.

"You go around that side," one cop said to the other. The cops jogged to the front of the house, one on each side.

Lou opened his eyes and breathed again. He was about to whispered to Gavin when an army truck pulled into the restaurant parking lot. He listened to the truck engine come to a stop and immediately heard the sound of boots striking the concrete. He estimated by the sound ten to twelve soldiers jumping out of the back of the truck.

"Ten-shun!" a voice called out. The sound of boots snapped in unison.

"Listen up, soldiers!" another authoritative voice said. "The governor doesn't want us wasting time out here. We're needed back in Rosemont a-sap so let's wrap this up quick. Two of the six terrorists were spotted crossing the street here and running right through this parking lot."

A helicopter flew noisily over the vicinity, making the officer pause.

When the helicopter moved on, he continued. "Our whirly birds are scanning the area so if they got any brains they're probably hiding.

"Check every house and garage. Kick over every stone. Try to bring Rizzo and Miss. Gorgie in alive, but kill them if they don't immediately surrender. Any other scavies you find, you are ordered to kill. They're part of a terrorist group that's dangerous to our country. Now let's move. We're pulling out by nineteen hundred hours."

"Lets go! Get with your group!" the voice who called them to attention said. "Each group will search the entire block they're assigned to. Then move three blocks west and search that block. Roberts, your group has Natoma, the first street right there. When you finish, go three blocks west to Newcastle."

"Yes sir!" a young man's voice said.

Three soldiers ran toward the fence and climbed into the yard.

This time Lou kept his eyes open and saw the legs of the soldiers come through the bushes toward them. For that moment he wished he could pray to a God that could intervene, though he would not be praying for himself; he would be praying for Teresa.

The soldiers were in the middle of the yard.

"You take the garage and the outside perimeter. You follow me," the young man ordered. One soldier went to the garage and kicked open the door. The other two rushed up the back steps and were standing on the deck almost right above their heads. The back door was kicked open, and they entered the house.

Lou crawled over to where an old sheet of plywood was lying on the ground. Gently he dragged it a few feet to the back of the house and set the end of it on the concrete ledge of the foundation.

Gavin crawled over to him, his face displaying frightful despair.

"Lie flat on your back against the ledge," Lou whispered. "Hurry, that guys gonna look under here when he's done with the garage."

Gavin slithered against the ledge and got on his back with the plywood by his feet. Lou was dismayed to see his protruding belly was considerably higher that the foundation ledge. He saw an object toward the front of the deck and wondered if he had time to pull it over there.

He sprang out and began crawling toward it, knowing the soldier would be coming out of the garage any second. He reached it and put his hand on it. It was a fifty pound bag of woodchips. He pulled it, and after dragging it only a foot, he stopped because of the noise it made. It was too risky to pull the bag any farther. The men might hear it.

Just then a helicopter moved back into the vicinity, casting its strident noise over them. He began to pull the bag again when a noise from the garage made him look up to see the soldier's legs come out of the garage door, stepping back into the yard. The helicopter was at the loudest point so Lou moved as fast as he could. He pulled the bag of woodchips up to the foundation, right over Gavin's head. Then he quickly lay down next to him. He reached down and grabbed the end of the plywood, pulled it over them, and rested the end of it on the bag of woodchips over their heads.

The helicopter moved on, and they could hear footsteps moving around the deck. The footsteps paused while the soldier squatted to look under the deck. He pulled out a flashlight and scanned assiduously. They held their breath with tightly closed eyes. Gavin was deep in prayer. Lou was expecting someone to crawl under and uncover them at any minute.

No one did.

They stayed under the plywood in darkness and silence for the next eighty minutes.

Lou finally broke the silence. "If they had bloodhounds we'd be dead," he whispered.

"Hell yeah," replied Gavin. "We're lucky they don't train dogs anymore, or maybe since a lot of dogs got eaten after the economy collapsed, they can't find any to train."

For the next twelve hours, they remained lying there in relative silence. It was excruciating for Lou who constantly worried about Teresa. He did manage to doze off a bit, but even his subconscious mind feared Teresa would be caught. He told himself she was safe, but then he would think of her hiding in close quarters with Reilly, and surely that scoundrel would try to seduce her.

With difficulty he was finally able to employ meditation

techniques. He managed to clear his thoughts and rest his mind. Peace came in the form of broken sleep.

Chapter 22

It was early twilight when Lou and Gavin pushed the plywood off of them. Perhaps it was still too light out to move, but they both had to pee, and neither of them could wait any longer. Both middle-aged men groaned from back pain as they sat up. They crawled to opposite sides and relieved their bladder in awkward positions.

They crawled over to the corner where they came in from and sat there silently, listening for any sounds. They had not heard a helicopter for hours now, and by all sensory indications, it seemed like the search had been called off. Still, Lou felt great trepidation about getting out from under the deck.

"I think it's still too early to set out," he said.

"Its nearly dusk, and its dead calm out there," Gavin replied. "Let's head for the cemetery once we have a drink. Let's see that backpack."

Lou had almost forgotten he was even wearing the back pack despite lying on it for the last twelve hours. It had actually made lying there more comfortable, providing and extra layer. He took it off and removed the sheepskin flask. They each drank some water. Lou became suddenly irate.

"Goddamn it, I'm gonna kill that Reilly."

"What's wrong?" Gavin asked.

"Me, Scooter and Joe Bob have water in our packs. Teresa is with Reilly, and he doesn't have any water. That bastard better keep here safe. I swear to God I'll-"

"Take it easy, Lou," Gavin interrupted. "Reilly's no stranger to this. He's been on every emancipist mission from the start. They'll make it to the cemetery, and she can drink then."

Lou appreciated Gavin's confidence and nodded. Then he grabbed the lattice and pushed it off the posts. They crawled out and slowly got to their feet. Lou replaced the lattice while Gavin was already walking through the backyard. They cut through the bushes and crouched down where they remained for a few minutes, observing the desolate street.

"They're probably keeping this street monitored with surveillance cameras," Lou whispered. "We better wait here another ten or twenty minutes for it to get darker."

Gavin nodded, and they both sat under the bushes. The night remained quiet until the sound of gunfire off in the distance crackled. A moment later they could hear a truck engine accelerating, the sound coming from the same vicinity as the gun fire. The army truck turned onto Milwaukee Avenue and sped off. Gavin and Lou looked at each other wide eyed.

For twelve agonizing minutes they remained still. Lou kept inadvertently thinking about how much he hoped if somebody got killed it was Scooter and Joe Bob and not Teresa. *Please not Teresa.*

The remaining light was finally gone. Lou rose to his feet and carefully climbed the fence with Gavin following. They trotted through the restaurant parking lot, trying to avoid open areas the best they could.

After careful inspection, they sprinted across the street and into the woods. Then they climbed the cemetery fence. Both of them were breathing heavy as they trotted toward the statue.

Once they reached the courtyard it appeared no one was around. The overcast sky filtered out most of the quarter moon's light, making the cemetery dark and eerie.

Lou sat on a headstone off to the side of the courtyard. Gavin kneeled in the grass nearby with his hands pressed together. His eyes were looking up at the monument of Jesus Christ. Then as he bowed his head and closed his eyes, Lou observed his lips moving. Gavin was praying to his Lord.

A snap of fallen twigs crackled. The flesh over Lou's spine tingled. Something was approaching. Gavin's eyes opened, and his head turned to the direction of the rustling. Gazing northward, a silhouette of a soldier, who was carrying a rifle, emerged from the darkness.

Lou froze with fright while Gavin slowly rose to a crouch. The soldier was coming right at them, inexorably closer with each passing second.

Lou's focus sharpened. Now he could see it was two figures approaching, both pointing assault rifles in their direction. Lou managed to move his trembling hand to his chest and place his fingertips on the gun handle. He gripped it and slowly removed it from the holster. He took aim while he squatted down beside the headstone.

Suddenly Gavin stood up, displaying himself to the enemy.

Lou held his sight on the leaders head prepared to squeeze.

"Paw, that you?" Scooter's voice softly called.

Lou emptied his lungs, dropped his head, and lowered his hand. Gavin went to them as Lou holstered his gun and got up.

"I knew the Lord was still looking out for my boys," Gavin said as he patted Scooter's back and then Joe Bob's.

Lou looked up at the statue with a sort of mystic admiration. He tried to imagine how a prayer would go.

Oh God . . . or, aaa, Lord Jesus . . . well both you guys I guess . . . if you can really help people here on earth, please keep Teresa safe for me. Thank you and amen.

Lou began walking toward the men when suddenly he stopped and looked back to the statue.

Actually Guys, if you are planning on answering my prayer, maybe you could also help us take over the government and, you know . . . save us from the evil guys. Thank you. God be praised and Jesus too.

He did the sign of the cross with his left hand and walked on.

"I wasn't sure we was gonna make it," Scooter was saying. "They had every jarheads and their mothers out looking for us." He turned to Lou as he approached them. "They must wanna get you pretty bad, old boy."

"Any idea if Teresa made it?" Lou asked.

"Nope," Scooter replied. He detected Lou's anxiety and put his hand on his shoulder. "Don't you worry, Lou. She's with Reilly, and that old boy can hide like a rat."

"That's because he is a Goddamn rat," Joe Bob added and chuckled.

"Shut up, Joe Bob," Scooter said. "Reilly's a survivalist. Maybe he got too big an ego fit in his head, but he's an honorable fellow. He won't get caught. Your woman will be fine. Just give it some time. We got here early."

They moved under a tree and sat in the darkness near the statue.

Lou's thoughts were scattering as if he were drugged again. He contemplated about how he should treat Reilly if they return. His mind favored visions of punching his face before saying a word.

Suddenly Joe Bob shushed them and sprang up to his feet. Everyone went silent and turned their heads southward.

Lou heard a clank coming from the fence. He sprang to his feet and dashed off.

"Get down, fool," he barely heard Joe Bob say.

After he covered the first hundred yards, he glanced back. No one was following him, and only then did he realize how irrational it was to be sprinting toward possible danger. He heard a clank from the east, turned to his left and ran toward the sound.

When he saw a figure standing next to the fence, he slowed up and jogged quietly as he pulled his gun out of his holster.

The closer he got, the figure of a soldier was revealed, looking upward to the top of the eight foot fence. He looked up and there she was. He could tell it was Teresa just by her outline in the dark, even from that distance he knew that beautiful, slim, dainty figure at the top of the fence was the woman he loved. He walked quietly now, looking in contempt at Reilly dressed up in the army fatigues.

"Come on, honey, you can do it," Reilly was saying, holding his arms up toward Teresa.

Lou grinded his teeth and realized he was still pointing his gun at Reilly.

"That's it, honey, just get that other foot over."

Then he heard Teresa whimper. Anger, directed at Riley,

raged in him, and he intended to pistol whip him for calling Teresa, honey.

"I'm stuck. My shirt is caught."

Teresa's voice snapped him out of his rage. He finally became aware that it was abnormal for him to feel this aggression and realized something was wrong with him. He took a deep breath and exhaled slowly, holstered his gun and approached them.

"Hey soldier," Lou said. Reilly flinched and gasped.

"Jesus Christ, you scared the shit out of me," Reilly said, frowning at him, but as he picked up the intensity in Lou's eyes, his own expression softened.

"How's my girl?" Lou said.

"Oh my God, is that you, Louis?" Teresa said, her voice quivering.

"She's just fine," Reilly insisted. "We found a nice cozy spot to hide and kicked back all day."

Lou was breathing deeply, attempting to remain calm. He looked up at Teresa.

"She's just having a little trouble getting over the top of the fence. Just give her a minute." Reilly looked up at her. "Come on, honey, you can make it."

"My shirt is snagged. I can't get it out." She sounded flustered.

"Put your hands together, and give me a boost," Lou demanded.

He stepped into Reilly's hands and got boosted up to where he could grab the top cross pole with his fingers, being careful not to touch the sharp ends of the metal link fencing.

"Okay, just hang on, Teresa. I'm gonna swing my arm and leg over you." He held with his right side and swung his left side over her and grabbed the cross pole so that she was in between his arms now. He lifted his leg and pushed the front of his boot into a link hole. "Use my leg for leverage now."

She put some weight on him but didn't lift any higher.

"Teresa, you have to put all you weight on my leg and lift yourself up higher. Then you can un-snag your shirt." She managed to lift up enough to loosen the tension and get her shirt free. Once her shirt came free, she fell into Lou with more weight and he had to squeeze the pole as tight as he could to support her.

The cut on his hand, which he got from old school window, opened up and began to trickle blood. He climbed down with her, and when they got to the ground, he gave her a hug.

"God, I was worried about you," he said then turned to Reilly.

"Thanks for keeping her safe. Good job, soldier." He patted him on the shoulder. "Just remember, Teresa goes with me from now on. Don't you ever run off with her like that again."

Reilly blew through his lips and turned away.

Lou grabbed his shoulder and turned him back. "You hear me, Reilly? She's with me."

"Yeah, whatever," he replied and turned away again. "Where are them slow witted Edwards boys? They make it back?"

Lou pointed at the statue, and he walked off toward it.

After he made it ten paces, Reilly turned back to them. "So what's the deal, Rizzo? Are you guys married or something? Cause if you not, you should know slavery is illegal in America, so the lady can make up her own mind about who can protect her better."

Lou hated him at the moment. He and Teresa walked toward the statue, and he took her hand.

"What the hell is he talking about? What's wrong with that asshole?" Lou said.

"He's having a tough time dealing with his friends dying. Give him a break," she replied.

Lou felt she was defending him and implying that he was being insensitive. The haze of rage clouded his mind.

"What the fuck are you talking about? You don't run off with another man's woman to deal with pain. Why are you defending him? Did you do something with him?" His voice was scolding. She looked as if she were about to cry.

"You bastard," she said and ran off ahead of him.

He froze. Watching her disappear with Reilly into the murky night brought on a dreadful feeling he only experienced after being drugged. He lost control.

The feeling of total emptiness took hold of him, the way it did back in the holding room of the gate station after Teresa had deserted him. The experience, coupled with the neurotoxin's downside affect, caused him to smash his head on the ground in a suicidal attempt.

This time he fell to his knees and pulled the gun from his holster. As he slowly lifted the gun to his mouth he muttered idiotically. "I can't even keep a woman for a week, not even close. No one respects me. Why the hell would they? Who gives a shit anyway? This country's fucked. No one ever listens to people like me."

His words were garbled now that the tip of the gun was in his mouth. Tears streamed down his face as he gripped the trigger. He closed his eyes tightly and began to squeeze.

Snap, crunch, snap.

The sound made him open his eyes and remove his finger from the trigger.

She could be in danger!

He lowered the gun and turned toward the sound. Someone was approaching; he could hear the footsteps crunching on the ground. He got to a squat and scampered toward the nearest tree for cover. Pointing his gun into the darkness, he waited for a shape to emerge.

It was still over twenty yards away when his eyes focused on it . . . a shape that stood tall, dark and graceful. Lou stood dead still waiting for a head to emerge.

When one did he thought of it as beautiful. He put his gun in his holster and walked toward it, finally stopping ten yards away from an adult buck with a grand pair of six pointed antlers. Lou and the deer were looking eye to eye for a moment, both creatures at ease, sensing each other's passive auras.

"I guess I'll be giving up on you guys too, huh Mr. Buck." His voice made the buck bob its head and begin to back off. "Don't worry, my friend. I'll fight for you." The deer took one last look at him and trotted off.

"Animals don't deserve to get nuked. Humans . . . I'm not so sure."

As he walked back to the courtyard, he thought about two things he was now unequivocally sure of.

Okay, what have we learned? One, my mind is unstable now cause that Goddamn, boot licking, agent sprayed me with poison; and two; I'm a bonafide lunatic with some crazy love for Teresa that can cause me to snap.

Then he considered what he didn't know. *Is this psychosis permanent, or can I fight it? Do I tell anyone about it?*

The murmur of their voices suddenly stopped when they noticed him approaching. Joe Bob stood forth, his chest flexed as he confronted Lou.

"What's up with you?" he howled. "Ain't you got no sense?"

Gavin got up and broke in. "Everything okay back there, Lou?" They were all staring at him silently. Teresa was standing next to Reilly, frowning at him.

"Yeah, everything's fine. I thought someone was following us, but it was a big old buck, a nice one too, six pointer."

Scooter and Gavin chuckled.

"I had one scare the shit out of me not too long ago," Scooter said. "Remember pa? I told you about it. These Illinois deer come right up to you like you was gonna feed them or something." There was a moment of awkward silence after that.

"I guess since nobody else is gonna say it, I will," Reilly said. "Nobody wants to do your plan, Lou. It's too risky, and it accomplishes nothing. It's best we just go our separate ways now."

Reilly was looking at Lou, but everyone else was looking down, avoiding eye contact. He looked at each of their faces and took a deep breath.

"Okay, listen up everyone," Lou began somberly. "Essentially, we're just a group of strangers with a lot of tension between us, and I admit the idea of us working together as a team seems insane right now. Hell, only yesterday I almost killed Joe Bob and Scooter after they almost killed me; and what they did to Teresa was indefensible. Now, since Reilly joined us, it seems the only one you're getting along with is Teresa." He stared down Reilly and waved his finger at him, "I know there's no love lost between you and the Edwards boys and I know you hate me because you blame me for the death of your friends."

Reilly sneered and quickly looked down to escape Lou's gaze.

"We broke out of jail and ran like hell. That's all, Reilly. It's not my fault."

Reilly looked back up at Lou with a hint of understanding in his cold, brown eyes.

"We may not all like each other but we're here together for a reason. Now, I never believed in that preordained destiny mumbo-jumbo, and I've never believed any religion. I still don't, but I'm feeling something extraordinary going on here. We've been gathered here to do something. I mean, we didn't assemble this team; something brought us together. If there is a God, and he roots for the good guys, he's definitely on our side. So let's do something together, something worthy of all those people like us that died fighting for freedom. Let's try to alter the fate of our country for them and for the next generation of Americans. In life, our actions are what define us, and despite our differences, we all have something in common. We are not inactive people. That's why we're here together. We are brave enough to take matters into our own hands. It's up to us to inspire the inactive, and we have a group here brave enough to act. If we work together with respect and trust for one another, we can do this. You guys with me?"

Everyone seemed to be in their own world gazing away from each other. "Well don't all answer at once, for Christ's sake!" Lou roared.

"I'm with you, Lou," Gavin said. Lou smiled at him. "Maybe I can still make you a believer and save your soul before we're done."

"Maybe, my friend," replied Lou. "I believe anything is possible."

"Me and Joe Bob is with you too," Scooter said.

"Thanks, Scooter, but I need to hear Joe Bob say it for himself." Joe Bob glowered at Lou who scowled right back.

Finally Joe Bob seemed to lighten up as a slight grin crossed his mouth. "I'm with you, old boy . . . Lou," he said and held out his right hand.

Lou shook it and smiled. Next he stood in front of Reilly and Teresa. It was Reilly he was looking at, but Teresa was first to speak.

"I guess none of this fate and destiny shit concerns me," she snapped. "Since you don't want me with you for the mission, I might as well be leaving now."

Lou jerked his head to look at her.

"If she's leaving," Reilly said, "I'm going with to look after her."

Lou jerked his face back to Reilly's. "Sure you are, Reilly, Dream on, buddy." Lou flexed his chest, staring furiously at him and got right up in his face. This was an act he was not familiar with, but he liked it. He was prepared to fight and was just waiting for Reilly to give him a reason to throw a punch.

"Why not, Lou?" Teresa asked, grabbing at his arm. "Your plan is to call some rich lady and have her take me away to the gated city where I can hide like a mole. Maybe I'd rather take my chances with Reilly. I'm a free woman, just like he said."

Lou turned back to her with a stern face. "Things have changed, Teresa. I thought we were gonna have more men for this mission, and you could be somewhere safe till it was over, but now it's just the six of us, and I need your help. Your country needs your help. You're a free woman now because people like us were brave enough to fight for it. I need you. We all need you. You're smart and decisive, and I honestly believe we can't succeed without you."

She was staring at him wide eyed and fervent.

"What do you say, Teresa, will you fight with us?"

"I wanna fight with you, Lou," she said, moving close to him, and those dark, innocent, baby doe eyes returned. "That's why I risked my life to break you out."

A smile broke out on his face, and he gushed with elation and hugged her. He let her go and stood before Reilly again.

"Well Reilly," he said, "can you accept the way things are and fight with us? We really could use your covert expertise, and this is the best way to honor your friends who'd be fighting with us if they were here."

Reilly looked at Teresa slowly and then the Edwards boys and finally back to Lou. "Yeah, okay," he finally said. "You fools are going to need me since I'm the only one who's got any common sense around here."

"Good, its official then," said Lou. He patted Reilly on the shoulder and turned to Scooter and Joe Bob. "Break open those backpacks, boys. Let's eat up some beans and tomatoes or whatever you got in there. Then we'll head out. There's no time to lose. I wanna be on T.V. tonight."

They shared two cans of cold chili between the six of them, and each drank some water while Lou explained how this plan would work.

Later they found their own secluded grave sight, relieved themselves, and headed out toward the street.

They traveled cautiously down Milwaukee Avenue, staying under tree cover the best they could.

When they reached the intersection of Devon and Milwaukee, they headed west down Devon. They traveled swiftly and quietly, being extra careful when they crossed each inter-section. They covered a mile and a half in less than twenty min-utes. They stopped when they came to a six way intersection.

"This street is Northwest Highway," Lou said, pointing, "and that's Harlem. Teresa, which one do we take?"

"Neither," she answered, "we stay on Devon a few more blocks until we hit Canfield. Then it's only a few blocks north."

They ran across the intersection, staggered in groups of two, running to the tree cover on the other side.

It was about another mile farther than Teresa had thought to get to Canfield, which they covered in eighteen minutes. Once they reached Canfield, they headed north. Seemingly, out of nowhere the sound and lights of the upscale North Chicago district hit them. They traveled slowly now, keeping totally out of sight by staying behind bushes, trees, or houses. It seemed a convivial sight to see the glow of street lights again and hear a vehicle drive by once in a while.

Lou felt like a man who had just found his way back to civilization after being banished to a desolate, savage world.

A car racing down canfield was coming toward them,

and everyone dropped to the ground. As it went speeding by, Lou saw the blur of a red sports car. He could tell it was an expensive, vintage, foreign car with more that eight cylinders.

"Wow, was that a Ferrari," he said after it passed.

"It's just some spoiled rich prick tooling around in his toy," Teresa told him. "The Park West Club is a couple blocks away from here. I'm sure that's where he's coming from . . . probably trying to impress some high class scank."

They moved on and began to hear the bass of the poorly contrived dance music, leaking out of the upper class night club into the quiet streets.

After covering another block, Teresa pointed to a building ahead with its windows lit up and a neon sign over the front, illuminating the dark street with a blue tint.

"That's it up there with the blue light," she said.

It was on the next block ahead of them. A news van was parked in front, along with five cars.

"This is crazy," Reilly said. "Look how busy that place is. There's gonna be security guards in there who'll call the gate cops the minute they see us."

"Not if our two brave soldiers here are good actors," Lou replied.

Joe Bob looked at scooter and blew through his lips. "Great, we fucked then. Scooter's as worthless as a lump of shit when it come to acting. You give him a two word sentence to say, and he'll probably reverse the Goddamn words." Scooter didn't bother to defend himself, only looked down at his feet while Lou stared at him.

"I'm afraid he's right, Lou," said Gavin. "You got to be good at lying to act, and Scooter, well, he can't hide anything from anybody. He's a loyal boy though." Gavin clapped Scooter's shoulders to cheer him up.

Lou took a few deep breaths and shook his head. "Goddamn it! *Now*, you tell me this!" he roared. "Switch clothes with me, Scooter." They began undressing. "I didn't wanna be dressed in military fatigues for this. It's not a good signal, but it's critical the guards are convinced for my plan to work."

They swapped clothes. Now Lou and Reilly were the

ones wearing the military jacket and pants. Lou took the assault rifle from Scooter and gave him his gun. Reilly traded with Joe Bob as well.

"Okay," Lou began while rolling up the sleeves that were too long for his arms, "we'll cross here two at a time and run to the alley. Then we'll sneak up from the back of the building. I want to peek in any windows we can reach and get an idea of where everyone is."

He was relieved no one objected or even spoke. They just followed his orders and crept their way over.

The alley behind the news station was dark and provided good cover for them to creep up to the back of the building. They designated a safe zone behind the dumpster where they could talk quietly.

Lou snuck around and inspected the perimeter of the building. It had only two exits, the main and the rear. He and Reilly peeked in the front window and got and idea of how the lobby was set up.

They converged behind the dumpster again.

Lou looked them over one at a time. Now he looked at them with a stern, warrior's gaze that oozed intelligence, and it gave them confidence. They were now mutually devoted to the mission, each with different reasons. It was clear in their expressions.

Joe Bob and Scooter wanted to impress their pa, the man whom they respected more than anything in the world.

Reilly wanted to fill the emptiness and rage that devastated his mind ever since his friends were blown up, and being semi-suicidal, he realized it was better to risk his life for a cause, rather than just blow his own head off. He felt like his life had no meaning once his friends were gone, but he did like Teresa. She gave him the needed reason to exist.

Gavin did this for pride and a sense of duty. He was a man of action and firm in his beliefs. He recognized Lou was special and had the intellect to lead. Gavin felt proud to follow him.

Teresa never felt so alive. Her mundane life she led before meeting Lou gave her no satisfaction. She always secretly resented the government and how they were handling things, yet she did everything she was ordered to do, and it left her feeling insignificant. She also recognized Lou was special and wanted to remain by his side, but she now realized she wasn't doing this for him. She did everything for her own sense of worth. For the first time, she felt proud of herself. She was making her own decisions. She felt free.

Lou did this for his country.

"We can do this if we execute," he said. "Teresa, you're gonna have to play my role of the deranged lunatic since I'm a soldier now."

She gasped.

"I know you can do this better than I would have, and since you're a pretty woman, they won't feel threatened and call the cops right away. But you have to be convincing for this to work. Got it?"

She nodded boldly.

"Scooter, you watch the back door. Make sure nobody runs out till we let you in. Gavin and Joe Bob, you watch the front and come in the moment we signal."

They nodded.

"Now, before we go in, we're gonna plan our escape."

Taking some time, they plotted out an escape route where they would run afterward. They designated a place where they could hide out until things were safer. It was the utility room in an old abandoned funeral home a few blocks away. If that was unsafe and they get separated, Lou told them all to head east down Devon Avenue until they get to the forest preserve that surrounded the Des Plaines River. Then all they had to do was follow it south until they get to dam number four in Rosemont, the place the British were supposed to rally with the Emancipators.

Planning the escape route gave them optimism that they may live through this, but as they walked back to the dumpster behind the news station, apprehension grew in all of them, especially Teresa, who was beginning to feel sick to her stomach.

They huddled behind the dumpster for one final meeting. Teresa Looked pale and nervous, but Lou was not disturbed by this because that's exactly how she should look for the plan.

"Alright, this is it," Lou began, his eyes looking over each of them. "We have the plan and the right people for the job. I can see in your eyes that we can all count on each other, so just stay sharp and follow my orders." He focused on Teresa, "Teresa, you okay, girl?"

She nodded nervously.

"Just do exactly what I said, and this will work. Give me your keyphone. I need it for a prop."

She dug in her front pocket and handed it to him.

"Remember, we're not really going to shoot anyone, but make sure they believe you will, and if you have to whack someone on the head, so be it. Alright, let's do this. Let's get a message to the people that it's time to stand up to the oligarchs. This is how it begins, right here with us. Lets go."

Lou and Teresa were the only ones who knew what oligarchy meant, but they all understood the context and felt the enormity of what they were about to do. They took off their backpacks and left them by the dumpster. Scooter went to the back door, and the rest of them walked together down the gangway along the side of the building. Lou peaked around the corner to make sure no one was coming in or out.

"Alright, honey, you're on," he said to Teresa. The thought crossed his mind to give her a good luck kiss, but he only patted her back like he would do to any of the guys. Ever since her outbreak at the cemetery, he decided to treat her like a team member rather than a lover.

She looked him in the eyes and exhaled. Then she darted off.

"Get ready," he said to Reilly and peeked around the corner to see Teresa open the front door and run in.

The first thing Teresa saw as she flung open the door was the red carpet. The walls of the reception room were blue and the ceiling white. Painted in grey bold letters on the wall in front of her was American Airways Chicago. Below it was a door. She headed for it.

From her left, a heavy security guard with a pot belly, wearing black pants and a white shirt, stopped watching his T.V.

and got up from his stool. "Can I help you Miss?" he bellowed.

Teresa stopped and turned toward him. "You have to hide me!" she shrieked. "Please don't let them take me back!"

The guard looked completely bewildered and began approaching her.

Teresa ran past him to the hallway entrance door he was hired to guard and pulled it open.

"Hey, you can't go in there! Come here!" The guard yelled and waddled quickly toward her.

She slipped through the door and into the hall.

The security guard was about to pursue her when the front door flew open again. This time two soldiers came in, and he stopped in his tracks.

"Sir," one of the soldiers called to him. "was that a woman with dark hair that just ran in here?"

"Yeah, I have to get her out of there," he answered, pointing at the door.

"Do not follow her, sir. We have the back exit covered. We'll take care of this," Lou said. He whipped out the keyphone, hit a few buttons, and held it to his ear. "Sir, we have her trapped in a building. All exits are covered. What does the general want us to do?" He paused a moment. "It's the American Airways studio." He paused again. Turning to the security guard, he asked, "How many people are in this building?"

The guard quickly waddled to his desk and looked at the log.

"Eight," answered the guard.

"There's eight civilians in the building, sir . . . We're with the security guard now . . . Understood . . . Yes, sir." He closed the phone and put it in his pocket.

"What's your name, sir?" Lou asked him.

"Mike. What's going on here? Who is that woman? She asked me for help."

"Did you come into contact with her," Reilly asked him.

Mike's eyes widened, and he shook his head.

"Okay, Mike," said Lou, "everything is gonna be fine. I just need you to get everyone in the building out here in this room right away."

"What? Why? The control room technicians can't leave their posts."

"Mike, this is military top priority. That woman is carrying a deadly virus. Now get everyone in here now!"

"Oh my God," Mike said. "What about the girl? She could be infecting people already."

"No, I'm sure she's hiding somewhere," Lou said. "The general is on his way with Doctor Garvey. They will remove the girl. We've been ordered to gather everyone in one room. Now let's move."

Mike sat on his stool behind the desk and nervously fumbled for the intercom microphone and hit the button. "Attention everyone, this is Officer Mike. I need everyone to come to the reception room now. This is no joke. Even technicians get out here now. We're under military orders." Mike stared blankly at Lou.

"Sergeant Reilly, open the door and make sure they all get in here without her touching anyone."

Reilly held open the door and looked down the hall. As Mike looked toward the door, Lou reached down and snatched his keyphone off the desk and stashed it in his pocket.

A balding, white haired, middle-aged gentleman walked in. "What the devil is going on here, Mike? I have to switch to network feed at ten!" he yelled then looked strangely at Lou.

"Take it easy, David," said Mike. "There's a woman with a contagious virus on the loose."

David looked suspiciously at the grubby soldiers.

"It's for you own protection, sir," Lou said to him. "We're under quarantine by military order."

A minute later nine people were standing in the room: five men, two women, and two grimy men dressed like soldiers.

"That's seven. Where's the last?" Lou said to mike.

Mike looked around to see who was missing. "Hey, where's Frank?" said Mike. "I didn't see him leave, and the van's still outside."

"Probably still in the crapper," a dark haired young man said. "He takes forever in there."

"Call him on the intercom again," said Lou. He noticed

David was staring at him and looking more suspicious. Mike went to the intercom, but before he pressed the button, Frank, the driver, casually waddled in.

"What's up?" he said.

"We're under quarantine, sir," Lou told him. "Now, I need everyone to move to the back wall here."

As they slowly moved to the back, Frank was studying Lou's face and frowning. "Hey, you look familiar," he said.

"I get that a lot, sir. Now please move to the back," Lou said firmly.

Suddenly, Frank's eyes widened, and his mouth dropped. "Oh my God, you're the guy from the protest story!" he yelled.

"What guy?" David asked.

"From the protest story that Tim got in trouble for airing. He's the guy that wanted to run for president. What's his name . . .? Rizzo, that's it."

"Hands up," Lou said, pointing his rifle at them. They were undisturbed.

"Rizzo, the terrorist?" cried David. "I knew something wasn't right."

"Call the cops, Mike!" a woman yelled.

Reilly shot off a round at the ceiling and exploded a light.

Screams arose.

"Everyone, get your hands in the air, now, or we open fire!" he yelled.

Everyone raised their hands except for David, who quickly grabbed his keyphone out of his pocket and flipped it open.

Reilly stepped up and kicked him in the stomach. David doubled over, fell to his knees, and dropped the phone. With one hand, David held his stomach, with the other, he reached for the phone in a last ditch effort.

Reilly smashed it with his boot, just missing David's fingers.

"Anyone else wanna try that? Just keep your hands in the air!" Reilly yelled, aiming his rifle at the rest of them.

Suddenly Gavin and Joe Bob rushed in with their guns out.

"Holy shit, it's a terrorist cell!" a man yelled.

"Oh my God, they're gonna blow us all up!" a woman screamed.

Gavin locked the door behind him.

"Search their pockets, and take their keyphones away," Lou ordered.

While he and Reilly kept them at gunpoint, Gavin and Joe Bob searched them all and confiscated everyone's keyphone.

Lou gave his rifle to Joe Bob and took back his gun. "Keep them covered," he instructed them. "Everyone, sit on the ground and relax, and nobody will get hurt. We're not terrorists; we're freedom fighters, and we're not here to blow anything up or kill anyone, but if you try anything, we will shoot." He looked over them all, trying to read their faces.

"I need to broadcast a message to the people, and this is the only way to do it, so follow my orders and we'll all get through this safely. Now, please sit down."

Their faces looked terrified, but they all calmly sat down, except David, who was still on his knees, gasping short breaths.

"I need two technicians," Lou announced, "one to work the studio floor and one in the master control room. Who's qualified here?"

No one immediately answered.

"Well, who's it gonna be?" Lou demanded.

"Well," Mike started to say, his cubby chin trembling,"David, the guy who got kicked in the gut, is the television director." He looked sympathetically over to Frank, a man just as large as he was. "And frank knows about production. He does all the on-scene reports."

"I'm the Goddamn driver, Mike, not the production manager!" Frank said irately.

"Come on, Frankie," Mike pleaded, "you know you can do that stuff. Just do what he says so we can get out of here."

"You know how to record, Frankie?" Lou asked.

Frank nodded, causing his flabby jowls to shake.

"You know how to make it go to air and switch on the network feed?"

"You're going to need *him* for that," Frank answered, pointing at David.

"Alright, let's go, Frankie," said Lou, pointing his gun at him. "Lead me to the studio floor."

Frank began walking to the door.

"You guys keep them covered," Lou told Joe Bob and Reilly. "Grab him and follow me," he said to Gavin.

Gavin grabbed David by the arm. "Let's go, old boy," he said and pulled him up to his feet.

Frank led the way down the hall to the studio floor.

The dressing room door opened when they passed it, and Teresa came out.

Once they entered the studio, Lou turned to her and smiled. "Nice job. Can you find the back door and let the Scootster in and then come back here?"

She nodded and left.

"Let's do this!" he yelled. He walked over to the stage and stood before the news desk. "Where should I stand . . . here?"

"That's fine, just stay right there," Frank said and moved the microphone boom over him. Then he centered the camera on him. "David, switch on camera one and the overhead mic. I think it's line three."

David let out a repugnant moan and glanced at the gun Gavin was pointing at him. Then he blew through his lips and switched on the camera. "Test the mic, Mr. Terrorist," he said. He turned on the amplifier and raised the level on line three.

"You can call me Lou. In fact, I insist on it, David. Check one two, check one two…"

Teresa and Scooter entered the room.

"Keep an eye on them, you guys," ordered Lou. "Make sure they record me right." He placed the gun inside his front pocket, took his army jacket and his shoulder holster off, and then set them on the ground. "We almost ready or what? Let's go."

"Alright, it's all set up," said Frank. "You ready?"

Lou cleared his throat and took a deep breath with his eyes closed. He exhaled, opened his eyes and nodded to frank.

"I'm hitting record in five, four, three, two, one."

"My fellow Americans, I'm Louis Rizzo, and I need to speak to you. Our failed government doesn't want you to hear me, so listen up because armed government employees will be coming to silence me the minute you see this. My friends, our democracy died, and we need to restore it. This is the darkest time in our country's history. Our leaders, or should I just say the people with obscene amounts of money, have had permanent power for far too long now. They created a two-class society by draining the life out of us so they could maximize their profits. We paid the taxes, and they paid the government to allow economic injustice. Now that they destroyed our economy and sucked all the money away from us, our illegitimate leaders are preparing for war. Their plan to create a new world economy failed because people in Europe rebelled against the central bankers and their sellout leaders. The rest of the world wants to unite and move on to a brighter future, but our corrupt government remains intact and is provoking war.

"We borrowed trillions from foreign countries and won't negotiate payments. In fact, our government won't negotiate at all.

"We must gain control of our government now, or we cannot avert the horror to come. You have no access to this information I'm telling you because the government controls everything you see and hear and cut us off from the world, but I assure you it's true. I was able to keep in contact with the rest of the world while you have been isolated from it. That's why they confiscated my computer and call me a traitor. The truth is the world fears and despises our government and wishes to overthrow it, and our government declared they will use nuclear weapons if attacked. Listen to me, my fellow Americans, they're preparing for this. When the nuclear warheads fall on our great land, they will survive in the bomb shelters they made in the gated cities. The people with all the money will survive, along with some police and military members, and of course, a small minority of servants to do the physical labor. But the rest of us are shit out of luck. I'm talking about massive population decline here. The government networks will immediately be telling you

I'm guilty of treason and out of my mind while denying this truth. They will call me a terrorist, and to them, I truly am one, but to you, the people who weren't born into wealth, the workers, the cops, the soldiers, and all the good, honest, working Americans, I'm a true statesman and a freedom fighter. I call upon you now. It's our duty to overthrow our own government, not some foreign coalition that will provoke nuclear war and devastate most of our great land.

"No sir! Americans take care of their own problems. I'm qualified to temporarily lead our country after we overthrow this destructive government. Then we can deal with the world sensibly, avoid war, restore elections, and bring true democracy and prosperity back to America. We, the common people, must do this! It is our right and duty as Americans. The time is now or never. I declare that starting tomorrow we, the common people of the United States, are on strike. Tell every worker not to work and every soldier and cop not to take orders until President Burns steps down, and I am allowed to take charge.

"I will immediately open friendly relations with the world, avert nuclear war, and restore our rights.

"Starting tomorrow, all who can make it must meet me just north of Chicago in Rosemont Illinois outside the convention center where our government now secretly resides, and we will take back our country together. Spread the word; no work till we're heard."

His voice rose and his eyes were blazing. "Tomorrow we unite in protest, for life, for liberty, for all of humanity and every splendid creature that still roams our lands. It is up to us to make our future secure again."

He had no idea how fast government agents would be able to cut off his message so he got that out as quickly as he could.

"If this transmission hasn't been cut yet, perhaps good people at the networks around the country will continue to let me be heard. I'll explain the situation we face."

He cleared his throat and continued. "The great American economic crash was knowingly caused by the malice and greed of our government's true masters, the super rich plutocrats. Now our money is useless outside the country. The lack of imported oil caused death and suffering because we never advanced alternative energy, thanks to the oil barons. The people should have overthrown our government decades ago . . . when the plutocrats were allowed to buy it away from us. Our fathers and grandfathers are guilty of not fulfilling their duty. But they fooled us with their propaganda, didn't they? They bought all our media and had us divided on the left or right. Now they're so damn good at controlling everything we hear and see, very few of us even know what's going on in the world.

"Our government devastated our economy and our livelihood. We used to be the breadbasket to the world, the biggest exporters of wheat, soybean and corn, and people are starving in its absence, but our government decided to give the world the finger because they won't accept our totally devalued dollar. The only way we can repay our debt is in food, and instead of agreeing to the W.U.N. trade accord and keeping us working, our government let us fall into despair, and many good people died while they focused on building gates to secure their only true constituents, the rich.

"Now the W.U.N. sees us as the biggest threat to global stability and wishes to invade our country and replace our leaders. We still have the greatest military in the world and the most nuclear missiles, and our government is geared up for nuclear war.

"I remember a saying I heard: In order to be happy, you must accept that the world isn't fair because you alone cannot change it. Well, I swear to you, now is not the time to accept unfairness. Our lives depend on our action. Alone, we are nothing, but if the American people unite, we are the mightiest power on earth. Every Chicago worker must not work tomorrow and walk over to the Rosemont Convention Center, and we will take back what once belonged to us, our government. Spread the word; no work till we're heard."

He jumped off the stage and put his jacket and holster back on.

"I hope you got all that," he said, walking over to the control board.

David and Frank were looking at him strangely. They seemed frightened.

"Is all that true?" David asked.

"It's all true, and we don't have much time either," said Lou.

"Jesus Christ, I feel so oblivious," David said, scratching his head. "It's like we've live in a fictional existence ever since we were cut off from the rest of the world."

"Essentially, that's correct," agreed Lou. Everything you hear on this network is fictional. Now let's get this on the air."

Now David was looking at him in awe, as was Frank who was speechless.

David ejected the tape, grabbed it, and walked out of the studio. Everyone followed him to the production control room. Gavin wasn't even pointing his gun at him anymore, and it dangled at his side.

David set up the tape quickly like a man with a purpose. "Someone needs to be here to hit *play*," he said, "while I switch the *on air* signal in the master control room at the same time."

"Who will see it?" asked Lou.

"Everyone who gets our local signal here in the Midwest until someone shuts it off from here. The rest of the country will see it through the network feed, but it can be turned off at each of the regional television stations anytime they want, so who knows how long it will stay on in other states."

"Okay, listen up everyone," Lou said. "I want everyone out of here once the transmission starts. We'll lock the doors, run like hell, and hope the message is heard."

David went to the master control room while Gavin followed him.

Lou watched the American Airways monitor. Oddly enough, the show being broadcasted was about American military might. A general was explaining how, despite extremely low pay and harsh conditions, soldiers were proud to wear the uniform, and America has never had so many people enlisted in the armed forces.

"Ha," Lou mocked, "that's true. I guess I was wrong to say everything is a lie. They can take this terrible situation and make it sound like a good thing."

"Okay, I'm all set here." David's voice came through the intercom. "Go ahead and play it, Frank. In five, four, three, two, one."

Frank ran the tape, and David hit the switch. Lou saw his face suddenly appear on the monitor, and he grimaced at how grubby he looked.

"*My fellow Americans, I'm Louis Rizzo, and I need to speak to you.*"

The audio sounded fine so he jumped into action as if a fuse had just been lit.

"Let's get the hell out of here!" he yelled. They all ran to the front reception area where Joe Bob and Reilly were still pointing their rifles at the station employees that were sitting on the ground.

"Get everyone out now!" Lou yelled, startling them. The people were quickly let out the front door with Lou holding it open for them. Frank was the last one out. He turned to Lou before leaving.

"I set it on a loop so it keeps replaying. Good luck, Louis."

"Good luck to all of us. I'm not in this alone, and I expect you to be in Rosemont along with everyone else from Chicago. The American people are on strike. Spread the word, my friend."

Once they were out, he locked the door. He faced the five of them that were anxiously awaiting his orders.

"Good job, people. We did something amazing tonight. Now let's get the hell out of here. Out the back door, hurry!"

They ran through the building, Teresa leading the way. Lou was the last one out. He pushed the door shut, locking it so no one could easily gain entry. Everyone was running for the alley, except Teresa, who waited for Lou. He placed his hand on her back, and they ran off, side by side. He swooped up his backpack from behind the dumpster and put it on as they ran. Once they reached the alley, he could hear the faint sound of sirens.

As they cut through the yard of an old abandoned two flat, they were running as a group on the way to the funeral home.

Suddenly the ominous sound of helicopter blades cut through the night air. As they crossed the street and headed for the next alley, they could see the searchlight from the helicopter, scanning the street east of them. They all remained on the path to the funeral home, until suddenly, rising above them, another helicopter appeared over the tree line. They all stopped as the searchlight was cast down upon them. There they stood, all six of them, frozen under the light. Their eyes were stunned by the brightness the moment they looked up.

"Remain where you are!" an amplified voice commanded. Then they heard a Fsssssssss . . . a noise that sounded like a tank of compressed gas being released. Lou saw a cloud of white smoke falling toward them.

"Hold your breath and run! Meet at the dam!" he yelled. They all dispersed in different directions. Lou and Teresa had to run back toward the direction they came from and where the other helicopter was lurking.

The area was bursting with activity. Squad cars were racing up and down the streets. Male voices yelled out from the direction of the studio. Not wanting to get any closer to the T.V. studio, Lou and Teresa headed north, down the street they just crossed moments ago. From behind them, a squad car turned onto the street, tires screeching. They ran down a gangway of a small brick house. Lou pulled Teresa behind an evergreen bush just before the spotlight from the car shined on them. They continued north, cutting through yards and jumping fences.

There were moments when Lou felt they were doomed. Car doors slammed, and cops were now on foot. He knew it was a matter of minutes before they were caught if they didn't hide somewhere fast. He stopped near a garage door and jammed it open with his shoulder.

They entered the garage to find it was cluttered with junk. He closed the door and pushed an old snow blower behind it to hold it shut.

"We'll sit down and rest a little," he whispered. With the door closed it was pitch black in the garage. Teresa blindly reached out for Lou and grabbed him around the waist. He carefully led her a few paces back, waving his arm in front of him like a blind man and felt out some room to sit down on the dirty floor.

Both of them were becoming skilled at the art of elusion. They madly wanted to speak, but both knew better and remained in total silence.

Their instincts served them well because moments later they could hear the sound of rocks crunching. It was coming from the alley. A car was slowly approaching the garage from the south. Only the crunching sound the tires made on the alley gravel could be detected. Lou couldn't even hear the quiet hum of the hydrogen fuel cell engine until it was right outside the garage where it suddenly came to a halt.

"Did you see that?" a cop's voice said. Suddenly the car door flew open, and a cop jumped out. They could hear him whip open the alley gate with his boots clumping along the concrete gangway leading right to the door.

As they held their breath, the cop ran past the door and into the yard.

The cop's strides sounded powerful and swift to Lou. He suddenly felt scared and vulnerable, like a feeble, old rabbit hiding from a wolf pack.

He grabbed Teresa and lay on the ground so they might be at least somewhat more inconspicuous when they kick in the door and shine a flashlight in. He prepared for the worst while the mix of grease, gas, and old stains on the garage floor assaulted his nose.

Footsteps returned to the concrete gangway. This time he was walking . . . right past the door and back to the quietly idling car in the alley.

They could hear him sit in the car and speak to his partner.

"It was nothing, just a soldier . . . fuckin' Jarhead sprinting through the yard like that. I thought it was one of them." The door shut and the car pulled slowly away.

They remained in silence for forty-eight more minutes, listening to car, truck and helicopter motors, droning in the distance.

Then the eventful night's sounds got more sporadic and finally became eerily silent.

"I have to pee," Teresa said, finally breaking the silence.

They got up slowly and meandered to the door. Lou quietly slid the snow blower aside and opened the door. The night seemed bright after being in such darkness for nearly an hour. He stepped into the yard and scanned the surroundings. Nothing stirred so he motioned for Teresa to relieve herself in the yard. He turned his back to her and walked back to the garage door, hearing her forceful stream splash to the grass.

He poked his head into the garage, the moonlight seeping in from the open door, brightening it somewhat. He noticed something toward the back that interested him: handlebars.

Teresa returned.

"Wait here. I'm going in to unlock the back door," he instructed.

She stood there confused while he made a ruckus. When he came out, they walked to the back of the garage. He checked up and down the alley then suddenly turned the door handle and slowly pulled up the overhead door. Teresa felt like the noise was excruciatingly loud.

She slapped Lou on the shoulder. "Stop it," she muttered, scowling at him.

He glanced toward her but continued lifting the door.

"Look, look," Lou said, gazing at the bicycle like an amused child. Teresa didn't share his excitement.

Lou pulled the bike out and inspected it. It was an old trek mountain bike made around the turn of the century. The tires were mushy but not completely flat. He held the handle bars and stepped over the frame but didn't sit on the seat.

"Hop on the seat and hold onto my waist."

"Oh come on, there's no way we're riding double on that thing," she replied and crossed her arms.

"Let's just try it a couple blocks. We got a few miles to hike, and this could save us some time and energy." He patted the bike seat. "Hop on the Louie Express, baby."

She smirked. "Fine, but you better not crash us." She lifted her leg over and climbed on the seat, shaking the bike as she tried to balance.

"Try to rest your feet on the frame for stability. Just don't hit the spokes with your shoe."

She managed to balance. He pushed forward a few steps, and off they went. The bike swerved left then right, and then he was in control. He leaned forward as he peddled with his chest over the handle bars so he wouldn't be pushing Teresa off the back of the bike.

She was clutching his waste tightly and let out a little gasp each time they swayed, but Lou boldly rode out of the alley and across the empty street. He turned onto the sidewalk and headed west.

They were going at a good steady pace. He coasted when they approached the first intersection. After looking both ways, he pumped his legs hard. A quick glance to the street sign confirmed he was on Touhy Avenue, and he picked up speed. The next intersection Lou didn't bother to slow down. He put all his energy into gaining speed.

He wanted to cover as much distance as they could before Teresa's butt got too sore to continue, and he was leaving the two of them exposed.

G.A.T.E. cops were currently patrolling the area, but they covered four more blocks without one driving down Touhy Avenue. To the north, the sky was brightened by the lights of the gated city. Lou coasted, advancing more carefully now.

"You okay back there?" he asked.

"My ass is getting sore, but I can handle it a little longer."

When he glanced back, he saw headlights approaching from the rear. He pumped hard and turned sharply into a gangway and grinded to a halt next to the side of the house. He turned back to watch the vehicle pass. It was taking frightfully long for the car to pass. It must have slowed down.

"Come on," he said and stepped over the frame. He held the bike as Teresa climbed off. Just then the front of the white G.A.T.E. car appeared and a searchlight shone down the gangway. "Down," he grunted, and they squatted against the wall of the brick duplex. The light moved slowly past, and they scampered down the gangway toward the backyard. The light suddenly stopped and returned to the gangway just as they reached the yard and lunged behind the building. A car door opened and shut.

Running to the back of the yard, Lou suddenly dropped to his hands and knees in front of a row of evergreens and desperately crawled between two of them.

He held up the prickly branches and motioned for Teresa to crawl under and move to the fence in back. They sat silently and motionless as a gate cop walked into the yard, shining his flashlight. He just stood for a moment, listening for movement. Lou slowly pulled the gun from his shoulder holster. The cop shined his light on the bushes, but the dense evergreens revealed nothing.

"Anything?" a voice crackled from the radio clipped onto his front breast pocket.

"I don't know. Maybe they jumped a fence. Meet me one block over."

"Got it," a voice crackled, and the tires screeched as the car in front sped away.

The cop immediately got on his hands and knees and began crawling between the bushes in the same spot they just entered. Lou held the gun in both hands and raised it to his chest. The cop's head came through, and Lou smashed down the butt of the gun on the back of his head. The cop whimpered in pain as his arms collapsed, and his head fell to the ground. He began to rise, and Lou smashed it again and again and once again. He could only move his arms a couple feet up and down with all the branches, so the cop was hurt but still struggling to get up to a defensive position.

"Go," he muttered. Teresa began to climb the fence.

The cop got his arm up and looked at his assailant. As their eyes made contact, Lou came down with all the strength he had and struck the side of his head. He holstered the gun and lunged toward the fence. Teresa had fallen when she jumped into the next yard. Once he popped over, he helped her up. For a fleeting moment, they looked into each other's eyes with panic and uncertainty. Then, dashing east through the yard, they climbed another fence and went back to the block from which they just came from and ran like hell.

They cautiously meandered their way westward, hoping to make it to the forest alive. When a helicopter scanned the area, they stayed hidden behind trees or bushes while they caught their breath.

For another hour, they led an erratic path, which brought them a mile out of their way, but the G.A.T.E. police units were thrown off by his path, searching houses and garages east of them.

Now, only three blocks ahead, lay the beautiful outline of the forest preserve that lay just beyond the empty tri-state toll way bridge.

They carefully covered the last three blocks, sprinted across the street and under the bridge without stopping. They finally reached the woods and found a path in, both exhausted and breathing heavy, but the trees made them somehow feel secure, like the forest was a sanctuary.

Deeper in the woods, they found a trail that led down to the river. A clearing with a fire pit neatly encircled with rocks lay thirty feet up from the river.

They sat on the ground near it, opened the backpack and finished the rest of the water.

"We should rest for twenty minutes. You want to lie down?" asked Lou.

"Shouldn't we try to find the rest of the guys first?" she asked.

"Our path took us a bit out of the way. That was Oakton Street where we went under the bridge, so we're still a few miles north of Rosemont. I'm afraid we have some more hiking to do before we get to dam number four." Lou took off the army jacket and laid it on the ground between them.

"Let's have a lie down. It's so peaceful here with just you and me. We have plenty of time to find them, and the British won't get here till tomorrow night. Let's enjoy some time alone." He gently grabbed her shoulders, helped her lie down, and slid the backpack under her head as a pillow.

"I'll be right back," said Lou. He grabbed the empty sheepskin flask and walked down by the river. Climbing down to the edge, he squatted, reached his arm into the river and filled the flask with cold water. After he climbed back up, he urinated on a tree and then pulled his pants all the way down and began to pour the river water on his genitalia.

"Ahh!" he shrieked the moment the cold water splashed his balls.

After giving it a good rinse and rub, he stretched the bottom of his shirt down and patted the area dry. He pulled up, buttoned his pants, and walked back to Teresa, who was sitting up and looking at him nervously.

"What the hell happened?" she said.

"Oh, aw . . . that was nothing."

"Goddamn it, Louis, tell me what it was. Did you see a bug or an animal?" She pulled her legs up to her chest and hugged them while looking around in fright.

"No, relax, like I said, it's nothing."

She scowled.

"Fine, I was cleaning my cock with river water. It was cold, and I shrieked, okay."

She began to laugh.

"You wimp. You can't handle cold water."

He knelt beside her, blushing.

"Well, don't I get to clean up?" she asked and tried to take the flask from his hand, but he pulled it away.

"Sure you do, but maybe I should . . . you know, help. Let me clean it for you."

She giggled and used her other hand to reach behind him and slap his butt.

"You don't sound like a man ten years older than me." She pulled the flask away from him and walked off.

"That's because you make me feel young again, baby." Lou stretched out on his back and gazed up at the tree branches, watching the leaves gently dancing in the breeze.

They were in great peril, but Lou somehow achieved a wonderful feeling of contentment for the moment. Making it to the forest was an achievement he was most proud of.

When Teresa returned, she lay on her side next to him on the jacket.

"You're right. That water is cold," she said and shivered.

Lou rolled onto his side and embraced her. Reaching behind her, he began rubbing his hand over her rump, but she didn't seem responsive so he stopped.

"Are we staying here all night," she blurted. "or are you planning on leaving soon?"

In a final attempt, he rubbed her rump again, this time squeezing it passionately and pushing his chest out to touch hers.

"Let's just relax. I don't care if we stay here all night. I want to be alone with you more than anything right now." He kissed her lips, but she pulled back.

"Okay, but I'm not in the mood for sex right now."

Lou released her and rolled onto his back abruptly.

"Oooooh," he whined like a child. "What's wrong? Don't you want me anymore?"

"It's not that, I'm just stressed out, I've been through a lot if you haven't noticed."

You had no trouble screwing me last night after being raped, he thought and almost said. *What happened? Were you already screwing Reilly this morning?* Then his sanity returned for a thought. *What's wrong with me? I'm not like this. I savagely beat a man's head with the butt of my gun earlier, and now I wanna fuck. They messed up my mind good. I gotta try to fight it. I can't tell anyone about it, or they will never accept me as a leader.*

"Fine," he muttered and closed his eyes.

She put her arm across his chest and snuggled up to him. He loathed her now and wanted to toss her arm off of him and turn his back to her. He knew this woman was corrupting his emotions and reducing him to an immature brat. His plan to have glorious sex before getting down to the business of overthrowing the most dangerous government in the world had been shot down, and he was utterly disappointed. He wondered if he even loved her anymore.

shit, I don't even like her right now.

It was agonizing just to lie there with her. Since he

couldn't have her, he wanted to get up and hike to the rendezvous area. He looked up at the leaves and tried to clear his mind. It didn't work.

After twenty minutes, he eventually calmed his mind, and his sex impulse diminished. Still, he didn't want to stay there anymore. Teresa sounded like she had dosed off by the sound of her breathing. He rolled away from her and got to his feet. She slid onto her stomach and woke when he moved, now looking up at him with sleepy eyes.

"What's wrong?" she asked.

"Nothing, we should get moving now. It's better to travel at night."

He sounded callous, and his tone stung her as he walked off toward the river. She got to her feet quickly. Feeling light headed, she grabbed the jacket off the ground and trotted after him. She was frightened. The man who said he loved her and promised to protect her with his life had turned cold, and she instantly knew it. When she caught up, she handed him the jacket.

"Thanks," he said, not looking at her. "We can just follow the river path. Probably be some branches we'll have to climb, but we should be there in an hour or so." He walked away, never looking at her.

His tone chilled her to the bone, and again she became light headed.

"Louis," she called, standing still as he walked away.

He turned around, frowning at her. "What?"

"Why do you sound so cold toward me? It's like you don't want me with you all of a sudden."

Yeah, you know why bitch, he felt like saying.

"Don't be silly. Now let's get moving."

She began to cry. He had already turned away and didn't see her body convulsing as she gasped short sobbing breaths, but after a few paces, he heard the whimpering and turned back. The callous attitude he was determined to take with her melted away in an instant, and he suddenly felt terrible for his strange behavior. He walked to her and embraced her.

"Are you mad at me because I didn't want to have sex?"

she asked, stuttering through her trembling jaw.

He held her tighter.

"Yes . . . I'm sorry for acting like a jerk. I respect your decision, and I still love you, Teresa. Let's just put this behind us and move on."

"I'm sorry, but I really didn't feel like having sex. I mean, we just had the chase of our lives. I watched you beat a man's head, and I'm scared shitless. It didn't seem like a good time to me, but if it means that much to you, let's just do it now. I just wanted to wait till we're done with the mission, and it would be nice if we have a shower and a soft bed."

"I understand. It's just the testosterone that made me act that way. We'll wait till we get to the White House before we make love again." He looked her in the eyes and smiled. The charm was back in his eyes.

She smiled."We can do it sooner if that takes awhile. Let's just get through tomorrow night first."

They walked along the river path, hand in hand. The flowing water, the leaves rustling in the breeze, and the crickets were the only sounds they heard as they covered over two miles. They passed under a bridge a mile ago, and Lou knew they made it back to Touhy Avenue. After they passed under the second bridge, he knew that was Devon Avenue.

"We're close to dam number four now," he said. "Keep your eyes peeled for those guys."

They covered another few hundred yards, and they could hear the water crashing over the dam. Another sixty yards and they were parallel to the dam. The noise of the flowing water dominated the night sounds. They both stood staring at the river for a moment, mesmerized by the flow.

"Well, this is it," he said, almost yelling to be heard. "Let's find a place to hang out for awhile, see if anyone shows up."

He turned his gaze away from the river. Suddenly his body flinched, and his heart palpitated. Twenty yards away was a soldier holding an assault rifle, and he was running toward them. He reached inside his jacket for his gun.

"Reilly," Teresa squealed cheerily and ran toward him.

Lou exhaled deeply and walked over.

Teresa gave Reilly a hug.

Lou blew through his lips. *She's awful bubbly all a sudden.*

"You made it," she said as Reilly squeezed her with his free arm.

"Yeah, we all did," Reilly said.

It was the first time Lou ever saw him smiling. His face looked strange without the scowl he had grown to know.

"We found an old campground not far from here," he said, staring at her.

Then he turned to look at Lou. "We broke into the counselor's cabin. The Edwards boys are there. They got a little fire going, and that crazy Scooter wanted to shoot deer. I told him he better not because someone will hear the shot. I swear, I couldn't stand being alone with those goofy hillbillies so I volunteered to wait for you guys first."

"Thanks, Reilly," said Lou. "Hey, you were great back there at the studio. Man, when you fired off that round, it scared the shit out of those people. If you hadn't of done that, I would have lost control of the whole situation."

They exchanged mutually approving glances and nodded to each other.

"Come on, follow me," Reilly said.

He led them at a steady pace. There was no trail where he led. The woods were dense, and the ground was littered with fallen branches. Reilly charted his own path, looking behind him periodically to make sure Teresa didn't trip on a branch. Lou was a few paces behind her and stumbling the most. His foot caught a tree root; he staggered, and softly fell to the wooded ground. He slowly got to his hands and knees. Smiling, he looked up to tell Reilly and Teresa he was okay. They weren't in front of him. They had kept moving and were a good distance away already.

They must not have even heard me fall, he thought.

He got up, brushed the twigs off him and trotted after them. He was attempting to run. Not wanting to fall again, he kept a close watch on the ground.

After twenty yards, he looked back up and didn't see

them anywhere. He stopped to listen for their footsteps, but nothing could be heard. He started hiking toward the direction he last saw them and sulked.

How could they not have looked back for me by now?

He quickened his pace. At the moment, he wanted to find them only so he could lecture them.

You don't leave a man behind in the dark woods, who doesn't know where he is. We're supposed to look after each other. He took a deep breath, bracing himself for the next thought. *Maybe they're trying to ditch me and run off together.*

He covered a few more feet, and there they were, about thirty feet ahead. The land sloped down, dropping them out of his sight until he reached the slope. He caught up to them as they were crossing a ditch at the edge of the forest line. Beyond the ditch was a gravel road.

Reilly jumped the ditch and stood on the other side, waiting to catch Teresa. He grabbed her around the waist when she landed and led her by the hand up to the road.

When Lou got to the ditch, he was surprised to see that it was not such an easy jump. He just stood there, crossed his arms and watched them get to the road, wondering if they were going to look back.

Teresa stopped and looked back after a few paces. They both looked at him standing there with his arm crossed while gawking at them.

"You all right with that jump, Lou?" Reilly called out.

Lou was going to insist he come back to support his landing, but he changed his mind and took a few steps back, then ran forward and jumped as far as he could, kicking his right foot high like a hurdler. He came to a graceful landing on the other side and used the momentum to pounce up the incline and jump onto the road. He walked up to them, acting cool.

"Yeah, I'd say I'm alright with it." He walked right past them.

The gravel road was cluttered with branches and seemed unused for years.

A few minutes later they came to the camp entrance. The rotting wooden entrance sign read FORT DEARBORN. There were eight dilapidated wooden shacks in a row led by a brick cabin.

Lou could see only a hint of smoke rising from the chimney.

"At least they know enough to use only dry wood and keep the smoke to a minimum," Lou said, sort of thinking aloud.

Reilly became defensive and stopped in his tracks to confront Lou. "They may be uneducated hillbillies, but they're expert outdoorsmen. All emancipators are," he said in a scolding way.

Oh yeah, well your friends were puffing smoke this morning, and it got them blown up, Lou thought but didn't consider saying. He assumed Reilly knew this, and that's why he reacted the way he did to his comment.

Scooter was keeping watch and saw them coming. He opened the door and patted each of them on the back as they entered the counselor's cabin.

"We was worried you wasn't gonna make it!" he exclaimed, smiling.

Gavin got up to greet them. Everyone was smiling and genuinely happy the group was back together. Even Joe Bob was grinning, and they all enjoyed a moment of jubilation.

"Piece of cake for this team, huh?" Joe Bob roared, and everyone laughed.

"Your crazy plan worked like a charm, old boy," said Gavin.

"We did something special tonight," said Lou. "We threw a wrench in the engine of government mind control. We gave people a glimpse of truth in their world of lies."

They were silent for a moment as feelings of triumph washed over them until Reilly grounded them.

"You think many people even got to see it?" he said.

The room seemed to deflate.

Lou scrunched his face and looked upward. He considered this question deeply before answering. "Yes, yes, I do, Reilly. I think a lot of people saw it . . . maybe not the whole thing but I got the important stuff out first. The people who saw it will talk about it, and the message will get out. It's inevitable now."

"He's right." Teresa spoke up. "The government will have to publicly respond to this, probably say Louis is a lying terrorist and that kind of stuff. Then they'll bombard the public with pro Compatriot propaganda." She looked at Lou and added, "That's inevitable."

"Right you are, my dear," said Lou. He was happy to hear her contributing to the conversation, "and the people will have to decide who to believe. Win or lose, we did our job."

They settled in for the night. Joe Bob suggested they finish off the whiskey and for Lou to have the first shot.

"Take a big one, old boy," he insisted as Lou tilted the bottle to his mouth.

Gavin had been boiling something in empty tin cans that he placed over the fire. He called it critter steak. When the meat was cooked, he let the cans cool and drained the water. He took out a grey chunk and popped it in his mouth. He held out the can to Teresa. She declined to have some, despite Gavin explaining how the protein would be good for her.

He handed it to Lou, who was sitting next to her. "Eat a few chunks of meat and pass it on," he instructed.

Lou tentatively reached in and pulled out a chunk of meat, a particularly large one, he noticed, while examining it closely. He glanced up to Gavin, who was staring at him, so he popped it in his mouth and nodded as he chewed the juicy, disgusting meat. He passed the can to Scooter, who hastily gobbled up three pieces while Lou still tried to swallow his one. When he finally swallowed, he shook his head like he had just downed a shot of harsh vodka.

Scooter passed the meat to Joe Bob and got up. He went to his backpack and dug out a can, opened it and placed a plastic spoon in it. Everyone watched as he walked in front of Teresa, squatted down and held it out to her. She looked at the can of cut green beans, then slowly up to Scooter's eyes. She took the can, being careful not to make contact with his fingers.

"Thank you," she softly said and dug in.

"So Gavin," Lou said, "what kind of critter was that anyway? Raccoon? Possum? I know you didn't catch a squirrel.

The Illinois deer might be easy prey, but our squirrels are too smart for you southern boys."

Reilly laughed.

"Yeah, it was like a squirrel," Gavin said, "It had four legs and a tail. That's what we call a critter in the South." The Edwards boys laughed.

Ironically, a moment later, Lou heard a rustle and a starching sound coming from the murky, back corner of the cabin. Gavin heard it too and threw an empty can toward the sound. Lou glanced calmly at Teresa. She was too busy enjoying the green beans to realize what Lou just learned.

Thank goodness she didn't eat the rat meat. I better keep her close tonight.

Chapter 23

L ou woke up, relieved to see Teresa was still sleeping next to him. He had an awful dream that she had been taken away by soldiers but couldn't recall many details. Still, it made his first impression on the new day a disconcerting one. Living as a necessitous American was a stressful existence for most. Lou understood this and empathized, although he always found comfort in saying to himself: *I can't get stressed out because others have it worse than me.* Today was different. His stomach felt uneasy, not the kind of intestinal uneasiness that might come from a diet of beans, tomatoes and rat meat, but an uneasiness caused by nerves. He thought of his working class father, who was always a pleasant and thoughtful man. Everyone loved to be around him until he was wore down to the nub from the stress he endured by trying to pay the mortgage, taxes and support his family during the recession of 2009. His physical appearance changed for the worst, as did his personality. The once pleasant man could no longer find joy in anything. It was then when Lou was still a young boy, that he told himself he would never become that stressed . . . no matter what life dealt him.

He sat up, crossed his legs, and stretched his arms and back. He and Teresa were currently the only ones in the cabin. He used the quiet moment to meditate. Clearing his mind turned out to be a task he could not realize, but he did discover it was not nervousness that made his stomach uneasy. It was fear. A helicopter thumped through the air somewhere in the distance, and the sound gradually got louder.

Teresa suddenly woke and sat up abruptly. "What's happening?" she said, grabbing Lou's arm and squeezing it.

Suddenly it was clear to him they were about to bomb the cabin. He was sure of it. **This cabin was about to blow!**

"Come on," he yelled and sprang to his feet. He grabbed her by the wrist and helped her up. They ran to the door, the helicopter thumping loudly and nearby. He flung the door open, and they ran out, sprinting toward the trees, taking cover just as the helicopter cleared the forest and flew over the camp.

Lou tucked Teresa's head under his arm, held it to his chest and braced for the explosion.

There was none. The helicopter never even slowed. It just kept moving toward Rosemont.

Teresa pulled her head away and looked at him oddly.

"I thought for sure they were coming for us," he said. "Now I feel like they aren't that interested in us anymore."

"Maybe they have bigger things to worry about," Teresa said but didn't really believe it. Surely the government can multitask.

They went back into the cottage and lounged for awhile. The Edwards boys and Reilly came back a half hour later with cans filled with water from the river; however, Joe Bob brought back something different. He was holding two dead male ducks by the neck, one in each hand.

"We feast before we meet the British lads tonight," Gavin announced, speaking with and old English accent. "Do you fancy duck, my lady?" he said to Teresa.

"Sure," she answered, smiling.

They spent most of the day in the cabin, talking, plucking feathers and resting. It was pleasantly uneventful and quiet all day . . . so quiet that it began to concern Lou as dusk approached. It seemed too easy somehow. Despite this odd feeling, he enjoyed the time they shared together that day. Teresa, who seemed bored, still wouldn't talk to Scooter and Joe Bob and still avoided looking at them, but she wasn't overly quiet.

When asked, she told them about what it was like working for the G.A.T.E. department, and they were all amused. She had a charming way of telling stories when people were really listening to her. Lou could tell she enjoyed it.

They boiled the water in the cans, cooked the ducks and shared the meat.

It had been dark for a few hours, and they had a final

conversation and made plans for every scenario they could come up with. Then they set out.

They walked together down the gravel road and entered the forest, walking in a staggered formation quietly and cautiously toward the dam. Lou was getting used to traveling through the woods at night, but it still frightened him, and this night he felt particularly uneasy. As they approached the river and the sound of rushing water emerged, his senses heightened. He didn't know what to expect from the six British military specialists. He felt confident when he was in charge, but surely the Brits would assume control of the group when they amalgamated. The Brits had a plan, a plan they were willing to risk their lives for, and they wouldn't be concerned for Lou and his clan's safety.

When they reached the riverside path, they scanned the area . . . nothing.

Reilly was the first to detect something. "Look over there across the river," he said, pointing. "You see that light? It's a flame. The fools are camping out over there, and they got a fire going in the open air."

Everyone saw it. It was a small fire, barely a flicker, and the distance between it and them was only a couple hundred yards.

"We're gonna have to go back to Devon street to get across the river," said Lou.

Nobody moved or spoke for a moment. They just stared at the flickering flame.

Finally, Joe Bob said what they were all thinking. "Y'all sure we ought to do this? We ain't even sure it's them. Even if it is, I ain't so sure we can trust these guys."

They all Looked to Lou, waiting for an answer.

"Hey, I didn't make the plan with the British," he said. "All I know is what you guys told me." He was looking at Gavin. "If the plan was to meet in this area, on this night, it'd be an incredible coincidence if that wasn't them."

"Yeah, he's right," Gavin said. "That's gotta be them. We come all the way here. Be kind of stupid if we don't talk to them."

"We don't gotta trust them, Joe Bob," Reilly said. "We're

not unarmed bush men here." He raised his rifle. "We're just as powerful as them, and we don't have to do anything we don't wanna do."

"That's true," said Lou. "If they want us to be sacrificial patsies so they can make a getaway, we won't be playing that game."

"Yeah, fuck them," said Scooter. "We got our own group and our own leader." He patted Lou on the shoulder.

Lou began nodding his head and became filled with pride. "Yeah, that's right," he said, still nodding, "we don't take shit from anybody. This is our country."

"Yeah," the others grunted.

"We're emancipators and proud of it," Reilly said.

They all set off down the river path without another word, walking proudly and assuredly.

When they reached Devon, the street was dark and deserted. They ran across the bridge two at a time without any problems and hiked their way back toward the dam, cautiously. All of them began feeling trepidation now. Reilly was in front, followed by Lou and Teresa with the Edwards boys behind them.

When they got closer, Reilly suddenly halted them to look and listen. They could see the figures now. Four men were sitting, and two were standing.

"Yeah, that's them," Gavin whispered. "I can tell by the tan and brown uniforms." Reilly walked toward them, and they followed. Closer, they crept to the group of men. They could hear their murmurs now.

Lou was suddenly terrified at the thought of startling them, which could cause them to open fire in response.

Suddenly one of the men whipped his head in their direction. He must have heard the crunch of their footfalls.

"Oy, who's there?" he called. The rest of the British went silent and turned at once with rifles aimed.

"Take it easy, dudes," Reilly said. "It's just us, the emancipators."

The men who were sitting got to their feet.

"Well come on then. We've been waiting for ya," said the

British guy. They emerged from the trees, into the clearing, one by one.

"Ello," another British man said to Reilly. "How many lads are in your group?"

Lou never liked the sound of a heavy English accent, but this guy sounded awful.

"There's six of us," Reilly answered, "and that's all that's coming. We had serious trouble along the way. A lot of good men died."

"I see. Well, that is sad news," said the British man.

They were all at ease now. Their rifles were hanging off their shoulder straps and pointing at the ground.

"Come by the fire. We have some tea on the boil," another British guy said.

Lou found his accent to be dreadful as well.

They all walked up to greet the British soldiers.

"You know, we should put out the fire," Lou said as he approached them. "We're not far from the street here."

"Take it easy, lad," one said, extending his hand to Lou.

Lou noticed all the British men had their right hands extended and the other in their front pocket. He reached out to shake the man's hand and watched the British man, who was shaking Reilly's hand, pull his left hand out of his pocket. He was holding something that glowed blue.

"Noooooo!" Lou yelled and pulled back his hand.

Zap! Reilly shuddered and fell to the ground. Zap, zap, zap, zap . . . the sound of more bodies falling.

The British man standing before Lou lunged at him. He grabbed his sleeve with his right hand and stabbed at him with his blue glowing left hand. Lou caught his arm and held it away from his body, but someone stepped up behind him and pressed a mini bolt blaster to the back of his neck. A shock shot through his body, causing him to see only white for a moment. Then he collapsed to the ground.

Chapter 24

When Lou came back to consciousness, he moaned as his eyes blinked and slowly opened. The white ceiling was still blurry, and he tried to rub his eyes. He panicked when he found his arms were strapped down as well as his legs. He might have begun struggling against his binds and screaming because he hated the feeling of being restrained, but after days of sleeping on the ground, the bed he was strapped to felt so good on his back that he remained calm. He lifted his head off the pillow and saw the room was completely white and empty, save the bed and a television mounted on the wall in front of him.

The door opened, and a man in a white doctor's jacket came in. He was holding a syringe and walking while gazing downward.

"Oh, you're awake," he said, once he looked up to Lou's head. He took out a communicator from his pocket and pressed down the button. "He's already awake," he said and began walking back to the door.

"Give it to him anyway," a voice, familiar to Lou replied.

"Oh, very well," the doctor said. He turned around again, walked back to Lou and administered something into his vein. Lou was still groggy and hadn't yet figured out what happened, only knew he was a prisoner.

"Please, get me out of here," he said, sounding weak and dry.

"I'm sorry, I can't do that, sir," the doctor said. He showed a look of sympathy. The doctor left, and Lou began to remember what had happened. He began to weep loudly and struggle against the straps.

A moment later the door opened, and one man walked

in. Lou immediately went silent to hide his weeping, but his face was wet with tears.

"Well Mr. Rizzo, I'm glad you returned to us," agent Joe Gerbuls said. "That was quite a prank you pulled. My bosses are extremely upset with you."

Lou felt immense anger when he saw who it was. "Oh shit, you again," he moaned. "I figured they would have got someone smarter for this, but I guess a smarter person wouldn't be as loyal as you."

"I'm glad you're happy to see me," said Gerbuls. "Don't worry, this will all be over soon. All you have to do is read a statement for everyone to see, and we can avoid a whole lot of ugliness." The door opened again, and a man pushing a cart came in followed by a guard armed with a bolt blaster. The man with the cart unbuckled Lou's straps and handed him a bottle of water.

After Lou drank half the bottle in desperate gulps, he let out a large burp. Whatever he was injected with was revitalizing him.

Gerbuls took a shirt off the cart and tossed it in Lou's lap. "Get changed," he ordered.

"Fuck you," said Lou, lying down again.

Gerbuls went to the T.V. monitor and turned it on.

"Okay, tough guy, have a look at this." Lou slowly turned his head to view the screen.

He saw a jail cell or perhaps a holding room because of its large size. It had a long bench connected to the wall, and the camera was angled so the entire wall was in the shot.

It must be a closed circuit link, he assumed. He counted ten people sitting on it. His heart sank.

Teresa sat between Reilly and Gavin with Scooter and Joe Bob on the end. Next to Gavin sat five men he never saw before, but he instantly knew it was the real British militia group. Lou assumed the absent sixth member of the group must be dead. Brigadier Roger Gilmore sat in the middle of them, looking completely dejected. His face looked bruised, and his head was slumped forward.

"I gotta tell you, I am impressed," Gerbuls began. "You really pulled off an amazing feat. Your little terrorist, propaganda speech was viewed nationwide. Half the people didn't show up to work today, and more left by noon. You managed to piss off the most powerful people in the world."

"They wouldn't be so powerful if people like you didn't follow their orders," Lou said while he internally rejoiced and loved his countrymen again.

"I'm sure you realize we need you to speak to the people, get 'em back to work. So maybe you figure you can be a tough guy because we need you alive." He walked over to the side of the bed, grinning devilishly down at Lou. "Well, we got a bunch of terrorists right there." He pointed to the monitor. "And we don't need any of them alive." He pulled a communicator from his pocket and spoke into it. "Show him."

Lou looked at the monitor and saw two armed guards walk into the holding room. They walked to the British man, slumping on the end and grabbed him by the arms.

"Leave him alone," the man next to him yelled and grabbed at one of the guard's arms. The guard smashed him in the face with the butt end of the bolt blaster.

Lou heard Teresa gasp.

"What are you doing? Stop this!" Lou shouted.

The guards held him up by the arms in front of the camera. Another man came into view and stood before the dazed British man. In his hand he held a long knife. With a swift move, he grabbed the man by the hair, held up his head, and cut his neck open. Teresa screamed, and the rest of them grumbled. A British man lunged off the bench and was blasted before he stood up. The man with the knife moved to the side so Lou could see the blood gushing down his chest.

"You son of a bitch!" Lou yelled, glowering at Gerbuls. "You didn't even give me a chance to save him."

"Now you know what happens next time you don't listen to me," Gerbuls said caustically.

The guards let the body drop to the ground and left the room. Teresa was crying, and Reilly held her around her shoulders.

"You are responsible for every death, Rizzo, not me. We caught those British scumbags two days ago, all thanks to you for letting one of your painting buddies know they were traveling from Crystal Lake to Rosemont. And you liberals said torture doesn't work. Freddy will assure you it does."

Lou closed his eyes so hard he saw red.

"We had groups of highly trained gate officers dressed like scavies search out every estimated course they could take on their way to Rosemont. It was a piece of cake . . . found the British idiots alongside the Des Plaines River in the Elk Grove woods. The first British scumbag died before telling us where the rendezvous point was, but the second was very obliging, and it turns out his information was correct because here you are. Torture definitely works.

"Hey, come to think of it, that guy who just got his throat cut was the squealer. Does that soften the blow?" Gerbuls laughed. The awful noise was poison to Lou's ears.

"Now get dressed, or the next one will be from your group, maybe the girl." Lou's eyes were filled with rage as he scowled at Gerbuls.

"Yeah, her, she'll get cut next. You see, I assured the president you would cooperate because you love her too much to let her die. I'm not sure if it's a true love or a neurotoxin love, but it's there, and a bleeding heart pussy like you can't let her throat get cut along with a lot of other peons you probably care about."

Lou opened his eyes wide and took in a deep breath. He sprang from the bed and grabbed at the scoundrel's head. He got him by the ears and squeezed with all his might as he yelled like a savage. The man, who pushed the cart in, ran out of the room. The guard froze momentarily in shock. Lou pushed Gerbuls all the way to the wall, slamming his head against it, wanting to pop his head like a melon. He let go of one of his ears and punched him in the face. Gerbuls was dazed. He pulled his arm back to punch again this time he would break his nose. Before he could throw the punch, the guard grabbed his arm. Another guard ran in and grabbed him around the neck and began squeezing. Gerbuls dropped to the ground. They got Lou down on his stomach, and a guard put his knee and all his weight on Lou's back to handcuff him. They left him there on the ground while they attended to

Gerbuls and helped him up. They assisted him out of the room, locking the door behind them.

Lou managed to get to his feet with his hands cuffed behind his back and plopped down on the bed, face first.

It was about an hour he was alone.

Finally, the door opened again, and a guard came over to Lou and took off his handcuffs. He sat up and saw two large G.A.T.E. officers were standing there with bolt blasters in their hands. Then Gerbuls toddled in. He had a red swollen cheek and a gauze bandage around his head, covering his ears.

"You're gonna be sorry you fucked with me," he said. His voice sounded solemn, and his gaze was pure fury. He took the communicator out of his pocket, and pointed at the monitor. "Two are gonna die for that, you stupid prick."

"No wait," Lou pleaded. "I'm sorry I lost my head. Please don't kill anyone else, and I'll do whatever you say." Lou took his shirt off and started to change into the clothes they brought him earlier. Gerbuls reluctantly put the communicator back in his pocket.

"You'll do whatever I say, or all of them get their throats cut, starting with the girl!" Gerbuls yelled.

"Fine, just don't harm them," Lou said, sounding firm. "Fuck it all, let the nukes fly." He looked at the armed guards and said, "Is that alright with you guys? We'll just sit back and let them take us to war. You gonna follow their orders to the death, huh." The guards didn't move or speak. He turned back to Gerbuls, "I want them treated well if I'm gonna sell out my country, you hear me, agent ass kisser. Give them food and drink and somewhere comfortable to rest."

"You're in no position to make demands, Rizzo, but I'll see they are treated well as long as you cooperate."

"Well, let's get the show on the road. Where's the statement you want me to read? You gonna record me here?" Lou said just as he finished dressing.

"No," said Gerbuls, "we're gonna record you reading it live to all the degenerates gathering outside the convention center."

Lou lifted his head, and his eyes grew wide. He felt his

heart warming and a kindle of hope.

"How many people are out there?" was all he could think of asking.

"I don't know," Gerbuls said disgustedly. "Who knows how many of these dumb fucks are going to show up, but they keep coming, and it's your Goddamn fault. You're gonna say what we tell you to say. Any deviation will mean death to your little posse and a bullet through the back of your head. Then we'll shoot down the mob if they try anything. So a lot of lives depend on your actions. Understand?"

Lou nodded.

The two large officers took him to a locker room where he showered and shaved under guard supervision.

Then they brought him to a large cafeteria where he ate a chicken burger, fries, and drank some sort of artificial fruit punch.

He considered how good it was, eating fresh duck and drinking boiled river water at his last meal and how different everything was, not so long ago.

He tried to work on the guards while he ate . . . teasing them about their acquiescence to a destructive government, trying to explain to them the urgency for change, but they remained expressionless and silent. They had been instructed to ignore everything that came out of the terrorist's mouth.

Lou was persistent for awhile, but he became silent near the end of the meal. His thoughts became devoted to Teresa. He considered if he had sent her away like he planned to, and it was just Reilly and the Edwards boys they were going to kill, would he go out there and lie to the people.

No, I would sacrifice them and try to spark a revolution, he thought and hissed angrily.

Next they led him down a hall. At the end of it an electric motor cart awaited on the concourse of the convention center. He sat in front next to the driver. The two beef head officers sat behind him, never taking their aim off him. The driver sped away. He honked at some rich, elderly, white congressmen, who were too slow to move aside. Then he accelerated in urgency.

Lou stared at him. "Hi, I'm Lou Rizzo!" he said, yelling to

be heard. "You know . . . the guy that wants to save our country." The driver looked over and smiled. The beef heads must have noticed because suddenly the one directly behind Lou smacked him with an open hand, hard on his left ear.

Lou yelped and cringed forward, holding his ear as it rang and stung.

"Keep your mouth shut!" the beef head yelled.

Lou did keep quiet, feeling embarrassed for yelping in front of the driver like that. He was like a defenseless infant at the hands of the scolding beef heads.

The ride ended at the north end of the convention center where they got on an elevator and went up twelve floors. They got out, walked down a hall and stood before suite twelve eighteen.

One of the beef heads knocked, and Gerbuls opened the door. Lou didn't move so they pushed him forward, forcing him to walk into the room.

A handsome man with dark hair sat behind a large desk. Sitting across from him was an older man with white hair, who stood when Lou came in.

Lou didn't immediately recognize them. It had been a long time since he had seen them in person.

"Rizzo," Gerbuls said, "meet President Burns and his Chief of Staff, Bill Trump." Bill extended his hand toward him. Lou ignored him and approached the desk.

"Bud, please don't do this," he pleaded. "We have to talk with the W.U.N. I don't know what this greedy, old fuck has been telling you." He motioned toward Trump. "This is insanity. It's pure evil to let this happen . . . hell on earth."

The beef head guards grabbed him by the shoulders and pulled him away from the desk.

"I wouldn't call it evil," Bud Burns said, "The world is overpopulated, you know, and the world that will arise from the ashes will be more like paradise than hell, and we will rule it."

"We are completely prepared for what is to come, Mr. Rizzo," said Trump.

His confident, dainty voice made Lou's skin crawl.

"Everything was planned for and going perfectly until your little stunt at the T.V. studio."

"Yes," President Burns injected, "and now you're gonna straighten things out with the public."

Lou looked down, shaking his head.

"It's the only way to prevent a bloodbath," Gerbuls said from behind.

Lou sharply turned toward him.

"A blood bath is inevitable, and you know it," he snapped, causing Gerbuls to flinch. Lou turned back toward the president.

"I wish, even if for just a moment, you people could really believe all men are created equal." He exhaled loudly as if admitting defeat and said, "At least then you might know the feeling of guilt."

Burns and Trump looked at each other and smirked.

"Yes whatever, Mr. Crusader," Burns mocked. "Your ideal society doesn't work. A socialistic society fails because common people are not inherently good. They need to be ruled by a wiser class of elites."

"This is the end game, Mr. Rizzo," Trump said. "It's time for America to use its might and establish a permanent empire. We'll control the world and create a perfect free market when the dust clears."

Burns stood and began to walk around his desk. "There'd be no more starvation, no more war, no more overpopulation," he said blissfully while walking toward Lou.

"No more rebellions," added Trump.

"Only a fool would believe that," Lou snapped.

The president was standing taller, thicker and physically stronger before Lou. He was frowning down at him. He took in a deep breath and let it go. "Here's the deal, Rizzo," he said sternly. "This war is coming! There's no stopping it now. They already have aircraft carriers in Cuba, and we've detected nuclear subs off their coast."

"Cuba will be our first nuclear strike in response," Trump interjected.

Lou began trembling. He felt like this moment was surreal and didn't know how he would react. After what he had done to Gerbuls, he suddenly feared his anger could not be repressed and he would make a last gasp effort to rip the president's face apart.

I'll fish hook his cheeks and pull until his skin rips apart.
His mind conjured up the image.

"You have a choice," Burns said. "You can do this right, and we let you live to be a part of the next great empire."

"And we let your friends live too," Trump added, as if it were a signing bonus.

"Yes, of course," said Burns. "Agent Gerbuls was telling me you were caught with the woman who broke you out of jail. Surely you would want her to be in the bomb shelter with you, right."

"Mr. Rizzo," Trump began, "we're willing to pardon you of all your crimes and appoint you as an advisor to the president once the war ends."

There was a moment of silence. They wanted to give it time to sink in and were amused that a working class hero was just offered the chance of a lifetime, a chance to live among the leisure class.

"Humm," muttered Lou, "so would I be rich like you guys? Maybe I can take his position when he tips over," motioning toward Trump.

"Or you can choose the alternative," said Burns. "I believe you already know what that is."

"Indeed he does," Gerbuls said from behind.

"So can we count on your cooperation, or does you legacy end here?" asked Burns.

Lou Looked at him and reluctantly nodded.

"Good," Burns said, turned and walked to the window. "Take a look at the problem you created."

Lou walked over and looked out. Beneath them was the courtyard, beyond that, the parking lot and River Road was beyond that. Lou swayed and felt like he might faint, seeing that the courtyard and most of the parking lot was filled with people. His mouth dropped open, and his heart soared.

They really came. The people are ready. For his whole life and generations before him, the American people were apathetic to challenging the government. The crushing drudgery of their daily lives played a large role in their apathy. Lou never gave up hope in the people, no matter how brainwashed they were by corporate media, no matter the fake two-party system that had amalgamated decades ago, no matter how weighed down by their necessitous lifestyle, no matter how poorly educated, duped and oppressed by unregulated bankers and the market forces. He never gave up hope in them one day rising up to take back their country because he never gave up on himself.

For a moment the weight of the dire situation faded, and he felt a warm rush of proud triumph.

"You see the podium they set up?" Trump said.

Lou saw they were using the veranda as a stage, and a podium was set up with a microphone. Workers were assembling the sound system presently. He also noticed armed guards lined the stage and the perimeter of the courtyard.

"That's where you'll give your speech," Trump continued. "There is a monitor built into the podium that will show your speech and highlight each sentence you're on."

"It's great; I use it all the time," Burns said. He walked to his desk, picked up a folder and handed it to Lou. "Here's your speech. We're going to do this as soon as the P.A. and the news cameras are set up. You got about a half hour. Is there anything we can get you while you get familiar with the speech?"

"Whiskey on the rocks, no . . . I want scotch and soda." Lou licked his lips. "And make it a big one, not some tiny glass filled with ice." He smiled to himself because he said it in a way that made the president seem like a personal servant.

"Agent Gerbuls, you wanna go down to the bar and get that?" Burns ordered. "Have a seat." He motioned for Lou to sit behind the desk.

Lou sat and opened up the folder. He let out a moan of disgust after reading the first two lines of the speech.

"This is terrible speech writing," he said, shaking his head.

"You'll make it sound just fine. You're an old pro," said Trump.

"Hey!" Lou shouted, "I never read speeches. I just jot down a few topics and points, and I improvise. I say what I feel! That's why people believe me, cause I'm openhearted and honest, the complete opposite of your breed."

They were staring at him, expecting more, but he just looked back down to the speech.

Burns cleared his throat and sucked his lip a few times, thinking of how to respond.

"Let me just make sure we're straight here," he said, walking closer to Lou. "Do you give me your word that you're gonna stick to the planned speech, or are a lot of people about to get killed?" His stare was piercing and unyielding.

Lou looked into his gaze for a moment, and then he blinked his eyes and nodded ever so slightly.

Burns held out his hand. "I got your word. Say it and shake on it."

Lou didn't hesitate. "You got my word," he said and shook the president's strong hand.

Burns immediately walked out of the room, followed by trump, without saying another word. Just the beef head guards stood in the room with him.

Lou's mind was so stressed that he couldn't read the speech. He kept starting over before he finished the first paragraph.

How the hell am I gonna do this? he kept asking himself.

Moments later, Gerbuls walked in with a scotch and soda. He set it on the desk and pulled the chair toward the window where he sat and gazed out of it silently.

For the next twenty minutes, Lou sipped his drink, read and re-read the speech, while the two beef head guards and Gerbuls remained silent.

Suddenly, a ringer broke the silence, startling Lou. Gerbuls answered his keyphone on the second ring.

"Yes . . . on our way," was all he said and ended the call. He got up from his seat and stretched his arms over his head while moaning.

"It's show time Rizzo. Let's go."

Lou got up and followed him out the door with the beef heads following close behind him. He felt like the weight of the world was crushing down on his lungs. He took short rapid breaths to stay conscious.

He sat on the electric cart, feeling lightheaded as they drove off. The ride gave him a tour of the south side of the center's main floor. As they passed a guarded door, a high ranking military officer was entering the room as Lou watched.

That must be the Command Center, he noted.

When the ride ended, they walked him through the concourse to the veranda doorway. Six armed guards were standing along the hallway with Secret Service agents by the door.

Gerbuls halted, turned to face Lou, and took the folder out of his hands. "You don't need this. Your speech will be on the podium." Then he put his hand on Lou's shoulder.

He felt violated to have this wicked hand upon him.

"You do this right or that pretty brunette is the first to get it."

Lou looked at the guards around him to see if they heard, and if they had a reaction in their expressions.

Gerbuls looked out the door, waiting for a signal. A moment later he lifted his hand. "Alright, get out there. You're on," he said and held the door open for him.

Lou walked out on the veranda and approached the podium. Some of the people up front began yelling and applauding when they saw him, and soon the crowd erupted in ovation. He could hear a group of people farther away begin chanting, "Spread the word; no work till we're heard."

The fresh, sunny afternoon air and the sound and sight of the people made his spine tingle. He looked at the guards at the back of the veranda and sensed some of them felt uneasy. Then he looked at the faces of the people upfront. In them he recognized the sense of duty and determination that was missing from Americans for far too long.

Chapter 25

He walked up to the podium and looked down at the speech. Bending over the microphone, he lowered it closer to his mouth.

"Hello," he said quietly. He decided to take the wireless microphone off the clip so he could hold it closer to his mouth. "Thanks to all you people who refused to work and came out here to support my cause. I was allowed to talk with the president." Lou paused before reading the next line and looked out at the faces staring back at him. He thought of Gavin, a good religious man who would never give up his freedom . . . also Reilly, Joe Bob and Scooter, tough outdoorsmen, who wouldn't even consider conforming with the Government Action Act.

But it was Teresa's image that was forefront in his mind, so vivid and real he could smell her scent and feel her body heat. He shut his eyes, trying to embrace her image, and tears flowed down his cheeks.

"The entire U.S. government heard the people today, and we reached an agreement." His voice was trembling. "I can guarantee you this." He took a few steps away from the podium and his eyes widened. "They're going to," he sprinted to the front of the veranda, "start a fuckin' nuclear war!" he yelled.

"Take him down," Gerbuls ordered, just as Lou reached the edge and leaped forward into the crowd. A spatter of bullets rang out, and people were screaming as Lou fell into the crowd. He knocked down two young men and a heavyset woman. They all fell to the ground as four more people struck by bullets fell right next to him. Lou saw blood flowing out of a man's neck while his gurgled screams abruptly ended. Another man, who never had a chance to scream, had a bullet take out the front of his head. Brain matter and blood drizzled down on Lou's arms and the back of his head. He got to a squat and quickly scampered forward, dodging between legs, sinking deeper into the crowd.

"Cease fire!" Lou yelled into the wireless Microphone he was clutching in his left hand. "All Guards and soldiers hold your fire immediately. Do not shoot your fellow countrymen. Stand with us. It's time to take back our country." Massive feedback shrieked through the speakers as the P.A. was quickly turned off. Lou threw down the mic and veered to his left.

The gunfire died down and stopped, but people were still screaming.

He scurried toward the perimeter of the convention center where guards had been positioned all along the building. Now, daring to run more upright, he bumped into a burley man, who looked at him with surprise.

"Come on, we have to get the guards to join us!" Lou yelled to him and kept moving. "Its time to rise up!" he yelled, looking around at the faces surrounding him. His eyes blazed, and he raised his fist into the air and screamed, "Let's take back our country!" He ran at the guards. "Take their weapons!" he yelled to the people running with him. As the group charged, more people joined in the stampede, growing with every stride.

To the guards it looked like a landslide of people suddenly falling toward them like a powerful wave just before it crashes to the shore.

"Halt!" one of them yelled, and all the guards futilely pointed their rifles at the charging crowd.

"Lay down your weapons!" Lou tried to shout over the roaring crowd.

"Stay back!" a guard yelled.

The first shot rang out and the young, blond haired, blue eyed, American, charging side by side with Lou, fell, screaming in pain.

"Take the guns!" Lou yelled as the mob narrowed the final space between citizen and service man. More shots randomly fired, hitting more Americans. Every time a body fell, the crowd roared louder and advanced quicker.

Some of the guards began to retreat toward the veranda entrance, while others dropped their rifles and held up their arms.

The guard closest to Lou made a break for it. He and two other men tackled him. A bald man began throttling the guard in the back of the head with his fist. Lou pulled the rifle out of the guard's clenched hand.

"Stop, you're gonna kill him!" Lou yelled and grabbed the bald man's arm before he landed another blow. "Don't kill them! Just take the weapons!" Lou yelled loudly to the mob.

The bald guy frowned at Lou and stood up. He got in Lou's face, breathing heavy and completely enraged. "This son of a bitch killed Vinny!" he yelled. "He was my best friend. Don't tell me what to fuckin' do."

Lou nodded. "We're not done," he said to the raging bald man. "Come on, let's do this for Vinny." He slapped the man on the shoulder and ran off toward the veranda, yelling to people along the way.

"Come on, we have to get to the command center!" He knew time was short. All the guards that were going to make it inside had, and they were holding the doors shut. In a matter of minutes, they could lock down the whole convention center and have their defenses organized.

He saw two young black men holding rifles that they just acquired from guards who received beatings.

"Everyone, follow me!" he called out. The black men followed him as did everyone who caught sight of him, and like a snowball rolling down a fresh snow covered hill, the horde grew.

He was twenty feet away when he could see guards trying to wrap a chain around the glass door's handles. They nervously looked up, directly at Lou. He held his arms up and slowed the horde to a walk. Staring directly at the guards, he began to preach.

"Fellow countrymen, open the doors and join us!" his voice was booming.

The people quieted down, and the guards remained transfixed on him.

"Stop taking orders. It's time to overthrow the greedy tyrants. They bankrupted our country, and now they're gonna start a nuclear holocaust. Open the doors and join us." After a deep breath, he yelled, "It's time to take back our country!"

The crowd erupted and charged the doors.

The soldiers backed away, retreating to a presumed safe distance. A dozen people got there before Lou. They burst open the doors and infested the building. Shots were fired, glass shattered, people screamed.

Lou boldly entered the building, deranged and suicidal. To his left, guards laid down their weapons and put their hands in the air, pleading for mercy. He quickly turned to the right and spotted the two guards taking aim from about twenty-five yards away.

"Don't shoot! Lay down your weapons!" Lou yelled. One of them squeezed off a shot, hitting a tall man next to him. The man groaned with rage, aimed his rifle, and began shooting at them. The two armed black men joined in. Lou was fearlessly running toward them to get a better shot. A soldier took aim at him, but a black rebel shot first and got him in the head. He stopped and watched the guard fall to the ground, while others rampaged past him.

That guy almost killed me, he realized.

"To the command center!" he screamed. People stormed into the concourse. Lou looked upward to see guards were on the second level, pointing their rifles down over the rail. There was about to be a massacre.

Some began shooting, **but a revised sense of American decency emerged in many of them, who couldn't bring themselves to randomly shoot fellow countrymen, fighting for their rights!**

"This way!" Lou screamed and headed toward the corridor that led to the command center. "Come on!" He began to sprint and noticed a guard taking aim at him from above. He dove forward as a shot ricocheted off the concrete floor behind him. He tucked and rolled but was moving too fast and couldn't spring back to his feet. He fell to the ground like he had been pushed. Someone returned fire next to him, reached down and grabbed him under the shoulder.

"Come on man," a familiar voice said while pulling him

up. "I got your back, dog, now move." It was Tyrell, armed with a rifle!

Lou looked at him, smiled for a second, and dashed toward the corridor. Once he was safely out of the concourse, he turned back. Tyrell was shooting up at the guard on the second floor that almost killed him.

"Come on, Tyrell," Lou yelled.

Tyrell fired a last shot and began to run. Just as he got one stride, a bullet entered the back of his head and splattered out the front. Lou's bodyguard's immense corpse fell to the ground.

"Noooooo!" Lou screamed, falling to his knees. Another black man picked up the rifle Tyrell dropped and ran to the corridor.

It was Deron! He pulled Lou to his feet, and they jogged down the corridor as a horde began to grow behind him.

The corridor seemed to stretch on forever. Lou knew this was the most vulnerable place to be. A few grenades could kill most of them and cut off their access to the command center. He was fearless until he witnessed Tyrell's death. Now he remembered if he dies, so does the revolution, and Tyrell's sacrifice was for nothing.

Then he realized, *Teresa, oh God, I sacrificed Teresa.*

Chapter 26

Teresa kept her eyes closed tightly and her face buried in Reilly's chest. Seeing that British man's throat get cut open and spew blood horrified her, and she didn't want to open her eyes ever again, but she did. Peaking ever so slightly, she glanced at the body.

Mesmerized by the gory sight, she took a long look before sobbing and hiding her face on Reilly's chest again. Reilly was whispering to Gavin some kind of contingency plan, but she didn't try to listen.

After the guards killed the British man, the captain had announced that if Mr. Rizzo did what was asked of him, they would be released. She was at least confident that Louis wouldn't let her die, so she wasn't interested in any contingency plan. Time passed slowly.

She was so thirsty but didn't dare ask one of these murderous guards for a drink of water.

Finally a keyphone rang, and she lifted her head to peak at the Captain, who answered.

"Jesus Christ, are you kidding me?" he shouted. That caught everyone's attention. "Holy shit! That's fuckin' crazy! What do we do?" the captain exclaimed with a look of sheer shock. "Okay," he said and closed the phone. "They want all gate officers to get over to the convention center to guard the command center. Moore, Beck, you two take care of the prisoners and meet us over there." The captain pocketed his keyphone and walked off.

"This is it," Reilly said, looking down the bench at the others.

All the guards left except for Officer Moore and Beck. They raised their rifles and walked to the front of the holding cell.

"Alright people, just remain seated," said Officer Moore. "We're going to get you out of here, so just relax." Moore unlocked the door.

"Get under the bench," Reilly told Teresa and pushed her toward the floor. She went to the ground and scurried under the bench just as the guards stepped into the cell.

Without saying another word, Moore and Beck aimed their rifles and began shooting. Two British soldiers were hit where they sat and fell to the ground as they screamed. The rest of the men sprang off the bench and charged the guards, each screaming their primordial death cry as all but one was struck with bullets.

Teresa was tucked in a fetal position under the bench. The ghastly sound of gunfire and bodies falling was horribly surreal to her as she awaited her fate.

She opened here eyes seconds later when the shooting stopped. Only two sets of legs remained standing and were right in front of her.

Both men were groaning and straining loudly against each other. She could tell by the shoes, one was a guard and the other, she hoped, was Reilly. It was half a minute before she heard a snap and a head struck the bench as the body fell to the ground. For a moment all was silent. Then the only surviving man in the room squatted down to look at her.

"Teresa," Scooter called, "we gots to get out of here." He extended his hand. She took it and got pulled out and up to her feet.

Gasping as she looked at the dead bodies, she began to cry when seeing Reilly's corpse face down on top of the guard he killed by breaking his neck, before he died from the bullet wounds in his chest. She began to fall to her knees, but Scooter grabbed her and held her up.

"We ain't got time to cry now," he said and swept her out of the cell.

He pulled her through the lobby of the interrogation chamber, located in the basement of the Rosemont G.A.T.E. station, and put his hand on the exit door handle. Teresa stopped weeping, and suddenly he heard boot heals clacking the concrete from outside the corridor. They were approaching fast.

Scooter let go of her, and she collapsed to the ground. He ran into the cell and picked up a rifle.

As Scooter scrambled to locate ammunition and reload the weapon, her mind kept repeating, *How could he let this happen? How could he let this happen!*

Chapter 27

As Lou and the horde of rebellious citizens neared the end of the corridor, he saw sunlight from the glass atrium illuminating the hastily erected, concrete barrier. The soldiers and cops were lined up behind it and a grenade launcher, aiming right at them, sat on top of a dedicated Illinois National Guardsman's shoulder.

"Halt, or we shoot!" someone shouted through a loud speaker.

"Stop! Everyone stop!" Lou yelled and slowed to a walk. "Please don't shoot!" he yelled to the troops. "We have to stop them before they destroy us all! Please, join us!"

"It's all over. This state is under martial law," the loud speaker man announced. "If you come forward, we will open fire. This is your only warning. Turn around and go back to you places of residence now."

Lou continued walking slowly, and the people followed.

"I just need to talk to whoever is in charge. Please don't shoot."

They were in range now. He could see how they were positioned to kill anyone who comes out of the corridor, like shooting fish in a barrel.

"Halt, or we shoot," the loud speaker man issued his final warning.

"Don't you care about your country?" Lou screamed, "You don't have to obey an order to kill your fellow countrymen! Help us set this country back on the right track, to prosperity, not war!"

"It's him!" a cop near the front yelled.

"That's the guy," some of the guards were saying as word spread.

The next chilling moment silence fell, filling everyone with nervous anticipation.

As the fate of the country floated in the ether Lou felt them taking aim. He could sense their thoughts. They were going to take him down, cut off the head of the snake.

They're giving the order now. Even if a majority of them refuse to shoot me, at least one of them will. I'm about to die. How foolish. How fuckin' foolish am I?

He cowardly stepped backwards, bumping into a portly man, willfully, even hopefully planning for the shot to hit someone else, anyone but him.

Deron was standing to his left.

"If they shoot, aim for the guy with the grenade launcher first," Lou murmured. The fatal moment stretched, and he tried to slink behind the portly man, but the big man would have none of it and sidestepped to keep Lou in front of him. Lou dropped to a squat and desperately pushed in between the legs of brave citizens, cowardly seeking cover from his eminent death. **Then...**

CRASH! The sound of windows being smashed erupted, and glass came crashing to the ground. The guards tuned to see a horde of scavies charging through the broken glass wall of the front of the convention center.

They were armed with guns, bows and arrows, and military assault rifles they acquired from guardsmen and officers they had already killed outside.

The interior forces didn't expect a separate attack from the front of the convention center. Nobody did, except the Emancipators who quickly planned a frontal attack when they saw most of the crowd entering the convention center from the courtyard. The Emancipators got word about Lou's televised message and as many that could make it were in attendance. They remained in back standing out by River Road, keeping close to the woods until now.

Gunfire broke out immediately. The guard holding the grenade launcher turned around and fired toward the broken glass opening where the scavies were charging in from. Bodies and limbs were propelled in the explosion, and many good men died in the first wave.

Lou got up and charged. As he ran forward, he held up his rifle to eyelevel and tried to hit his target. The guard turned back and aimed the grenade launcher right at him. Lou stopped to aim better and fired again. He missed, and the guard targeted his weapon, but a split second before the guard fired, a bullet entered his head, making him fall backwards, discharging the grenade straight up instead of right at him.

"Yeah boy," Deron celebrated after making the brilliant shot. The grenade hit the ceiling and fell back to the ground, exploding and killing the guards behind the barrier.

"Nice shot, Deron!" Lou yelled, astounded by the luck.

"To the Command Center!" he shouted, and the charge began.

Lou's horde stormed forward, spilling into the atrium as a second wave of scavies also charged from the front.

Lou was in the middle of a chaotic battle. He shot two guards in the back before return fire barely missed him, but many other citizens were killed. The guards were caught in the middle, and friendly fire from the scavies soon became the biggest danger. Being overwhelmed by the two sided attack, servicemen began laying down their arms, but many Americans continued to die in those bloody ninety seconds before the gunfire began to settle down.

At the first available moment, Lou looked around and located the doors to the largest executive meeting room in the convention center. It was the newly relocated National Military Command Center. Two guards were still standing in front of the doors taking potshots at any civilian they saw. These brainwashed interior guardsmen were going to fight to the death.

"Deron!" Lou called, made eye contact with him and ran toward the doors.

Once close enough, he slid down to his knees, took aim, and shot a bullet into one of their chests. The other guard turned, took aim at Lou and had a bullet pass through his neck, courtesy of Deron.

They charged to the doors. Lou pulled on the handles

of the locked double doors and idiotically began to throw his shoulder into it. Before precipitously crashing into a room filled with Secret Service members, he came to his senses.

Once these doors open, they'll open fire.

He backed to the side and pulled Deron next to him.

"We gotta get these doors open!" he yelled, hoping people would volunteer to be the sacrificial soldiers of liberty. Some people began banging their shoulders into the doors. Finally, two men charged it together, and with savage rallying cries they struck the door jointly. The door flew open, and like prophecy, gunfire mowed them down as they stumbled into the Command Center.

"Wait!" Lou yelled before more people charged in. He stood next to the open door and yelled, "Surrender your arms now, and I personally guarantee you will survive to be a part of the newly liberated America!"

A moment passed, and suddenly a voice from inside called out. "Don't shoot!" a Secret Service agent yelled and began running out of the room.

"Get back here, Buchanan! That's an order!" President Burns yelled.

Buchanan made it to the door, but a bullet hit the back of his head before he escaped the penalty of insubordination. It was Bud Burns himself who shot him with his personal side arm.

The President ran to his laptop computer on his desk. "Keep em out!" he yelled to the remaining Secret Service and presumably began sending the authentication codes to the launch facility in Okeechobee County, Florida, where an intercontinental ballistic missile was programmed to make the short trip to Cuba. This was the first target in a series of launches that were planned to strike key W.U.N. countries.

It immediately dawned on Lou what was happening.

He's pulling the old spoil sport routine.

"We got to stop him," he said to Deron. They gathered up a group of armed men and surrounded the door.

"Throw your guns down, and raise your hands! We will not shoot unless fired upon!" Lou spoke loud and clear. The president's staff started to squirm.

"For Christ sake, don't kill us!" one of the advisors yelled.

"This is suicide," General DeMay said and got up from his chair at the table. "Lay down your arms, men," he ordered.

"Not yet, DeMay!" yelled Burns.

The general ignored the president and walked near the doors. "We surrender!" he yelled. "You hear me, we threw down our arms; don't shoot!"

Lou nodded to Deron, lifted his rifle and moved in.

Deron grabbed his shoulder and pushed him to the other side of the door. He scowled at Lou and shook his head. Then he nodded to another armed man, and they went in first. Lou's heart swelled with admiration for Deron as they went through the door, rifles pointed.

Not a shot was fired, and a few more men went in before Lou.

"Get your hands in the air!" Deron yelled.

Once Lou entered, he saw everyone in the room had their hands raised except for President Burns, who was standing over the laptop, typing away. Deron had his rifle aimed at him.

"Search them all and take their arms!" Lou yelled to his fellow revolutionaries, "And let's all be cool! Nobody gets hurts! The people have reclaimed their government!"

Dozens of citizens came into the command center to help confiscate arms from the Secret Service and the president's staff, who were now the peasants and being treated roughly.

Lou walked toward Burns. "Bud, it's over. Get away from the computer now."

Burns looked at Lou for a moment. "Ha, what a surprise . . . Rizzo." He looked back down to the computer and hit a few more keys.

"Move away now, Burns!" He screamed.

Burns looked at him again. "You claim to be a man of your word, Rizzo, but you sure broke your word to me. Why should anyone trust you?"

"Last chance, Burns, move away now."

Burns started to raise his right hand, but with his left he hit the enter key and sent the codes he entered. Then he grabbed his gun off the desk and took aim.

Lou saw it and immediately fired a shot. He missed, even from such short range.

Then Burns shot. The bullet struck Lou's right shoulder and buried itself in muscle, between the scapula and clavicle bones, turning him sideways as he fell to the floor.

A second shot popped off, and Burns fell to the ground. Deron got him right in the chest.

Lou was on the ground screaming bloody murder like his arm had been bitten off by a shark.

A man fell to his knees and pushed his hand down on the wound to slow the bleeding. "You're gonna be okay, man. Just relax."

Lou continued to scream until Deron knelt next to him. Once Lou saw his face, he stopped his loud bawling and shifted to moaning deep breathes.

"Man, you sure is a terrible shot," Deron said, smiling.

Lou suddenly broke out in laughter, wonderful, uncontrollable laughter, momentarily making the pain secondary and the triumph of victory primary.

Chapter 28

A young rebel eagerly took off his shirt and ripped it into strips for his new leader. He helped Deron tie them around Lou's shoulder, slowing the blood loss considerably. Deron and another man helped Lou up and over to the large, plush, brown, leather seat at the head of the table. The same chair President Burns used to sit in.

"I want the former presidential staff back at the table now," Lou said groggily, looking at the business suited men lined up against the wall, some still being searched for weapons.

"You heard the man!" Deron yelled. "All you suits, get back to the table now." The president's immoral executive cabal apprehensively returned to the table after they were roughly frisked by poor people.

Lou spun his chair and faced a Secret Service man who was standing at gun point against the wall behind him. "You," Lou called to him, "get a medical team up here. I want to be fixed up right here in this chair."

The Secret Service man nodded.

"You guys watch him," he told the men, covering him with their shiny new guns.

"General," Lou called to the large, five star general, Brian DeMay.

The general most always had a stone cold serious expression on his pale face and was bald on top of his head with short white hair on the side.

He looked at Lou. "Go to his desk. Get that computer and find out what that crazy bastard did before he shot me." The general walked over to the president's desk, stumbling as he stepped over the body.

"Deron," Lou called.

"Yo," he answered and scampered over to him.

"You're my right hand man, Deron." They engaged serious eye contact for a moment and Deron nodded. "Have people get the word out; the people have assumed control of our government. Stop all fighting. You got it?"

Deron nodded.

"Get television cameras in here, and I'll address the nation."

Deron hopped to it, yelling out orders to fellow rebels in a boisterous manner.

Lou turned to the man who dejectedly was forced to sit closest to him. "You're the Secretary of State, right?"

The man nervously nodded. He was a lean blond haired man with thin, gold framed glasses that almost seemed invisible on his narrow nose.

"I can't remember your name."

"It's Steve Jolston," the man said, trembling slightly.

"Alright Steve, you're my new chief of staff. Cause I sure don't want that slime bag working for me." He pointed with his left hand toward Bill Trump, who sat sulking at the end of the table while armed citizens stood about, some of them pestering him.

"Get someone over here to swear me in as the president. I don't suppose the chief justice is in town."

Steve was speechless and confused.

"Just take care of it, Steve."

"I-I can't," Steve stuttered, "They took my keyphone."

"Whoever took this guy's keyphone, give it back now!" yelled Lou. Then he turned his chair towards DeMay. "General, what's the hold up? Get over here with that computer."

The general gently picked up the laptop, walked to the table, sat near Lou, opposite side of Steve Jolston.

"I'm not exactly sure what he did," said the general. "It's hard to pinpoint…"

"Deron!" Lou yelled, cutting off the general. "Put you gun to his head and get ready to blow a hole in it."

Deron immediately pointed his rifle at DeMay's large, shinny head. His eyes grew wide with fear.

"I'm gonna ask you once again, General. A lot of good

people died today, so no one minds if we kill some more of the bad guys. This is your last chance. Tell me what he did!"

The general took a deep breath and opened his mouth.

"Don't tell him a thing, DeMay!" Trump suddenly shouted as he stood up and grabbed a rifle from the hands of a skinny scavie standing near him.

Lou began to dive under the table as Trump tried to shoot him. A man behind him smashed trump in the back of his head with a punch. As trump fell forward, the closest armed citizen shot at his head. Trump was dead before his face hit the table. Twenty more bullets filled the corpse before the shots ended and blood spilled off the edge of the table. Lou got back in his chair, unshaken by this event, but he had to hold his wound harder now to slow the blood that was soaking through the bandages.

"What the fuck did he do, General!" Lou yelled as the pain flared.

"He sent codes for a nuclear launch," DeMay blurted.

"I fuckin' knew it! Goddamn spoil sport!" cried Lou, "He ordered the first strike on Cuba, right?"

"No sir, he ordered the second strike." DeMay paused.

Lou frowned, irritated to be waiting for him to finish.

"Hong Kong," he finally said.

"No, not China. Goddamn that son of a bitch!" Lou cried.

"We have to get into the bomb shelter right away!" DeMay implored, "There's a state of the art Military Command Center down there."

"I'll bet there is, you bunch of sick fucks!" Lou shouted. "Get me the soldiers at the launch facility, now," he ordered to DeMay.

Then he turned to the rest of the staff. "I want another computer with an open link to the World Wide Web. Call some secretaries here. Hurry up, your lives depend on it."

The general reached the two soldiers in the hot seat at the launch facility in the middle of the Mojave Desert at the Fort Irwin Military Reservation. The web-camera showed bo⌐ soldiers monitoring their computer screens.

"I got them," the general told Lou.

"Well," said Lou sarcastically. "Order them to stop the fuckin' launch."

A team of paramedics entered the room. One plopped a med kit on the table in front of Lou. The other opened it, grabbed a scalpel and began cutting off Lou's right sleeve.

"Gentlemen, this is General DeMay. We have a situation here."

"Sir?" one of the soldiers replied.

"There's been a revolt. The presidents dead," DeMay said, sounding remorseful.

Lou saw red. He groaned loudly, reached for the computer and pulled it over to him, making the paramedic accidentally jab him with the scalpel. He positioned the monitor in front of his face.

"Stop the launch at once! That's an order!" he yelled to the direction of the microphone hole.

Both soldiers looked up at the monitor to see who was yelling. They both silently stared at Lou's large, close-up, facial.

"This is Louis Rizzo, the acting Commander and Chief. NOW STOP THE LAUNCH!"

That got their attention. One soldier shook his head, shaking his jowls as if to snap himself out of a trance.

"Sir," he said, looking down at his flight monitors. The missile is already in flight."

A news crew burst into the room. The cameraman was already shooting live, slowing to show the dead bodies by the entrance and panning up as he walked into the room.

Lou closed his eyes hard.

Come on, think. What do I know about I.C.B.M's? Now the cameraman spotted Lou and walked closer, bringing him into a clear view.

"How long till the missile reaches mid-flight?" Lou calmly asked.

"Sir, it's approaching mid-flight," the soldier replied, "beginning descent . . . re-entry in . . . . six minutes."

"Has the post boost vehicle been jettisoned yet?" Lou asked with his eyes closed and his fingers crossed.

Another tense pause took place.

"No sir, not yet. It will be before the final stage."

Lou exhaled deeply.

"Okay, listen to me, soldier. Use the post boost vehicle now! Guide it away from its target. Hong Kong is a southern coastal city. You have to try and make it come up short and south of the target. Sink it in the South China Sea. You understand, soldier?"

The soldier leaned his head over and talked with his partner for a moment.

"Yes sir, our best chance is to try to force an early re-entry."

"We're all counting on you, gentlemen. The whole country is," said Lou. "Make that missile miss!"

A paramedic poured something on his wound, and the other one went in for the bullet. Lou grinded his teeth and moaned, despite it being numbed. The bullet was removed, and they began stitching him up. His blood was smudged all over the fine leather seat. It was all being documented on American Airways. The six year reign of government controlled media ended with a bang, **live coverage of the second American Revolution!**

Lou felt dizzy and closed his eyes. The voices around him distorted, and his head tipped forward.

The next thing he was aware of was something tapping his forehead. When he opened his eyes, Deron was standing next to him, trying to get him to notice something. Whether he passed out for ten seconds or a minute, he didn't know, but he felt better, as if he took a nap. The paramedic finished bandaging his shoulder.

"Thanks, man. Good work," Lou muttered.

A few female secretaries were standing by the table now. A tall slender one with luxurious blond hair walked in last. She looked at the body of Bud Burns lying on the ground, gasped and ran to him.

"Where's my open link, General!" Lou yelled.

Startled, DeMay turned toward the tall, blond secretary, who was now kneeling over Burns' corpse. She was crying, and when she grabbed Burns' hand, she let the laptop computer she was holding fall to the ground.

"She should have it," the general said. "That's Bud's secretary, Sharon Brown."

"Sharon, get over here! Your country needs you!" Lou shouted at her. "Go get her," he said to Deron. "You, young lady," he said, pointing to a dark haired, chubby secretary, "get over here and work with the general."

She scurried over to their side of the table, and Lou leaned closer to DeMay.

"I want you to communicate with the military. Contact every general. Let them know we're in control here. I want the Air Force and every missile defense squadron on high alert."

He looked down at the screen in front of him, displaying the hot seat soldiers in California who were desperately trying to guide the missile downward prematurely. He pushed the computer toward Steve Jolston. "Here, watch these guy's for me."

Just then Lou noticed the T.V. camera pointing at him from across the room. "Hey, are you guys recording!" he yelled, pointing at the camera.

"Yes," the crew answered in unison.

"Get closer, I want to address the nation."

Citizens stepped aside so the cameraman could move closer. Deron led the weeping Sharon Brown over to his side.

Lou looked up at the tall blond and said. "Not the time to weep, Sharon. I lost someone very close too, but millions more could die if we don't do our best right now. I need your help. Understand?"

She nervously looked over to the camera then back to Lou, sniffled and nodded smugly.

"Set up next to me here. Log on to the world wide web and send an instant message to deputy p dot m dash t dot swan. Got it?"

She closed her eyes to memorize the address and nodded. "Write this: it's Lou Rizzo, urgent, must connect with Tony."

She set down the computer next to him and got to work, still standing and was hunching over to reach the table. An astute citizen grabbed a desk chair and rolled it over to her so she could sit.

Lou struggled to his feet, facing the camera. "My fellow

Americans, we, the people of our dear country, have done our duty and overthrown our corrupt government. As the leader of the people's revolution, I, Louis Rizzo, will serve as acting commander in chief until fair elections can be held. All fighting between us must stop. The biggest battle we must win is in each of our minds. Our inherent differences are gone. We are all equal now and must face the future as united Americans. Together we face a moment of crisis, but if all of us stand united, Americans can overcome anything. Today we took back our democracy, but it came at a price for not doing it sooner."

Sharon Brown patted his wrist. He bent down and read the reply message (Never heard of a Louis Rizzo).

"God dang it! Click on the camera icon and tell them to hit video link. Say it's really Lou, and I must talk to Tony immediately."

He looked back at the camera. "Listen up, America! Our former president ordered a nuclear missile launch as his last act to attempt to drag us into a nuclear war. What a guy, huh? I'm going to do my best to avoid a W.U.N. nuclear counter strike, but we must stay vigilant, especially those of you in the military. I welcome American Airways, now a free media source, to continue coverage while we try to work through this crisis."

Lou sat back down and faced the computer screen. "Steve, update me on the missile."

"They've altered the trajectory," Jolston said, "but they estimate wind sheer could change it during the final stage."

"Tell them to try to keep the nose low as long as they can," Lou ordered.

Just then the face of Tony Swan appeared on the screen.

"Louie, is it really you?" His voice sounded skeptical.

"Tony, it's really me!" Lou exclaimed, pulling the computer in front of him. "Listen, we have successfully overthrown the government. In fact, this is being broadcasted to America as we speak."

"That's unbelievable," Tony said.

"Yeah, well, here's the problem. President Burns is dead, but before he died, he ordered a nuclear strike on Hong Kong. We're trying to divert the missile into the ocean. China must be informed that the launch was a mistake. People in the city and near the southern coast should find shelter. There's not much time, Tony."

"Dear God, the W.U.N. will counter strike immediately."

"That's why I need you to link me with the head of the W.U.N. right away. As acting president of the United States, I want to propose an immediate peace accord."

"Yes, of course, this is quite overwhelming, but let me be the first to say congratulations, America."

The people within earshot erupted in applause.

"Hurry Tony!" Lou yelled over the noise.

The deputy prime minister of Australia sent his staff in motion. The Chinese government was informed of the potential danger. A call for an immediate W.U.N. meeting was sent to every country involved, and the message that America had overthrown its government began to circle the world. Tony sent Lou a link to the W.U.N. video conference site. When Lou logged onto the conference site, his face appeared in a small box with his name and country next to an American flag emblem. A second box appeared with the Australian flag under Tony swan's face. A moment later an Asian man, bald with thick, black, framed glasses appeared with the Chinese flag and his name, Hu Kung. He spoke Lou's name in an almost humorous way and completed a sentence in Chinese. He paused and a computerized voice translated it.

"So Mis-ta Vizzo are we expected to believe this missile was fired unintentionally?" The words also appeared at the bottom of the screen. More boxes were popping up, but Lou focused on China, knowing they were the military powerhouse of the W.U.N.

"Yes Sir, Mr. Kung, the American people have reclaimed our government, but just before we stormed the command center, our former president ordered the launch." Lou paused for translation.

Kung spoke before he could continue. He was shouting furiously. The mechanized voice translated.

"You expect us not to assume this is an American tactic

to slow our response." The moment it was translated, voices of other representatives spoke in support of the question.

"Yes, how can we be sure you're really in charge?" the British man asked.

"We are sure of nothing," said the Russian, followed by a cacophony of agreeing words.

"Look here, my esteemed colleagues," Lou said. He stood up and tried to lift the laptop but his right arm was useless. "Pick it up and follow me," he told Sharon Brown. She picked it up with the screen facing her chest and followed him toward Burns' corpse.

"Turn it around," he rudely snapped at her, "so the camera is facing me, for Christ's sake." Once she managed to turn it around, Lou squatted next to the body, reached under and sat it up. "Get in close with the camera," he told Sharon. "This is the body of our former president, who, as you can see, was shot in the chest and killed, I'm sure at least some of you can identify this face as Bud Burns.

When he knew we were about to seize control, he ordered the launch." Lou held the body up for a moment longer and let it drop. Then he reached out to the laptop and made Sharon point it directly at him. "As acting president and representative of every American citizen, I, Louis Rizzo, swear that I do not lie and would never dream of lying to the W.U.N." He went back to the table and took his seat. As Sharon set the computer down in front of him, he could hear skeptic responses. The computer translated Kung's response.

"This is not conclusive proof of anything."

"No sir, it isn't," said Lou, "but my actions are. I've ordered Missile Control to try and divert the rocket south of Hong Kong into the South China Sea. I give you my word America wants peace with China, and I want to arrange immediate peace talks with the W.U.N. in which America will sign the nuclear weapons ban treaty, open trade with the world, and begin paying restitution and all of our debts to China. America has a new government now, and we're going to be a friend to the world."

Lou took a few questions from other representatives before Hu Kung responded.

"Let us pray your missile does not cause much suffering." Pause for translation. "China would like to congratulate the American people for overthrowing their evil government." Pause. "It is our honor to support you in this difficult time of transformation by sending peace keepers to assist you until your government and country is stabilized."

Lou gasped when he heard that. Blood rushed to his head as he tried to act natural.

"Thank you, Mr. Kung, we're honored by China's kindness and understanding, but peacekeepers won't be necessary. I'm in complete control of the military, and the American people will stand united behind me."

All the representatives were silent for a moment.

Finally, Mr. Kung responded. "We are pleased by your optimism; however, we must insist on a peace keeping mission." Pause for translation. "If things are good as you say, they can be out in a year or two."

Lou debated, attempting to seek support from other nations, but none was found. They all seemed to agree that China sending troops to America was a good idea.

As time quickly passed Lou felt like he was losing creditability.

Suddenly General DeMay interrupted him. "Sixty seconds to impact," he announced.

"One minute to impact," Lou announced to the W.U.N.

The Representatives went silent.

DeMay counted down from ten.

Lou shut his eyes as if in prayer.

"Three, two, one, impact."

The missile splashed into the South China Sea only twenty four miles off the coast, between Hong Kong and Macau.

"We hit water!" the soldier announced, and the room erupted with cries of joy.

Lou congratulated the soldiers and felt relief pour over him like a soothing cool breeze. Then exhaustion hit him. He wanted to rest, but he feared the moment he was alone with his thoughts, the memories of Teresa would reduce him to misery.

Foreign representatives began voicing accolades once

they were informed the missile was diverted into the sea. Everyone refrained from debate until Hu Kung received the reports.

It was nearly ten minutes when he returned to the W.U.N. emergency video conference. He began to speak in a somber voice, adjusting his glasses when he paused for translation.

"On behalf of The Politburo Standing Committee of the C.P.C. and the people of China, we accept President Rizzo's assertion that the missile was fired by the former president, and war with China is not the intent of the new one." Kung continued.

Lou became so anxious that he wished he could understand Chinese so he didn't have to wait the extra ten seconds for translation.

"We thank you for the quick actions that diverted the missile away from our densely populated city; however, great damage has been done already. We have lost contact with many ships in the impact vicinity. The damage that has and will continue to impact us could be great."

Lou began to consider the disadvantage he was at.

Kung continued. "We acknowledge this not to be an act of war, but China is still in danger from further nuclear attacks while America is unstable." Pause for translation. "We have the right, and it is our obligation to oversee and assist America in securing its new government and stabilizing their country. We seek approval from the W.U.N. and President Rizzo." Kung's Chinese sounded harsh on his next line and he stared right at the camera. "However, for the safety of China, we will proceed as planned, even without approval. We suggest America open communication to the world at once, including their media outlets."

A murmur of voices surfaced through the laptop speaker once it seemed Mr. Kung was finished.

"Mr. Kung," Lou said before he could leave, "give us one week before you send troops. Allow us to host the treaty signing here in America, and we will prove to the world our country is stable."

Once Kung heard the translation, he wrinkled his face and spoke at once. "The W.U.N. meeting should commence in no longer than two days, only to allow for travel time, and I am certain no representative will agree to travel to your unstable nation."

"Then give me your word you will not deploy troops until after the treaty. We must be given a chance to state our case against this."

A wry smile crossed Kung's face. He sort of bowed to the camera and spoke. "See you at the meeting, Mr. Rizzo. Good day, gentleman." He got up and walked off the screen. Then his link ended, and the box disappeared.

He never gave me his word. That little bow doesn't mean shit, thought Lou.

Representatives began signing off, some of them wishing him luck first.

Lou was instructed to keep his link to the W.U.N. always open and to open their satellite transmissions to the world. Lou agreed, and the meeting ended.

Lou stood up and whispered to Deron to take the laptop out of the room.

"America, here are my guidelines," Lou said as everyone went silent, giving their full attention while the camera panned a close-up on him. "We will reopen all communication with the world, including this television network, American Airways; however, I want to keep the Freedom Forever Network a source for communicating with America in private. That will remain our secure, domestic link.

"Because of this nuclear incident perpetrated by our former President, I fear we cannot trust the Chinese government, who may see our situation as one of weakness. If they send troops to our country, like they intend to, I believe they will try to take us from within and try to rule us under their form of autocracy. This is a foreign country with a standing army of two and a half million members. I will never allow them to put active military members on our land." His eyes widened as he took pause for breath.

"Our military shall stay on high alert, and defenses shall be prepared along our east coast. The U.S. government, the military, and all law enforcement members are now here to serve and protect America and all our citizens.

"I declare the gun ban terminated as of now, and every able-bodied citizen should be armed. I want confiscated weapons distributed to our citizens.

"No American shall commit a crime against another American, for we are all in this together. Anyone who commits a violent act against an American citizen should be punished immediately.

"Everyone must be prepared to defend our land against foreign invaders. Every American must stand united for our democracy.

"We must all help each other through this vital period. Today we celebrate our second revolution and mark this glorious day as a new holiday. Tomorrow we get back to work, producing, harvesting, and distributing for our freedom, prosperity, and our future. We will conduct government like our founding fathers intended. We will have a large, thriving middle class again, and everyone will have the right to proper education, healthcare and retirement benefits. Hard work will be rewarded, and the American dream will be real for everyone. Let history remember that this generation of Americans rose to the challenge of monetary oppression and created a bright future for the next." His voice had risen at the end. He paused again, taking a deep breath and continued at normal tone.

"I will go to the W.U.N. meeting and ask for peace, but if China wants to challenge us and threaten our democracy, I feel secure in saying America will fight for its freedom. We will never have our lands occupied by foreign troops. Are you with me, America?"

Everyone in the room, except Steve Jolston, began yelling and applauding.

When the noise died down, Lou looked back at the camera and said, "Celebrate our independence tonight, but tomorrow everybody must return to work. Service city workers will be given a higher hourly rate. Owning a home and a car and raising a healthy family without fear of financial desperation will come fast. To all of you in the leisure class, get back to work tomorrow. The world is open to new deals and trades, and start new small businesses throughout the country. Although you will no longer be able to hoard enormous sums of money at the expense of our prosperity, you are still to be admired and allowed to live a life of luxury for your success.

"To the people in the wild: the scavies, the emancipators, the patriots, who helped us achieve this victory in such a big way, come out and work with us. You are our standing militia. Join society again, and power will return to small towns that have been forsaken for so long by our past government.

"A fair and wonderful new society awaits us if we work together for it." Lou felt woozy. His mind was working too hard, and there was still so much to do.

"That's it for now," he said and nodded to the camera. He plopped down in his chair. Leaning forward, he addressed the administration.

"So gentlemen, a couple hours ago you supported a plan for global nuclear war where perhaps billions of people would have died for some crazy world dominance idea. It's so sick and evil, it would seem justified putting you all to death right now."

Citizens around the table grumbled and moved closer while the camera kept rolling.

"But I believe men can change if they want to. You can amend yourselves if you help me keep the government working. Everyone needs to know if you're with the people now that we have spoken. Can we trust you to serve us?"

"Yes," DeMay said first. They all nodded except Steve Jolston.

"What about you, Steve?" Lou asked.

"I think if you try to negotiate with the W.U.N.," Steve shouted, "we're ALL gonna be learning about Chinese communism real soon!"

His candor, even as his life was in jeopardy, impressed Lou. He hated Steve's world view and all like him, but he knew that this was a man, who in his mind, never had a reason to lie.

"Alright, I'm keeping the cabinet together so things run smoothly. Every decision goes through me for now, and some of our citizens will be watching you at all times, just to make sure you're serving us well."

Lou looked back at some of the people standing behind

him. "Can one of you brave citizens reach into that lump of shit's pocket over there and bring me his keyphone?"

Two men scurried over to Burns' body. Each reached into one of his pockets. The man who got the right pocket pulled out the keyphone, trotted over and handed it to Lou with pride.

"Here you go, Lou," he said smiling.

"Thanks, man," he answered, returning a smile.

He turned forward. "Call me on this keyphone for every decision. General, that means every military decision."

He turned to Jolston. "Steve, get the chief justice over here to swear me in. If he's dead or something, get one of the other rich, conservative, bastards in the Supreme Court to do it. We'll have an inauguration ceremony in the courtyard."

Jolston nodded.

"The rest of you, I want to address the congress here in Rosemont tomorrow night. Arrange it." He closed his eyes and took in a deep breath. "Alright, meeting adjourned." Falling back into the chair, he felt like he could pass out in half a minute if he closed his eyes. The staff members got up and nervously tried to leave the room. "Look after them, people. Make sure they don't get hurt and they stay loyal," he announced to everyone.

Steve Jolston was about to scurry out of the room.

"Steve, get over here!" Lou yelled.

Steve kept walking.

With a nod from Lou, Deron dashed after him and forcibly led him back to Lou's side.

"I already got in touch with Chief Justice Connors," said Lou. "Can I please go and see if my wife is okay?"

"I wouldn't mind if you see your wife," replied Lou, "but you also have a lot of greedy friends that used to be powerful, and they might not want to accept the way thing are, and when a group of you sociopaths start scheming, bad things happen."

Steve began looking frightened as Lou coldly stared at him.

"Please just don't hurt me. I'm not gonna scheme against you."

"Were not gonna kill ya," Lou said, softening his gaze, "but you're gonna have to stay with me. I need a rich asshole for an advisor, and you're the only one who tells the truth." He struggled to his feet. "Now, where were they keeping my friends locked up?" Steve was silent for a minute as Lou stood face to face with him. Steve shook his head, adjusted his thin glasses and looked down. "Where are they?" Lou repeated.

"What's the point? They're dead. Look, I heard about the girl and all but those soldiers were ordered to kill, and I'm sure that's what they did."

Lou just scowled at him and began breathing deeply, like he was about to attack.

"Okay, relax," Steve said, holding up his hands. "They were at the Rosemont police station a couple blocks away from here."

"Let's go," he said.

The three of them left together. Steve led the way followed by Deron and Lou.

The convention center was filled with citizens celebrating. They were looting alcohol and food from the cafeteria. Once Lou was recognized by someone, a crowd of people would gather. Lou would smile, wave and make short remarks as they continued out of the building and onto river road.

Out in the streets it seemed somewhat chaotic at first. People were yelling and stomping about, but it appeared the violence had ceased. It was no longer rage that the people felt; it was triumph that filled them, combined with apprehension to sudden anarchy and an uncertain future.

As they made their way down River Road, a crowd gathered around them. Deron was doing his best to tell people to stay back, but their excitement could not be controlled. It was like the way teenage girls would act when they saw one of their heavily commercialized teen idols back in the days of corporate sponsored entertainment. Everyone wanted to get near him, talk to him, touch him, or just see him up close. Men were crowding him, holding out their arms, and Lou began to shake some of their hands. People farther back began to push forward, and Lou was bumped in his wounded shoulder. He cried out as he was bumped from behind and collapsed to the ground.

"Get back!" Deron yelled. "Give the man some room. He's hurt."

The people around him were shocked when Lou fell, and they began yelling for people to move back. Deron helped Lou to his feet. "We ought to get you some rest. I'll take you to the hotel," he said.

"I can't sleep until I know for sure. Please take me to the police station," Lou said, sounding weak.

Deron looked around and saw a G.A.T.E. car slowly moving down the crowded road. "Yo man! Stop that car! Mr. Rizzo needs a ride!" he shouted.

Citizens rushed to stop the car and pulled open the doors.

"Get out of the car! The president needs a ride!" one man yelled.

The officers nervously got out, holding their hands in the air. Deron helped Lou to the car and eased him into the back seat. Then he looked around for Steve and saw him trying to force his way through.

"Man, let that dude in the suit come through!" Deron yelled. Once he got Steve in the car, Deron got in the driver's seat and drove off, honking the horn and yelling out the window. "Get out the way."

Steve told him where to go, and they pulled into the Rosemont Police Station parking lot a few blocks away. They entered the main entrance. The place was deserted.

"Take me to where they were holding them," Lou told Steve.

He led them to the stairway where they went down to the basement.

When they entered the hallway, it was completely silent, except for their footsteps. The body of an Illinois National Guard soldier lay on the ground ahead of them. Lou stopped to observe that the soldier had been shot. Closing his eyes, he wondered if he could go through with it. He opened his eyes, breathed deep, and walked forward. Deron and Steve were already in the holding room.

"Aw man, that's nasty," he heard Deron say.

Preparing his mind for the worst possible sight he could imagine, he entered the room, looked into the holding cell and stared at the carnage. His heart sank, and his stomach felt nauseous. Corpses littered the ground. The blood from each of the bodies had created a large, burgundy puddle.

He first saw Gavin's face turned up to the ceiling, his jaw and eyes wide open and his chest stained in blood. Lou fell to his knees, moaning and vomiting. The awful acid taste burned his throat, and his eyes dripped streams of tears. Crying, coughing, and heaving, he fell to his hands and knees, consumed in emotional and physical pain while his wounded shoulder throbbed. He was responsible for so many deaths: Teresa, Reilly, the Edwards boys and the British men, who were apprehended because of him carelessly letting Freddy overhear the information Tony Swan gave him. He loathed himself and wanted to die.

"I told him not to come here," he heard Steve say.

Suddenly anger pushed away the suicidal thoughts. He struggled to his feet with Deron's help, being careful not to look into the cell. He began to stagger out of the room. His gaze fell to the soldier's body in the hall, and he suddenly stopped. His intellect returned, and he wondered why a soldier had been killed down here. He was afraid to see Teresa's body, didn't want the image haunting his dreams, but now he knew he had to inspect the bodies.

He turned around and walked back to the cell. Gavin was closest to the door. Five dead British soldiers were easily identified by their uniforms.

Reilly's body was face down on top of another body. The body under him was a guard. Another guard lay dead near the bench. His body had no bullet holes, but his head rested in a way that looked like his neck had been broken. Joe Bob was face down next to him with the back of his head splattered with his own blood and brain matter. Lou glanced over all the bodies again.

She's not here.

Sudden optimism accelerated his heart rate.

"She's not here!" he shouted.

"What you talking about? Who ain't here?" said Deron.

"Teresa. She's not here." He looked around again. "Neither is Scooter." His eyes grew wide while he gazed at Deron. "They got away."

He left the building at once and got back into the cop car. They drove back to the Hyatt Regency Hotel, located next to the convention center. Deron parked right in front of the main entrance. The hotel was occupied by politicians, their wives and other government employees, but in the last hour, common citizens had overrun the hotel, looting food and liquor while partying in the lobby, at the pool, and in the bar.

As they walked through the lobby, word spread that Lou was there. A crowd gathered while they waited for the elevator. They respectfully began to applaud. Lou raised his good arm and pumped his fist in the air. When the elevator door opened, he held his palm out to quiet them.

"Together we took our country back!" he shouted. "Celebrate tonight, my friends, but be respectful, and let's get back to work tomorrow. We have a lot to do." The doors closed, and they went to the top floor.

They brought him to the presidential suite. Steve unlocked the door with his keyphone, and they went in. Lou sat on the bed, ready to give in to the drowsiness.

"I want you to hire some men to work for you," he told Deron. "I need armed citizens watching over me at all times. If a group of big wigs attempt a counter revolution and kill me, this country would slip into chaos. I leave it all up to you, Deron. I have complete faith in you. You're going to need a crew, say six to ten people.

"Maybe get scavies. They're all unemployed and bold minded. I want good people protecting me at all times."

Deron nodded and held out his fist. Lou bumped it with his left fist and smiled.

Then Lou turned to Steve. "Steve, I want you to contact the media. Put out the word that the president is looking for Teresa Gorgie. We have to find her. She means a lot to me. You find her for me, and you will gain my trust and have the job of presidential advisor, you got it?"

Jolston looked stunned. This man, who was once his

enemy, was now asking him to do something that obviously meant a lot to him. How can he be so trusting and naïve?

Steve felt conflicted. He had no affection for this liberal idiot, but he was amazed by him and perhaps beginning to admire him.

"Alright I'll see what I can do," he said and walked out.

Lou lay on his back and easily got comfortable on his state-of-the-art mattress. It felt like he was lying on a cloud.

Deron was standing across the room talking on his key-phone.

"Keep me safe, Deron. I need to rest," Lou said and closed his eyes.

"Don't you worry, man," replied Deron. "I got some of my boys coming over to watch you while I find some new recruits."

"Good man," said Lou."

Moments later he was fast asleep.

Chapter 29

Lou became aware of voices in the room as he slowly awoke . . . just murmurs of a different dialect, until he fully awoke and comprehended.

"Damn boy, we thought you was dead."

"Man, I'm telling you, Jerome popped that soldier boy right before he got me."

Lou opened his eyes, turned his head, and saw a group of armed black men loitering. He was confused at first and almost yelled at them for being there. Then he realized they were Deron's friends, left here to guard him.

He pulled Burns' keyphone out of his pocket. There were three missed calls. He checked them: General DeMay, Sharon, and John. He was hoping Steve had called, and he swore in anger.

"Hey, Mr. Rizzo's up," a black man said, noticing Lou was awake.

They greeted him enthusiastically. "How ya doing Lou?" "Hey Mr. Prezz."

"Hey guys, thanks for watching out," said Lou while waving his left hand.

Before returning his missed calls, he went to contacts, found Steve, and hit send.

"Yeah," Steve answered.

"Haven't you found her yet? She can't be far away," said Lou.

"I looked up her file and put her picture on the air and said the president wishes to see her. I gave my number out, and I just got a call from someone that said she's at the Radisson Hotel with some hillbilly scavey. I'm going to check it out now."

"Good, thanks man. Go get her." As he ended the call, his heart soared, and he smiled to himself.

I guess it's true. Even the losers get lucky sometimes.

He returned his missed calls and gave every order with confidence. He felt like a new man with an aura of optimism surrounding him, like he could take on the world now.

For the next two hours he was inundated with calls. People began meeting with him in the presidential suite. He was served a good meal, and Sharon Brown came over and set up her secretary station on the desk.

He was so busy talking to people and making decisions that it was five hours later when he finally began to wonder what was taking Steve so long. He took out the keyphone, but before he could call him, Sharon called to him.

"What is it, Sharon?" he said, walking over to the desk.

"Tony Swan is sending the information now. The W.U.N. meeting is in two days in Beijing China. I'll inform Air Force One. You'll have to leave tomorrow night."

"China!" Lou yelled, "Goddamn it! They must be running the whole show. I wanted more time before I leave the country. This is bullshit." She stared at him wide eyed and confused. "Oh well, we better get this over with. Go ahead and make the arrangements, and I want you to come with me. A president is lost without a good secretary."

He walked away and called Steve. When the phone rang, he heard a ringtone in the room. He looked around at the many faces in the room and noticed Steve was sitting on the couch with a drink in his hand. He closed the keyphone and walked over to him.

"What the hell? How long have you been here!" he shouted.

Everyone went silent.

"I don't know . . . a while I guess," Steve said, not looking up to Lou's eyes.

"Start talking, Jolston. My blood pressure is rising. Where is she?"

"I found her for you. It's just ahh . . . " He ran his hand through his thin blond hair and exhaled. "She doesn't want to see you."

"What?" Lou muttered and began to feel faint. "Why

didn't you bring her here, Goddamn it?"

"I couldn't. She refused to come with me. What was I supposed to do, have her seized? People would have killed me. It's still anarchy out there, you know."

"Where is she now?" he asked solemnly.

"Forget about her, Rizzo. You got a country to run. She knows you left her to die along with the others, and she's not going to change her mind. She went through a traumatic event. It's nothing short of a miracle she and that hillbilly got out."

Lou forced his anger to pass without allowing it to seize him. Not expecting her to react like that, he was stunned and felt stupid.

He tried to empathize with how she must feel.

"Come here," he said to Steve and walked over to the other side of the room. "I want someone to secretly watch over her, make sure she's okay. Put a good man on it. When I get back from the meeting, maybe she'll change her mind."

Steve nodded and walked back to where his drink was while he pulled out his keyphone.

Chapter 30

The next day in the courtyard of the convention center, on the same stage that Lou dove off of, he was sworn in by the very conservative chief justice of the Supreme Court. A huge crowd gathered, and it was all televised, not just to Americans, but transmission was opened to the world. His improvised speech was magnificent as he told the world, "America is once again a true democracy, of, by, and for the people, and money will never again influence political decisions, and we are now a friend to every peaceful nation."

Then he addressed congress. Though he despised every affluent and out of touch with the common man, member of congress, he demanded that they work with him to rebuild America and restore a strong middle class.

He declared elections would be held next year, and every seat would be contested. If they wanted a chance to be re-elected, he said they'd better prove to the people that they wanted to improve the lives of their poor constituents. Lou promised the people would be involved in every major decision the government made via the internet and town hall meetings.

It was nothing short of a miracle how smooth the transition of power happened. A general feeling of unity prevailed in the minds of most Americans. People returned to work; law enforcement was respected, and the military was compliant under the new commander in chief.

That evening, he boarded Air Force One at O'Hare airport. Things had been going so smoothly that Lou began to feel uneasy about it and suspected that if a group was planning a counter revolution, they would try to blow up the plane on the runway, and surely Jolston would be a part of it, so he insisted he come with him along with an entourage he hand picked. He had the runway surveyed by guardsmen, and he interviewed the pilots, who seemed to be fine citizens and in support of him.

Still, as the plane took off, he felt vulnerable. Going back to his time as an Illinois senator, he hated flying over oceans, and much of the journey to China was unpleasant for him, though the luxury of Air Force One astounded him.

It was the first time he had ever been to China, and the smog of Beijing was worse then he expected, despite knowing China was the slowest country to limit the use of fossil fuels.

Most W.U.N. representatives pleasantly smiled and shook his hand upon meeting him. However, Hu Kung, although polite, seemed standoffish to him.

The meeting was filled with excitement. It began by the chairman requesting Lou to tell the story of how America overthrew its government. Lou gave a captivating and detailed account of his last incredible week.

When he reached the part about how they were going to kill his friends if he didn't lie to the people, his voice grew somber, and his eyes saddened. Explaining how he dove off the stage just before gunfire erupted thrilled everyone, including himself. "What happened next can only be described as three miracles," he said and talked about the scavies' timely attack, Deron's last second potshot and Burns' near miss that got him in the shoulder instead of the heart. His recounting was so exciting, it seemed unbelievable, even to himself, but he ended by saying, "I found out hours later that Teresa actually got out alive, but now she doesn't want to talk to me cause I left her to die." He got choked up trying to finish. "I guess I don't blame her."

He could say no more and sat down, fighting back tears. His candor in that moment won over their trust.

"Bravo, America," the Italian representative said and clapped. A few more joined in, and then the entire room applauded passionately.

After that they got down to business. Lou agreed to all terms asked of the United States. He signed the nuclear weapons ban treaty, in which China had added that during the long period of time it would actually take to eliminate all existing nukes, no nation shall use nuclear weapons, even if a nation was in danger of losing a war, and using nukes was its only hope to prevail.

They claimed it was to protect the Middle Eastern countries where wars were still probable because of the enduring hate over religious differences that still permeated the psyche of Muslims, Christians, Jews, and Hindus. Lou had other suspicions.

After that, Hu Kung made his case. He explained in detail the terrible events caused by the nuclear missile that barely missed Hong Kong, how it affected the fishermen and costal regions. He explained how a country still in the chaos of post revolution, one that had so many nuclear weapons, must have W.U.N. supervision until their government is stable. His case was well presented and convincing.

He requested that China be allowed to send two hundred and fifty thousand peace keepers to America for no more than two years to ensure China's safety by overseeing America's governmental transformation and for keeping its new president safe. He added that America owed trillions of dollars to China, and it was their right to make sure that they would be fairly remunerated by this new American government.

When it was Lou's turn to speak, he argued that China had no right to place soldiers in his country. His life was not in danger, and his country was already stable.

When all the members voted, by a slim majority, they agreed to permit China to bring in troops to America, but no more than one hundred thousand. A force larger than that would seem like too aggressive of an action. Hu Kung was content, and the proposition was passed.

Lou asked to make a final comment before they adjourned.

"Esteemed colleagues, I feel confident that many of you now know me and trust me, and you're right to do so because I am inherently a man of my word. The agreements I have made will all be met. We will begin paying back China at the start of our next fiscal quarter. Humanitarian aid, in the form of grain and wheat, will begin being delivered to Africa this week, and we look forward to fair trade with every nation that wants to do business with us. However, if foreign troops try to invade or occupy any part of our cherished lands, it will be interpreted as an act of war, and we will be forced to defend our homeland. My friends, I cannot allow Chinese soldiers into my country. I'm sure all of you can understand why." He stared at Kung as he finished, who flashed an evil grin back at him. Voices murmured as he gave Kung a steely stare.

"Mr. Rizzo, the vote is final," said the sitting chairman from Russia. "This meeting is adjourned."

Every member seemed to get up at once, anxious to depart. Lou felt like yelling for them all to sit the hell back down and listen to him, but he didn't. He was a man who did not waste a moment of time on something he knew was futile. It was over; no one would go against the will of mighty China, especially after one of their major cities was nearly nuked, and their relentless, expanding, economy and military gave them clout.

Not wanting to get back on the plane right away, Lou had dinner with Tony Swan later that evening. They had great, non-political conversation most of the night. Tony acted as if Lou was like a super hero, asking about what it was like to lead a revolution.

Eventually Lou changed the subject and talked about his son. "God, it's going to be so great to see him. I'm going to come to your country as soon as I can. I wonder if he'll wanna come back to America with me or wanna stay in Australia. If he doesn't want to leave, I would never force him to."

Lou was quiet after that, thinking about how America was not safe yet. As they were about to end the night, Lou got political.

"Tony, can I count on Australia's support. I need some allies. With America back in, the W.U.N. can keep China in check."

Tony sucked air through his teeth and ran his hand through his hair. "Yes, they certainly have asserted themselves as the new empire on the rise. Perhaps you're right. With the U.S. back, maybe we can take a harder line with China. You know I'll be doing my best for you, Louie, but I can't promise you the Prime Minister will see things our way. I suggest you go along with it for now. The last thing you need is a war with China. Let them come in and observe how well your government is running, and then you can request they leave in six to eight months."

"That's not what they have in mind, Tony. They don't intend on ever leaving once they get in, believe me. I'll try to negotiate, but allowing foreign troops in my country is out of the question."

Tony eyes grew wide and fearful. "Lou, please," he began, but Lou held up his hand and shook his head.

"Don't bother, Tony. Why waste words?"

Tony frowned and nodded his head. They shook hands. Tony stared into his eyes for a moment as if getting a last look at a legend.

"We'll keep in touch, mate," he said and walked away.

Outside the door, Chinese authorities apprehended Tony for questioning.

Lou had another drink at the table with his entourage before they all left together. When they got to the airport they boarded Air Force One.

The pilots had been sufficiently rested, and Lou requested they leave at once.

Ten minutes later, they had not moved. The captain walked out of the cockpit and asked to speak with Lou.

"Sir, we requested clearance and it was denied. They say they can't give us clearance for another few hours."

"What?" Lou shouted and rose to his feet, startling everyone around him. "Why the hell would we have to wait? The weather's fine. You telling me they can't get clearance for Air Force One!" he looked upward in thought. "What was their reason for the delay?"

"Its strange, sir," the short bald pilot said, "They didn't really give us a reason. Said the runways are being cleared for an emergency of higher priority, and the information is confidential."

"Yeah, right, they're stalling us, and I hate to think why," said Lou. He walked up to the pilot and put his arm around his shoulder. "What's your name, captain?" he asked.

"Bill Schivo sir," the captain answered.

"Alright Bill, let's go back to the cockpit. We can't sit around here all night." Lou walked with the pilot and co-pilot back to the cockpit and told them to take their seats.

"Get me General DeMay through the plane's secure communications."

The co-pilot tried to reach DeMay's keyphone through the Air Force One link.

"Sir, our link is scrambled. They're jamming us," said the co-pilot. "The source must be coming from the control center."

"Aw shit, this is bad. Get us the fuck out of here!" Lou shouted.

"But sir, we haven't been granted a runway. It would be dangerous to move without clearance," said Bill.

"I don't doubt it, but we're getting out of here. Look…" They saw police cars were coming down the runway, heading right toward them. "Pick the nearest runway that's clear. Let's go. I want the quickest takeoff you ever made." The pilots looked at each other for a moment. "Let's go," Lou repeated. As they taxied to the runway, the control center immediately told them to halt. The police cars continued to chase them.

"Air Force One, you are not cleared to take off. Stop at once."

The co-pilot looked back at Lou.

"Tell them we have a medical emergency and must get back to the U.S. as soon as possible, and we will not stop."

The co-pilot said what Lou told him while Bill accelerated, causing Lou to sway.

"You better sit down and strap in, sir," Bill told him. Lou took a staff seat in the cockpit and buckled the seat belt.

The plane quickly accelerated down the nearest runway, which was completely clear, confirming Lou's suspicions. They ascended without a hitch.

Only moments after they broke through the clouds, Lou told them to check the communications. It worked now and General DeMay was called through Air Force One's secure communications. DeMay answered at once, seeing Air Force One on his caller I.D.

"DeMay," he answered.

"Its Rizzo. We may have a problem here."

"Mr. Rizzo, how did it go with the Chinese?"

"They got W.U.N. approval to send troops into our

country. I told them if they do, it will be taken as an act of war. We'll have to wait and see what they do in the next couple weeks."

"Aw . . . actually you wont have to wait that long," said DeMay, "They have a fleet of ships just a few hundred miles off the coast of California. It's a mighty fleet too: battle cruisers and aircraft carriers, and they have another fleet about a half day behind them around the Hawaiian Islands. They say they have permission to land at Monterey Bay."

"Goddamn those sneaky bastards!" yelled Lou, "They didn't wait for W.U.N. approval. They sent out the fleets days ago.

You tell them they are not cleared to land. If they come within fifty miles of our mainland, it will be taken as an act of war."

"Good idea, sir, you can't let these chinks waltz into our country," said DeMay. Lou closed his eyes and rubbed them, he thought about all that was lost during his life long endeavor to bring justice to the American people. He thought about Teresa and how she gave him strength, only to lose her in the end.

"All my life I've fought my country's corrupt government. I've been in conflict every day because I never gave up believing we would some day overthrow them and a fair, diplomatic government would emerge. We finally did it. We fought and won back our country, and what do we get . . . another Goddamn war to fight. Conflict is cyclical, thanks to the evil of men."

There was a moment of silence.

"Sir," DeMay finally said.

"I got a feeling Air Force One is in danger, General. I wish we still had a military presence in the Philippines. Maybe we could get some jets to escort us. We need help, General, but there is not enough time."

"What are you talking about, Rizzo?" DeMay shouted into his phone, sounding half angry and half concerned.

"Sir!" the co-pilot shouted, "radar shows three planes following us." Lou's heart sank, and he filled with rage and self-hatred.

"Just like the president I replaced," said Lou, "the

Chinese want world domination too." He looked at the pilots, who glanced back at him. They noticed his eyes were tearing. He looked disgusted with himself. "Do your best to evade, gentlemen."

"What's happening, Rizzo?" DeMay shouted again.

"General, I declare America is now under military order, and you're in charge. China is about to commit an act of war." He exhaled deeply, "Beat these bastards, General, and then allow America to have free elections and restore true democracy. Those are my orders. Give me your word you will follow them."

Lou closed his eyes and thought of two people he wanted to see one more time so badly.

"I give you my word, President Rizzo," DeMay replied while the Chinese jet fighters closed in on Air Force One...

LaVergne, TN USA
30 January 2011
214432LV00001B/72/P